"The truth is ...
It i...
Book-...

"Davies spins his yarn with characteristic humour.
... *The Cunning Man* is a novel that stays with you."
The New Brunswick Reader

"Nobody but Davies could have written this novel.
How many writers ever achieve such distinctiveness?"
Calgary Herald

"*The Cunning Man* is vintage Robertson Davies...
a strange and compelling story."
The London Free Press

"Davies turns a tale with the grace and deftness of a
19th century novelist.... Whether he is navigating the
arcane waters of Anglican hagiography or humanity's
quirky sexual mores and hygienic habits, Davies's vision
embraces life in all its idiosyncratic splendor."
The Hamilton Spectator

"Life in its brightness and its darkness is the stuff
of Davies's novels, as brightness and darkness are
the stuff of life itself, and that is what gives them
their universal appeal."
Winnipeg Free Press

PENGUIN BOOKS

THE CUNNING MAN

The son of a journalist, Robertson Davies was born in 1913 in Thamesville, Ontario, and educated at Queen's University and at Oxford. He has had three successive careers: first as an actor with the Old Vic Company in England; then as a publisher of the *Peterborough Examiner*; and most recently as a university professor and the first Master of Massey College at the University of Toronto, from which he retired in 1981. He now holds the title of Master Emeritus.

It is as a fiction writer that Davies has gained international recognition. His work includes three critically acclaimed trilogies: the Salterton trilogy, composed of *Tempest-Tost, Leaven of Malice* and *A Mixture of Frailties*; the Deptford trilogy of *Fifth Business, The Manticore* and *World of Wonders*; and the Cornish trilogy, *The Rebel Angels, What's Bred in the Bone* and *The Lyre of Orpheus*. He has also written *Murther & Walking Spirits*, available as a Penguin paperback. His latest book is *The Cunning Man*.

The Cunning Man

a novel
by

Robertson Davies

Cunning men, wizards, and white witches, as they
call them, in every village, which, if they be sought
unto, will help almost all infirmities of body and
mind....

The body's mischiefs, as Plato proves, proceed
from the soul: and if the mind be not first satisfied,
the body can never be cured.

ROBERT BURTON, *The Anatomy of Melancholy* (1621)

Penguin Books

PENGUIN BOOKS
Published by the Penguin Group
Penguin Books Canada Ltd, 10 Alcorn Avenue, Toronto, Ontario,
Canada M4V 3B2
Penguin Books Ltd, 27 Wrights Lane, London W8 5TZ, England
Penguin Books USA Inc., 375 Hudson Street, New York, New York
10014, U.S.A.
Penguin Books Australia Ltd, Ringwood, Victoria, Australia
Penguin Books (NZ) Ltd, 182-190 Wairau Road, Auckland 10,
New Zealand

Penguin Books Ltd, Registered Offices: Harmondsworth, Middlesex,
England

First published as a Douglas Gibson Book by McClelland and Stewart, 1994

Published in Penguin Books, 1995

10 9 8 7 6 5 4 3 2 1

*Publisher's note: This book is a work of fiction. Names, characters, places
and incidents either are the product of the author's imagination or are used
fictitiously, and any resemblance to actual persons living or dead, events, or
locales is entirely coincidental.*

Manufactured in Canada

Canadian Cataloguing in Publication Data

Davies, Robertson, 1913-
    The cunning man

ISBN 0-14-024550-2

I. Title.

PS8507.A75C8 1995   C813'.54   C95-930089-9
PR9199.3.D38C8 1995

For Brenda, and our daughters
Miranda, Jennifer and Rosamond

AUTHOR'S NOTE

I record with gratitude my indebtedness to Dr. Richard Davis for advice on certain medical matters. I am also grateful to Moira Whalon for help in regularizing the chronology of the narrative.

Errors, however, are all my own.

The only portrait from life in the book is that of the City of Toronto. All other characters are imaginary and no reference is intended to any person living or dead.

The quotation from Nevill Coghill's translation of Chaucer's *Canterbury Tales* is used by permission of Penguin Books, Ltd., and the trustees of Nevill Coghill's estate.

I

The Cunning Man

SHOULD I HAVE taken the false teeth? In my years as a police surgeon I would certainly have done so; who can say what might be clinging to them, or in the troughs that fit over the gums? I would have been entirely within my rights. But in this curious situation, what indisputable rights had I?

To begin with, I was no longer a police surgeon, but a physician; primarily, I suppose, a diagnostician, in private practice, and also a professor in the Faculty of Medicine (Diagnosis). I was thus a rather unusually qualified bystander when poor old Father Hobbes died right in front of the High Altar at St. Aidan's, on the morning of Good Friday. Instinctively, like a firehorse when it hears the bell, I darted forward as he fell. I was still not old enough to know that a doctor should never be in a hurry. When Charlie waved me back, hissing, "This is holy ground. Leave it to me," I did not want to insist on my rights, or at any rate my privileges, as a medical man. Charlie was insisting on his rights as a priest in a way I resented, but I did not want to get into a tit-for-tat quarrel with him. We were members of two rival priesthoods, he the Man of God and I the Man of Science, and in the circumstances I thought my priest equal if not superior to his. But I did not want to show pique or press a petty advantage. We were in a church, Holy Communion had begun, and the dying man was behind the altar rails, so I suppose I thought Charlie was on his own turf and must be respected accordingly. Was this chivalry toward the weaker, or snotty contempt for a lesser creature? I suppose it was a little of both.

If I had taken the teeth the story that this young journalist tried to extract from me would have been very different. A better story? I cannot say. But I was certainly not going to tell Ms. Esme Barron, of the *Colonial Advocate*, everything I knew. If I leave a few notes on the story in my poorly kept Case Book, somebody may find it when I am dead. What they will find is much more than "a few notes" but when I wrote this I did not know how much my story would possess me. I had no intention of confiding in this very attractive, tactful young woman, whom I did not trust an inch.

She has asked a question, and I must answer.

"Yes. I signed the death certificate. I saw the body as soon as it was removed to the vestry."

"Who moved it?"

"A couple of deacons who were helping to serve Mass."

"What's a deacon, exactly?"

"A sort of priest-in-training. It's the lowest rank of the ministry in the Anglican Church. A deacon is working his way up to becoming a fully ordained priest, and he has some clerical functions, but he can't celebrate Communion or give the Blessing. Nor can he hear confessions, which was heavy work at St. Aidan's."

"It was what they call High Church?"

"Very High Church. As high as the Bishop would tolerate. This Mass of the Pre-Sanctified on Good Friday morning was very High Church stuff."

"Daring, would you call it?"

"Well, if you think it daring to revive a ninth-century ceremony in 1951 in Toronto, which hasn't what you might call strong medieval roots."

"What was it like? Very fancy?"

"Fancy isn't the word I'd choose. It gets its name from the fact that the bread and wine for the Communion are prepared and blessed the night before, and kept in a side chapel. It was something special for Good Friday, and at nine o'clock in the morning the full forces of St. Aidan's were present: the gallery choir was there, with the famous Dr. DeCourcy Parry at the organ, and the chancel choir—they did the plainsong bits—with the notorious head of the chancel plainsong choir, Darcy Dwyer, wearing the robes appropriate to his office—and the much-loved old Father Ninian Hobbes as celebrant, assisted by Father Charles Iredale, whom I knew well, and nearly two hundred of the faithful in the church—"

"What kind of people? Who went to a place like that?"

"All sorts. A typical St. Aidan's group. Some obviously well-fixed, some obviously poor; all sorts of people, from white Anglo-Saxons to black people, because St. Aidan's drew heavily on the black population of Toronto, many of whom at that time were employed as porters on the railways. Now and then some of them acted as servers at Mass; they and some of the congregation used to joke about Black Masses; that was the sort of joke St. Aidan's people loved—a whiff of gunpowder amid the incense. There were nine nuns of the Order of St. John there; they had a convent and school nearby. Oh, it was a very close community at St. Aidan's, and as it drew people from every part of Toronto, it had quite a wide influence. The diocesan authorities—"

"Excuse me. The what?"

"The Bishop, and the clergy who worked under him

to administer the whole church district. St. Aidan's was a thorn in the flesh because it carried such a strong hint of Rome with it—"

"A hint of Rome? How do you mean?"

"Ms. Barron, if I am to give you elementary lessons in Church history, we'll never be finished. You know that the Anglican Church is a Protestant Church? Of course you do. But there is a branch of it that insists that it is a Catholic Church in every sense except that it does not acknowledge the sovereignty of the Bishop of Rome. Some people have rather fine-spun notions about its descent from the pre-Augustinian Celtic Church in Britain—"

"Yes, I understand. I'm not stupid, you know. But I have to write for a lot of people who don't know any of this stuff, and I've got to make it plain and interesting. So tell me how Rome would get into an Anglican church in Toronto?"

"Usages, not very significant in themselves, but they mount up. Calling the parsons 'Father,' and calling the Communion 'Mass' and bowing and crossing yourself during service, and lots of incense and—dozens of things—"

"Yes, yes; I get it now. But I'd like to get back to the moment when the old man died. Tell me exactly what happened."

"Everything seemed to be going splendidly. Because the bread and wine had been blessed and prepared the night before, they were brought to the altar in solemn procession after the Adoration of the Cross—some wonderful plainchant, for that. Lots of incense. Then Father Hobbes recited the pre-Communion prayers, took the wafer that had been laid out for him, held it up for everyone to see, put it in his mouth—looked odd, then dropped to the ground. There was the briefest possible pause, because I think Iredale supposed the old man was genuflecting. But why had he not done that before he took the Host? Forgetfulness of old age? But in an instant it was plain that he had fallen. Father Iredale and the deacons rushed to him and lifted him partly—but it was clear to me that the old man was already dead."

"So quickly?"

"I would have put it at less than ten seconds."

"How did you know that he was dead?"

"Long experience. In war, as a police surgeon—you get to know the look. Something has gone."

"How would you define that?"

"Just in those words. The soul has gone."

"The soul?"

"You seem surprised."

"I am. You, a doctor, talking about the soul."

"As you say."

"I've heard Dr. Roseveare, at the General, say he's operated on over a thousand patients and he's never yet met with anything inside them that he could identify as a soul."

"I know. I've heard him say it, too."

"But you wouldn't say that?"

"No. I wouldn't say that."

"I suppose that's why you were on hand that day when old Father Hobbes died, right at the foot of the altar."

"Partly that."

"Partly—?"

"Let's leave it at that."

"Okay. Now when can I come again?"

"When do you have to complete your article?"

"There's no hurry. Several of us are working on a series: *The Toronto That Used To Be*. I'd like to see you a few more times, if that's all right."

"Quite all right."

"But, just before I go, tell me—I'm trying to get the real story about this death, because there was some talk of a saint, later on, wasn't there?"

"Could we leave that for next time? I hear that a patient has arrived in my waiting-room."

As I ushered Ms. Barron out, the question nagged again: should I have taken the false teeth? Charlie Iredale was eager for me to sign a certificate of death then and there, but of course I don't carry the proper form about with me, and as I had to return to my office to do that, I could very well have insisted on taking the false teeth, for some simple tests, to see if they gave any evidence of the cause of death. As it was, I did not insist, and when one of the deacons called for it I could have sent the certificate and the teeth over to the rectory that afternoon, certifying that the old man had died of cardiac arrest. As everybody does, one way or another.

If I had any doubts, they soon vanished.

[2]

I SHALL HAVE to watch my step with Ms. Esme Barron. Not that there is anything in the least dishonest about her, but she has the unresting curiosity of the really good journalist, and a technique of cross-examination that is worse than anything one usually meets with in the law courts. I have been an expert witness many times, especially in my police surgeon days, and I know that lawyers like to be subtle, even when they have little gift for it. But journalists like Esme are not subtle; they ask direct, intrusive, and disconcerting questions, and are quick to spot any evasion. They will stick to a point when you are eager to get away from it; they are implacable, and, if you do not answer a question, they will hint that you are furtive.

In my way I am just as clever as Ms. Barron. I have much to conceal, and I shall do so. I shall give her other things to dig into, without going into all the trouble that arose after the death of Father Ninian Hobbes.

Who cares now if an old priest dropped dead while celebrating Communion, so many years ago? The answer to that, I know very well, is that thousands of people will be interested if Ms. Barron can serve them up a hot and spicy dish. She is very keen on what she calls "the public's right to know," which means her right to blat anything she can uncover that is scandalous or prurient. But mine is a profession sworn to priestly secrecy.

I think I knew about this series of articles on which she is engaged—*The Toronto That Used To Be*—before she did. It was an idea that came to her boss, and her boss is my godson, Conor Gilmartin. He is also her lover, or she is his; I never know quite which way the pussy jumps in such affairs. He puts the plums of the series in her way, because normally it might be expected that an article on St. Aidan's Church and its environs might be done by the *Advocate*'s religious editor (ambiguous expression) Hugh McWearie, whom I know well, and who would do it much better. Certainly it was Hugh, when the three of us were talking about the series, who said that the parish of St. Aidan's was, or had been, one of Toronto's most interesting villages, and should be thoroughly explored and written up.

It was one of Toronto's better mayors who had started the "village" idea. The big city, he said, was of special interest in North America, because it was composed of a number of neighbourhoods, or "villages"—the Chinese, the Italian, the Portuguese, the Muslim, the Taiwanese, and many more, to say nothing of the Jews, whose

Orthodox community was virtually unknown to most of us. All tended to live in identifiable sections, with their own shops and places of assembly, even in some cases their own newspapers, and within the communities there was a neighbourly concern for the safety of children, for religious observance, for the old, which did much to keep down the rate of violent crime. The mayor's concept of Toronto was substantially, if not wholly, true. The *Advocate* wanted to write it up and promote it, and discuss how the villages came into being and how much of their character persisted among second- and third-generation immigrants.

The parish of St. Aidan's was interesting because it was perhaps the only remaining Anglo-Saxon or Anglo-Celtic village, the dominant presence in which was its large and active church.

Had there been some talk of a saint, Esme had asked. Indeed there had been, and if there was any revival of it, I wanted to do whatever I could to steer it in the right direction. That was something I could do for my poor old friend, Charlie Iredale, who had made a sacrifice greater in his terms than I could possibly conceive, to bring it about. But I should have to watch my step, because Esme was no fool.

[3]

"I suppose I ought to call you Uncle Jack now."

"Please don't. My name is Jonathan, and I've never had a nickname. Doesn't go with my character. So, Uncle Jon—if you must."

"No I mustn't, if you don't like it. I didn't want to be familiar. But as I'm married to Gil, I thought Dr. Hullah seemed a bit formal."

"Don't call me uncle anything. Call me Jon if you like, and I'll call you Esme."

Much had happened in the rather short time since last Esme Barron sat in the patient's chair in my consulting-room. Because I have a consulting-room, and not an "office" like so many of my colleagues; I'll tell you why when the time comes. Esme and my godson Conor Gilmartin had been married, and married in a church, what's more, which surprised me, because I thought Gil had grown away from all that. It was a quiet affair and the guests were few. Esme's parents, who were an unremarkable couple from somewhere in Western Ontario, where I gathered they had a big market garden and greenhouse, looked a little out of place; she was round, like a barrel or a zero, and wore bifocals and grey stockings; he was small, seemed very fit as a gardener might well do, and wore his best suit, which looked indestructible and was of that grey material that suggests an old corrugated iron roof. Gil's parents, Professors Brochwel and Nuala Gilmartin from Waverley University, were old friends of mine, and rather more than friends. Otherwise, nobody except Hugh McWearie, who acted as Gil's best man, wearing his usual look of resigned regret (which was deceptive), and a young woman whose name I never caught, who "stood up" with Esme, who looked as if she did not need, and never would need, anybody to stand up for her except herself. But Esme made a pretty bride, for she was a handsome young woman, and it's a poor bride who cannot call up a look on her wedding day. She did not wear a white dress. Sensible girl.

I was there as a kind of general friend of everybody, and attending physician in case Gil fainted at the altar, as he looked rather likely to do.

Now Esme had returned to my consulting-room and

her job of digging up whatever was interesting and picturesque about the "village" that surrounded the Church of St. Aidan.

"The saint bit," she now said. "What was all that about?"

"Oh, just a little local enthusiasm," I replied. "Father Hobbes had been very popular. More than popular, really. He was loved. Because he was a very good old man, you know."

"Good in what way?"

"Didn't heat the rectory properly. Didn't dress himself in anything but ancient clothes that he must have had for thirty years. Ate awful food, and expected the priests who lived with him at the rectory to do the same. Gave every penny he had to the poor. At least that's an exaggeration in our time; he gave every penny that the government didn't grab or that wasn't demanded for immediate expenses, to the poor. He used to roam around the parish on winter nights, up and down all the alleys, looking for bums who might have dropped down drunk, and who might freeze. Time and again he brought one of them home and put him in his own bed, while he slept on a sofa—and the rectory sofa was penitence for a saint, let me tell you. There was some talk because he was very generous to whores who were down on their luck. He made their more prosperous sisters stump up to help them in bad times. Got the whores to come to Confession and be scrubbed up, spiritually. He used to joke with them, and they adored him. You should have seen the whores at his funeral! Got into trouble because he let the church fabric run down, giving away money that should have gone for heating, and leaks and fresh electric bulbs.

"Of course with an example like that, money rolled in. St. Aidan's wasn't a rich parish by any means, but people stumped up astonishingly to help Father Hobbes, because he never spared himself. Father Iredale did everything he could to keep the church decent, and got a lot of help from people who gave vestments for the clergy, and paid the considerable bill for candles, so the services were always handsome. The whores, again, loved paying for incense. Whores can be very devout, you know. They need religion in their business. Everybody chipped in. DeCourcy Parry, who looked after the music, could have doubled his salary anywhere else, but he loved the feeling of St. Aidan's and made its music the best in Toronto. Dwyer worked selflessly— and if you'd known Dwyer you'd know what a lot of self he had to subdue—because he loved the plainchant and the intricacies of ritual. There was an extraordinary atmosphere about the place.

"So it wasn't surprising when poor old Father Hobbes died, in full view of a lot of his people, at the foot of the altar which was sacred to him as the true table of God, they declared that he had been a saint, and wanted to do something about it."

"So what did they do?"

"There was nothing to be done. The Bishop sent one of his archdeacons to preach a sermon in which he explained laboriously that the Anglican Church no longer created saints, without in the least diminishing the greatness of the saints of the pre-Reformation days—this was a typically Anglican example of eating your cake and having it too—and after a while it all quieted down."

"That's not what I heard. I heard there was quite a ding-dong about it, and even talk of miracles. Didn't the Bishop have to take strong measures?"

"Oh, people love to exaggerate these things. You can take it from me it was all a tempest in a teapot. I was there, you know."

"Didn't the Bishop throw Iredale out?"

"Heavens, no! Father Iredale was in the course of time transferred to a parish in the northernmost part of his large diocese. I suppose the Bishop thought he might be glad of a rest from the over-heated atmosphere of St. Aidan's."

"Jon, I smell a rat. You're not a rat, are you?"

"The farthest thing from it. But I have a well-cooled memory, which isn't common."

"You knew Iredale well, didn't you?"

"Well—we were at school together."

[4]

At school together. Everything that I say to Esme about Charlie is conditioned by that fact. Everything that I say to Esme is conditioned by the larger fact that I am who and what I am: Jonathan Hullah, M.D., F.R.C.P., with a wide reputation in the treatment of stubborn and chronic diseases, and a somewhat murky reputation among some of my colleagues because of the methods I use in such treatment. Everything I say to Esme is rooted in my childhood, and in the totality of who I am and what my experience of life has been. Does she understand that? She is not a fool, by any means; indeed she is a very keen-witted young woman. But she is a journalist and an interviewer who does not dig very deep, because if she did so she might blur the clarity of the "story" she will eventually write for her paper. There are depths in me that Esme will never explore, nor do I suppose she wants to do so. But those depths lie below anything I may tell her. And they must be explored in some degree in this narrative in my Case Book.

How many interviewers, I wonder, have any conception of the complexity of the creature they are interrogating? Do they really believe that what they can evoke from their subject is the whole of the "story"? Not the best interviewers, surely. Esme is not bad, but she desires clarity above all else, and clarity is not a characteristic of the human spirit.

What I shall tell her will all be true so far as it goes, but in terms of the reality of the "story" she is seeking, with the energy of a terrier after a rat, what I shall tell her will not be even half what I know.

Everything I am lies behind everything I say. So—Charlie and I were at school together.

"Gilmartin?"

"Present."

"Hullah?"

"Present."

"Iredale?"

"Present."

"All new boys? God, what's happening to this school? What names! Gilmartin; Hullah; Iredale! This used to be a school for white men! Where do you bastards come from?"

"Salterton," said Gilmartin.

"Salterton," said Iredale.

I remained silent.

"Well, come on, Hullah? Where do you come from?"

Forced to the wall, I answered, "Sioux Lookout."

"Never heard of it. Where is it?"

"Northern Ontario."

The interrogator was a misshapen lump of devil's dung who was the prefect on duty to take the four-thirty roll-call; his name was Salter. Salter L., because boys at Colborne College did not have given names: they had surnames and initials.

"Sioux Lookout! God, what next?" said Salter, feigning deep grief. Then he went on with roll-call. But we three new boys—Brochwel Gilmartin, Charlie Iredale, and I, were linked together in sympathy as not being "white men," as defined by the troglodyte Salter, and we became friends from that hour.

I needed friends. I had not been in Colborne College forty-eight hours, but already I was aware that all the other boys seemed to be cousins, or at least second cousins, and that they were all Tories by birth. I had no relatives, and my parents had always been Liberals. At that time political and religious loyalties were even more important in Canada than knowing who was related to whom, and roughly how much money they had. I felt deeply bereft, and saw myself nobody at all, but that did not last. Salter proclaimed loud and long that I hailed from an unknown place called Sioux Lookout, which must unquestionably be a dump, and I was quickly dubbed Nature Boy, a denizen of the woods.

I was laughed at because I said "Look *out*" with a warning emphasis of the second syllable; I had never heard the name spoken otherwise. And it was a reasonable pronunciation, for Sioux Lookout was a point at which the Ojibwa, for centuries, had met and resisted their enemies from the south, the Sioux. So—Sioux Look*out*. Why not?

Colborne College was an admirable school, but of course that does not mean that it was a comfortable, agreeable place; the most strenuous efforts of the most committed educationalists in the years since my boyhood have been quite unable to make a school into anything but a school, which is to say a jail with educational opportunities. Schools, since their beginning, have been devised to keep children out of their parents' way, and in our time they have the added economic duty of keeping able-bodied young folk off the labour market. But they are so organized that only the most inveterate block-heads can enter at the bottom and come out at the top without having learned a few things.

At Colborne we learned not only the set curriculum, but also the intricate politics of community life, how to behave toward our elders and presumed betters, and a certain sophistication, shallow but useful. We learned how to bend, but not break. We learned to take the rough with the smooth. We learned not to whine or lay claim to privileges which we were not able to carry successfully. We found, and adapted to, what was probably going to be our place in the world. And in the midst of all this we learned a high degree of cunning in concealing what our true nature might be. You could be an artist, or an aesthete, a philosopher, a fascist, or a con-man at Colborne, and only a few people would guess your secret.

It was this last important lesson, the acquirement and concealment of cunning, that I had already some aptitude for and which, when I came to Colborne, I looked for in others, and found at once in Charlie Iredale and Brocky Gilmartin. Our oddity, and the thing we had to keep to ourselves, was that we knew where we were going.

So many of the boys seemed to feel that some path would open to them after they had left school, and doubtless the university or the military college; they did not give much thought as to what it might be. They lived in a world where their parents had taken paths that they had not chosen with determination, but which they followed more or less contentedly as lawyers or stock-brokers or people caught up in the huge array of inex-plicable jobs that go under the heading of "business."

We three could define our ambitions: Brocky wanted

to be a scholar and university teacher; I wanted to be a physician; Charlie—this had to be kept dark indeed—wanted to be a priest. Yes, a priest, as the word is used in the Anglican Church. To most people at Colborne that word meant a Roman Catholic. There were a few R.C.s in the school, just as there were a few Jews, but they would never have dreamed of questioning the straight Anglican line taken by the Headmaster. I think they even enjoyed it, making mental reservations, no doubt, but savouring the fine prose and the gentlemanly formality of the whole thing. They did not seek to emphasize their differences.

Colborne, a good school but of course not a paradise, offered a fine spread of learning useful in all three of the professions we had chosen so early in life. The masters were pleased that Brocky liked to dig deep under the surface of the lessons he learned in classics and modern languages; I could make the most of the physics and chemistry labs if I did not shirk classics; Charlie was good at history, and at nothing else.

[5]

NATURE BOY. They could have given me worse and less appropriate names, because when I went to Colborne I knew more of the wilderness than the lads whose acquaintance with nature meant a summer home at Georgian Bay and some water-sports on much-travelled lakes. I was born and passed my first fourteen years in and around Sioux Lookout, which was nearly two thousand miles north-west of Toronto. The southern world reached us by the daily appearance of the transcontinental train of the Canadian National Railway, which dropped mail and parcels when there were any. Most of the mail was for my father's mine. It was not really his mine, but one of many mines that belonged to a company of which he was a part owner; its product was iron pyrites, an uninteresting mineral, but of value in the hardening and refining of several other metals, and in the preparation of green vitriol, which was used in the manufacture of inks and dyes.

It seemed to me then that my father was the king of the place. Certainly he was its most substantial citizen. But I now understand that he cannot have been a man of much ambition, as he was content to live in an out-of-the-way place, managing an easy mine, and without much company of his own degree of education or cultivation. What he really liked was hunting and fishing, and he was able to do that all the year round, because there were no forest rangers very near to question him, and as the Indians on the adjacent reserve hunted and fished legally whenever they pleased, a man doing the same thing would have attracted no attention if a ranger had passed through.

My father was a man of kindly, easygoing disposition. He was very good to me, teaching me quite a lot about engineering and mathematics without actually making lessons of it, and taking me with him into the forest, and canoeing on Lac Seul. With him I learned to know the trees, the white and the black spruce, the balsam firs, the jack-pines, the queenly birches growing in stands by themselves, and the trembling aspens that threw such a varied and magical light when the sun shone, and offered a shuddering, nervous presence in a forest otherwise still and at times alarming. Not that I was alarmed, except when there was an unexpected storm; I will not say that I loved the stillness of the forest, because it was too much a part of my life to be singled out for notice, but that stillness became for me the measure and norm of what life should be and I carry it in my soul still. When I am most in need of rest in the racket and foolish bustle of modern Toronto, I lock my doors and close my curtains and try to recapture the stillness of the forest in which I grew up, and shared with my father.

My mother was quite a different sort of person. She had been well-educated, in the manner of her youth, which meant that it never occurred to her to go to a university, but she acquired a cultivation and a range of knowledge that few university-bred girls seem to have. I think she did what many women did in her time, and allowed her life to be conditioned by the circumstances of her marriage and the tastes of her husband. He was an engineer and soon after their marriage became the boss of a mine in Sioux Lookout; very well, to Sioux Lookout she would go and see what it had to offer her. What it offered was a wide range of possibilities for nature study and botanizing, and she took to these with enthusiasm. It offered what was much valued by women of her sort at that time, and that was an opportunity to "do good," to help those less fortunate than herself, to teach new ideas of sanitation and child-care, to make my father "read the Riot Act" to drunks who beat their women, and to try to help, when help was needed, the Indian women on the reserve nearby. She was a Good Influence, and though that is much mocked in our time, it was an indisputable fact in her time, and she filled the role with good sense and enthusiasm. Everybody liked and respected Mrs. Hullah, even though they didn't always want to do what she thought best.

In the home, she was determined that I should not be what she called "a woods child," and very often the C.N.R. train dropped parcels of books and gramophone records from Toronto, and our house rang with Beethoven and Brahms (this was before the craze for

Mozart had begun) and on Saturday nights with Gilbert and Sullivan, which my father loved. I took in the Savoy operas almost before I could speak, and liked them better than *Faust*, which my mother had complete in large albums of records. I liked the Devil, but I didn't know how Faust had wronged Marguerite, and nobody thought it proper to tell me.

I look back on those days in Sioux Lookout as if to a lost paradise. I was a lonely child, but I liked loneliness and like it still. Despite my mother I was a woods child, and what the woods taught me is still at the heart of my life. And unlike so many of the people I meet in my consulting-room I loved and admired my parents and was grateful to them, and am so still. Oh, of course, I had the usual adolescent revolt, but it passed as childhood diseases should.

[6]

NOT, HOWEVER, as all childhood diseases do. When I was eight I fell ill of scarlet fever, and I bear some of the marks of it still.

How did I get it? (Or should I say how, and why, did I "catch" it, for as a physician I have always been aware of the wisdom that lies in the notion that one "catches" a disease, rather than being caught by it.) From time to time I wandered down to our little railway station, which was not much more than a shed, and stared at and mingled with the passengers who got down on the platform for the five minutes or so that the train halted, to stretch their legs and perhaps to wonder at the nearness of the forest and the great silence that enwrapped it. Did some infected carrier of the disease cough or sneeze near me? That was the received wisdom of the time about scarlet fever. That was how it was passed on.

One day a queer thing happened, which I never told my mother. The train halted, and among the passengers who stepped down to the platform to take the air were three girls, rather older than I—eleven or twelve, I should say—and they eyed me curiously as I scowled back at them. They whispered and giggled among themselves, and then the boldest—she had ringlets and wore a white bunny-skin coat and overshoes trimmed with the same fur—darted forward and kissed me full on the mouth. They hurried back into the train, squealing with juvenile sexual excitement, and left me, red in the face, in the middle of a group of laughing adults. Was that how the infection was passed on? Whatever, or however, I think I caught scarlet fever from that young hussy, and after a few days of moping, sore throat, and occasional vomiting, I was extremely ill.

My mother consulted the clinical thermometer. My temperature was 103 F, and I was covered with a flaming rash. Dr. Ogg was called at once.

Dr. Ogg was not an ornament of the medical profession, and he was rarely called to our house except in extreme emergencies. Dr. Ogg was a drunk and a failure. His wife had run away long ago to pursue a life of shame in Winnipeg, which must certainly have been more lively than life with Dr. Ogg. Since her departure the doctor had declined into dirt and moral squalor. His livelihood was earned chiefly by writing prescriptions for bottles of gin, whisky, and brandy, required regularly by the few hundred citizens of the village for ailments that Dr. Ogg identified. This was an era when the sale of intoxicating liquors was forbidden by law in Canada, but a qualified physician could prescribe them when they were imperatively needed, and qualified physicians regularly did so, though rarely on the scale of Dr. Ogg. As there was no pharmacy in the village, he kept the stocks in his own professional premises, and thus had the advantage of being able to sell them at his own prices. He was, in fact, a bootlegger, raggedly cloaked in a physician's gown, but when there was an emergency it was still remembered that he was also a doctor.

Dr. Ogg appeared at my bedside, smelling strongly of disinfectant and brandy. He was reasonably sober, for he feared my father, who could have made trouble for him if he had become too much of a local disgrace. He examined me, and sniffed at me (I have never forgotten that), and beckoned my mother out of the room, to tell her that I had scarlet fever, probably in the form of *scarlatina miliaris*, and that it was an extremely dangerous disease. For the present there was nothing to be done except to keep me as comfortable as possible, and let the fever take its course.

When he left, he went to my father's office at the mine, and told him that it would be necessary to quarantine our house. Everybody had forgotten the fact, but Dr. Ogg was Medical Officer of Health in our district, and this was part of his duty. If the disease got to the Indians, he said, there would be hell to pay, because they had no resistance to it, and the consequences would be frightful. So, some telegraphing was done, and next day the east-bound train brought several red placards from Winnipeg, which were duly tacked on all the doors of our house, warning the public to keep its distance, because something not too remote from the plague lurked inside.

My father, deeply reluctant, had to move out and camp in his office at the mine. Inside the house remained my mother, the Indian girl who served as "hired help," and myself. My mother was my nurse, living in an adjacent room. Dr. Ogg visited us twice a day, and became more and more depressed and despondent. Why did not my mother and Dr. Ogg get the disease to which they were daily exposed? Why have I, in all my years of practice, never "caught" anything from a patient? I think I know but my theory would not look well in a medical journal.

My temperature went from 103 to 105 and stayed there for several days. I was twice daily put in a "cold pack"—a sheet soaked in cold water, enclosed in a blanket—to reduce the fever, but without success. At last the thermometer rose to 106, and Dr. Ogg told my parents that I was not likely to live overnight.

What happened then I know only because of what my mother told me many years later. As evening fell on the day when Dr. Ogg gave the bad news, some Indians began to appear on our lawn, outside my bedroom window; they made a clearing in the snow and set up a tent, a simple affair of poles leaning inward and bound together at the top—a tepee, or wigwam, covered in skins. My mother did not understand what was happening, and it was my father who told her, when he came for his usual sundown visit. She talked to him out of a window.

"They've sent for Elsie Smoke," said my father.

My mother knew who Elsie Smoke was—a "wise woman," a herbalist who sold charms against various misfortunes, and mixed some tonics and lenitives from stuff she gathered in the woods, and now and then applied mouldy bread to axe-cuts or serious injuries of the sort. This was before the discovery of penicillin, and Elsie's remedy seemed to people like my mother to be dirty, irrational, and, if efficacious, it must be because of luck rather than any knowledge of the healing powers of mould.

"What are they going to do?" said my mother. "We can't have Elsie Smoke here. You know what Ogg said.

I've got enough to bear without some sort of interference like this. Tell them to go away."

"I don't think we should do that, Lily," said my father. "I told you how grateful they were that you're doing your best to keep the infection in our house and away from the reserve people. They want to help, if they can. It would be mean-spirited to turn them away. Not that I'm sure they'd go," he added, remorsefully. Like my mother he had faced the fact that I was virtually certain to die, and that for both of them this would be a cruel blow. It is a measure of the confidence and love between them that my mother did not insist further that Elsie Smoke and whatever came with her should be driven away.

Of this, as I have said, I knew nothing, and my recollection of what happened subsequently is a mixture of what my mother told me and some phantasmagorical recollections of my own, in which she had no part. The tent was completed, and about seven o'clock at night Elsie Smoke made her appearance, carrying a number of objects my mother could not identify, and went into the tent, without nodding to or in any way recognizing the Indians who stood about, and who shortly afterward went off to their own homes. Not a sound or a sign of life came from the tent, until about ten o'clock, when bird-calls began to be heard from time to time. Bird-calls, on a night in the dead of winter; what could that be? After a time the bird-calls were intermingled with low animal cries, in which the howl of a wolf, not at full strength but low and as if at a great distance, was predominant. And then the tent began to shake, and it shook and it shook as if it would fly into the air. The bird-calls and animal voices gradually tapered off, and a very low drum-beat was heard in their place, and this went on, and on, until my mother said it seemed to be hypnotic, for she at last allowed her weariness to over-come her—she had been nursing me night and day for at least three weeks—and she laid herself down on her bed, partly dressed, in case I should call out in the night.

I heard none of this, for I was in what I now know was a coma, and perhaps approaching death, for my fever was at its worst. But about midnight, I somehow became aware of the drum-beat and, although I had been most strictly commanded not to get out of bed, and although I was so weak and feverish that I could barely drag, I managed to creep to the window and look out at the shaking tent. The window did not fit per-fectly, because no windows ever did so in those days, and some cold draughts crept through the crevices at the sides; I snuffed them up eagerly, although they almost made me vomit, in the condition I had reached. And there, I cannot tell for how long, I huddled on my knees, in my nightshirt, staring at the shaking tent and listening to the drum-beat which, as my mother said, was truly hypnotic.

When my mother came in at six o'clock the next morning, I was lying on the floor by the window. She gave a shriek, for she was sure I was dead, but I was nothing of the sort, and was quickly huddled back into bed and—oh, how often this happened during that ill-ness!—my temperature was taken, in my armpit as I could not bear to have anything for long in my swollen and painful mouth. To my mother's astonishment it had dropped to 104 and by the time Dr. Ogg came at nine o'clock it was 102. I was sweating profusely.

Ogg was delighted and quick to claim credit. "The crisis has passed," he declared; "that's what I had hoped for."

"But you said—"

"I know, Mrs. Hullah, but I thought it best to prepare you for the worst. But I never gave up hope. Not personally, that's to say. That has been my watchword, always. Never give up hope."

It was then that my mother thought to look out of the window. The tent was gone, and the only sign that it had been there—and what a sign!—was a patch of sere grass where the tent had stood. Not less than two feet of snow and ice had melted away beneath it.

My mother told Ogg what had happened, though she had no idea of what importance might be attached to it. But Ogg had, and was very angry.

"Damned interfering old slut," he said, with a very red face. "Her and her shaking tent and her damn-fool rubbish! I'd have her run out of this place if she wasn't on the reserve and a little bit outside the law. She just keeps up superstition and gets in the way of the advance of science."

The good news was quickly taken to my father. The important Ogg did that, to gain whatever credit he could for my improvement, although he warned that too much significance should not be attached to my drop in temperature.

It continued to drop, however, though not so dramatically, and in about a week it was normal or a tittle or so above, and I was able to embark on the long course of egg-nogs, very lightly flavoured with rum, with which my mother was determined to bring back my strength.

It was ten weeks, however, before I was in any real sense recovered. There was a long and disgusting period when I had to scurf off the brown flakes of skin that were left behind by the fever. Ogg had a fine word for that. "Desquamation," he called it, and insisted that I be gently brushed down while standing on a square of newspaper, and that every flake be gathered and burned, as it was still infectious, as was I. My mother was to wear a mask, so as not to inhale any of my body-dust.

All this time my poor father was sleeping in his office, but at last I was able to wave to him out of the window of my room. As soon as I was declared non-infectious, Ogg demanded that the whole of our house be disinfected, which at that time meant plentiful swabbing and daubing with carbolic acid in solution. It ruined the finish on the furniture and of course it destroyed all the wallpapers, but my father was so delighted that he promised my mother a jaunt to Toronto for a complete refurnishing.

This could not take place until after my mother's illness. Ogg was officious about that, but it was perfectly plain that she was worn out with anxiety and nursing, and needed "building up" with one of Ogg's most powerful tonics. It was an era of medicine when great faith was still reposed in tonics, which were chiefly composed of iron and a few bitter herbs mixed with cheap sherry. My father added tonics of his own, admirable wines from his cellar. He had always been a keen lover of wine since his student days in Montreal, and had plentiful stocks that saw him happily through the rigours of Prohibition. Ogg was sure his nostrums "made blood." My father was equally sure his wines "made blood" and he even extended his theory to include me, and I had plenty of wine diluted with water every day, forming a taste that I have never lost. But of course this was "medicinal" and only incidentally pleasurable.

Thus I suppose something like four or five months passed to include my convalescence and my mother's, before my parents, armed with measurements of all sorts, took the train to Toronto to refurbish our house. It was decided—O joy beyond all telling!—that I should accompany them. They thought, kind folk, that after my brush with death I deserved a treat.

It was thus that at the age of nine-going-on-ten I made my first descent upon the city that has enveloped my life and which I hold in great affection. London is romantic and historically splendid; Paris is infinitely beautiful and has an air of louche aristocracy; Vienna has an ambiguity of spirit—a bittersweet savour—which enchants me. But Toronto—flat-footed, hard-breathing, high-aspiring Toronto—has a very special place in my heart, like a love one is somewhat ashamed of but cannot banish. I was lucky to visit it first in spring, when the trees were coming into leaf, for it is a city of trees and they are its chief beauty, all through the year. If ever it loses its trees it will be like a woman who has lost her hair.

We stayed at the King Edward Hotel and, while my parents spent long days in Eaton's, choosing wallpapers and hangings, I was left in the hotel library, where various hotel people kept an eye on me. But I was up to no mischief; the library was the usual characterless hotel assemblage of books, except that somebody had furnished a tall shelf with a long run of the *Illustrated London News* extending back into the eighties and nineties, over which I pored in a kind of enchantment, forming a totally erroneous idea of the appearance and life of the capital city of the British Empire. Best finds of all were pictures and accounts of the first appearance of many of the Gilbert and Sullivan operas, and to me they were as if written yesterday. We made one memorable visit to the theatre, the Princess on King Street, long gone to make room for University Avenue, where we saw Fritzi Scheff in *Mlle. Modiste*, and I experienced my first conscious stirrings of sex as I gazed at her beautiful legs. I had never been in a theatre before, and to this day even the most heavy-breathing drama of degradation and social injustice has a certain glamour for me; I always hope that a leg may appear to lighten the darkness.

By far the most significant part of this swoop upon civilization was a visit to an eminent physician, Dr. James Robb, who was to look me over and pronounce on my condition. He took a long time about it, and I now recall him as a thorough and expert diagnostician. Not much of a psychologist, however, for when he had listened and probed and punched me, he proceeded to tell my parents what he had discovered, while I was still in the room, standing by my mother's chair. I was, he said, "delicate" and must be treated accordingly; scarlet fever had left me with a somewhat dubious heart and a considerable loss of hearing in my left ear. All things considered, I had come off lightly from my encounter with a dangerous and insidious disease, but I must under no circumstances be overtaxed.

This was of utmost importance to my future, because whoever declares a child to be "delicate" thereby crowns and anoints a tyrant.

[7]

SCHOOL WAS the problem. How was I to get any sort of education? I was already ten and had never been to school in my life. The local school was a Catholic mission school where the nuns spent all of each morning teaching prayers and the Catechism. That would never do for my parents, who never went to church, even when that was possible, but whose Protestant prejudices were unimpaired. There was no school on the reservation; the Ojibwa could attend the mission school if they wished, and they did not wish. The only solution was for my parents to teach me.

Not a bad solution, as it happened. My father was a

good mathematician, in the engineering mode, and algebra and geometry were at his fingers' ends. With them, he mingled some science, as it related to engineering, which was much more practical than any science I learned later at Colborne. More interesting to me were his demonstrations, on our walks, of the essentials of geology. My mother took on geography and Latin, and they united on history (my father was greatly concerned about Napoleon's campaigns), and literature, which meant unlimited reading and much memorizing of poetry. Every morning I had lessons; every afternoon I was free to read, or play, or roam.

If I roamed, however, it had to be under the care of Eddu, and I loathed and despised Eddu, who reciprocally loathed and despised me.

He was a Métis lad, about thirteen, I suppose, who had a bad leg because long ago he had been caught in a trap in the woods. Mrs. Smoke had given him her bread-mould treatment, but he still walked with a hirpling gait locally called the string-halt. His disability was supposed in some mysterious way to create a sympathy for me, the delicate child, but it did nothing of the kind. There was a notion that I would learn some French from Eddu, but at its best his French was a patois and when he wanted to tease or humiliate me it retreated into a muddle of French, English, Ojibwa, and a dash of Gaelic that was called Bungee, or Red River dialect, which baffled me. Eddu's real name was Jean-Paul, but he was called Eddu for no reason I ever heard.

My dislike for him might be called snobbish and fastidious, but in my experience snobbery sometimes means no more than a rejection of what is truly inferior, and if mankind had never been fastidious I do not suppose that *haute cuisine* would ever have displaced hunks of meat parched over a smoky fire. I did not like Eddu because he suffered from the most overwhelming adolescent sexual erethism I have ever encountered. Put more bluntly, Eddu was unappeasably horny.

The very first day that Eddu, officially charged with the guardianship of my delicacy, took me into the woods, he stopped as soon as we were among the trees and showed me his penis, which was in a high state of excitability. He demanded that I should show him mine, which I refused to do, less because of modesty than from fear of where this might lead. Not that I had any notions as to where it might lead, but I sensed that this was dangerous business. He jeered at me, and said I probably had nothing to show. He wanted me to touch his, to test its heat and rigidity, and I did so tentatively and without enthusiasm. He was like that all the time, he said, and it explained his somewhat stooped and loping walk. The girls in the village and on the reserve all knew about him and some of them permitted him the favour of a "feel," so that he was an expert on the subject of local female adolescence or, as he said, "How they was comin' along." There were others who allowed him an intimacy he called "stink-finger." As described by Eddu this game seemed as prolonged and ecstatic as anything in the *Kama Sutra*. I could watch him with the girls, if I liked. I did not like. Without knowing precisely how or why trouble would come of that, I had a deep intuition that I should keep clear of it.

I was not ignorant of sex. I had read a good deal about it in the works of Sir Walter Scott. Love, I knew, was a very fine thing, and for me it took the form of an idealization of Fritzi Scheff. Like any country child I had seen animals "at it" and vaguely discerned what it was they were at, but I did not make the leap from the animal to the human experience because animals were, after all, animals and we were not. My parents never said anything about this matter, assuming perhaps that I was too delicate to know about it, and anyhow, what was the good of putting ideas in a boy's mind, where they would occur in plenty of time. About Eddu they had no inkling whatever.

I very quickly reached an arrangement with Eddu; I would go my way and he would go his, and he could collect his dollar a week for guarding me without any fear that I would tattle on him. I have never since thought of Eddu as an exemplar of natural man; he was not like an animal because animals have a sexual restraint that Eddu lacked, and they have their chief business to attend to, which is getting enough to eat to keep them healthy. Eddu was a product of civilization, which has made it possible for a man to devote his whole attention to sex, to make a primary pastime and hobby of it, and indeed to live for it. Eddu's future, I know now, would have been happiness as he understood it until he was about eighteen, after which he would spread syphilis among his male and female companions, and would be barking mad before he was thirty. This is not nature: this is civilization gone askew.

So I was blessedly free of Eddu, and wandered at my own sweet will. Sometimes I went into the forest, which was right at the edge of the village, and loved it and responded to it, but not in the literary fashion that would have pleased my mother. She coursed me through *Hiawatha*, explaining that he had been an Ojibwa, and that the shores of Gitche Gumee really meant Lake Superior, which was a considerable distance south of us, but near enough to be an exciting literary association. *Hiawatha* did not take with me; I did not "catch" Longfellow as I had "caught" scarlet fever. I tried loyally to think of the North West Wind as Keewaydin and Gitche Manitou as God in an Indian war-bonnet, but as there were Indians all around me and they did not carry on like that I could not delude myself with high-flown nonsense. I could swallow *The Lay of the Last Minstrel* and *The Lady of the Lake* without a blink, because there was nothing in my real world to contradict them. But not *Hiawatha*; the reality, or what was left of it, lay too near.

To me, the forest was peace and loneliness and freedom to think and feel as I pleased. It was tangible nobility and it struck into my being without literary interference. Later in my life, when I was far from the forest, I found the same thing in music.

[8]

MY ILLNESS, and my importance as a delicate child, coloured all my thinking, and I was anxious to know everything about it that I could find out. I haunted Mrs. Smoke.

I choose the word with care. I would manifest myself in her cabin and sit quietly on the floor without speaking a word, although I knew that she was aware of me. I would watch her at her endless messings, as she boiled or soaked plants, scraped and rubbed up bits of bone, chose or rejected scraps of dirty fur, and seemed never to be finished or pleased with what she was doing.

I found out, as time went on, what she was doing. Diuretics for unfortunates with stone, or gravel, concocted from bearberry and dandelion. Alum root, boiled in milk, for suspected cancers. Burdock for the woefully constipated, a numerous group on the reserve; blackberry boiled in milk for the occasional sufferer from diarrhoea. These were comparatively harmless remedies that never killed and now and then might cure. But Mrs. Smoke dealt in other nostrums not so innocent.

Bittersweet for "female complaints"—yes, perhaps. Spasm root for help in childbirth—yes, that worked most of the time; but there were abortifacients, sought by the overdriven mothers of ten or eleven hungry children, and sometimes these brought death, but never brought a Mountie to Mrs. Smoke's door; the Indian and Métis community was too secretive for that.

She prepared decoctions of foxglove for weary old hearts, and doubtless these sometimes hastened a death that was already on its way, because digitalis has to be handled with more discretion than Mrs. Smoke knew. Her brews of deadly nightshade for palsy and epilepsy, and for a well-established cancer, I cannot now bear to think of. But the decoction of willow bark she gave for fevers and agues I now recognize as being a carrier of salicylic acid—a primitive form of Aspirin, no less, and much what I prescribe daily.

Mrs. Smoke's patients were exclusively Métis and Ojibwa, with one notable exception, which was supposed to be a secret, but in communities like Sioux Lookout there are no secrets. The exception was Père Lartigue, the missionary priest, who suffered dreadfully from piles. But he could not appeal to Doc Ogg because Doc Ogg would have demanded that he hike up his *soutane*, and let down his pants, and show the afflicted part; Père Lartigue's Jansenist modesty could not endure such an exposure. So every Saturday night old Annie, his housekeeper and the source of all rectory gossip, called on Mrs. Smoke for a jar of fresh butter in which boiled yarrow had been generously mixed, for the priestly anointing.

All this I knew from keen observation and eavesdropping in Mrs. Smoke's grimy one-room hovel. Her cabin was squalid, and stank—an old, inveterate stench of decay but not of death. She had skin bags, and cloth

bags, and bags that had begun to grow moss on the outside because of whatever was on the inside. There were
no corners in her cabin; wherever a corner might have
been expected was a heap of rags and pelts and odds and
ends that did not look like anything anybody had ever
used or made. There was no chimney, but a hole in the
roof—a small hole—through which most, but not all, of
the smoke from her fire disappeared. The fire was partly
contained in a stone structure that was part grate, part
stove, part kitchen table, and on it something smelly
was always on the boil. The floor was of pounded earth
and after long rains or the spring thaw it was soft and
moist to the foot. The ceiling was low and black. The
one object that was not wholly utilitarian was a doll, the
foundation of which was a rough crucifix that hung on
the wall, covered with beads and feathers. Above it hung
a smoke-blackened mask of a face divided down the
middle into a red and a black half; the nose and mouth
were twisted to one side in an expression that might
have been derision, or madness. I once asked what it
was, but Mrs. Smoke gave no answer.

She rarely gave answers. The Indians and the Métis,
merry enough among themselves, were morose and taci-
turn with me. But Mrs. Smoke was the most uncommunicative of them all. I could tell from the look of her
back, and the sound of her breathing, when she might
be inclined for conversation. But despite these difficulties I had many a fine talk with Mrs. Smoke. It would
be tedious to recount them, and impossible to render
her part in comprehensible English, because when she
wanted to push me away, so to speak, she drifted more
and more into the Red River patois of which I did not
understand one word in ten. So let me give you the drift
of all those talks in a single dialogue, in which I put
Mrs. Smoke's words in ordinary English, as a few of the

Indians spoke it; that leaves out a great deal of the flavour of what was said, but what else can I do?

Myself: I've decided what I am going to be, Mrs. Smoke. When I grow up, that's to say.

Mrs. Smoke: (No words, but an almost imperceptible grunt, which I take for encouragement.)

Myself: I'm going to be a doctor and cure people. Like you, Mrs. Smoke.

Mrs. Smoke: (Says nothing, but from the heaving of her shoulders I know she is laughing.)

Myself: Do you think that's too ambitious? I'm a worker, you know. Both my parents say so. I learn quickly. I'm going away to school when I'm stronger.

Mrs. Smoke: You go to a doctor-school?

Myself: Oh no, not yet. I have to learn a lot of other stuff first. A doctor has to know just about everything there is.

Mrs. Smoke: Like Doc Ogg, eh?

Myself: No, not like Doc Ogg. And you know why.

Mrs. Smoke: (Does not rise to this bait, and after a time I go on.)

Myself: Who cured me when Doc Ogg said I would die? You know, Mrs. Smoke. It was you, wasn't it?

Mrs. Smoke: No, not me.

Myself: Who, then?

Mrs. Smoke: Never you mind.

Myself: But I do mind. You had your tent right outside my window, and there were noises and drumming, and the tent shook till it looked as if it would fly away. And I began to get better from that night. Not that I'm completely better yet. I'm still delicate, you know.

Mrs. Smoke: Shit.

Myself: What?

Mrs. Smoke: Strong as a bear. You don't fool me. You live to be an old man.

Myself: Oh, I know. But I'll always be delicate. I'll always have to be very careful.

Mrs. Smoke: You fool everybody else. But you don't fool your own self.

Myself: I really am delicate, you know. Even Eddu says so.

Mrs. Smoke: You'll see Eddu under the ground.

Myself: The sooner the better, so far as I'm concerned.

Mrs. Smoke: What's wrong with Eddu?

Myself: He's bad. He talks about bad things.

Mrs. Smoke: What bad things?

Myself: Girls. You know.

Mrs. Smoke: (She has an unusual fit of giggles.)

Myself: You should respect women. Even girls. My mother says so.

Mrs. Smoke: (She is not to be drawn.)

Myself: What's more, he hath lain with a beast to defile himself. Père Lartigue's dog! The priest's dog! How's that for defilement?

Mrs. Smoke: You get sore prick doin' that. Bitch very salty.

Myself: What if the bitch has something? Something half-dog and half-Eddu? What'll people say then?

Mrs. Smoke: Sell it for a show. Make Eddu rich.

Myself: Mrs. Smoke, I don't like to say this, but sometimes I think you aren't serious.

Mrs. Smoke: (Says nothing but is seen to shake.)

Myself: Mrs. Smoke, will you take me for a pupil? Teach me all you know about medicines and cures? Teach me about the shaking tent? I'll work hard. I'll be your slave.—Will you, Mrs. Smoke?

Mrs. Smoke: No.

Myself: But why? You'll never get a better pupil. Who'll carry on after you?

Mrs. Smoke: Can't do it. All wrong.

Myself: What's all wrong? Here I am, crazy to be a great doctor and help people, and you won't teach me.

Mrs. Smoke: I said: all wrong.

Myself: But why?

Mrs. Smoke: Wrong colour. Wrong eyes. Wrong brains. It would kill you.

Myself: What would kill me?

Mrs. Smoke: What you have to go through.

Myself: Worse than university, you mean? I'm not afraid of that.

Mrs. Smoke: You God-damn better be afraid if you want to learn. You God-damn better. You have to go crazy, starve, sweat nearly to death. Then maybe you ready to learn. But you wrong colour. Wrong colour outside, wrong colour inside. Wrong eyes. Can't see except what white person see. Wrong brains. You gab, gab, gab all the time; never watch; never listen. Never *hear* nothin'. Wrong brains.

Myself: Then help me to get the right brains. I'll shut up. I'll be like a mouse. Teach me to see the way you see. Teach me to hear. Please, Mrs. Smoke.

Mrs. Smoke: No.

Myself: I thought you were my friend. But you don't take me seriously.

Mrs. Smoke: (A long pause, then—) What's your animal?

Myself: My animal? I haven't got an animal. Not even a dog.

Mrs. Smoke: Your animal that goes with you and helps you.

Myself: Oh, I get it. You mean like in *Hiawatha*? My totem. I haven't got one. I guess I could choose one.

Mrs. Smoke: You don't choose him. He chooses you.

Myself: Haven't I got any say?

Mrs. Smoke: No.

Myself: Then how would I know?

Mrs. Smoke: You'd know all right. *(A long pause, during which I try to understand what Mrs. Smoke is saying; respectful as I am toward her, I have a certain feeling of superiority, as one who can read—which she cannot—and has been to Toronto, which seems to me to be an Athens. At last—)* You want to try?

Myself: About the totem, you mean?

Mrs. Smoke: Look in the basket beside you.

The basket is one of several, but this one has a cover. Consumed with curiosity I lift the cover quickly, and start back with a gasp, for I have heard the warning. In the basket, on some leaves, are two of our ground rattlesnakes, the Massassaugas, about which I have been repeatedly warned; roused from their torpor they give their warning rattle, which is not loud but to my ear has terrible menace. My father has warned me against these creatures: my mother has a great horror of snakes and cannot bear to hear them mentioned, and she has infected me with her fear. Have I turned white? Probably, for Mrs. Smoke laughs her silent, shaking laugh. She dips her hand into the basket and pulls out a snake, which writhes around her arm. She grasps it behind its ugly head. She pushes it toward me, urging me to touch its black-blotched head. I shrink back and whimper, for I fear the dreadful fangs. Long afterward I learn that the bite of these creatures is rarely fatal. Rarely—what sort of reassurance is that to a boy, already convinced of his delicacy, confronted by an old woman who he suddenly sees as quite other than himself, not simply in race and age, but in the deepest truth of her being, who is giggling and pushing the dreadful snake—(it is really only about twenty-four inches long but to me it has the menace of a dragon)—toward his face? At last Mrs. Smoke drops the creature back into its basket and replaces the lid.

Mrs. Smoke: Don't like your totem, eh?

Myself: It's not mine. It can't be mine. It's awful.

Mrs. Smoke: Totem can be awful. You knew it when you saw it. What did you think? A pet?

I have sat down on the dirt floor, as far from the horrible basket as possible. I must have looked unwell, for Mrs. Smoke, unwontedly, hands me a mug of tea. Her tea is a fearful concoction, and not all tea, I think. But I manage to gag down a few sips of it, and feel better. My determination to leave the cabin, and never speak to Mrs. Smoke again, gradually gives way to my curiosity.

Myself: I'm sorry if I was yellow.

Mrs. Smoke: (Makes no answer.)

Myself: Would I ever get used to it, do you think?

Mrs. Smoke: Yes.

Myself: Mrs. Smoke, what's your totem?

Mrs. Smoke: Ask no questions you'll hear no lies.

Myself: Does it help you to cure people? Did it help you to cure me?

Mrs. Smoke: I didn't cure you.

Myself: Who did then, if it wasn't you?

Mrs. Smoke: (After a very long pause) Them.

Myself: Who's them?

Mrs. Smoke: The ones who came.

Myself: To the shaking tent, you mean?

Mrs. Smoke: (Says nothing.)

Myself: Your helpers, you mean?

Mrs. Smoke: You ask too many questions. Go on home, now.

[9]

As I LOOK back toward those days, I think I must have been a hateful child. I understand that the judgement of an old man, and such an old man as I have become, on his childhood self cannot be truly objective, and certainly there were people who liked me, and I know my parents loved me—my mother with a maternal intensity as her darling snatched from the jaws of death; my father, I suppose, looked on me as his posterity—as someone who would continue his respectable, professionally competent, unaspiring life. But the child I see as I look back is a rotten little fixer, cocksure in his judgement of his elders and convinced without ever putting it into words that he was the cleverest thing in the world of Sioux Lookout.

One of the people who liked me was Dr. Ogg. He had decided that I was the most spectacular case that had ever turned up in his dismal practice, and my survival was entirely owing to his patience and sagacity. Physicians are not permitted to advertise, but Doc Ogg took care that I was a daily reminder to the whole community of his skill.

After my dark encounter with Mrs. Smoke, when she insisted that the hateful, poisonous serpent was in some deep and primitive way united with my fate and my observation of life, I began to pay more attention to Doc Ogg. Vainglorious little wretch that I was, I thought I would match his medicine against Mrs. Smoke's, which I had begun to think had failed me. Not the mystery of the shaking tent, but the horror of the black-spotted snake. The village doctor was not promising as an approach to the white man's medicine, but he was all I had to study.

Doc Ogg was a lonely man, for good reasons. He had a depressing personality and he was a bore. To Indian eyes the horns of the cuckold were plain upon his bald brow. He drank too much, because the drink was always handy in his pharmacy and he hadn't much else to do. Day after day, when he had picked up yesterday's issue of the *Winnipeg Free Press* or the Toronto *Colonial Advocate*, according to the way the train was going, and read it to the bone, the rest of his day stretched before him without incident. A week might pass without his receiving a visit from a patient; an accident in the woods was a godsend to him, provided the patient did not prefer the attentions of Elsie Smoke. His meagre income rested on his activities as an unacknowledged, but clearly recognized, bootlegger.

Consequently a visit from me was always welcome. He thought I came to admire him, to marvel at his learning and skill.

"Science, Jon; science rules the world. Take Père Lartigue, for instance. Not a bad fella, for a Frog, but what's he got to give the people here? Magic. That's what he does in his church. He lets on to turn water and wine mixed, and a piece of bread that old Annie his housekeeper bakes herself, into the blood and flesh of a magician that he tells us lived long ago in the so-called Holy Land. Imagine! And he expects the Indians to swallow that! The Indians aren't fools. Don't you think it. They laugh at him behind his back."

I thought of Eddu and Père Lartigue's dog, and of the many sly insults that were offered to the dull, discouraged, haemorrhoidal missionary priest. But I didn't swallow all of what Doc Ogg had to say about Jesus.

"You don't believe in Jesus, Doc?"

Doc Ogg thought it wise to cover his tracks. If it got around among the better element—six English-speaking families that were somehow associated with my father's mine, and a few women among the Métis—that Doc Ogg thought poorly of Jesus, it would not add to his slight reputation.

"I believe in a modern, scientific way, Jon. It's just this magic I won't put up with. Mind you, I suppose ignorant people have to be told what they can understand, or think they understand. They can understand miracles a lot better than they can understand science, because science takes brains, and that's where we've got it all over them. Science rules the world, Jon. Hitch your wagon to science."

I did that, so far as my circumstances allowed. That is to say, I became by degrees Doc Ogg's pharmacist. It was not demanding work. Once I had mastered the apothecary's scale of weights, with its 480-grain ounce and its 12-ounce pound I was ready for work; as I already knew the troy weight system from my father, who used it for the odd scraps of precious metal he found here and there in the district, the apothecary's system was easy. So there I was, in Doc Ogg's kitchen which also served as his dispensing-room, mixing up the totally ineffective tonics, rolling the few pills that were called for, and occasionally pounding up a salve with mortar and pestle (for Doc Ogg had only the simplest elements of an apothecary's laboratory), and gaining an insight into the medical life of Sioux Lookout which gave me a sense of being a privileged insider.

Mrs. Chambers, Mrs. White, and Mrs. Owen all took the same tonic, composed of a pinch or two of medicinal rhubarb and Indian senna, suspended in a cheap red wine Doc bought by the demijohn, and I assume they followed instructions and shook it well before the twice-daily tablespoon. Not all tonics were mixed with wine; if a Métis woman had such a bottle, it would be her husband who would drink it at a draught. Tonics for them had to be bitter without being positively noxious, and were suspended in distilled water. Doc Ogg's water was distilled from the product of his own well, and I did the distilling.

"That's where the profit comes," the Doc would say

as I lined up the bottles of water and nastiness, to be picked up at seventy-five cents a bottle.

Doc had a fair trade in rheumatic ailments of one sort or another, though he never made much distinction among them. Salicylic acid in one form or another, suspended in alcohol, was the preferred treatment, with a salve of Vaseline mixed generously with oil of wintergreen to produce heat and a strong healing smell. Of course this stuff was virtually useless, but rheumatics, as I quickly observed, are often career-invalids, and they did not so much want to be cured as to be a focus of concern and attention. In really severe cases among Métis who paid on the nail for their medications, Doc sometimes ventured on dosing with arsenic, or iodide of iron, or both, and now and again he had the luck of finding a suggestible patient who improved, for a time.

Of course among the rheumatic patients were many who had gonorrhoeal arthritis, and Doc dosed them with quinine, for which some of them formed a genuine liking. Venereal diseases were common, and the Doc took a most unscientific and highly moral attitude toward them. I was not supposed to know about these, but the Doc was too loose-tongued and lonely to keep his mouth shut, and mumbled about people who did not wash enough (though he was not himself an obsessive washer) and who came hobbling into his office with a well-developed chordee.

I see now how many ailments were the consequence of a water supply that was confined to a few wells, many of them too near a seeping privy. When all water has to be carried inside in pails, bathing is a foolish indulgence and Doc often asserted, probably with truth, that some of his patients had not had a bath since the day they were born. But as things were, there was a great deal of scurfing and scabbing, and the formation of cheese-like substances in folds of skin. It is paradoxical that the more often mankind gets into hot water, the better off it is.

Gonorrhoea in all its Protean forms was everywhere; children were born blind, or simple, men had gleet and their women had "the whites" and sometimes "pus in the tubes." Mucus dripped from places where no fetid mucus ought to have been.

Now and then a teamster from the forest appeared with glanders, which he had caught from his horses.

In spite of these ills, however, the town was not a walking sick-ward. People went about their business and discharged it pretty adequately. Their ailments and Doc's remedies were the subjects of long, deliberate, anecdotal evening conversations.

Some illnesses, of course, were very bad. Syphilis Doc dosed with mercuric pills, and a few sufferers pranced about the town with the high-stepping gait of their kind. Tuberculosis was common, but only when it was incapacitating did Doc turn to his program of "unloading the disease through the bowels," done with a mixture of boiled hops and molasses, followed by a starvation diet, to rid the body of excess carbon—which was, of course, the cause of the disease. Where this fantastic notion came from, I have no idea, but before antibiotics, treatment for tuberculosis was highly imaginative.

It did not take me long to discover that the Doc did not really know very much, and had not added anything to his knowledge since he received his degree. That degree, from the University of Toronto, was attested to by a framed certificate which hung, always crooked, on his office wall; it was signed by a number of indecipherable names, but Doc could identify them all, and invariably spoke of them with familiar affection as

"Old So-and-So" from whom he had learned the science which meant so much to him. But later, when I was myself a student at that medical school, I took the opportunity to look up Doc's record, and discovered that he had graduated near the bottom of his year and not a prize or a distinction had ever come his way.

"But keep this clearly before you, Jon," he would say, when he had been too many times to the brandy bottle in the kitchen cupboard, "Science rules the world. Cling to Science, boy, and keep clear of superstition. And there's lots of that. Did you ever hear of Christian Science? That's a what d'ye call 'em—an oxymoron, and don't you ever get to be that kind of a moron."

Doc loved that joke and trotted it out often.

However, I must not be ungrateful to Doc. I cannot say that he taught me pharmacy, because he was himself too shaky-handed and slovenly to mix anything with real accuracy, but he showed me how to teach myself a few of the elements of it. He made it possible for me to look at sick people professionally, and without either pity or contempt. And he taught me what a bugaboo Science can be in the mind of a man who, whatever his ill-luck and his limitations may have been, was simply a fool.

That was the harsh judgement of a boy. As indeed my whole judgement of Sioux Lookout is that of a child, egotistical as children must be to survive; I am sure my vision of the place must be juvenile, but not trivial so far as it goes. Since then I have met so many fools who were vastly more learned than Doc Ogg, and a few holy fools whose lives provoked awe and sometimes terror, and scores of common or garden fools who nevertheless managed to muddle their way through life, skating on the very thin ice that divided them from any real knowledge of themselves or the world about them, without once falling through, that I do not regard the term "fool" as dismissive or even severe.

I have myself played the role of fool in so many guises that I feel a kinship with fools, much as I try to avoid being infected with their folly. For folly is one of the infections toward which Doc's much-vaunted Science has never turned its Cyclops eye.

But I realize that Esme is expecting me to speak. All that has gone before in these jottings in my Case Book, and which forms so much of the underpinning of my life, has presented itself to my mind in a pause of no great length. But now I must speak.

[10]

Esme is eyeing me expectantly, and I realize that I have not answered her question about Charlie Iredale. But as I have explained, questions can now bring back to me such a flood of feeling that I must take heed of it before answering, or I may say something I would rather keep quiet. Especially about Charlie. I suppose I have been silent for fifteen seconds.

"Oh, of course I remember him well. We shared a room in our first year."

"Was that usual?"

"Yes. The school did not have dormitories for boys older than twelve. There were rooms that served as studies and bedrooms. Very bleak they were, too."

"Bleak. How do you mean?"

"The furnishing consisted of two army beds, two pine desks with one drawer, two chairs, and two clothes-presses for us to keep our things in. Oh, and a small mirror and a washstand."

"What's a washstand?"

"How lucky you are not to know. It's a small cupboard

on top of which sits a china jug and a basin and a soapdish. We had no running water in rooms; it had to be fetched from a tap in the corridor, and it was never really hot. In the cupboard underneath there ought to have been a chamber-pot, but we did not have such Persian pomps, and for our creatural needs we traipsed up the hall to the room where the urinals and bathtubs and W.C.s were."

"Sounds Spartan."

"It was Spartan."

"And your parents paid big fees for that?"

"No; they paid for the education. The amenities for the body were kept at a minimum. I speak of the boarders, of course. I suppose there were a couple of hundred of us, and twice as many day-boys. We boarders regarded ourselves, reasonably enough, as the heart of the school."

"You could have lived better than that in jail."

"People who get into jail need luxury; they have no intellectual resources. You're not going to trap me into moaning about the simple conditions of daily life at Colborne: I am sick to death of writers who whine about their school-days. Let's get it over with: the food was dreadful and the living accommodation was primitive, but we knew we weren't there to enjoy life, but to be prepared for its rigours, and on the whole I think it was a good program."

"Very nineteenth century."

"Not entirely. But it had nothing to do with the country-club concept of a boys' school that one hears of, for instance, in the U.S. I have said many times, and I'm saying it again to you, that a boy who can go through a first-rate boarding-school and emerge in one piece is ready for most of what the world is likely to bring him."

I am not going to tell Esme about the fagging system, which still flourished at Colborne in my day. Boys in their first year—New Boys—were assigned to boys in their third and later years to act virtually as servants; clean shoes, brush clothes, get the laundry ready to go out and count and put it away when it came back, polish the buttons on the Rifle Corps uniform and, if the fag-master happened to be an officer, polish the sword; run errands, wrestle the trunks up from the basement when holidays came, and in general do everything they were told without complaint. Some boys hated it, of course. Shelley hated it when he was at Eton, but the world cannot afford many Shelleys. For myself, I don't think it's a bad thing for a privileged boy to find out what it is like to be a servant.

There were occasional tasks of an unusual character; my fag-master, a Hitler-in-embryo named Moss, conceived a passion for a girl in Bishop Cairncross's school for girls, a few streets away; as he had no literary talent, he demanded of me that I prepare a poetic tribute to this goddess, and I laid on his desk, within an hour, a version of one of the innumerable *Odes to Celia* concocted by Elizabethans who were suffering from Moss's malady. Unhappily, the goddess's name was Putzi (for Prudence) Botham, and so my recension began, rather lumpily—

> *My lovely Putzi, heavenly fair,*
> *   As lily sweet, as soft as air,*
> *No more torment me, but be kind*
> *   And with thy love ease my troubled mind.*

This love-garland was duly dispatched to Putzi, but as Moss had none of the cunning of a lover he sent it on college paper with the crest on the back of the envelope, so that when it had been handled by the girls who distributed the mail, it was all over the school that Putzi had received a mash note, and the demands to read it were too great for Miss Botham. The girls were not Elizabethan maidens, but tough lacrosse-playing little Toronto sprouts, and they thought the poem hilarious; Putzi agreed and gave Moss the air, by telephone. Understandably, Moss blamed me for this tragedy, and made my life a burden for a few days, but I was not without a valet's resource, and spat in the glass of water he demanded every night during study-hours. Nevertheless, I gained face of a certain kind, as one who could produce a love poem, authentic if perhaps overstated, on demand.

Of course I shared the secret of the poem with Brochwel Gilmartin, who was delighted by it, and used to make gestures of mock-reverence whenever he met Moss in the halls, as tribute to a true lover and poet.

> *"A breathing Poem—woman's smile—*
> *A man all poesy and buzzem,"*

Brocky would murmur, looking at Moss with doglike admiration. Moss suspected that this was cheek, but on the other hand it might be admiration, of which he could never get enough. As I've said, Brocky was one of my two great resources and friends during my onerous first year at Colborne. The other was Charlie Iredale, and through sheer luck I shared a room with Charlie.

That was good for me, and good for Charlie, as well, because some of his habits might have caused him trouble if he had another room-mate. The very first night he surprised me by kneeling beside his bed, and praying for at least ten minutes. I was not one to pray, myself; my parents, though nominal Christians, had no Christian observances except the festivals of Christmas and Easter. But I had heard about prayer, and was surprised to see it in one so young; I had thought it was something people came to in old age, if at all. I do not suppose there was another boarder in Colborne who prayed as Charlie did, though a few may have muttered something as they lay under the sheets. Prayer was a thing you did in obligatory church, on Sunday morning. But there was Charlie, obviously devout, kneeling by his bed.

I would not have mentioned it, but he did, a week or so later.

"I never see you pray," he said.

"I don't."

"How do you keep your accounts balanced?"

"What accounts?"

"Your life. How do you keep track of which way you are going, and if anything's wrong, why is it wrong, and how do you ask for help when you need help?"

"What's that got to do with praying?"

"Everything. That's part of what praying is."

"Part? How do you mean, part? Isn't prayer just asking for stuff?"

"What a benighted heathen you are, Hullah! Listen—"

And then to my astonishment Charlie, who was just my own age, gave me a brief but pithy lecture on the three modes of prayer: Petition—asking for help and strength for oneself; Intercession—asking for help and strength for others, and for the world; Meditation—placing yourself, silent, before the greatness of God.

"And you think that does some good?"

"I know it does. And so would you, if you thought about it. It's an important part of the big struggle against the Devil. And everybody ought to get into it. You just let everything slide, and then complain when the Devil gets to work on you."

I was not at that time much worried by the Devil, nor was I persuaded to become a prayer myself, but I thought too highly of Charlie to scoff at him. My attitude, I now see, was that of millions of grown-up people; religion may be a very good thing, but it's spooky and too many nuts believe in it, and I didn't want to be bothered. Charlie had other customs, too, not so impressive, which I observed without comment, but which I thought—well, possibly unwholesome.

He fasted on Fridays and on some other days; not obviously, but he ate little and of the plainest foods at table. Nobody noticed, or if they did they thought he was not well. And every day he read in a little black book, which was not quite an ordinary prayer book, called *The Monastic Diurnal.* And when he had any leisure for reading (which was not often because he was slow at school work and needed every minute of study-time to get through the heavy preparation for the next day's lessons) he read a thick book which I could see was called *The Golden Legend.* As he kept this and the *Diurnal* in his desk—and it was a point of honour not to snoop in anybody's desk—I never had more than a passing look at it.

Apart from this unboylike preoccupation with religion, he was a normal schoolboy, or a little brighter than normal, though not at school work. Brochwel Gilmartin and I both thought highly of Charlie because of the charm of his character, and his wit, which took the form of a rattling, gossipy kind of conversation which was full of pointed comment on the behaviour of some of the boys who were at the top of the school, and thought well of themselves and did not understand why everybody else should not do the same. Charlie was never spiteful, but he was observant, and his recounting of a conversation or any sort of encounter with one of these great ones had just enough merrily ironic edge to make it irresistible to Brocky and me. It was as though Charlie saw life from a special angle, as of course he did, for he was describing our Colborne life *sub specie aeternitatis*, in so far as a schoolboy may. He laughed, and laughed infectiously, and Brocky and I were delighted with his company.

This would not have been odd, if we had not been separated by a gulf which is very important in school; Charlie was not clever at school work, except that he really understood history and in the end, after an undistinguished school career, won the History Prize in his last year. But he was often in hot water for tests not passed, or work not done up to a sufficient standard, and by the end of the week he usually had a load of PDs—punishment drills—to be worked off, so that his Saturday afternoons were not free. Brocky and I, however, were good at our work, and won prizes and distinctions, and if we got a PD or so, it was for an ill-defined but clearly understood offence called "cheek," which was impudence toward, or failure in reverence to, our elders and supposed betters. Brocky was full of cheek.

It was the cheek of a boy who knew himself to be intellectually superior to virtually all the other boys in the school, and a few of the masters, as well. For the masters were the usual mixed bag, ranging from men of genuine learning, wide experience of life, bravery in war or something else that made them worthy of admiration, to dullards who drudged efficiently through the same lessons year after year, clods untroubled by a spark. Brocky came from a home dominated by a father who was a self-made man, and unlike some in that category he had made rather a good job of himself, and had given his son the outlook on life of one who has seen the world as it appears to somebody who is getting, and keeping, his head above the waves. Brocky wanted a life of scholarship but he was under no illusion that it was a superior life to that of those more immediately engaged in politics or industry. Under his father's tutelage he had acquired a strong objection to what in those days it was fashionable to call "boloney," and which was to be discerned everywhere. "That's boloney," he would comment several times a day, and usually with good reason. But he was not a shallow scoffer. He distinguished what was worthy from what was unworthy in many things; as he sometimes said to me, when I had confided to him that my father's work was the extraction and refinement of iron pyrites, he knew fool's gold from the real thing.

"At that age? You've got to be kidding." Esme thinks I am playing the old man's game of glorifying the past.

"I'm not. You'd be surprised how early the distinctive strain asserts itself in a really good young mind. Brocky had a very good young mind, and he's become a distinguished scholar, as I expect you know."

"Don't, I'm afraid. That sort of thing doesn't often turn up in my work."

"Then perhaps you'll take my word for it. And he did it by sifting the boloney out of much of his realm of scholarship, which is rare. Universities are not free from boloney. Or had you heard?"

"Oh I've heard. But go on about school life. You must have been an odd lot at Colborne."

"No. But we had at least one weekly admonition from our Headmaster, which bit into the fabric of my mind and many another mind in that school. 'Much has been given to you,' he would thunder, 'and much will be expected from you.' And he was right. It wasn't entirely a school of rich people's boys, but everybody there came in some sense from a background of privilege. And the

Head dinned it into us that we had to justify the position we had inherited. Of course we made fun of him, but we remembered what he said."

This may be putting it rather strongly, but I sense that Esme is not one for subtle distinctions. I tell her that I think the Head was sometimes puzzled by Brocky and Charlie and me, because we lacked the proper boy-like enthusiasm for sport. It was because we didn't care who won in a game where there were strict rules, and where to be a good loser was regarded as almost better than winning: we were getting ready for the game that came after school where the rules were subject to sudden change, and we were determined to win. As we have done, in our various ways. Esme doesn't like that.

"In what way were you winners?"

"I've told you. Brocky has a very wide reputation as a scholar and writer on his scholarly speciality. I am not unknown to the medical world as a man with a few uncommon ideas about disease. I've published a handful of papers which have attracted attention, and I have earned a somewhat murky reputation as a diagnostician."

"Murky? Why murky?"

"I shouldn't have said that, perhaps. It doesn't really fit in with what you wanted to talk about."

"I see. Well—what about Charlie? Has anybody ever heard of him?"

"Perhaps some day they will. He was a man of almost saint-like resolution."

"Ah—there's the saint thing again. Aren't you going to talk about that?"

(Not on your life I'm not, young woman, and I must guard my tongue. How can I steer her away from that subject?)

"If you want to understand Charlie perhaps you should hear more about his school-days."

"If you say so."

[11]

SCHOOL-DAYS; what a lot of boloney—in Brocky's term—has been written by people about their school-days! Innocent souls who recur to them as to a Golden Age, when the world was young and when a few disappointments served only to throw into prominence the splendid moments, and a succession of unsophisticated love affairs gave something like third-rate poetry to every existence. Contrast with them the sophisticated souls, who hated all subjection, suspected all precept and instruction, found love a cheat and life itself a prison, who threw themselves upon the thorns of life and bled copiously into depressing autobiographies. And yet almost all of both groups learned to read, without necessarily comprehending what they read; and to write, without necessarily being able to convey any coherent thought or opinion in what they write; and to figure, or cipher, enough to make change and do ordinary banking, but without much comprehension of what the world of figures means. It is not often that school-days are utterly lost days.

The belly-achers who hated school are usually bores, but the larger group who saw nothing much in school except as a background to growing up, are to be gently pitied, for they began early lives crippled by incomprehension, which might, long afterward, bring them into my consulting-room, complaining of vague, but to me revealing, ailments.

After Brocky and I had met, or at least become conscious of one another, at roll-call (where Salter declared that we were not "white men" because our names seemed unusual to him) I found myself facing him in the corridor, and there was a glint in his eye.

"You're a very tall chap," said he.

"Am I?" said I.

"Who's your tailor?"

"Tailor? I haven't got a tailor."

"So I had divined, with the almost uncanny intuition which is one of my outstanding characteristics. Don't you think you ought to get one?"

"What are you talking about?"

"Sorry. I was initiating a conversation along the lines of Mr. Toots, when he first met little Paul Dombey. You've read *Dombey and Son*?"

"No."

"Not well up in Dickens?"

"I've read *A Christmas Carol*."

"Saints preserve us! And in Sioux Lookout, too!"

"Look, Gilmartin, I've heard just about enough about Sioux Lookout. So shut up, do you hear me?"

"O Great One, I hear and obey. But I must explain: I was beginning a conversation with you along the lines taken by the immortal Mr. Toots when first he meets little Paul Dombey at Dr. Blimber's Academy. Sorry to be so damned literary, but it's the colour of my mind, you see. What's the colour of your mind?—Well, we'll find that out later. But—and you understand I took the literary tack because I didn't want to be too offensive— Mr. Toots asked little Paul who his tailor was because little Paul was so funnily dressed, and do you know what little Paul replied?"

"What?"

"He said: 'It's a woman makes my clothes as yet. My sister's dressmaker.' I don't suppose your clothes are made by your sister's dressmaker?"

"I haven't got a sister. Are you trying to be offensive?"

"No, but I'm obviously not charming you. I just wanted to throw out a literary hint, which hasn't really worked—has it?—that your clothes are likely to make you an object of jocose comment here, from primitives like our friend Salter."

"What's wrong with my clothes? They're what the school Clothing List specified."

"Aha, that explains everything. But you ask what is wrong. My dear man, that collar—!"

"I don't see the other fellows wearing them."

"No, and you won't, except perhaps at Hallowe'en. When did you last see a slim youth (that's you) wearing an inch-and-a-half stiff collar which has already made a red ring around his innocent neck?"

"Aren't they obligatory?"

"No. I won't elaborate; just No. Have you got any money?"

"Some." I had a good deal which my father had left with me, but I was too downy to tell anybody, and kept it buttoned in an inside pocket.

"Then the day after tomorrow, being Saturday, you and I will go downtown and get you a few things that will bring you out of the nineteenth century. Till then, I suppose you must go on with that terrible horse-collar."

Brocky was right. My parents, who were overjoyed when I passed the examinations (which I had to write, to my astonishment, in Doc Ogg's office and supposedly under his supervision, as he was the only university graduate other than my father in Sioux Lookout) that admitted me to Colborne College, were very much astonished by the school Clothing List, which came with my letter of admission. It asked for puzzling things—a dozen stiff collars and a dozen white shirts to which they could be attached, long-sleeved undershirts and pants to match, three lounge suits, one at least to be black or dark blue, and a hard hat, of the kind called a Derby; spats might be worn if desired. But when my father took me to Toronto he dutifully purchased these things, though the haberdashers were surprised that they were for a boy of fourteen; they still kept a few of the stiff collars for their older customers, whose necks had grown leathery with age from wearing such gear. My father murmured a little, for he sensed that the school Clothing List had not been revised since the turn of the century. But he assumed that these were the customs of distinguished old schools, and if the List had demanded a liver pad, or a reversible dicky, he would have ferreted one out, somehow.

Saturday was a deliverance for me, because my appearance was already a subject of ribald comment among the boys in my house, and even the Housemaster, Mr. Norfolk, looked rather askew when he saw me. Brocky had gone through my clothes and declared that the suits, shoes, socks and whatnot were all right, but the terrible underclothes and the shirts and especially the collars had to go, and he suggested the Grenfell Mission as a suitable recipient, for the Esquimaux (as they were then called) were notoriously given to hard stand-up collars. We got some decent soft shirts with attached collars, and some underwear which did not turn a September day into a Turkish bath, and I was a being transformed. Indeed, that was the way Brocky put it:

"*The Deformed Transformed*," said he. "Dramatic poem by the great Lord Byron, unread by virtually anybody but me, and I assure you it's no place to go for a laugh. But the title is remarkably handy for situations like yours, don't you think?"

Brocky and Charlie opened a new world to me, for

here were boys of my own age with minds that were grounded in worlds of which I had never dreamed. I must have been an intelligent boy, but I was like a strong youth who had never been called on to use his muscles; my mind was attuned to dreaming in the forest, and to sharp observation in the different consulting-rooms of Mrs. Smoke and Doc Ogg, but I had never before felt intellectually inferior, which is certainly one of the spurs to intellectual growth. I had never before been in a world where I was not the cleverest boy around, who therefore did not need to exert his brain.

I had read a lot, but I never thought of using what I had read as an inexhaustible source of reference and mental high-jinks, like Brocky; when he quoted from the *Bab Ballads* to cheek Moss I almost jumped out of my skin, to discover somebody else who knew and treasured them.

I had felt much and felt it deeply in the forest, but it had never occurred to me to associate such reflection with anything as remote and generally repugnant as religion, about which the little I knew was barbarous, and Charlie woke me from an ignorant stupor. The school work at Colborne gave me no trouble, but the worlds of Brocky and Charlie made my head spin.

Of course I had been a lonely child, and to be suddenly dropped into a noisy, rattling world of six hundred boys who worked under the dominance of masters who were jocose, acerbic, dowdy-minded and, in some instances, plain bloody-minded; masters who had distinguished themselves in war, and had now taken to the only profession open to men trained for nothing but war; masters who had travelled over the whole world and had fetched up at Colborne; masters for whom great hopes had been entertained when they were young men, and who had felt those hopes fade as the decades passed; masters who were born teachers and made learning an adventure; masters who were obviously engaged in that dismal traffic between those who did not want to learn and one who did not want to teach—not that these, in their ironic despair, were not sometimes the most revelatory of all; all of this was confusing, but breathtaking, bewildering. I had been jerked into another world suddenly, and every day brought several surprises.

One of these was that I had only recently begun to be visited by those dreams that come to all boys, in which sexual experience presented itself in a variety of forms, always terminating in an explosion of copious, hot semen which stained the bedsheets and made the pyjama trousers as stiff as those awful collars from which Brocky had delivered me. I did not know what to do about them, tried without effect to restrain them, and vaguely wondered if I were in some way unnatural, a monster of sexual desire. It was an astonishment therefore when Brocky came into my room—my room and Charlie's—one morning, whistling cheerfully, and announced:

"Gents, I'm on top of the world. Last night La Belle Dame Sans Merci had me in thrall, and that always brings a great clearing of the head."

"What are you talking about," I said, grumpy in the first half-hour of waking.

"You know—the lady whom one encounters in sleep and yields to—oh so gently, until gentleness gives way to ecstasy—full beautiful—a faery's child. A couple of times a week, on average, she takes me to her elfin grot and then—whoopee! One wakes, alone and palely loitering, but one soon feels very much better. I rather pride myself that she comes to me in that splendid romantic guise. There are troglodytes in this school who can be heard snorting and blowing in their sleep whenever the dark fit is on them, and I shudder to think in what form Lilith the Succubus descends on— well, for instance, on my fag-master Salter. He dries his pyjamas on the heating-coils, and his room reeks of the baking Salterian sperm. What will his posterity be, one wonders."

Charlie was blushing furiously. I knew he hated these night visitations, and did his best to conceal them, but, as I keep saying, I am an observer. I wondered in what form Lilith the Succubus—Lilith the Old, Old Mother—came to him. Too well I knew how she showed herself to me. Sometimes she came as a melting young beauty, and I did not know where I learned to form any such image, for melting young beauties were not part of my waking world. I then believed that the waking world was the only world in which truth was to be found; my acquaintance with the wisdom of the dream world came later. Sometimes the succubus was a repulsive hag, and more than once she was Mrs. Smoke, brandishing a rattler in my face and laughing hatefully as I yielded to the irresistible urgency of the dream. The boys at school all talked of these dreams, but Brocky was the only one who had anything to say that gave a broader significance to a common human experience. La Belle Dame Sans Merci—yes, that was one of the forms of that dream—love in which man is the victim, the creature who undergoes ravishment.

Charlie never spoke about sex. When the talk among a group of boys turned in that direction, as so often and so understandably it did, he was silent and crept away as soon as possible. Once, when I got him in a corner, so to speak, he told me that he recognized it as an inescapable and necessary part of the human condition, but it was one he intended to offer up as a sacrifice to the work for which he knew he was intended. It was then that he confided to me that he wanted to become a priest.

Not that he made any secret of it from anyone who knew him. At a Hallowe'en evening at school he turned up at dinner with his bathrobe turned into a cassock, and a bedsheet folded to become a surplice, and he had hung a scarf around his neck as a stole; it was a great success, and certainly one of the most complete of any of the improvised costumes that were on show. But these were the external trappings of priesthood; the essence was kept very close to his heart.

Thus we journeyed through Colborne College. We were members of the Music Club and attended concerts which meant more to me than to Brocky; he had the tin ear not uncommon among people of strongly literary temperament. He knew it. Like Yeats, he said. But he learned, though I wonder what music really meant to him. Later I knew he took great pleasure in Tschaikowsky, and while I would not say a word against that great, underestimated master, he certainly isn't Bach, who was my special, and somewhat puritanical, admiration. I was a Bach-snob for years.

Who would not become a Bach-snob under the tute-lage of Richard Craigie, who was the senior of the two music-masters in the school? Under his guidance one might range pretty far in the fields of music, but one always returned to home-base, and home-base was Bach. I fell very much under the dominance of Mr. Craigie, and I now understand that he led me in a direction that was to open out into one of the chief interests of my life, and that was the cultural development of the city of Toronto.

Of course I did not think of it in such terms then, for, in comparison with Sioux Lookout, Toronto was an

Athens, and everything that happened there in the world of music was a revelation to me. The symphony orchestra, making yet another hopeful beginning, would not pass muster now, but it was brave and persistent. In those days musicians of good quality might be found in the orchestras of movie theatres, because this was in the mute era of film, before sound; quite large orchestras played appropriate music while films were shown. The musicians, sick of playing Tschaikowsky's "None But the Lonely Heart" and the finale of the *William Tell* Overture night after night, gathered themselves into an orchestra, and when they could escape from their servitude to Bebe Daniels and Colleen Moore—which meant at five o'clock in the afternoon—they gave concerts of music of assured worth. Mr. Craigie told me they got less than five dollars a performance, but their souls were refreshed, as were ours. Sometimes the performances were rough; now and then an amateur had to be called in who played some unusual instrument (I remember a small Anglican clergyman who would appear shyly with his bass clarinet when he was wanted); but it was a bigger orchestra and a better one than most of its audience had ever heard, and its long-suffering conductor, Constant Gebler, called forth more music than might have been expected from what was, in the opinion of sophisticates who based their judgements on the radio broadcasts of great orchestras from the States, a scratch band.

A dozen or so musical enthusiasts from Colborne had leave to attend these concerts, and I never missed one. To this day I am indulgent toward orchestras that are trying to lift themselves in the world, while critics are busy assuring them that they are not the Vienna Philharmonie and never will be.

Charlie and Brocky came to the concerts as well, but

what they liked better were the first Toronto stirrings of operatic production; *Hugh the Drover*, which Mr. Craigie assured us was very fine, and he was right. It is still the only "grand" opera to base its romance on the outcome of a fist-fight, which is an English rather than Italian way of deciding who gets the girl; Hugh the Drover and John the Butcher have to be pugilists as well as singers, and perhaps this accounts for the neglect of a fine work. There was also an ambitious production of *Hansel and Gretel*, with fourteen real angels in the Vision Scene, who occasionally moulted a feather as they did their stately dance around the sleeping children. And of course there were visiting opera companies, like that of Fortune Gallo, who thrilled us by announcing an *Aida* which would be given a special, almost Egyptian, character by the fact that the title role would be sung by a young Red Indian soprano. Also, a *Faust* with designs by Norman Bel Geddes, which seemed very advanced to us. *Faust* puzzled me then and puzzles me still; if Faust was so clever, why did he sell his soul to deflower and impregnate Marguerite, who is manifestly a nice girl but a simpleton? Brocky had some light to throw on that question: men of brilliant intellect, he said, were often stupid about women. He proved this to be true, though not quite fatally, soon after leaving Colborne.

We haunted the gods of the Royal Alexandra Theatre; almost every Saturday afternoon we were in the topmost gallery, and when a company of Shakespearean actors from the Festival Theatre at Stratford-on-Avon visited Toronto for several weeks we gobbled eight Shakespeare plays, and digested them as well as our inexperience would allow. It was the discovery of a splendour of which we, as children of the New World, had little knowledge. The splendour of Shakespeare as he wished to be encountered—in performance. Here was a vast ocean of myth and poetry, in which Brocky had waded, though he never seemed to get in over his head; but Shakespeare acted brought total immersion, from which I, for one, never recovered. We had met with Shakespeare plays at Colborne—*Julius Caesar* and *Henry IV, Part One*, as works comparatively free from disquieting women, and *As You Like It*, with the supposedly dirty bits omitted, but I am of the firm opinion that Shakespeare in printed form should be kept from children; if they cannot meet him in the theatre, better not to meet him at all. One might just as well ask children to read the symphonies of Beethoven.

"I've got leave to go out this evening to have dinner with my father," said Brocky, one day, "and I thought I'd take the opportunity to book for the four Saturdays that the D'Oyly Carte will be here. I suppose you want me to book for you, as well?"

"What's the D'Oyly Carte?" I asked.

"My God! the voice of Sioux Lookout! Hasn't heard of the D'Oyly Carte! Yet he quotes freely and intelligently from the works of the great W. S. Gilbert, and has been heard to troll a stave by Arthur Sullivan. Don't you know, you poor boob, that the D'Oyly Carte Opera Company is the one undoubted and apostolic guardian of the Gilbert and Sullivan operas? Don't you know that Richard D'Oyly Carte— known to the mockers as Oily Cart—was the manager who drew and held those two unlikely geniuses together, to produce the operettas you know so well? And that this company of unassailable authenticity, still conscious of the burning eye of Sir William Gilbert on every move it makes, is to be here in two weeks' time, and will do just about everything one could wish to see, in the true Gilbertian style, and that we can drink it all in and be refreshed? Give me some money, and leave all the rest to me."

Brocky was not mistaken. Shakespeare had been overwhelming; this was pure delight. Toronto had a snobbish fit over the D'Oyly Carte people; Sir Henry Lytton (imagine, a real knight, but as funny as a crutch, and able to dance like a teetotum, and actually wears a monocle *off* stage!) and the imperial Bertha Lewis, and the oleaginous Leo Sheffield, and the mock-ferocious Darrell Francourt; they begged them to come to lunch, and to appear at charity affairs, and read the lessons in fashionable churches, and do all the things famous English players were expected to do in the outposts of Empire. I sat entranced through eight of the operettas that I had known since early childhood from the phonograph records, as they unfolded in their charming, whimsical splendour on the stage of the Royal Alex (which is what we theatre aficionados always called it, now that Alexandra was no longer Queen, and no *lèse majesté* could be imagined) and lost my heart agonizingly to Winifred Lawson, who was so comically pathetic as the Plaintiff in *Trial by Jury*. What has Nature produced more totally ravishing than a beautiful, witty soprano? And all of this musical indulgence was approved by Mr. Craigie, because it was English, and the D'Oyly Carte people were models of proper English speech, and Arthur Sullivan had been a Mendelssohn Scholar at the Royal Academy of Music, just as Mr. Craigie himself had been, many years later.

"You said school was rough; it sounds to me as if you'd had a high old time," says Esme.

I realize that in giving her some excerpts and impressions from the foregoing, I may have become lyrical, as old men do when speaking of the past.

"Those theatre and concert adventures were a few hours stolen from hard work and Spartan living. But you mustn't suppose the school itself offered no recreations. We had all sorts of clubs."

Oh, indeed we had clubs, ranging over a variety of the things—though not all the things—that could interest boys of alert, or less than alert, minds. There was the Stamp Club, with a large membership, because the school seemed to be hopping with people who, as Brocky said, could get into a fever about little pieces of paper that strangers had licked. There was the Travel Club, presided over by Lieutenant-Commander Daubigny, who taught French and German but had had a lively career in the Royal Navy and was rumoured to have eaten raw human flesh at a cannibal feast. There was the Chess Club, dominated by an English master, Mr. Crowe, who was no chess-master himself, but had in full measure the solemnity that goes with that game, and could reduce himself to a near-death stupor before making a significant move. There was the Art Club, but it did not flourish. There was the Music Club, of which Brocky and Charlie and I were keen supporters. And at the top of the tree was the Curfew Club, reserved for stewards, prefects, and the top boys of the Sixth Form. Brocky was a member because he was an obvious prefect, capable of keeping order and dealing out the high, the middle, and the lesser justice in anything that did not need to be brought to the attention of the housemaster, Mr. Norfolk. I was a member, though not as a prefect, because I became, in my last year, editor of the school magazine, which carried literary recognition; I was what was called a Steward. We Curfew Club members enjoyed a dizzy eminence in the school, for we were the only boys who were permitted to smoke in the school building. We met on Sunday nights in a room in the tower, an architectural mishap, for it was fifteen feet tall, and its windows were at the ten-foot level; the tower clock was accessible through a trapdoor in the roof, and could be heard mumbling and cursing to itself at all hours.

Our meetings varied greatly in the degree of their intellectual strenuosity. There were members who wanted to talk about philosophy, because it was around that time that a cheap edition of Dr. Will Durant's *The Story of Philosophy* appeared and intelligent boys were drunk on the great popularizer's "attempt to humanize knowledge by centering the story of speculative thought around certain dominant personalities"; you see how well I conned his pages and deluded myself for a while that I was thinking profoundly. There were members who were mad for science, and I suppose I ought to have been more supportive of them than I was, but I had had a whiff of real science—at least of geology— from my father, and I tended to dismiss the enthusiasts as amateurs. And they had small regard for me; geology was not rated very highly by the germ enthusiasts. Brocky liked nothing better than to stand the Curfew Club on its head.

"The collective colour of the Curfew Club mind," he said, "is a sort of grey-green, greasy Limpopo River colour, and it needs clarifying; are they grey or are they green or what are they? Only determined stirring and boiling will tell."

He certainly boiled them the February Sunday night he read his paper titled *A Knotty Point of Shakespeare Criticism Untied: Where Did Hamlet Hide the Body of Polonius?* This sounded so meaty, so solemnly literary, that Mr. Thomas Norfolk, the senior English master, decided to grace us with his presence, in addition to one of the junior English staff, roly-poly, witty Mr. Sharpe, who took an unschoolmasterish delight in Brocky's mischief. There we sat, puffing away at our strictly legal cigarettes (Mr. Sharpe smoked a pipe with a bowl of extraordinary size) as Brocky unfolded his manuscript and began.

The problem of what Hamlet did with Polonius, said Brocky, had been neglected because so many other matters of greater immediate interest were raised by the famous scene (Act Three, scene four) where Hamlet has his great confrontation with his mother, and treats her to a most unfilial roughness of tongue. The scene moves swiftly, as the finest of Shakespeare always does, and indeed not twenty-five lines have passed until Hamlet detects the presence of Polonius behind the arras, and stabs him, without knowing who he is. What then passes between Hamlet and Gertrude is so laden with significance—Brocky said that he would not even attempt to deal with the suggestions of an incestuous passion in the Prince, and Mr. Norfolk nodded sagely in approval of this scholarly reticence—that we are apt to neglect Hamlet's declaration—

I'll lug the guts into the neighbour room

—until after the next scene when Hamlet appears, declaring—

Safely stowed.

Clearly he has hidden the body of the good old counsellor, but where? When Rosencrantz and Guildenstern question him, he says that he has "compounded it with dust whereto it is kin," which would have tipped off the two court toadies if they were not so stupid. We know better; we remember that "dust" means not only the flesh that remains when the spirit has flown, but any cast-off rubbish or human waste matter, and in the circumstances, what might that be? It is made plain enough when Hamlet is questioned by the King, and at last says that they may find Polonius by his stench—if they take their time looking in the right place. "If you find him not within this month, you shall nose him as you go up the stairs into the lobby."

Now, what does this tell us? Is it not as plain as day? Hamlet has hidden Polonius in a room reserved for the King which the King rarely frequents, a room to be found off the stairs. In such a castle as Elsinore, and indeed in any castle of the sort that would be well known to Shakespeare, who had visited several such castles with his troupe of travelling players, that room off the stairs would be the privy, built on the outward walls to overhang the moat. Hamlet who has a nasty and decidedly dirty tongue—consider the way he talks to Ophelia before the play-within-the-play begins, with everyone listening!—is hinting that the King does not often go to the privy, and is indeed constipated.

Was this a deadly insult? Consider the reference the Prince makes to his uncle-father: he calls him "the bloat king" and describes his kisses as "reachy" which we know means rancid. Did the King then suffer from halitosis? Was not Hamlet being inexcusably personal in thus taunting a man who had the power of life and death over him?

Can we utterly deny ourselves some speculation as to what significance such a taunt may have had for Shakespeare himself? It is often said that it is dangerous folly to attempt to plumb the depths of an author's mind by finding apparently significant hints of personal preoccupation in his work. But—we are only human; may we not seek to find out anything about the Prince of Poets that he has inadvertently let slip? It is surely worthy of notice that you may seek a Shakespeare Concordance from end to end without finding a single reference to constipation, although a plethora of other human ills are exploited to comic or tragic effect. Why this silence on a complaint so common, so vexatious, so sinister in its effect on the human spirit? Was Shakespeare attributing to King Claudius, through these taunts of Hamlet, an ailment that was his own secret, nagging, unremitting worry?

Brocky modestly left conclusions to others. He had not had time, he said, to sift the complete works for references which might throw light on this matter. But he threw it open for discussion by the Curfew Club. Was Shakespeare constipated? What do you think? Could it be made clearer that Hamlet heaped a final insult on Polonius—not a bad old soul, as Civil Servants go—by dumping him in the privy?

This was sailing dangerously close to the wind, and everybody knew it. I thought Brocky was going too far, but I marvelled at his impudent courage.

Mr. Sharpe was looking askew, and puffing his great pipe till it must have been red-hot. But to everyone's astonishment Mr. Norfolk took the lead in the discussion and was a model of insensible calm. The point made by Gilmartin, he said, was of a certain interest, which a young critic might excusably exaggerate, for one dearly loved one's own child, however feeble it might be. But when one contemplated the Mind of Shakespeare in one's maturity, one realized that such distasteful trivialities as the location of privies and the personal characteristics of characters who deserved the closest psychological study were far beneath the notice of true criticism. Others abide our question, Mr. Norfolk continued (and everybody including Mr. Sharpe knew that he was approaching one of his flights into the intense inane), but the Swan of Avon soared free. Question as we might, he smiled and was still, out-topping knowledge. Criticism at its greatest and best was but the foiled searching of mortality.

With closed eyes Mr. Norfolk was silent, lost in wonder at his own kinship with the Immortal Bard.

[12]

BROCKY'S DARING ASSAULT on the gravity of the Curfew Club was not the high point of the Club's history during our last year at Colborne. By an odd chance, that was brought about by Charlie.

Not that Charlie was a member. How could he be? He had never made it into the Sixth Form (we still had Forms in those days, and not Grades) but lingered in an academic Limbo called Five A Special, where boys were dumped who, for one reason or another, could not qualify for the final promotion. He had no distinctions; no, not even the Scripture Prize, because on his examination papers he knew too much, and wrote too much, and introduced doctrinal and historical matter which was outside the range of the college chaplain—a contentious young parson whom the Bishop did not want to appoint to a parish—and thus drowned in his own superfluities. Charlie was a failure, because he never seemed able to do anything to the satisfaction of authority. Yet everyone liked him because of his gentle but not mollycoddle way. Mr. Sharpe summed it up when he said that Charlie was not so much a lame duck as a lame dove.

There was to be a meeting of the Curfew Club of unusual interest, because one of the top masters—those who ranked just below the Head—was to speak on a subject on which he was an acknowledged authority. Acknowledged, that is to say, outside the walls of Colborne. Mr. Dunstan Ramsay, the head history master, was to speak about The World of Saints, and as he had written two or three very well thought of and often translated books about the most popular saints—the saints in whom tourists would have an interest—we expected something authoritative. And, as this was very much in Charlie's line, Brocky and I asked permission to bring him as a guest; because he was well-liked by everybody—well, almost everybody—in the school, there was no difficulty in arranging that.

When we assembled in that curious tower chamber on a March Sunday night (the last Sunday before the Easter break) we expected that Mr. Ramsay would run us through a few popular saints, tell a few amusing stories about saints, and we would then move on to coffee and doughnuts. But Mr. Ramsay surprised us by bringing, and displaying, the most beautiful book that until that time I had ever seen. It was William Morris's 1892 edition of Caxton's *The Golden Legend*, and for a quarter of an hour or so we gaped in wonder at the superb pages as Mr. Ramsay turned them. (This was my first lesson in the etiquette of book-collecting; you do not allow anybody to touch your treasures unless you know them well enough to trust them.) I was already bitten by the book-collecting bug, as was Brocky, and we spent many Saturday afternoons grubbing through the dusty second-hand bookshops that then existed on Yonge Street, between College and Bloor. We were always in hopes of discovering something unsuspected by the bookseller in those dreary assemblages of outworn theology, outdated encyclopaedias, fiction that had not outlived its season and kindred rubbish, and now and then we picked up something of interest to one of us, though I don't imagine many other people wanted such things. I bought old medical books, stuff discarded by students in the nineteenth century, not because I thought they could teach me anything of value about modern medicine, but because they contained interesting clues to the medical past. One book I treasured especially; it was a manual of bandaging, and from it one learned that the physicians of the mid-nineteenth century, however little they knew about antisepsis, could certainly truss up a patient after a wound or an amputation so that his own mother would not have known him. Brocky looked for first editions of poets, and never, to my knowledge, found one of the slightest significance, though he acquired a lot of amusing junk, published in the nineteenth century by hopeful souls at their own expense.

Mr. Ramsay introduced us to the beauty of the printed book, which comparatively few people understand, and which has in my time become the concern of small private presses. Faced with that Morris *Golden Legend* I fell in love, in one of the few really rewarding romances of my life: I fell in love with beautiful books, and now, as an old man, I have a harem which is by no means trivial.

Having shown us the book, Mr. Ramsay put a question: why, in 1892, did a great printer think it worthwhile to produce yet another edition, and that an immensely complex and expensive edition, of a book which had been one of the most popular in Europe for five hundred years? It was because *The Golden Legend* had been described as one of the ten books which, taken together, would give a coherent idea of medieval thought and medieval knowledge. Did all modern historians of the Middle Ages know it well, then? Some of them said they did, but a personal knowledge of the book might make their claim seem a little insecure. What was the book about? It recorded the legends of the saints, in the order in which they were celebrated by the Church, beginning with the Legend of St. Andrew on November 30, at the beginning of Advent, and working through the Christian Year to the following November 29, when the Saints Saturninus, Perpetua, and Felicitas exerted their benign influence. It was a book to which the devout could turn at any time for edification and—this should not be underestimated—a thrilling story. Never neglect the charms of narrative for the human heart, said Mr. Ramsay.

Never neglect the soft, persistent influence of the Middle Ages in the Modern world. How many wards, streets, and districts in Toronto—to say nothing of churches—were named after saints; look in the telephone directory and be ready for a surprise. Why was St. George Street, still one of the most fashionable in the city, so called? Who had cherished a little, half-understood cult for the warrior-saint when that street was named? Surely it might better have commemorated, as did Bloor Street, some prosperous brewer or distiller? Why not Gooderham Street? But no, St. George it was and would be for the foreseeable future.

A wag suggested that the garbage lane behind St. George Street might be called Dragon Alley, and Mr. Ramsay said that was good medieval thinking, and it could certainly be so. This interruption might have diverted the evening into a light-hearted discussion, if Evans had not intervened.

Evans was acknowledged leader of the Great Minds among Colborne's Sixth Form that year; he was a solemn, prematurely withered fellow who was expected to make a stir in the world, but precisely how was not yet apparent. Evans was intensely rational. I cannot call him scientific, because his curiosity was too heavily blinkered

What, Evans demanded, was a saint, and who defined

the word in modern acceptation?

The maker of saints, said Mr. Ramsay, was the Church of Rome, and it had an elaborate process of canonization, which gave the most careful consideration to the claims of anyone who was proposed for saint-hood, requiring evidence that would support the claim, and usually taking a considerable number of years before a new saint was proclaimed. A saint had to be a person of heroic virtue, whose manner of life and death attested to uncommon holiness, and who could be proven to have brought about a number—not less than three—of miracles, meaning benevolent happenings contrary to the normal order of things, or what might be called natural law. Once proclaimed, the saint might be invoked through prayer for help by believers, and in an earlier day many saints were thought to be particu-larly helpful in specific cases, as, for instance, St. Vitus, who could be invoked in cases of dog bites, snakebite, and of course Sydenham's chorea, long called St. Vitus' Dance. Then there was St. Anthony of Padua, invalu-able in finding lost articles. And of course there was St. Wilgefortis, to whom women might apply for help in getting rid of a disagreeable husband. There, said Ramsay, you have a good spread of saints: nobody knows just who St. Vitus was, but he appears to have been real enough, and St. Anthony was a well-attested historic figure, but Wilgefortis seems to have arisen simply because she filled a need, and there is no proof of her existence whatever. The Church has been anxious, in recent times, to show itself above such folk-saints as Wilgefortis, though shrines to her are still plentiful in Europe; Ramsay had himself visited several, and had photographs of the portraits of the saint, who rejoiced in the possession of a large beard.

"Which just goes to show," said Evans, "what an

imposture religion has always been."

"Don't you think that's rather too embracing a condemnation?" said Mr. Ramsay.

"Surely, sir, here in the Curfew Club we can be frank," said Evans, very man to man.

"Quite right; the lodge is tiled," murmured Brocky, and was silenced by a frown from Evans, who continued.

"Religion belongs to the childhood of the human race. You've made a reputation investigating some parts of it, but was it scientific curiosity—history's a branch of science after all—or some real concern with religion that pushed you on?"

"Real concern with religion, certainly."

"But a scientific concern? Not as a believer?"

"You suggest that science rules out belief?"

"In religion, surely."

"Why?"

"Because belief posits adherence to a creed, and a creed posits belief in a God, a Prime Mover, a Creator, and an Imminent Presence. And that won't wash."

"It won't? Tell me."

"Well, it's pretty widely accepted now among the advanced people—the molecular biologists, you know—that the recent investigations into basic organic stuff show clearly that all forms of life come into being by pure chance, through unpredictable mutation, and because of necessity probably rooted in Darwinian selection. And that makes it quite out of the question to posit any Master Plan, or Planner, or scheme of Creation. Simply won't wash."

This provoked some murmurs, for the Curfew Club, though very advanced thinkers, liked to keep one foot on shore, so to speak, and at that time Evans' kind of talk was strong medicine among the sons of the Toronto élite. But through the murmurs one voice was heard clearly, and though it was a voice I had never heard before it was issuing from Charlie. Heads turned, because as a guest he was not expected to speak. Not forbidden, but expected to preserve a certain humility, as not being a member.

"And that won't wash," said he.

"Eh? What do you mean it won't wash?" Evans was taken off guard and not pleased.

"It won't wash because it posits—to use your fancy philosophical term—a God with human limitations and human values—a kind of Big Man, in fact. Your advanced thinkers suppose that if God does not think like them He can't think at all, and therefore doesn't exist. What makes you suppose that what your advanced people call 'pure chance' means the same thing as what God means by 'pure chance'?"

"Are you positing a world in which everything is laid down and unchangeable, because of what our grandmothers called 'God's Will'?"

"Not at all. I'm not *positing* anything. But I'm suggesting that although God's Will must eventually prevail, individual parts of the creation have great freedom under what used to be called natural law, and they are often presented with situations where they have to use that freedom. If they make a mess of things, probably God will try again."

"You seem to have done a lot of thinking about this, Iredale," said Evans, in a voice which he meant to be a crusher, "so perhaps you'd favour us with a definition of God?"

"Out of the question," said Charlie. "That would be like a forty-watt electric bulb trying to define Niagara Falls. All the bulb knows, if it knows anything, is that without the Falls it would be a useless curiosity."

"No proof, then?"

"Not of any kind that would convince you."

"So why?"

"Faith. 'Believing where we cannot prove,' as the hymn says that we sing so often at morning prayers."

"Belief without proof can lead you up some pretty dark alleys."

"Belief where there is unquestionable proof would be possible only to someone who had final knowledge of all things. Someone with God's view of history. We have to put up with the knowledge that's open to us during our lifetimes. We can't have knowledge of future things; we have only a scrappy knowledge of past things. You know what the sailor said when he was told that King Solomon was the wisest man the world had ever known, or would ever know?"

"Can't say I do."

"The sailor said, 'If I had Solomon aboard my ship he wouldn't know a jib-boom from a poop lantern.'"

Evans alone of the Curfew Club did not think this funny.

The chairman intervened here. He was the Head Boy of the school, a decent chap called Martland. "I think we ought to get back to Mr. Ramsay and *The Golden Legend*," said he. "Let's hear about an era when firm belief was common. I think you said, sir, that for centuries people turned to *The Golden Legend* for thrilling stories. What kind of stories? Would we think them thrilling now?"

"Not in the same way, certainly," said Mr. Ramsay. "They tend to be pretty terse; not a lot of detail. They tell of martyrdom and miracles and, unless you think martyrdom for the Christian Faith a great and heart-lifting form of death, the story is simply a bloody story about a tyrant and a victim. The same with miracles. They are temporary interruptions of natural law. If you share Evans' point of view you may dismiss them as pious lies. But it might be hasty to suppose that there are no such interruptions. Things do happen, now and then, about which we hear in a newspaper account, probably written by a sensational journalist, or a cynic, and the truth is obscured in both cases. When we speak of a miracle nowadays we tend to think of it as happening in a hospital, or a scientific lab, where somebody does something that extends or contradicts what had been believed before."

"And which will stand examination for years after—examination and rigorous testing," said Evans, whose flame was not quenched.

"Will stand examination till the next scientific miracle shows that it was mistaken, or reaches beyond it," said Charlie. I was embarrassed, because I had introduced him—a non-member—into the Club for this meeting, and he was taking on airs as if he were an old hand. Martland thought so too, and intervened again.

"Let's hear Mr. Ramsay," he said; "that's what we're here for, after all."

"Please don't worry about me," said Ramsay. "I'm delighted to see some heat developing on a subject that I thought might only be of minor interest to you. Miracles are a fascinating study. When the Reformation came along they became an embarrassment to defenders of the Church, and a rare old scourge in the hands of the Lutherans. And so *The Golden Legend* came in for a lot of abuse from both sides. Even a man so finely balanced as Erasmus got hot about it and dismissed believers as fools if they believed tales of ghosts and devils and miracles."

"What did he make of the miracles of Christ?" It was Charlie, putting in his oar again.

"Christ was above the argument," said Ramsay.

"I'll bet he was," said Evans; he seemed to be developing into a rancorous atheist before our eyes.

"We must look at the situation from an historical point of view," said Ramsay. "For a thousand years, following the Dark Ages in Europe, the Church was the only really effective civilizing element, and stories of miracles reached people who would not have understood theological argument. They believed, as Iredale says, and they needed support for their belief. Consider how far even a southern French village was from Rome in the twelfth century; most people had been no farther from their homes than they could walk in a day. A local miracle or a local saint was worth more to them than any amount of fancy argument or Papal letters."

"So you are admitting that the saints and the miracles were inventions, to strengthen the Church's hold on ignorant people?"

"No, I'm not admitting anything of the kind, and you, Evans, are talking like an Ulster Orangeman. I am putting forward the idea that if civilization was to advance, it needed such aids, and the Church was the only civilizing element in a very rough time."

"But we can forget about saints and miracles today," said Evans.

"Unfortunately history doesn't develop as neatly as that," said Ramsay. "We still hear of miracles. Some impressive ones have been reported during the past century. I've visited places where they happened, or were said to have happened, and I have never met anyone who would admit to doubt. Just a year ago, in Portugal, I visited a great church at Milagres, which celebrated the miracle of Manoel Francisco Mayo. The church was a notable evidence of belief in something apparently incredible which was said to have happened, and attested to by people one would not think of as liars, not really so very long ago. I think we shall see miracles happening, and saints occurring, for quite a while yet, in this supposedly scientific age."

"But what *is* a miracle, exactly," said Nolan, who always wanted to get into any argument, to show himself keen.

"Bernard Shaw says a miracle is an event which creates faith," said Mestayer, who liked to show himself up to the minute. At that time it was still rather daring, in the kind of society that provided boys for Colborne, to read Bernard Shaw.

"Sorry! Shaw makes a character in *Saint Joan* say that," said Brocky. "Not the same thing. It's an Archbishop speaking. He defends miracles against the charge of being frauds, because frauds deceive, but an event which creates faith does not deceive, and therefore it is not a fraud, but a miracle. A nifty argument, but you have to remember it is an Archbishop speaking. For him that was the party line."

Charlie simply would not keep quiet. He struck in again: "Shaw always gives everybody a fair deal. In that same scene he makes somebody say that the Church must nourish faith by poetry. One of the defects of the scientific viewpoint is that it leaves no room in life for poetry."

"Poetry, meaning precisely what?" said Evans, who was determined to smash Charlie or himself suffer a severe loss of face. But Charlie was ready for that question.

"Poetry is the breath and finer spirit of all knowledge; it is the impassioned expression which is in the countenance of all Science."

"God!" said Evans.

"Not quite. Wordsworth," said Charlie.

"Well done, Iredale; you've got 'em on the run," said Mr. Ramsay laughing; he was enjoying himself. This may not have been the happiest comment, because, although it seemed to cover Charlie with laurels, it widened the gap between him and the anointed members of the Curfew Club; toward them his talk came dangerously close to being cheek because at that time, in that school, there was an almost Japanese respect for seniority But Evans would not admit to defeat or even a temporary setback.

"You'll never be a scientist, Iredale, if you lug in any authority who happens to suit your argument at the moment. What has Wordsworth got to do with anything? What about Erasmus? Didn't Mr. Ramsay say he had been very rough on miracles? And wasn't Erasmus one of the big guns of religious belief?"

"Yes, but Erasmus had the scholar's weakness," said Mr. Ramsay, again intervening to help Charlie, which may not in the long run have been helpful. "Erasmus wanted everybody to be as intelligent as himself and if they couldn't he thought they were simply being mulish."

"And Erasmuses are few," said Charlie. "Simple folk are many, and simple folk are still the most numerous. Indeed it has been said that God must love simple people very much, He made so many of them."

"But not as many as he made of the *Spirochaeta pallida,*" said Evans, "so if we accept your argument, Iredale, God must love the Great Pox even more than the simple."

As argument went in the Curfew Club this was regarded as a knockout blow, and was greeted with laughter and applause. Charlie was silent, but everybody knew that though he may have lost the argument, he had scored some points.

Martland called the meeting to order yet once more, and for the rest of our time Mr. Ramsay talked about

The Golden Legend and the kind of society that throve on wonders and embraced belief. The word Legend, said he, did not simply as now it does something in the nature of myth or fable, but rather a "lesson" or a "reading." Respect for the *Legend* did not mean a rejection of the Renaissance or subsequent adventures of the mind. Rather it meant a sympathetic understanding of a past age, which might still, under examination, have much to tell us that would enlarge our lives. It was at our peril that we dismissed such minds as those of St. Augustine, or St. Thomas Aquinas. The truly historical view, he insisted, was not a tale of man's progress from barbarism or superstition to modern enlightenment, but a recognition that enlightenment had shown itself in the long story of man in a variety of guises, and that barbarism and superstition were undying elements in the human story. He had some sharp things to say about the rise of National Socialism in Germany, in support of his assertion that barbarism and superstition find new uniforms for old troll-folk. He called attention to the number of countries that still maintained slavery, in overt or slightly disguised forms. He talked of the subjection of women, and was perhaps a little tactless in attributing so much of that to the importation into European (and thus into New World) life of Oriental ideas of womanhood that hid under the Near Eastern skirts of Christianity; the chilly Romans, and even the hairy ruffians of Celtic Europe, treated their women better than Christianity did, and thus far Christianity, for all its great benefits to our lives, had its shadow side. Much of what he said, of course, was dismissed by the keener minds of the Curfew Club as the eccentric talk which held Ramsay back in his profession. A good teacher, but a crackpot. What was wrong with the position of women? To the boys of the Curfew Club it looked as if women had an easy ride.

[13]

CHARLIE'S BRIEF NOTORIETY after
the Curfew Club affair disappeared into disastrous disgrace after the Easter holidays. Disgrace, that is, as we
measured it at Colborne. After Easter everybody in the
upper forms was in a painful process of being wound up
for examinations. Wound up, in a few cases, until they
were like clocks that had been over-wound, and had to
be released from their tension by medical intervention.
The severest winding took place among those boys who
were to face the Matriculation Examinations, the key to
university entrance. In those days there were twelve such
examinations; twelve papers in a variety of subjects and
although some leeway was permitted—French was
obligatory but German was permitted—two of the
papers were in mathematics and two in science, as our
tentative dabblings in physics and chemistry were called,
dignifying them far above their desert. It was in these
four subjects that Charlie was not simply weak, but virtually incapable, and they had for years made his school
life a misery. As the dread month of June approached,
Charlie became visibly unwell; many boys looked pale
as the ordeal approached, but he had shadows under his
eyes and lost weight which, as he was spare already,
made him almost skeletonic.

It was the Headmaster's doctrine ("from those to
whom much has been given, much must be expected")
that was at the root of all this distress. Because Colborne
was not a school in the government system, supported
by taxes, but an old private institution relying on fees,
paid by well-to-do parents, it had to do well, and if possible brilliantly, in the general examinations applicable
to everybody. Colborne was a regular scooper of
Lieutenant-Governors' Medals, and similar distinctions;

only thus could it justify its assumption of privilege in the face of a world that did not like privilege for other people. It took upon itself the mantle of leadership, and it damned well had to lead when the Matriculation results were announced, vying with the other private schools for scholarly laurels. So the pressure was great, the overwinding zealous, and boys of unusual talent were groomed like racehorses by masters who gave them special time, and analysed examination papers for years back to cast some light on what questions might be asked, and what answers might most successfully be given. Brocky and I came in heavily for this sort of fine-tuning, but poor Charlie was a hopeless case and, although nobody was downright miserable to him, he felt the chill of exclusion as one who was simply not worth extra coaching.

Not that he did not try. He tried desperately in those last few weeks to reverse the ineptitude that had been inveterate in him for years. He sat late over his books—we were allowed to keep our lights on as long as we pleased in those last few days—but, although I now had a room to myself, being a steward, I looked in on him from time to time and tried to cheer him up. How do you cheer up a man for whom the guillotine is drawing nearer and nearer? I attempted a little coaching, but Charlie was reduced to a point where I felt that I was, in Dr. Johnson's words, assailing an unresisting imbecility. He was so fair that his hair was almost white, and there were times now when he looked like an old man. I was aware that he was becoming physically ill, and not simply from the anxiety which was in the air we all breathed. Something ailed him, and the headaches from which he suffered were more than the result of fatigue. I bought a clinical thermometer—the first of a porcupine of such things I have owned—and took his temperature; it was never below 100 degrees. I urged him to see the school doctor, because of earaches that came and went, and a good deal of pain in his eyes. This he did, but the school doctor, who was no Galen—was, indeed, not much more than Doc Ogg in a clean shirt— patted him on the shoulder and talked soothingly of "exam fever" and gave him some Aspirin. I urged him to see another doctor, but to my surprise he refused.

"It's all imagination," he said. "I must conquer it."

"Charlie, for God's sake don't be a mental Strong Man," said I. "You're sick. It's obvious. You can't go into examinations like this. It isn't imagination."

But nothing would move him. He knew what the trouble was: he was malingering, his body was betraying him, and he wouldn't put up with it. He would show his body who was boss. I knew that he prayed a great deal, of course for help in the examinations. But subsequent clinical experience has convinced me that God is not particularly interested in examinations, just as he won't be dragged into the Stock Market, or being a backer in show business.

Without my being in the least aware of it, this illness of Charlie's was the strong influence that led me to become a physician, and the rather special kind of physician I am. It wasn't his body that was betraying him, and it wasn't possible for his mind to bully his body into subjection. It was something else, some more profound and radical Charlie that was trying to keep him out of a contest in which he would certainly be hurt. It was my fondness for Charlie, and my sympathetic but also clinical observation of his illness, that did more than the murky lessons of Mrs. Smoke, or the shallow certainties of Doc Ogg, to make me determine to be a physician, in order that I might pursue this sort of observation as far as I could.

I understand now that Charlie was very ill—far worse than I could possibly know at the time—and that what ailed him could have led to quite possibly fatal mastoid infection, and was at the moment sinus infection of a kind that cried for immediate attention. It would not have taken much of a turn in his illness to kill Charlie. But it didn't, because disease doesn't work as inevitably or inexorably as that. Another element, too subtle to be purely physical and too profound to be wholly mental, was at work, some Third Charlie which made him very miserable and made his examinations a wretchedness like a prolonged martyrdom, but did not mean him to die.

June came at last. I saw nothing of Charlie during the actual examinations, because he was sitting the Junior Matriculation tests and I was in the Senior rank from which, if I were successful, I would enter on university work without having to do the obligatory First Year, during which attempts are made to teach people who will never do so in this world to write grammatical prose, and to instil a few basic facts relating to the accepted concerns of Western civilization into minds hitherto untouched in this respect. I had my own fish to fry, and very tricky fish they were. Every day I made my way from Colborne downtown to a huge drill-hall in what I believe was a Victorian armoury, and found the desk with my number on it. At that rickety and unstable desk I tackled a "paper" which was distributed by the invigilators who, under the eye of the Chief Examiner, walked the aisles and looked out for cheating, escorted girls to the lavatories improvised for them in the masculine armoury, or went with bursting boys to the urinals, where the keenest watch was kept to see that no aids to knowledge had been concealed within the flies of a pair of trousers. The invigilators must have walked miles in that vast room, but their expression of melancholy detachment never altered; if one of them had asked me what I would like for my last breakfast before the walk to the gallows I should not have been much surprised. It was an ordeal, extending over several days until all the papers necessary to my particular case had been completed.

It was a very long time since I had thought of myself as "delicate" and I certainly was not delicate in my approach to the examination ordeal. I was as well prepared as it was possible for anyone of my abilities to be, and under the guidance of several masters who gave me special tutorials at Colborne I had acquired a pretty good notion of what these examinations were likely to ask. It would be vainglorious to say that I "sailed through," but I emerged on the last day feeling that I had not done too badly; there had not been a question on any paper I could not have attempted, and because there were options I was able to choose the ones on which I thought I could make the best showing.

Except for occasional meetings I had not had much time to attend to Charlie during the examination two weeks. I had looked in on him, of course, but anybody who has undergone rigorous examination periods will know that I was taken up with my own concerns, and had not much time for anybody else. But now, on the final day for both of us, when I had handed in my last paper, I hunted him out. When I knocked at the door of his room at the school there was no answer, so I peeped in, and there he was, sitting at his desk, looking worse than I had ever seen him.

Without being aware of it, I did my first physical examination, there and then; I took his pulse, looked at his tongue—yellowish and heavily coated—listened as well as I could to his heart, with a tube of rolled-up foolscap; fever, loss of appetite, headache continually—

not uncommon symptoms but indicative of something wrong, accompanied as they were by a leaden pallor and deep exhaustion; all indications strongly unfavourable, though of course I did not know how unfavourable, and within an hour I had phoned my parents in Sioux Lookout, and they confirmed my opinion that I should defer my return home and take Charlie to his home in Salterton, as fast as I could. They knew a little of Charlie; had met him on visits to me in Toronto, and had been charmed by him. I knew they wanted me home—they were lonely—but they believed me when I said this was an emergency. Also within the hour I telegraphed to Charlie's parents to be ready to meet him when we arrived, later in the evening, at Salterton and where presumably there would be some sensible and affectionate care for Charlie.

I had more money than Charlie and when I bought the tickets I did the thing in style, and secured us places in that long-vanished bastion of luxury and privilege, the Parlour Car. We sat in fat chairs upholstered in dusty green velvet, on revolving bases, and thought ourselves great swells. Indeed, the bustle and sense of emergency I created raised Charlie's spirits. For the first time in weeks he was being taken seriously as a person, and not as a dubious examination candidate. So as we sped through that unpromising land which lies east of Toronto, toward Salterton, which is halfway toward Montreal, he told me about his humiliations of the past two weeks. He thought he had not done badly in history papers, Ancient and Modern, and creditably on the papers in English Literature and Composition; he had been secure in French Grammar and Authors, and strong in Latin Grammar and Literature; but in the sciences and the maths—disaster. He knew he had failed, and felt the full ignominy of failure as it might apply to a Colborne boy.

Colborne boys were not supposed to fail, but to succeed; it was to train them for success, in whatever they attempted, that their parents sent them to a private school. Without being too lurid, the Headmaster sometimes told us what failure meant: what employment lay open? He was not specific, but we could divine his meaning; surely the collection of garbage, or even of night-soil, would be the fate of one who did not pass his university entrance. Success was the aim, but not success in the most vulgar and crass sense—no, no, it was success as conceived by the great Dr. Arnold of Rugby that was to be sought. It was success in some worthy enterprise, success in the achievement and maintenance of character, that mattered, and money was a secondary, if not really an unworthy, aim. The Headmaster was not tied to Dr. Arnold, however; he was, for his time and profession, a daring man, and he quoted to us the words of Bernard Shaw: the true purpose of life, said that sage (still of a somewhat sulphurous savour in the nostrils of Tory Toronto), was to devote oneself to a great purpose and to exhaust oneself in that devotion, and not to live a life limited to self-satisfaction. But it was inconceivable to the Head that anyone should enter on such a life without achieving university entrance, even if he should decide not to follow that path. University entrance, in his mind, and in all right-thinking minds, was a rite of passage without which entry into true and effective manhood was unthinkable.

So—Charlie was a failure. And I was taking him home to face his parents.

Charlie's parents were a puzzle to me. They seemed so distant, without being in any way neglectful or unkind. They were affectionate enough in their way; Professor Iredale sometimes called him "old man" and his mother called him "dear" but that is a term with many intonations, and the one she chose was not the most intimate. I had visited them two or three times during my school years, at mid-term breaks, and they had always been charming and agreeable but not accessible, like my own parents. I put this down to being what I thought of, with mental quotation marks, as "high born." The Professor came of a family who had, in England, long been university dons or clergymen or both, and he was Head of Classics at Waverley; his mother was a Miss Merriam of Montreal, and like so many of the English Montrealers she had never spiritually left that city, and her talk was full of references to balls and toboggan parties, and her school-days at the establishment of the redoubtable Miss Edgar and Miss Cramp, who formed generations of Miss Merriams into irreproachable young ladies—irreproachable until you got to know them. She mentioned once—it was a family joke—that when she had announced her engagement to Herbert Iredale a concerned friend had said: "But Edith, what will you do? *Nobody* knows professors!" Nevertheless it seemed a successful marriage and it was plain that the Iredales "had money" and as this is uncommon in university circles it probably came from her side of the family; the Professor had brought Greek and Latin to the match and it appeared to work well. People were happy to know this particular professor. It seemed to me that his parents looked on Charlie as a man long before he had ceased to be a boy, and they took no heed whatever of the baby who lingers in us all, so long as we live, and whose demands must sometimes be met.

There they were, at the old limestone station of Salterton. They received Charlie with smiles, and his mother kissed him, and they greeted me with what seemed almost to be greater warmth, because I had "put myself out," as they said, to bring the sick boy home. It was apparent they did not think there was much the matter with him, and assumed that he was suffering only from examination fatigue, and the sense of failure—for they were not unaccustomed to Charlie's failures. But money is a great cushion against academic failure.

It was plain very soon that there was indeed something serious wrong with Charlie. The fever and the headache did not disappear after a few days of egg-nogs spiked with rum, and the leaden pallor increased. Charlie vomited too often even for someone whose stomach was freighted with unaccustomed egg-nog. The family doctor—who was a family friend, and not a man of keen perception, who took his cue from the parents, rather than from the patient—decided that somebody else, a "specialist," ought to look at him. Salterton was the most sophisticated medical centre between Toronto and Montreal; its university had a good medical school, and it possessed a decent hospital, so at last Charlie was assured of the attention he had, in my amateur opinion, long needed. The specialist hummed and hawed, and called in colleagues, and they announced after a conference that Charlie was suffering, at bottom, from badly impacted nasal sinuses—of which there appeared to be several—and these must be drained. The draining was undertaken, and worked pretty well, it seemed, but there were two—the medical terms meant nothing to me then, but they were the ones on either side of the nose, under the eyes—which simply would not drain, and probing revealed that they were so badly impacted that no draining was possible. The only recourse was to do what the specialists called a "fenestration operation" to open the stubborn sinuses. This would not have caused deep concern except for one thing: in the state of anaesthetics at that time, there was no sort of injection that would knock Charlie out during the operation—

everything was given by inhalation—and so the work would have to be done without anaesthetic. The doctors did not enlarge on this point, but it did not need great imagination to know what it could mean.

Charlie's parents received this news characteristically. His mother said, "Oh, darling!" at intervals, which was an advance on "dear" but it was plain that she had no way of meeting such a situation. His father was jocose, and said Charlie would just have to think of Nelson's men having legs sawed off in the bowels of a rolling ship, with nothing but rum and a bullet to bite on to keep them steady. I knew the Professor had been a soldier, and apparently a good one, in the First World War, and had seen dreadful things, but it was plain enough that he was brushing Charlie's approaching ordeal aside; he simply would not face it imaginatively. Nor, perhaps, would it have done much good if he had done so.

During the fortnight that this was going on, I hung about, for the Iredales had urged me to stay with Charlie. I am sure they knew that in some ways I was closer to him than they were. If I say anything about this to Esme, I shall have to be cautious; nowadays, and in Esme's world, any strong friendship between males is at once pronounced to be "gay," but Charlie and I were certainly not in that league. My attitude toward him was protective; his toward me was trusting. I did not lord it over him, nor did he lean on me, but that was how it was. I can swear with my hand on my heart that no thought of sex entered our minds, and if this now appears to be a limitation, it was one that Colborne certainly encouraged. I think this sort of strong male friendship has always existed, and needs to be understood by those to whom Sex is Lord of All. In his parents' home we shared a room, but most decidedly there were two beds.

During his illness Charlie lay for hours reading *The Golden Legend*. His old copy, which he had brought to school, had been a grubby little nineteenth-century reprint in Latin, and Charlie was adept at reading the bad, late Latin of the author, Jacobus de Voragine; his ability in the classical Latin we were taught at school was rooted in this experience. But after that notable meeting of the Curfew Club Mr. Ramsay had seen quite a lot of Charlie, and finding him to be an enthusiast for the *Legend* he had presented him with a translation into stuffy but serviceable Victorian English. Charlie cherished it, because he had won history prizes at school, and anything from Ramsay—known popularly as Old Buggerlugs—was a prize because of its rarity. There it was, with "To Charles Iredale from a fellow enthusiast, Dunstan Ramsay."

The night before the operation I think Charlie must have read and prayed all night; I slept, but I was aware from time to time that his light was on. I had taken a look at the English version of the *Legend* now and again, but could not long stomach the whoppers that were recorded as saintly acts. Charlie was not open to argument. "Moral truth overrides mere fact," he would say, and years later I was to hear this pronouncement more than once. That night I knew that he was fortifying himself with moral truth, as he understood it.

Charlie was reading his old Latin *Legend*: I was reading the English version. Why? Because the doctors who were to operate had pondered long on the subject of what might help him to bear the pain, which would be severe and of long endurance. At last they had hit on the most unprofessional plan of consulting the patient. And Charlie had said that he thought it would help him if someone read to him as the surgeons worked, and the doctors agreed to give it a try.

Who should read? Mrs. Iredale declared that it was utterly beyond her. The very thought appalled her. The Professor said he would have done so, certainly, but unluckily the Learned Societies were having their annual meeting at Waverley that week, and as Department Head he was compelled to chair a Classics symposium at the very hour of the operation and thus—we could see that his hands were tied.

So I was to be the reader. I agreed readily because I longed to see an operation.

The following morning Charlie ate no breakfast, as he had been bidden by his doctors, but I ate with a good appetite. We were early, because Charlie had to be at the hospital before eight o'clock. We walked together, in the morning sunlight, across the university campus, to the hospital, and mounted its front steps (for it was a building erected in the days when the number of front steps was an assurance of importance) and were met at the door by the lesser surgeon, who put Charlie in the charge of a nurse who hurried him away to be prepared for what was to follow.

"You're the friend, aren't you?" said the surgeon. "Neither of his parents here? Aha. It's very good of you to stick with him."

"Well," said I, not anxious to pose as a noble creature, "I'm very interested in medicine, you see. I'm hoping to be a doctor myself."

"So?" said the surgeon; "I understand you're going to help us. A novel sort of anaesthetist. Ha, ha. It will be longish, and it will be painful, but I know it will help him to have you near."

And so it was. I enjoyed "scrubbing up" and putting on a gown with the great men. At last the time came to go to the operating-room, and I was cautioned to sit behind Charlie's head on a high stool. Reader though I was I would get a good view.

Charlie was wheeled in on a table, looking thinner and more ill than I had ever seen him, but there was about him an air of resolution. I knew that he had been given some cocaine, but it had to be used very moderately, in these circumstances. I knew that as soon as blood began to flow, the effect of the cocaine would be greatly lessened. Charlie knew it, too. When the surgeon—not the junior but the top man, who was to do the work—whispered to me, "Ready?" I set out on the wonder tales of Saints Peter and Paul. My voice was strong and I read well. The head nurse handed the chief surgeon, a Dr. Hetherington, an instrument of some kind, and I saw Charlie's right hand move under his sheet; I knew he was crossing himself, and in that moment I understood what this meant to him. It was martyrdom. He would offer up his suffering to the glory of God, and he trusted in God to see him through it, or perhaps even to receive him, if that were not possible. I was sure the doctors had no doubts about the outcome, but doctors do not always know what is going on in the mind of a patient, and there can be great fear of death when experiencing something which does not, in truth, bring death close. I know that, after long years of practice, when understanding the patient has been my principal concern. The relationship of the patient to Death is not by any means the same thing as the medical probability of recovery.

The operation was long, and as I read I could not always keep my eyes from the spectacle in front of me. The head nurse cast a glance at me from time to time to see how I was holding up, but I stayed the course. If Charlie could do that, surely I, as a spectator and unconventional assistant, could do no less. Simply put, they thrust probes up Charlie's nostrils and cut holes sideways into the impacted sinuses. There should have been natural holes, but they had been clogged, or perhaps had grown together. I could hear, in the silence of the operating-room, the grinding as the bone was fretted away. It was like rats gnawing in a wainscot. I admired the calm and assurance of the surgeon, and the efficiency with which the head nurse directed everything apart from him in the room. My concern for Charlie was intense, but I kept my breakfast down, and what I felt for him was far beyond admiration. This, I thought, must be like what those saints of his endured, in one grotesque form or another, and his resolution was saintly.

I read as eloquently as I could. The circumstances made any colloquialism impossible; this called for the high style.

My only breach of operating-room etiquette was a loud sneeze, which I was able to quench with a handkerchief, and, of course, the mask I wore over my nose—not my mouth—was helpful. If I had sneezed into the room I think the head nurse might have murdered me, out of hand.

I do not know quite when it was—perhaps two-thirds of the way through the operation—Dr. Hetherington signalled to me to be silent, putting a rubber-gloved finger to his lips. I thought the reading must be too much for Charlie, and closed the book. The Victorian volume looked shabbier than before, because the chief nurse had insisted on spraying it with some sort of disinfectant and, though not sodden, it was damp.

At last it was over, and Charlie was wheeled away. The chief surgeon turned to me. "Sorry to cut you off," he said, "but you cannot believe how distracting your reading was. I found my mind wandering to the story, and that wouldn't do, would it? You held up remarkably," he continued; "I hear you intend to join us?

Good luck to you."

In that moment I think I grew a foot. Spiritually, that is to say, for I was already six feet tall and showed no sign of stopping just yet. But I felt I had been welcomed into the profession which was to be mine.

[14]

"WHERE WAS BROCKY all this time?" Esme spoke sharply. "I thought he lived in Salterton, too. Did he leave the whole care of Charlie to you?"

I was somewhat surprised to hear her speak of her father-in-law in this accusatory manner.

"Not at all. He came to see Charlie often, and his mother sent Charlie fruit and flowers. During the time Charlie was in hospital—people stayed a lot longer in those days than they do now—I was often asked to Brocky's home. We spent a lot of time together."

How odd it was, too. The contrast between Brocky's home and Charlie's astonished me, and astonishes me still. It also taught me a lesson about being a doctor: you can't really form an opinion about somebody until you have seen the place where they live.

It was a matter of taste, I suppose. The Iredales, or at least Charlie's mother, had unfailing Good Taste, in the sense that anything that could be reduced to a minimum in colour or design was so reduced; her walls were "off-white" with here and there a daring touch of a silvery hue; her upholstery attracted no attention, but was of wonderful materials; all the appointments of the table were so perfect you never noticed them; there were always fresh flowers in the rooms, but not what Mrs. Iredale would have laughed at as "cottage flowers," because every bloom was so well bred that it "knew its place" and was almost unnoticeable. The pictures on the walls were competent amateur water-colours; Mrs. Iredale had once "painted" but had not "kept it up." Charlie told me that his father said that you ought to be in the presence of a man for at least ten minutes before you noticed that he was impeccably dressed, and this principle seemed to assert itself in the house—everything was in such perfect taste that it was almost invisible.

Not so with the Gilmartins. Colour leapt up from the Oriental carpets on the floors, shouting a greeting to the walls, one or two of which were covered in red damask. Chandeliers that did not jingle and tinkle with crystal, glowed richly with ormolu, or the latten of the Low Countries. Anything that could be polished gleamed and glistened; everything that could carry ornament was loaded with it. It was plain that the Gilmartins loved "antiques" and worked on the principle that anything that was good of its kind went splendidly with anything else that was good of its kind, let it be what it might. With a result which was rich and wondrous, or The Old Curiosity Shop, according to how you responded to Brocky's parents. I liked them very much. There were lots of pictures, of every possible period and school, and they all rejoiced in big gold frames. Several were huge things of Welsh mountains by a painter named Leader. Professor Iredale was a learned man—professionally a learned man—but all the books in his house were confined to his study, except for an occasional novel, in vogue at the moment, which might lie artfully in view in the drawing-room. But the Gilmartins had books all over the place, and some were shiny and new and others were scruffy and old; some were superbly bound in leather but next to them might be a bundle of tatty cheap reprints; they subscribed to more magazines than I had ever seen before in one place and there were newspapers everywhere, because publishing newspapers was the way in which Mr. Gilmartin—he was not yet Senator Gilmartin—had gained his fortune. The house shouted with exuberance, and I suppose a great epicure in decoration like Mrs. Iredale would have laughed that it did not "hang together." But the Gilmartins wouldn't have cared if they had known, I don't think they had any notion of what "hanging together" might mean. To them stuff was stuff, and the more of it, and the richer the quality, and if possible the older, the better. They rejoiced in profusion.

The house was called St. Helen's, and it was on the waterfront. It was one of the oldest houses in the city and it was old in the sense that a Canadian house may be old; I suppose it was built during the first two decades of the nineteenth century. It was spacious, and friendly, and had all too plainly been built in a day when servants were many. But the Gilmartins did not seem to care; I don't think the conception of "convenience" ever entered their heads, and with an indoor staff of a houseman, an upstairs maid, a cook, and something called "a rough girl" they got along splendidly. There were two men in the garden, which was as uproarious and I suppose as tasteless as the house itself, but it was the delight of Brocky's mother's heart.

She was an invalid. This was immediately made plain, and like every well-to-do invalid she had a slave. The slave was her sister, Aunt Minnie, and one quickly sensed that Minnie was not quite like other people. I soon learned from Brocky that she had *petit mal*; that, although she did not positively have "fits," she had frequent "spells," when for a few seconds she was absent in spirit. "Away with the fairies," was the way Brocky put it. As for the invalidism of Mrs. Gilmartin it was a complexity of ailments, of which asthma was the foremost, and a number of others, not unconnected with habitual overeating, followed after. But her invalidism did not limit her zest for conversation, gossip, and judgements shrewd and sharp—and it must be said, witty—upon people and circumstances.

They all ate enormously, talked at once and often with their mouths full, and seemed to draw sustenance from the spoken word. Much about Brocky became clear during a meal with his family. Laughter, derision, irony, and every aspect of rhetoric were native to them; without, I think, being aware of it, they regarded language as the great unfailing plaything, and the play was unceasing.

Their very silences were rhetorical. I ate several dinners at St. Helen's and I cannot say with accuracy how often a silence fell over the table which was almost as though the Gilmartin family had been struck dumb, or had been silenced by some painful recollection or recognition. No, I cannot recall how often, but certainly it was often enough to impress me as a thing that happened often, and was to be dreaded. Their emotional variation was as extravagant as their taste in household furnishing and could drop from hilarity to a heavy silence without any apparent signal or reason. When it happened I kept quiet; this was a meaningful family silence and no attempt on the part of a guest to bridge the gap in conversation would have been tactful, or indeed thinkable.

Brocky spoke about it once when we had retired to his room upstairs after a dinner where one of these paralysing silences had fallen.

"You understand that this isn't a happy household," said he. "My parents simply don't get along, though they try—especially when there's a stranger present—and every now and then the conversational steam runs out."

I didn't understand about "not getting along." I had

no experience of family life except in my own home, where I don't imagine it ever entered the heads of my parents to consider whether they "got along" or not. They were married, and that was it. If they had anything to say, they said it, and if they had not, they did not find silence disquieting. Most decidedly they did not regard talk as an art-form, or an entertainment, or indeed anything except the common drudge that carried meaning. I suppose they were boring, but I do not think the idea of boredom had meaning for them, either. I said something of this to Brocky.

"You don't surprise me," he said; "when you first turned up at Colborne you hardly seemed to have a tongue in your head. But I sniffed you for a talker. You just needed to be uncorked, and I set to work to uncork you."

If Brocky had a fault, as a friend, it was just the tiniest assumption that he had created me out of some unlikely assemblage of oddments, as the young Frankenstein had created his Monster. I said so.

"Not a bit of it," he said; "keep your shirt on. No, no; I was, in so far as I was anything, the Pygmalion who released you, alive and talking, from the marble block—or I suppose I should say the Canadian granite of Sioux Lookout.

"What was that Monster's name? Was it Erik? I must look it up." And look it up he did. The Monster proved not to have a name. Looking things up was the family habit. Brocky's father—his name was Rhodri, and his wife called him Rod—told me that he was a self-educated man, and he didn't pretend that he had made an especially fine job of it, but at least he had persisted from boyhood in looking things up.

"For instance," he said, "you have an unusual surname. Hullah. Now where does that come from? You don't know? But it must come from somewhere, and if we knew we might find out a lot of interesting things about you. Brochwel, go and look in that dictionary of surnames, and see what you can find out about Hullah."

So Brocky had to leave the table, and Aunt Minnie put a cover over his plate, to keep his dinner warm. He was gone for about ten minutes.

"Nothing about Hullah in the surname book," he said, "but there's a Hullah in the *Dictionary of National Biography*. Here it is: John Pyke Hullah, born 1812—died 1884; composer and musical educator. He invented a system of reading music without notes—a system that was supplanted by Curwen's *Tonic Sol Fa*—"

"Oh, the Tonic Sol Fa!" said Mrs. Gilmartin. "Do you remember it, Min?"

"I certainly do," said Aunt Minnie, "and I never understood why we had to learn it. I always found it harder than reading ordinary music—"

"Go on, Brochwel," said Rhodri. "What about the family? What about the name?"

"The name is supposed to be Huguenot," said Brocky.

"Aha! then there we have it," said Rhodri. "Huguenot. There's an ancestor for you, and a bit of family background."

"But why do you think I'm related to this man?" said I.

"Oh, sure to be! Very uncommon name. Have you ever heard of anybody else named Hullah? Don't miss a chance to acquire an ancestor. I wish I had one—even one."

"You've got lots of them, Dad," said Brocky. "Their pictures are all over the house. Oh, I know you bought them all, here and there, but you can say what Major-General Stanley says in *The Pirates of Penzance:* 'I don't know whose ancestors they *were*, but I know whose ancestors they *are!*' Possession is everything."

"That's not the same as an unusual name," said Rhodri. "I'd hang on to John Pyke if I were you."

"I remember Hullah, now," said Mrs. Gilmartin. "He wrote 'Three Fishers.' We used to sing it, Min."

Then, to my astonishment, these two elderly women—they seemed elderly to me—began to sing, charmingly and musically, without a hint of asthma or age in voices that spoke of membership in really good choirs—

> *Three fishers went sailing*
> *Out into the West;*
> *Out into the West*
> *As the sun went down—*

On they went, to the refrain, with its insistent lap-lap-lapping sound, like gentle waves on the side of a skiff—

> *For men must work,*
> *And women must weep,*
> *Where there's little to earn,*
> *And many to keep;*
> *And the harbour bar is moaning.*

Very Gilmartin, this. Profoundly un-Iredale. Unthinkable to the Hullahs of Sioux Lookout. Singing at the table! Singing gently and movingly. A worse solecism, surely, than putting one's elbows on the table.

"I haven't heard that in donkey's years," said Rhodri. He wiped his eyes. "Thanks, Vina: thanks, Minnie. Thanks very much."

Minnie giggled and flushed. She giggled and flushed

at everything. Mrs. Gilmartin smiled, and suddenly I saw what may have drawn her and her husband together; they had been united by music, that siren who makes so many bad matches.

"I think I'll have to call you Pyke," said Brocky. "We can't go on forever calling each other Hullah and Gilmartin, as if we were still at school. Pyke. It's a very good name for you."

And it is true that to my few intimates I have been Pyke ever since.

[15]

ALMOST UNNOTICED, the summer wore away and, as so often with the summers of youth, I do not remember a day of bad weather. I lingered in the courtly old city of Salterton, made welcome, in their very different ways, by the Iredales and the Gilmartins. I came to know something of Charlie's father, who seemed to me to be a great eccentric, for he confided to me that when he travelled, even overnight, the first thing he packed was Liddell and Scott's great Greek Lexicon, in case he should feel the need to check the derivation of a word. This humanized him, in my eyes. The Greek and Roman classics were far more than stuff he taught to undergraduates and the occasional graduate who wanted to rise in the scholarly world; they were a passion, and I have always loved a man with a passion. Without the classics could he have survived his wife's impeccable taste? As it was, I think he regarded Taste platonically, as something related only to the world of sense and having no reality in the world of thought.

I stayed on because I was supposed to be coaching Charlie for the supplemental examinations he would attempt in the autumn. If he were successful then in improving his failure marks to pass marks, the universities would not be closed to him. We pegged away at chemistry and physics and algebra and geometry in what were, God knows, their barest and simplest elements, and with great difficulty I managed to get a few things into his head. But teaching in the garden, in the sunlight, was not the best atmosphere for that kind of drudgery and we wasted too many hours in talk, in which Charlie gave me some elementary instruction in theology, which he declared was the Queen of Sciences. He would not attach any importance to my protests against what seemed to me its kangaroo-like jumps in logic and its substitution of moving rhetoric for reason. But he did succeed in convincing me that it was another world of thought, and even in implanting some painful doubts in my mind about the logic and reason which I had assumed were the only approaches to important matters.

"Reduce everything to that," said he, "and your world crumbles to dust.

> The abdication of Belief
> Makes the Behaviour small—
> Better an ignis fatuus
> Than no illume at all."

"Who said that?" I asked.

"Emily Dickinson, if it matters. Pyke, you really ought to get over demanding authorities and attributions for everything. I suppose you pick that up at St. Helen's."

"All right. If you're happy with an *ignis fatuus*, it's your affair. But I like—"

"And stop arguing for victory all the time. Just listen, and let a few things sink in. Stop trying to win, and just let what's said wash over you, and see if any of it lingers."

"But Charlie, here I am trying to knock some stuff into your head which is rooted in proven fact. If everybody thought as you do, algebra and geometry and physics and chemistry would—what was it you said—crumble into dust—"

"I wish they would," said he.

"Look—we're trying to get you into the university—any university—and if you want to be a priest that's where you have to start. So do be a good fellow, and try to get the hang of this stuff."

Then we would drudge on. It was very unfair, because I was really sympathetic with Charlie's ambition and sometimes he treated me as if I were an enemy, who was bullying him about crass trivialities. Sometimes, too, he would play the invalid's dirty trick of suddenly looking ill and weary, as if I were pushing him too far for his strength. Brocky was no help. When he sat in on these lessons, if an argument broke out, he jumped from one side to the other, now dismissing Charlie's view of the world as priestcraft and moonshine, and at other times treating me as a boneheaded pedant who loved elementary science and baby math—which God knows I didn't.

He would quote Yeats to abuse me.

> *"A levelling, rancorous, rational sort of mind*
> *That never looked out of the eye of a saint*
> *Or out of a drunkard's eye—"*

he would declaim, and assure me that never had poet summed up my contemptible class of intellect so cogently. "But if you're bent on being a sawbones," he said, "I suppose that's the best sort of mind for you to have."

That always made me furious, and sometimes it seemed as though we might quarrel seriously.

Could I be angry with him, however, when he told me so much, and with the eloquence which was his heritage and his gift, about the difficulties in his home?

"It's a split at the very centre," he said. "In novels marriages are torn because the people can't agree about sex. I don't suppose sex ever was the top concern with my parents, Victorians as they are, at heart. It's a question of loyalty—"

"But surely," said I, "they aren't disloyal to one another? They seem to be so close. I'd have said they were tied together as tight as people can be."

"It's a loyalty to a country, or an idea of civilization, or just to roots. It's far beyond a personal thing, and yet it is deeply and inveterately personal. My mother, you see, is a real New World person. Old Loyalist stock, left the States at the time of the Revolution. Great-uncles killed defending Canada against the Yanks in 1812—the whole thing. She simply hasn't any attachment to the Old World at all. What she knows of it, she mistrusts. But my father—he's lived most of his life in this country, and he's done some quite good things for the country as well as for himself—but there's a part of him that's never left Wales. *Hen Wlad fy'Nhadau*—old Land of my Fathers—it's bred in the bone with him, you see, and she's jealous of it. Funny, isn't it, for a woman to be jealous not of another woman who has a hold on her husband, but of a country. But that's it. She wants to possess him utterly, as she wants to possess me, and he won't have it. You've seen what's happening in the past two or three weeks. He's packed his trunks and dashed off to the Old Land, explaining far too much that he must just look in on the house he has there, and the trees he's planted there, and—you heard some of it. But it's the pull of blood, if that isn't too melodramatic a way of saying it. But why not be melodramatic, when you're dealing with melodrama?"

"And she simply won't go with him?"

"Can't. Surely you see how it is, and you wanting to be a sawbones? No, no; he's thrown me to her as a solatium. I'm the one who has to be nailed to one loyalty or the other. No chance of compromise. And she insists she couldn't go. Not wouldn't, but couldn't. With her asthma, the sea-voyage would reduce her to nothing, and the climate of Wales would polish her off. That's the story."

"I simply don't believe it."

"Don't you, Dr. Hullah? Well Doc, the heart has its reasons which reason knows nothing of. Ever hear that?"

"No."

"I thought as much. Pascal."

"Never heard of him."

"Liar! But remember what he said."

Sometimes Brocky seemed old enough to be my father—my grandfather. He laughed at me because I was so pleased with the character of Salterton, which had—at least in its oldest, central part—a colonial charm that spoke of the last of the eighteenth or the first of the nineteenth century. Handsome, sober old houses built of limestone by Scottish masons who never skimped an iota of their work; noble old elms; a domed cathedral built to remind early settlers of Home; Waverley University, which hinted of Sir Walter Scott, and had been built with a sobriety that told of a Presbyterian regard for learning; and apart from these mute testaments of a colonial past, people who seemed still to be touched with a colonial spirit. I had never lived abroad and so had never experienced anything like it. I assumed that it was indeed the Old World, and at least in part that land of romance for which Brocky's father longed. I learned later that it was indeed the Old World, but seen through a diminishing glass. Like so much in Canada, its spirit was Chekhovian, clothing in a present dubiously accepted, a regret for a past which had never been. All of this, when I spoke of it, made Brocky loud and derisive.

"Do you think it's Cranford? Do you think it's a Jane Austen world? Do you think the commonest affairs of life have no place here? Come with me, and I'll show you something."

This was on a sunny afternoon in July. Brocky had one of his family's cars, and he piled himself and Charlie in the front seat, and me in the rumble, and sped to one of the exits of the town, where an old fort still guarded a bridge that crossed a river which at that point was joining Lake Ontario.

The fort looked implacable, treeless and hot in the midsummer sun, and showed no sign of life except for a sentry in a box at the gate. The sentry, as we approached and parked across the road, was having a hissed altercation with a strange figure; sentries are not supposed to speak except to utter formal challenges, but this one was angry and, though he spoke low, we could hear him plainly.

"Get t'hell outa here, you God-damned bitch! D'you hear me? Get out, or by Christ I'll call the sergeant and put you under arrest. Now gwan—beat it!"

But the figure did not move. When I got a good look at her I could see that she was a girl of not more than sixteen years of age, if so old. She was filthy, she was barefoot, and she wore a garment that would have been a smock if it were not so skimpy; but it was tight enough to show the very young woman's figure below. Her hair was long and dirty; her face was smeared with what might have been the remains of a piece of bread and jam. A child of about two, dressed no better, clung to her very short skirt.

"Aw c'mon, Jimmy. Give us a break will ya?" she said, and for another moment or two they argued, if argument may mean blasphemous abuse from the sentry, and coarse pleading from the girl.

"Okay, you bastard," she said at last; "but I got my livin' to make and I got t'get what t'eat somehow. So if I can't go in I'll fuckin' well stay outside. And yuh dursn't touch me."

She retreated across the road, very near to our car, and in a surprising cry, which I could never have expected from so young a creature, she set up her howl.

"A hunk fer two bits!" she shrieked. "A hunk fer two bits! C'mon, yuh cheap buggers, yuh'll never get a piece o' tail cheaper. A hunk fer two bits!"

She was near enough to us for me to touch her. I was frightened, as men often are by rowdy manifestations of female sexuality. Charlie was scarlet with embarrassment. But Brocky was in fits of laughter. He shouted at the girl—

> *"The harlot's cry from street to street*
> *Shall weave Old England's winding sheet."*

The girl rounded on him. "What are yuh yellin' about, yuh little prick? Hey, d'yuh want a hunk? C'mon, show me what y'got if y'got anything in your pants. C'mon!"

"Just quoting from our old friend Blake, Miss," said Brocky. "Just showing my friends the sights of fragrant old Salterton. How's trade? Thriving, I trust."

"You shut yer fuckin' mouth," said the girl. "Don't give me any o' that fancy shit. D'yuh want a hunk or don't yuh?"

By this time several soldiers, attracted by her hulla-baloo, were standing at the barrack gate, laughing and urging the girl on. "Don't you take any lip from Pretty-Boy, Maggie," shouted one, and "Hey, Mag, yuh wear pants?" shouted another.

Maggie rounded on them, with a screech of laughter, and hauled her skirt up to her waist. No, Mag did not wear pants. "A hunk fer two bits," she screamed, and Brocky took the chance to drive away, leaving the scene to resolve itself as it might.

"Now there, gentlemen, is something you haven't seen in Salterton. Maggie is a fixture at the barrack gate in fine weather, and so we must suppose she gets enough together to keep herself and that child. Is it her child? God only knows. Underneath the quaintness you admire so much, Pyke, the old houghmagandy is hard at work, and the harlot's cry is loud and clear."

"Poor soul," said Charlie. "I ought to have thrown her a dollar."

"Not on your life, Charlie," said Brocky. "She'd haunt you forevermore. A dollar! Why that's the price of four kicks at the cat! You'd spoil the market! Do you suppose nobody in this town knows who you are? What would your mother say if Maggie came a-tapping at your chamber door, some night?"

"The degradation!" said Charlie, shuddering.

"Perhaps. Or possibly a short life and a merry one, for Maggie. Remember her when you read books in which beautiful, scented Balzacian courtesans or Dostoevsky harlot-saints appear. She's the real thing, without disguise. A hunk for two bits, in fact."

[16]

I LEARNED SO MUCH from Brocky. His mind seemed to have taken shape so much earlier than mine. He was quicker-witted, and though I never felt at a serious disadvantage with him, he had seen corners of the world that were still unknown to me. The Funnies, for instance.

I was rather inclined to despise the Funny Papers, as they were then called; but Brocky was an avid reader, never missing a day with *Mutt and Jeff*, or *Maggie and Jiggs*, *Barney Google* and *Andy Gump*. He delighted in the Falstaffian braggings of Major Hoople, and occasionally spoke in what he imagined was the Major's voice.

"If you're too fine for the funnies, you're too fine for life," he would say. "They show you what the people are thinking who never read a book, never hear a sermon, and forget to vote. Does that make them worthless? Not on your life. The funnies give you the dreams and the opinions of *l'homme moyen sensuel*, and if you want to be a politician, for instance, that's the place to start. Understand the funnies, and you've made a good beginning on understanding mankind."

One day he took me to the headquarters of his father's newspaper, and there, after a brief colloquy with a sub-editor, he showed me the page-sized pink cardboard forms, embossed with what would be the funnies, when the sheets had been through the stereotyping machine, which would cast them in printer's metal.

"Here they are, you see. A full week's issue of hilarity and hard-bitten street philosophy on every one of these sheets. They are not called stereotypes for nothing; they embody what a majority of people believe, or accept as self-evident. They make every reader feel superior to what he can recognize as the stupidity or folly of somebody else. Whenever Mutt crowns Jeff with a spittoon, a million simple minds have a thrill of triumph. When Maggie hits Jiggs with the rolling-pin and a balloon reading 'Ka-Pow!' springs out of his head, a million painfully endured marriages are given a momentary discharge of tension. And it's all funny, you see. That's what you have to bear in mind. What might be tragedy if Sophocles got hold of it, is funny in the four or five daily frames of the funnies. While the funnies live, Aristophanes is never quite dead."

What does Brocky think today, I wonder, if he still looks at these repositories of basic folk belief and wisdom, conditioned as they are by our modern heaviness of spirit, and the eagle eyes of the seekers after political incorrectitude? I must ask him when next I see him. Has the Aristophanic freedom of our youth fled from the earth?

I might have been overcrowed by Brocky's worldly wisdom if I had not been, almost daily, a witness to what seemed to me to be a deep flaw in his character. Brocky was mad about a girl.

We saw a lot of girls, during that summer in Salterton. We sailed in the fine harbour in dinghies and sometimes in more impressive craft, always with girls aboard. We went to informal and improvised parties at the homes of girls whose parents liked young people, or at least presented a reasonable appearance of so doing. Sometimes we rushed along the roads, going nowhere in particular, in cars where the crowding was so great that girls were compelled—simply compelled—to sit on boys' laps, and sometimes in the darkness they found themselves being kissed, which they bore with whatever composure they could muster. For those were days that now seem impossibly innocent, when sexual approaches and sexual play were limited by fear of "going too far" with all the disgrace for the girl and the unwanted and oppressive, but inescapable, responsibilities for the boy that an illegitimate child—no no, never illegitimacy, for marriage would be demanded, for certain—would bring with it. There were marriages that were hasty, and babies from which the callous said it was necessary to brush rice off them, but such mishaps were rare. And in spite of strict limitations about what might be done— Eddu's game of "stink-finger" was rare among the better children of Salterton—a good time, as the social notes so often declared, was had by all.

Now and then there was a serious "affair," and one such which I saw take root and blossom was that between Brocky, who was just nineteen, and Julia Opitz, who was then seventeen. Julia seemed to me to be a nice girl, quite pretty and with a neat figure that looked well in a bathing-suit, a soft laugh, and a line of fashionable chatter which included every cliché and catchword of the time. Because Brocky was so engrossed with her I took a careful look at her myself and concluded that she was a self-preservative girl who would, in another five years, be a self-possessed and cool young woman; Brocky was mad about her, but I could see that she was by no means overset by Brocky, although she was flattered by his attention, his conversation, and the look of stunned adoration which, from time to time, could be seen in his eyes when he looked at her.

These things happen, of course. There were three or four "serious affairs" observable among the group we met almost daily in Salterton, at the Yacht Club, or wherever it might be, but I think that even the most serious of the couples were aware, some place deep in their consciousness, that this was not love for keeps, and that it was to be enjoyed while it lasted. This was not cynicism, but a quality hard to define except by the blunt old word gumption. But Brocky's gumption was in eclipse.

Looking back on that time, I blame his mother, though she, like Brocky, was working under influences she did not understand and could not control. Rhodri had packed his trunks and, making far too many excuses, had gone off to Wales and his country home there for ten weeks. Malvina had assured him that she understood why he had to go—had indeed urged him to go—but in the depths of her heart hated his going and felt it to be a betrayal. So when her cherished son began to bring home a girl with whom he was plainly infatuated, her outraged motherhood declared war on that girl, and she and her lieutenant Minnie waged it implacably.

Not obviously, of course. No, it was the armoury of sighs when Brocky went out for the evening, or controlled smiles and cool glances whenever Julia came to St. Helen's, of "bad turns" if Brocky was late coming home at night, and slight delays in acceding when Brocky suggested that Julia might come to dinner before a movie. Malvina made it plain, without anything blatant being said or done, that she found Julia a burden, but a burden she would bear, of course, if Brocky insisted.

Aunt Minnie had no such arts. She simply asked Julia if she could sew on a button, at need, and wondered aloud if she were not chilly in the scanty summer frocks she wore. And Minnie glared. She smiled as she glared, but her eyes glared, and sometimes when Julia was slangy or unsuitably vivacious (in Aunt Minnie's terms), she would turn her head aside and murmur almost inaudibly, "Oh, Lordy!"

Brocky missed none of this. Indeed, he would have had to have the insensitivity of a rhinoceros to miss any of it, and he had the thin skin of a lover. It drove him to seek in Julia what he could not find in the overwhelming femininity of his mother, and his antagonism to Minnie—who often managed to have one of her "spells" at the table when Julia was present—became venomous.

I now see what a very old drama this is, but it was new to me then and it made me uncomfortable, because it seemed to me to show up my friend as an ass.

My refuge was Charlie. I did my best to coach him in the things that were so repugnant to him, and the following autumn I had my reward, for he scraped through in all the necessary tests, and miraculously a letter came from Colborne saying that he had won the school's top history prize. That was something to dangle before any university to which he applied.

When mid-August came I had to return to Sioux Lookout. My parents had been very patient, and I knew they wanted some time with me before I returned to Toronto to enter the university. The day before I went, Charlie gave me his copy of Sir Thomas Browne's *Religio Medici*.

"You've got to read it," he said. "And you've got to reread it. It's absolutely your thing, and you've got to be a doctor like old Browne. What I want for you—what I pray for as your experience of God's blessing—is that like Browne you may 'assume the honourable style of Christian.' Do try."

In the emotion of parting, what could I say? "I'll try, Charlie," I said. "I really will." And at that time I meant it, as one means so many things when one is young which take on a very different colour as one grows old.

So—off I went, back to Sioux Lookout, and during the succeeding six years I saw Brocky infrequently, and Charlie not at all, for it is thus that the intensities of youth are reshaped and defused by the press of circumstances.

II

MY INTENTION was merely to write a few notes, to separate what I thought it prudent to tell Esme from what I know about Charlie and the affair at St. Aidan's, but I seem to be writing an extended memoir. Shall I go on? Yes, for a while, at least, because Esme promises to return to the attack as soon as she has completed some work she has in hand that calls for more immediate completion.

Why do I say "the attack"? Esme is not attacking me. She is discreet in so far as the work of a newspaper interviewer permits. What do I feel, in my innermost heart, she is attacking? Charlie, of course, but why should I defend Charlie? Loyalty to a friendship that was intimate in the beginning, but which lost that kindly intimacy as our lives progressed?

In my work I often have to deal with patients who are compulsively retentive; they protect what needs no protection, withhold information which is of no importance, and delight in saying "No." Am I becoming one of those? What is it about Esme that makes me defensive? Her youth? Her undeniable attraction? The fact that she has now married my godson, Conor Gilmartin, and, however absurd it seems, I feel that she is an intruder into the life of the Gilmartins, in which I have a clear and also a shadowy part? Am I becoming consti-pated, like my other retentives? I believe I am. Should I take the advice I give them and, instead of resorting to cathartics and blasters of one sort and another, search my mind for the origin of my undue retention? That is what I would advise them to do. Physician, heal thyself.

I am writing in my Case Book, a handsome leather-bound volume I bought a long time ago, when I first went into private practice, thinking to fill it with a record of my work. Fool! I soon learned that the modern physician must keep a card index and, nowa-days, a computer, if he can cope with one, or afford a secretary who understands the latest technology. My secretary and nurse, Mrs. Christofferson, would have nothing to do with a hand-written record. So my hand-some Case Book has only two or three old entries, and the pages beyond are virgin. But it shall not be wasted. I shall become my own *Case*. Physician, etc. Take your own medicine.

[1]

FIVE YEARS at Colborne had done much to make me superficially a city person and, in my own estimation, a sophisticate. But Sioux Lookout con-tinued to be my Eden, my place of origin in the spirit as well as in the flesh. As I made the journey from Salterton after that revealing and enlarging summer I may have felt patronizing toward Sioux Lookout, as a place that had nothing more to teach me. I felt myself to be an adult.

It seems to me that one matures by fits and starts, not by gradual process. At Colborne I had begun as a New Boy, as green as ever New Boy was, and at the end of five years I was a Steward—the highest level of prefect—and editor of the college magazine, a hardened smoker (five and six cigarettes a day, when the pressure of editorial work was intense), a member of the Curfew Club, and altogether a swell and a notable, held in awe by New Boys. An exemplary fag master: helped with homework, repressed cheek. Within the confines of the school I was a person to be reckoned with.

The Salterton summer reduced me, in some respects, to being a New Boy again. In the estimation of parents, for instance.

I was astonished by the coolness of the Iredale household. Coolness, let me insist; there was nothing cold about it. But Charlie and his parents seemed almost to be equals. His mother was polite to him. Polite to me, too. She always called me "Hullah," in the school way. My mother was polite toward me, of course, but in quite a different way; she called me Jon, and it would never have occurred to her to defer to my opinion about anything; she tended to order me about, not in an overtly bossy way, but as if I were still ten years old. I do not think I was ever more than fourteen, in my mother's reckoning. Charlie's allowance was paid by his father into a bank, where Charlie had an account, and he could spend it as he pleased. It was a much bigger allowance than mine, although I am sure my parents were far more affluent than Charlie's. Charlie bought his own clothes, and was never questioned about the style or the cut, whereas my clothes were still supposedly bought under the eye of my father, but in fact chosen by my mother, so that I tended to look as if my clothes did not quite belong to me; they were not allowed to say what I felt about myself, but to reflect the opinion of my elders and betters. Charlie already looked like a man, and I was sometimes aware that I looked like that awful creature "a growing boy," though I had done most of my growing. When Charlie had to have his important operation, it was his decision, although of course he talked to his parents about it. This was all puzzling to me; Charlie was off the chain in a way that I was not, but I know now that there was a warmth of concern in my home which was lacking at the Iredales.

I assumed that this was the English manner of upbringing. Maturity and individual judgement were expected and encouraged. It was not the Canadian way. Certainly not as I knew it.

Nor did the household at St. Helen's, so very different from the Iredale house, show me anything that I found familiar. Dominated by the mercurial spirit of the father, and revolving around him, it was continually surprising and sometimes embarrassing, when the parents quarrelled at the table, or when Aunt Minnie went off into one of her "spells" and scrabbled in the pickle dish with a groping, uncontrolled hand.

Brocky seemed to have as much freedom as Charlie, but he had to make a stand now and then to secure it. He had no money of his own, and had to ask for it; sometimes Rhodri forked over generously, with a laugh, but sometimes he made a fuss, and reminded everyone within earshot that money did not grow on trees, and that he had known times when he had to look at both sides of a five-cent piece. There was a furious row at dinner one night during my stay.

"You don't seem to do anything but loaf around and go to parties," said Rhodri. He was in one of his looking-at-both-sides-of-a-five-cent-piece moods. "I don't know why you don't look for a job."

"But Dad," said Brocky, "what kind of job could I do? I would have to find a labouring job."

"Well, I don't suppose it would kill you," said Rhodri; "some experience of that kind would give you a different outlook on life. Bring you up against some realities."

"You, the publisher of a newspaper, talking like that!" said Brocky, with exaggerated dismay. "Haven't you heard that we are in the middle of the worst depression of the century? Suppose I took a job? Suppose that I could find one? I would be taking it from some poor fellow with a wife and children who needs it desperately. What would my fellow-workers think of me? Indeed, what would they think of you? 'Young Gilmartin, who doesn't need a job, grabs one in the face of the thousands of unemployed who have no resource but the labour of their hands. Just look at Young Gilmartin, in his brand-new overalls, going home after work with his dinner-pail to St. Helen's, for God's sake, to eat a huge meal! The gall of it! Isn't that the way the rich have always behaved? Not content with what they've got they must snatch the crust from the mouth of the worker's child.' You know, it wouldn't surprise me if they ganged up and beat me to a pulp. And I wouldn't blame them! No, I couldn't find it in my heart to blame them! I would bow to their justifiable wrath! I would kiss the rod!"

Old Rhodri—he wasn't very old, but he had the authority which is suggested by the adjective "old"—was furious. This kind of high-coloured Welsh rhetoric was his own preserve, his accustomed art form, and he could not bear to have it turned against him by his long-tongued son. He roared. The word is not chosen carelessly. He roared. Beginning with his immigration to Canada, long ago, he rehearsed the ignominies and burdens of his youth, his determination not to knuckle under to Fate, his daring and high resolve in raising himself above the artisan class in which he had begun, and the Herculean labours which he had undertaken in order to—to what? It appeared that all of this had been undertaken in order that Brocky should never know the bitterness of poverty, the grinding necessity of acquiring a competence (Rhodri hated the word "rich" when applied to himself), and have the inestimable advantage of a first-class education, a boon denied to his father, who had had to struggle all his life under the dark shadow of ignorance. (This, from a man whose dripping-with-blood political articles, framed in fiery but grammatically impeccable rhetoric, were the delight of the Liberal Party, was coming it strong, but Rhodri did not deny himself anything; it was his delight, in the old phrase dear to Brocky, to "be somewhat at large, and have ornature.") With my eyes fixed on my plate, I listened to his ornature for at least ten minutes, which is a long time for a speech at a domestic table.

Then, suddenly, it was over.

"All right, you've made your point," said Rhodri. "Do you want the car tonight?"

"I don't think your mother enjoyed that very much," I said, as we drove off in the car to meet Julia and some friends of hers, with whom I was supposed to make airy chat while Brocky pursued his ill-starred wooing.

"No, she didn't. You know why, of course? Those rows are evidence of how close my father and I are. And she hates that."

"Doesn't want you to be on good terms with your father?"

"It isn't a case of 'good terms.' You know what Freud says: falling in love with one parent and hating the other forms part of the permanent stock of the psychic influences which arise early in childhood. But Freud seems to mean that you fall in love with your mother and hate your father; I've done it the other way round. I think lots of people do."

"You don't hate your mother. Do you?"

"Certainly not. I'm very sorry for her and try to be as

nice to her as circumstances will allow. But circumstances don't allow very much in that line. The way she thinks, not to be wholly on her side is to be a traitor. Don't you follow? Probably not. I suspect you of having a nice, happy uncomplicated home. A terrible start in life, let me tell you. The more rough-and-tumble you experience early in life, the better armed you are against what's to follow."

Brocky was full of that sort of easy wisdom. But nothing of his Freudian stoicism showed in his affair with Julia. As a bystander it seemed to me that Julia treated him like a dog. A dog she quite liked. A dog who could be petted when she felt blue, and who would lick her hand and gaze with doggy admiration as she pitied herself. A dog she would never beat, but whom she would readily board out at the vet's for any length of time when its presence was inconvenient. I was never on anything better than ordinary good terms with her, but nevertheless I learned a lot from Julia.

She was quite a pretty girl, though not the Venus Brocky thought her. What made her popular and drew enough admirers to make Brocky's life a burden was that she had a very good "line," for it was a time when girls had "lines." Her line was not remarkable or particularly original; it was composed of catch-phrases and scraps from popular songs, but she "put it across" with great vivacity and an air of being always about to burst into laughter, so that the small change of her conversation had an air of wit, though she never said anything funny. Brocky did, of course; he shone in the circle in which he and Julia moved, and she laughed with him, and at him, and made him feel that she particularly understood and appreciated what he said. She was a girl who seemed always to be in movement; she snapped her fingers, cut little dance steps when others were standing still, and I would say that she wiggled her hips if that were not to suggest a vulgarity of motion; she was a graceful wiggler. She seemed always to be moved by a breeze not palpable to others. She was like a girl in a musical comedy who seems forever about to burst into song—though she never did so.

Brocky's approach was to play up to her, and I found that embarrassing, because he was too intelligent to be doing all the wiggling and finger-snapping he attempted, without ever making it seem quite spontaneous. He now wore spectacles, great horn-rimmed things, and as he jigged and pranced their owlishness rebuked his levity. That was not all, however; he contrived, whenever he could, to get Julia alone and to talk to her seriously, and declare his love, as poetically as he could manage. Julia liked that, in moderation. Though I was never present at one of these "serious" times—of course I wasn't, for intimacy was the soul of the thing—I know Julia enjoyed them, moderately, because Brocky's admiration was worth having. But she was forever entreating him not to "get too serious," and he was set on being as serious as lay in his power. In love, he was a whole-hogger. What he thought would come of it, I don't know and I never asked. He greatly liked talking to me about his love, but I understood very well that he would resent it if I tried, however gently, to put it under the microscope.

Oh, how he liked to talk about Julia! And what a bore it could be, for an outsider! One of his follies was to see her in terms of the literature to which he was determined to devote his life, and he never seemed to see that this was loving at second-hand. He raved about her magnificent carriage—and indeed she did carry herself well—quoting Chaucer's description of Alison, the merry young wife in "The Miller's Tale":

Wincing she was, and like a jolly colt,
Long as a mast, and upright as a bolt.

This did not seem to me to be the happiest comparison, because Alison was rather a twister, and the way she treated her learned lover Absolon was funny, though not for Absolon. When, in the darkness, the poor scholarly booh begged her to lean down from her window and give him a kiss, she amused her handsomer lover, who had been enjoying her, by sticking her arse out of the window and letting Absolon kiss *that*.

Tee hee, quoth she, and clapped the window to.

Absolon, poor gull, was left marvelling that a woman should have what he took for a beard.

Coarse old ruffian that he was, Chaucer knew a thing or two, and I was reminded of it this very night. For when Brocky and I arrived at the Yacht Club, where she was supposed to meet us, she did not appear, and we hung about, Brocky dwindling by the quarter-hour, until just after nine o'clock when a canoe swept gracefully past the dock, with a Lieutenant Dorrington paddling, and Julia lying gracefully on some cushions. She spied Brocky, and waved and kissed her hand. Dorrington leered, as it seemed to me, in triumph.

Tee hee, quoth she, and clapped the window to.

She phoned the following day, and explained that Dorrington had asked her to go along while he picked up some of his traps at the barracks dock, and it had all taken much longer than she expected, but I don't imagine she hoped to be believed. It was simply the well-understood female privilege of changing her mind. The miracle was that Brocky believed her. Any self-deception rather than face the fact that Julia was a flirt, and half wanted to shake him, and half wanted to have as her slave the most amusing young man in Salterton.

It was sad, but educative, for me to see Brocky, whom I regarded as so far superior to myself, made the buffoon of such a silly piece of work as Julia. As friends will in such circumstances, I became self-righteous.

"You really ought to read less poetry and more Shaw," I said. I was very strong on Shaw at that time.

"Why?" said he, suspecting that a sermon was coming.

"Well—*Man and Superman*, for a starter. It's marvellous about sex. Goes right to the nub of the thing."

"So?"

"About how women are really looking for their best biological fulfilment. And that governs who they'll fall in love with. Or, more frankly, who they mark down as their destined prey. If that's not your role, you don't stand a chance."

"You're talking about me and Julia, aren't you?"

"I suppose so."

"Oh, you suppose so, do you? Listen, my friend; you're talking about something you know nothing whatever about. You've never been in love. Nor, I suspect, has your gabby old friend Shaw. In its highest form it's a mystical thing, and until you've experienced it, no amount of talk about it makes any sense."

"Like eating oysters, do you mean?"

"Don't be funny. I mean that it's something quite out of your ken, and I don't want to hear your opinions about it. Until you've been through it, don't twaddle about it."

"But you haven't been through it. You're bang in the middle of it, so far as I can see."

"And may be so forever."

Useless to talk to him. He even believed that if he loved Julia strongly enough, some magic would compel her to love him in return. Oaf from Sioux Lookout though I was, I wasn't stupid enough to believe *that*.

Looking back, I see how callowly I judged the affair. Julia was not a heartless flirt, as I supposed; she was just a girl testing her powers, which were not inconsiderable, and she was not burdened with any unusual understanding of other people's feelings. As for Brocky, he had perhaps read too much, drunk too much poetry, and was unable to bring his protective cynicism, which served him so well in other matters, to bear on his obsession with Julia. Fortune, who dearly loves such tricks, was having a little sport with them both, and Fortune may show a Chaucerian roughness when she cracks jokes.

[2]

SIOUX LOOKOUT, in mid-August, showed already a touch of autumn. No dramatic turning of the leaves, but a melancholy in the air and some chill at night. Not a sentimental melancholy; rather a sobriety as the year accepted its death. What was I to do? I had finished school, and had a couple of finely bound prize books to show my parents, who pretended not to be impressed. I was already pointed toward the university, but I had no idea what medical studies might offer me, and no intention of trying to ready myself for the future. So I wandered aimlessly, and read aimlessly, and ate a great deal and made it clear that I was now quite old enough to have wine as something other than medicine. My father had some good wine, though how he acquired it I do not know and thought it better not to ask. Prohibition, it was well understood, was a blessing for the poor, who "couldn't handle liquor," and a sop to its advocates, who were chiefly Methodists, but it was not to be taken seriously by people like ourselves, hereditary handlers of liquor. Luxuries were few in Sioux Lookout, and my father's wine was doubly precious in consequence.

Everything seemed peaceful, and even sleepy after the frenzied social life (as it seemed to me) of Salterton. It was not until much later that I recognized how provincial, indeed how colonial, and in the case of the older inhabitants, how Chekhovian that life was, and sensed the Chekhovian autumn that hung over it. I see now that Sioux Lookout was the enduring reality of my homeland, and Salterton a retreat into its past.

Young as I was, what impressed me chiefly was how old everybody was growing. Doc Ogg was now an old man, and an old man, what is more, who had habitually drunk too much of the cheap sherry and rough brandy in which he suspended his foolish medicines.

"You're going to the greatest medical school in the world, boy. Don't let anybody tell you different. McGill—pah! What have they got since they lost Osler? Johns Hopkins? Eh? A big name, but can they hold a candle to the U. of T.? I doubt it. And overseas? Germany's gone to hell since the last War. France was never anything since Pasteur. And the Old Country? Eh? Who's at Edinburgh now? Can you name anybody? No, boy, you're headed for the greatest medical school in the world. I know, because I was there, and it was the making of me.

"Now look, boy. I regard you as my heir, see? You're my child in a way no natural-born child can ever be. You're my child in science, and I'm going to give you something."

Here Doc Ogg, with drunken éclat, reached from under some clutter on his desk his battered, much-worn copy of *The Principles and Practice of Medicine* by William Osler, M.D.; its subtitle was *Designed for the Use of Practitioners and Students of Medicine*. Doc's was the Third Edition and I already knew that it was thoroughly out of date and that Sir William Osler had revised it substantially. But I received it with becoming modesty, as an aspirant to the scientific splendour of mind which was Doc's.

"Make that your Bible, boy, as I've done. Read it, read it, read it and burn it into your mind. Osler—the greatest. And never forget he was a Canadian, eh? We've taught the world more than the world knows."

"Insulin?" I suggested. I was not well up in medical discoveries, but everybody knew about insulin and how Banting and Best evolved it in a shed on the Toronto campus. "Nobel stuff, and a life-giver to thousands who don't know where it began."

"Yeah—well—insulin sure enough. From the old U. of T. My *alma mater*. The greatest medical school in the world."

"Who are the big men there now?" I asked. "Who should I look out for?"

"Oh—ah—well, it'd take a long time to name them all. Changed since my day. Everybody, I'd say. The cream. But never forget Osler. He's the *fons et irrigo*. God, thinking of it makes my Latin all come pouring back."

It was decent of Doc to want to give me a push in the right direction, even if he didn't have much idea of where it lay. His old Osler was dusty and yellow and spoke of neglect. But his heart was in the right place—as we so often say of people whose minds are sadly astray. I kept the Osler and have it still, re-bound and among my books relating to the history of medicine. What a lot of diseases there are now that the great doctor had never heard of! And what curious diseases he discusses, no case of which has ever come my way— such arcane ills as saturnine neuritis, rice-water stools, and scrivener's palsy. He lived in a world where noxious chrome yellow, a fairly serious poison, might be used by bakers to give cakes a pretty colour, and patients might appear in the consulting-room suffering from "railway brain." I do not speak in scorn; we have our fashionable, fleeting illnesses today and I see many of them in my own consulting-room.

I would not have dreamed of visiting Doc without a balancing call on Mrs. Smoke. Doc showed the wear of years, but she looked just as I had last seen her. In the old way, I entered her cabin, which smelt, if anything, more pungently than before, and sat for a while on the floor until she was ready to speak to me. She was scraping a skin.

"You seen Eddu?" said she, after a while.

Yes, I had seen Eddu, who had rushed upon his fate faster than I would have thought possible, and who was now a wreck, but whether from booze or girls I do not know and did not want to find out. When he had seen me he barked a derisive greeting from a distance but I, not possessing Charlie's notions about Christian charity, pretended not to hear.

"The town drunk, now," said Mrs. Smoke.

The ice having been broken, I told Mrs. Smoke about my next move in life.

"You remember when you first told me you wanted to be a doctor?" said she.

Indeed I remembered, and remembered her scorn of my ambition.

"Do you think I'm doing the right thing?" I asked.

"You got more sense now. Then you was just a kid."

"But do you think I'm doing the right thing?"

"What do you care what I think?"

"Oh, come on, Mrs. Smoke! Don't talk to me like that! Why wouldn't I care what you think? Do you suppose I've forgotten when I had scarlet fever and you saved me?"

Mrs. Smoke made no response, and her silence pushed me to talk in a way I had not intended, and which had in it an echo of Doc Ogg.

"You brought the shaking tent! That was magic! You can't do magic for me, and then shut me out and say I don't care what you think!"

"Not magic. Magic is shit."

"What do you call it then? That night in the tent— what did you do?"

A long silence, and then, when at last Mrs. Smoke spoke, it was in a voice I had never heard from her before, a young voice, not gentle but not weighted with experience, as was her common speech.

"I guess you're old enough to know. As much as I know, and that isn't much. What did I do? What does anybody do in the shaking tent? I went into the Great Time and I asked for helpers. I did it because your mother and father was good about not letting the fever spread among my people. Christ knows what it would have done if it had spread. So we owed you, see? We owed you our lives. My people wanted me to help you, so I had to ask for the Helpers. And they came, and you got better."

"What Helpers? Who are they? Where do they come from?"

"I don't know."

"Would they come for anybody?"

"No, they wouldn't."

"But—if there are these Helpers, oughtn't we to try to get them more often? Why did they come for you? What is the Great Time?"

Mrs. Smoke's face was like stone. I knew it was a foolish question. But since last we had talked I had read the story of Parsifal, and I knew what harm could follow if the right questions were not asked at the right time.

"When I told you I wanted to be a doctor you said I was the wrong person, going the wrong way. That can't be right. How can I be anybody but myself, and what way can I go except the university way, if you won't tell me about your way? The Helpers—I really and truly do want to know about them. Haven't I a right to know? Didn't they come for me?"

Again, a long pause. Conversation with Mrs. Smoke was not a thing of urbane chit-chat, and doubtless that was the best thing about it. At last she spoke.

"You got to find out for yourself," she said.

"Was that what you did? Did you find them yourself?"

"Nobody that taught me would teach you. You're the wrong person, going the wrong way. But maybe you could find out something for yourself. You ever get lost in the woods?"

"Lots of times."

"Well, you're here so you must have found your way out."

"In the woods the secret is not to go in circles. You have to look for the sun and blaze your way and sooner or later you'll come to something."

"Uh-huh."

"Is that how it is? Keep on, and blaze your way so you don't backtrack?"

"Maybe."

"Mrs. Smoke, please don't shut me out. Do you know what? You're a kind of second mother to me. When I was dying you brought me back—you and the Helpers. You gave me life. Don't shut me out now."

Another one of Mrs. Smoke's long silences. Then—

"Remember the snakes?"

"Do I! You scared the life out of me! Poisonous rattlers and I nearly put my hand in the bucket."

"You remember?"

"Of course I do."

Another silence, but I saw Mrs. Smoke shaking with laughter, though not a sound escaped her. Then illumination!

"Do you mean they were the Helpers?"

Mrs. Smoke almost made the great leap from her inner laughter to audible mirth. Almost, but not quite. For the first time she turned from the table where she was scraping the pelt and looked me square in the face.

"You're not as big a fool as you look," she said. "Now go home! I'm busy."

[3]

GOING HOME WAS not what it had been in earlier days. There was something uneasy in the air, and I could not grasp what it was. The Thursday nights when three other couples came in to make up two tables of bridge had been abandoned. My mother played endless patience; my father read. My parents had never been great talkers, and at meals my mother had initiated whatever conversation there was, but now she sat silent, and would not have spoken if my father had not asked her some direct, harmless question. Had she been out today? Found any new plants? Talked to anyone? She had noticed the new moon, of course? Visible in daylight, with a rim where the old moon had been, which suggested rain to come. I talked, but in the uneasy manner of a boy who does not want to discuss anything that is important to him. Nothing about the Iredales, though I gave details of Charlie's illness; nothing about the Gilmartins, except that they had a fine garden; nothing about girls, of course. A little talk about going to the university in a few days.

Sometimes my mother would rise from the table and leave us alone. She "went to her room," which had special significance because she and my father no longer shared a room; he slept in a poky little thing, not much better than a large cupboard, down the hall. No explanation of these sudden absentings was offered, but my father would sigh and offer me more wine.

It was my first experience of the way in which the malaise of one family member can infect a whole household and rob it of its spirit. Since then I have seen much of it. This is one of the things not always recognized about illness; many people other than the obvious victim may be strongly affected.

Unlike Parsifal I did not fear to ask questions.

"What's wrong with Ma?"

"She's just a little out of sorts. It will pass."

"Has she seen a doctor?"

"Of course."

"Not Ogg, I hope?"

"A good man in Winnipeg. Dr. Cameron says it will pass."

I suppose it did pass, at least in part, but not before a distressing scene between me and my mother in which she tried to involve my father, but the cause of it could not have been farther from his realm of understanding.

My father suggested that he and I spend a couple of nights camping on the shores of Lac Seul and pretending to fish during the day while in fact looking at the silent, calm beauty around us. We returned refreshed and as quiet in spirit as it was in our nature to be. But my mother was sitting in the living-room, holding a closed book in her hand and looking, appropriately, like something out of Greek tragedy. She held out the book to my father.

"Did you know he was reading this?" she asked. I had never truly understood what the word "fraught" meant, though it was popular in the fiction of the day. Her speech was heavily fraught, and her question was rhetorical, for my father took the book and looked at it uncomprehendingly.

"*The Interpretation of Dreams*," he read from the spine. "No. I never heard of it."

"If ever a book ought to be banned, *that* book ought to be banned. It's filth! The purest filth from beginning to end. Degenerate, German filth. I won't have that book in this house! You read it, Jim. You just read the pages I've marked with those slips of paper. Then you'll know! Then you'll see! I won't stay in the same room with that evil, vile, degenerate, filthy book!"

She rose, and "went to her room." My father held the book in astonishment. Neither of us had ever seen her like that.

"What in hell was all that about?" he said.

"I suppose Ma has been reading Freud and it has upset her."

"Well, let's have dinner and then I suppose I'll have to dig into this thing. It doesn't look like my kind of book. Is it really filthy?"

"Not in any way that would give pleasure," I said. It was a smart-alec remark and I should have held my tongue. My father gave me a glance that disturbed me more than my mother's rage. But I was angry that my mother had been snooping in my room. Mrs. Iredale would never have done such a thing. What was she looking for? Pictures of girls?

After dinner my father sat down patiently to read the book. He seemed the most unlikely reader for that work, with his bifocals halfway down his nose and his partly bald head gleaming under the light of the oil lamp by his chair; we still lit with oil in Sioux Lookout. He should have been reading something by John Galsworthy, full of controlled social consciousness, detailed but not probing investigation of character, and unimpeachable sanity, justice, and compassion. I was reading *Point Counter Point* which was new then, and gave me a warm illusion of sophistication. From time to time my father sighed, as I had heard him sigh over particularly tedious pamphlets about industrial mining.

It was about ten o'clock when my mother appeared. I had not thought she would be able to stay away all evening, and here she was, and loaded for bear, as we Sioux Lookouters say when we mean that somebody is in a peak state of fury.

"Well, Jim? What do you think?"

"Eh? Oh, well I can't say I've read very far. Not easy going. Fine style, mind you. Smooth as silk. But every two or three sentences you have to stop and think."

"And have you any doubts about what you think?"

"So far as I've got he makes a strong case for taking dreams seriously. This stuff about sleep releasing depths of the mind—I can see what he means. Anybody who gets really quiet—like in the woods, for instance— knows how stuff comes up that surprises you and sometimes startles you. But when he gets into interpretation, I'm all at sea. Symbolism. Not my kind of thing at all. That's really more your line of country. But I haven't come to anything yet that I'd call filthy, if that's what you're getting at."

"You've always been a slow reader—"

"Yes, yes; you say that often. But I really get hold of what I read. I can't skim a book like this and have a quick opinion about it."

"That book is a devilishly clever apology for filthy thought, and we all know that filthy thought leads to filthy action."

(Does it? Did Eddu behave filthily because he thought filthily or vice versa? It seemed to me then to be one of those chicken-and-egg things.)

"I can't agree with you there. We've all—I suppose I mean all men, because women are admittedly different—we've all had dreams we wouldn't like to publish in the *Winnipeg Free Press*. But we don't act them out. Maybe the dreams are a safety-valve."

"I suppose men haven't as much control as women; after all, they're not as fine-natured. But what you say has nothing to do with that book. It's not just about coarse thoughts; it's about the mainsprings of civilization, and human thought; it's about how we see one another; it claims to know our inmost wishes. And if that man is right every decent human feeling is tainted and Christianity is a fraud and we're no better than the beasts that perish. We're just slightly tamed monkeys. And that man is trying to drag us back. Where did you get that book?"

"Some of my prize-money was a credit on a very good bookshop. I got it there."

"Doesn't that school exercise any control over how you spend prize-money?"

"They give us credit for common sense."

"Jonathan, don't you speak like that to me! Are you insinuating that I haven't got common sense?"

"I just think you've misunderstood the book."

"I've understood it perfectly well, young man. I'm not a fool, whatever your witty friends might think."

"I didn't say you were a fool, Ma."

"Your whole attitude ever since you came home makes it quite clear what you think of your father and me—"

"Just a minute, Lil. You're going too far. He hasn't said or hinted anything of the kind to my knowledge and I've just spent forty-eight hours alone with him."

"Jim, if you're going to side against me I'd better go to my room before somebody says something they'll be sorry for."

"Ma, what's the trouble? What's chewing you, for God's sake?"

"Don't speak to me in that cheap, common way. And don't take God's name in vain. You know what the trouble is—that book—"

"But *what* in the book, Ma?"

"Yes, Lil; I haven't come on anything yet that I can't put up with. What are you talking about?"

"Look where I've put in that big bookmark. The Oedipus thing. Read it, if you can without gagging."

"No, I won't read it. You tell me. Oedipus. He was a Greek, wasn't he?"

"He was a Greek dogged by a dreadful fate. He killed his father and married his mother. And this filthy German says every man wants to do the same thing. And he carries on about it. That's what our son has brought home from school."

"Oh, come on, now. He's just somebody in an old story. What's it got to do with anything?"

"Now who's passing opinions about the book without reading it? Ask your son what it has to do with anything. Anything and everything, according to this man."

"Ma, let me explain. Oedipus is the hero of a story—a play, as Freud uses him—who acts out in dramatic form something that has its tremendous impact—because the play is famous, and has been for centuries—

because it is rooted in a primary experience of the growing child."

"Incest! Is that an experience of anybody except some of the riff-raff and hooligans out here in the woods—"

"Wait, wait, wait! Give me a minute to explain. Everyone recognizes Oedipus and feels for him, because they have been through his trouble themselves—but as children—as mere babies—"

"The innocence of children abused! Sex imputed to tiny babies. Innocent little souls!"

"Ma, are children really innocent? This stuff is supposed to happen even before they can speak! It's a very simple thing, and when you think of it coolly, it looks inevitable."

Here my mother burst into tears and made loud, frightening sounds, and looked very unlike herself. Since then, in practice and in personal experience, I have come to know those orgasmic cries. My father went to her and mopped her eyes, and soothed her, and suggested that she would be better off in bed.

"And miss this?" she cried. (A Freudian slip, Mother; if it was really intolerable, or unbearably offensive, you would surely want to get away from it. But nothing would budge you from centre stage in this great scene, and it is not until now, so many years later, that I see it fully.)

"What's this all about?" said my poor father. "You'll drive me crazy between you."

"Dad, it comes down to this, in its simplest terms: the infant depends utterly on its mother, and her face is the only face it has learned to recognize; she is food, warmth, coddling, and love. She is the Beloved because she is the whole of the universe and of life. But another element intrudes; an element with a deep voice and a different smell who wants to summon the Beloved of the infant's life away from it. So this second element becomes the hated one, and the infant wishes, with all the power of a single-minded, egotistical creature, that it could get rid of the Intruder. And there you have the tragedy of Oedipus as it is lived and acted out in every life. Before the child can speak the whole thing has pretty well cooled down, but it lies at the base of the child's experience. Babies are passionate little buggers, you know; just listen to them scream when they want something; there's bloody murder in every howl."

"You mustn't use words like that in front of your mother, or me, if it comes to that. But I see what you mean. I'd have to have time to think that over. It's pretty steep, looking at babies that way. But you hear what he says, Lil. It's just a medical theory."

"Not medical, Dad. Psycho-analytical."

"What? Well, whatever you call it. Just an idea. Can't hurt anybody."

"Oh no? That's stupid even for you, Jim. Can't hurt anybody! Don't you see what it does to me?"

"You're overwrought. You'll see it differently tomorrow."

"That I will not. Don't you *see?*"

"See *what*, Lil? I see what everybody else sees."

"You don't see what position it puts *me* in with my own son?"

"What position? I don't know what you're talking about."

"The mother and son—*as lovers!* Do I have to spell out every word? Aren't you disgusted? Can you stand there and have me involved in such filth? Your own *wife?* And his *mother?*"

"Now, Lil, we won't get anywhere talking like that. Let me help you upstairs. Then you have some of that stuff Dr. Cameron gave you, and get a good night's rest.

You're worn out."

Up the stairs they go, my mother sobbing, my father being as gentle as he knows how, but rather plainly thinking the whole business is a bore and he wishes to get out of it as soon as he can.

I was badly shaken, and for the first time in my life I had serious resort to my father's whisky. I had furtively pinched little nips before, but now I gave myself a good three fingers and poured in some spring water. My attempts at reflection took me nowhere, for my mother's outburst had quite unmanned me and I had no power of rational thought left in me. Those were the days when mothers had unbelievable mystical muscle, and the whole notion of motherhood was of a religious significance. All I knew was that I had created the worst row in our family's history, so far as I knew, and I had affronted my mother's modesty and sense of propriety, and worst of all I had unexpectedly revealed that my mother thought her husband stupid, and thus shown a rift in the family of which I had not previously had any knowledge. I wallowed in this morass of feeling for not less than an hour, making it worse with unaccustomed whisky. Meanwhile, upstairs, my father was doing his best to be understanding of his sobbing wife as he waited for Dr. Cameron's prescription of chloral hydrate to send her to sleep.

It was on the fourth day after this scene that I took the train to Toronto to get myself ready for the university. The house was very still during most of that time, and we all kept up an icy politeness. I suppose my mother wanted me to grovel, and burn Freud. But I saw matters otherwise.

My father did not refer to the matter again, except once, as we sat one night by an early September fire when my mother had "gone to her room."

"I've been thinking about that business, you know. That Oedipus business. I suppose in the terms that fellow is using to discuss it, it makes a kind of sense. I can see that. You look at babies—babies in the reserve, for instance, and you can catch a glimpse of what he is talking about. But one thing puzzles me: what about girls? Do they want to kill their mothers and marry their fathers? Doesn't really make sense because the father doesn't feed them and cuddle them and sing to them; he's still the Intruder, isn't he? What about girls? Are they so utterly different?"

I wasn't able to help him. "I don't know," I said. "I believe he discusses that in a later book, and I haven't read it yet."

"So you won't know what to think till you've read it in a book," said my father. And I knew well and truly that he was not stupid.

[4]

THE UNIVERSITY VERY sensibly insisted that anybody who wanted to study medicine must have a B.A. as a starter. There were eager young medicos who thought that was a waste of time; they had no idea of medicine as a learned profession and perhaps they should not be blamed, because who would have told them that it was so? The genteel tradition was on its last legs in Canada; its legs had never been particularly strong, but there was a lingering notion that some professions went with stiff collars and wives who employed maidservants and sometimes drank tea in the afternoon, and that aspirants to such splendours ought to have some dash of cultivation. The B.A. could not confer cultivation but it was a nod to a great tradition.

The B.A. gave me no trouble at all. At Colborne I had been taught how to learn (which most of my contemporaries from the public schools had not) and so I romped easily through the good but not demanding requirements and had lots of time to pursue my real education. Because real education, as I had already discovered, meant things you really wanted to know, rather than things other people thought you should know.

I read as much of Freud as I could lay my hands on, buying the books rather than getting them from the university library. At that time such borrowing might have attracted undesirable attention, for the prejudice against the great Viennese doctor was strong in Canada, and I was told that the medical faculty, and such psychiatric practitioners as then existed in Toronto, had decided that he was a flash in the pan—"a flash in the bedpan" as one witty neurologist had put it.

It was not that they were unaware of Freud. Those who had been in the university before the First World War remembered that one of his disciples had, for a time, been of their number, and they had not liked him. He was not a companionable man, and was apt to say sharp things. He could not conceal that he thought Toronto a backwater and its pretensions to culture risible. He made sour jokes about the word "provincial," which occurred so often in our governmental system, and defined his own appointment to the Government Hospital for the Insane; too much of what was said and done, he hinted, was provincial indeed. But there was more to it than that; he lived in Toronto with his sister and another woman, and who precisely was she? Suspicion gave way to certainty, and the portcullis of respectability dropped.

I quickly heard of this, and made my own enquiries, and often after that I would make my way to Brunswick

Avenue, which was then on the outskirts of the city, and gaze in awe at the house in which Dr. Ernest Jones, whom time would reveal as the most loyal of Freud's lieutenants, had written his classic study of *Hamlet* and his splendid monograph on *The Nightmare*. What if Jones did have a mistress? I would have had one myself if I could have found one, but the kind of girls whom I met at the university were not of the mistress type—or perhaps I was not as dashing as I hoped I was.

I was severely bitten by the bug of psychoanalysis, and read everything I could find about it, and was for several years wholly under its spell. Indeed, it took my service in the Second World War to lower my fanaticism and point me in the direction I have followed ever since. But during my university years and through my medical training I was a Freudian fanatic, though a muted one.

Time has changed the attitude of the heeding world toward Freud from hatred or fanaticism to something like patronage or indifference. I say "the heeding world" but perhaps it is on the unheeding world that his mark is clearest. Everybody now talks about "complexes" and "inferiority complexes," and attributes adult disasters to infant experiences, thinks dreams contain cryptic messages and understands a vocabulary of inexact gibblegabble derived from Freud, Jung, Adler, Klein, and God knows who, and thus far—not really very far—Freud's great aim is achieved. Because, it seems to me, from the beginning of the twentieth century Freud sent a loud wake-up call to mankind, to become aware of what lay beneath the surface of the mind, and to mend its ways accordingly. And mankind, as always through history, has half-heard the call of the prophet, half-understood what he says, and vulgarized and cheapened whatever of his teaching may come its way. But something has been achieved. A few holes have been thrust through the wall of human stupidity and incomprehension.

As for me—? I suppose my moderation of my earliest Freudian faith—the first religion I ever espoused—must be the matter of what I write in my Case Book, if I am ever, at my present advanced age, to see anything coherent in my personal and professional history.

One thing I did learn from Freud, which has never diminished and has indeed grown with the years, is a habit of careful observation, of heedfulness, in my relationship with the rest of the world. To learn to see what is right in front of one's nose; that is the task and a heavy task it is. It demands a certain stillness of spirit, which is not the same thing as dimness of personality, and need not be partnered with a retiring, bland social life.

My social life in my student years was lively, and was fed by two enthusiasms which might at first seem irreconcilable, but are not so: religion and the theatre.

As a half-baked psychoanalytical zealot I was of course a doubter and an infidel in religious matters. I had not been brought up in a strongly religious household, though Christian precepts and values were at the root of both my parents' behaviour. But to live in Toronto in my student days and be unaware of religion was out of the question. It seemed to me that the campus swarmed with chaplains and Christian Unions and undergraduates bent on saving souls, and this was a reflection of the spirit of the city. Churches abounded, and every sort of religious fare was offered to the religious shopper. Baptist zeal, Methodist self-satisfaction, Presbyterian Scots certainty about everything, Anglican social superiority, and a horde of evangelists and backstreet messiahs to suit every taste, as well as an undertow of prohibitionists, anti-tobacco crusaders, and warriors against prostitution, who were linked with the churches though not actually a part of them, seemed to dominate the mores of the city. The imperceptive, unselfconscious city prospered under its soggy blanket of shallow middle-class morality and accepted prosperity as evidence of God's approval.

Armed with my shallow understanding of Freudian doctrine and my youthful egotism I set about studying as much of this spirit of Toronto as I could, went to church twice on Sunday—a different church, to get as much of the flavour as I could—and had a high old time laughing and jeering at the faithful as the Baptists whooped; as the Methodists leaned forward in prayer, resting their heads upon the back of the pew in front, as though suffering from hangover; as the Presbyterians listened to their highly literate, carefully argued, and quite incomprehensible "discourses"; and the Anglicans met with the vicar at the church door, for reassurance of a superiority and not being as other men.

Of course I did not neglect the Catholics, and saw the excellence of a faith which permits its believers to behold God's flesh and blood every day of their lives, if they choose, and to find solace in unfathomable devotions. And all at the trivial price of psychological peonage. Do as the Church tells you, and all will be well. You need not stir an independent finger.

I did my best to miss nothing. I even ventured into the single Orthodox Church, and stood stolidly among people who seemed all to be under a Dostoevskian depression, and stared at me with feeble hostility. They did not positively tell me to leave, but spiritually they shoved me toward the door. The famed Orthodox liturgy was impressive, but often out of tune, and I was amazed when the priest produced a large yellow comb and arranged his hair and beard in mid-service. There I felt most strongly that Christianity is not the all-embracing faith that it is said to be. You must find the church that suits you, that you can stand and that can stand you, and stick with it.

[5]

Inevitably amid all this temple-hopping I found churches that appealed to me more than others, and my favourite was soon established; it was St. Aidan's, Anglican and very High. So High, indeed, that sometimes it seemed that the Roman Catholic Mass was a simplified version of their sung Eucharist.

It was a case of a strong-minded tail wagging a far from reluctant dog; the tail was Dr. DeCourcy Parry, the organist and choirmaster, and the dog was Father Ninian Hobbes, who knew nothing about music and had a tin ear, but who sensed a splendour in Parry's services that was appropriate to his ideas of Divine worship. For Father Hobbes, the humblest of men himself, thought nothing too fine for the acts of worship over which he presided, and he acquiesced in everything Dr. Parry suggested. Dr. Parry was a composer of gift, and he wrote a lot of music specifically for St. Aidan's, and thus brought it a distinction unapproached by any other Toronto church. He had a fine gallery choir of men and women who sang out of sight at the back of the church, where the organ was and where Dr. Parry was free to exhort, signal, and do all that a choirmaster must do, without being seen. In addition there was a plainsong choir of eight men who sang in the chancel, robed and solemn, led by Darcy Dwyer. The combination of Dwyer and Parry was unbeatable as a source of magnificent accompaniment to the services, but there were many (outside St Aidan's, of course) who thought that these two elaborated the services beyond what was defensible in terms of mainline Anglicanism and the spirit of the Thirty-Nine Articles.

The elaboration of ritual originated chiefly with Dwyer, and Parry was happy to agree to anything that made for a more splendid musical service. "Surely God must weary of this perpetual serenading," said one archdeacon at a clerical gathering, and the remark sped around the Toronto Anglican community. There were Low Churchmen who spoke of the splendid vestments as "millinery." But no Bishop quite liked to gainsay the formidable Dr. Parry, who had proof and example for everything he did, and foisted on Father Hobbes. Dr. Parry's talent and the money he sacrificed to remain at St. Aidan's, made him a privileged person. Dwyer also managed to secure for himself considerable privilege, and he did it by his agile wit.

He was a student of church ceremony and tradition and he wanted to include in the St. Aidan's services everything that he could discover that was picturesque or merely unusual. Lots of incense, of course; clouds of it whenever an excuse arose. Holy water, sloshed about lavishly, especially at funerals. Processions with banners, and these were no innocent advertisements for the Women's League or the Infant Band but handsomely embroidered depictions of the Instruments of the Passion, of the Virgin as Rose of the World, of the IXΘYC symbol, and anything else that a devout adherent of the church could be persuaded to pay the Sisters of St. John to work, with infinite patience, on a silken background. Ornaments abounded: chasubles, of course, with splendid orphreys to enrich them; copes, it seemed, without number; dalmatics, humeral veils, and tunicles whenever possible. And who said when it was possible? Darcy Dwyer, of course, and he could produce handsome and often rare books to prove it. It was he who pointed out that a candle should never be lit except with flint and steel, and a cigarette lighter filled the bill, infallibly. It was he also who persuaded the priests to wear soft slippers at Mass, so as not to kneel and show the dirty soles of their boots. Sometimes it was thought that he went just a little too far. When he suggested, for instance, that the deacons and subdeacons veil their eyes with their sleeves at the Elevation of the Host, as if they were blinded by the nearness of the Body of Christ, Father Hobbes vetoed it. Then, being an amiable man, he permitted it at certain high feast days, though he hinted that he thought it somewhat theatrical.

Theatrical? Of course it was. Darcy Dwyer may have been a banker by profession, but he was a theatre director and an actor at heart, and he was happiest when marshalling the forces at St. Aidan's for a truly stunning effect. "If it is uplifting and awesome, Father, is not that what we seek to create?" Father Hobbes had no answer, though in his heart he may have had doubts. I do not know. I never spoke to him or was near to him until the morning when he died so suddenly at the altar, which was long in the future.

At first I went to St. Aidan's for the show. But as I came to understand the meaning the elaborate ritual bodied forth I gained a greater pleasure in the services. Not that I believed, deep-Freud greenhorn that I was. Not that I did not equate much of what was said and done with the reductive spirit of Sir James Frazer's *The Golden Bough*, an abridgement of which I had read— once. But I could not resist the beauty of what I saw and heard. Especially the plainsong.

Dr. Parry's gallery choir sang splendidly the church music of the ages from Palestrina to himself; one of the secrets of this beauty was, I later learned, that he never allowed his forces to sing above a *mezzo forte*; there was no bawling, and the music seemed to float through the church. But it was the plainsong that seized me.

At first I did not know what it was. At intervals the eight men in the chancel choir, or sometimes Dwyer alone, would utter what sounded like speech of a special eloquence, every word clearly to be heard, but observing a discipline that was musical, in that there was no hint of anything that was colloquial, but not like any music I had met with in my, by this time, fairly good acquaintance with music. My idea of church music at its highest was Bach, but Bach at his most reverent is still intended for performance. This music was addressed to God, not as performance, but as the most intimate and devout communication. It was a form of speech fit for the ear of the Highest.

It was at this time, early in the third year of my university studies, that I met Darcy Dwyer, which I had never expected to do, because he seemed a remote figure, known to me only in church and on the stage.

The university had a good theatre of its own, built during the first enthusiasm for what was for so long called Little Theatre, marking it as amateur but of a seriousness not attempted by the amateur theatricals of the nineteenth century. Toronto had a lot of keen amateur actors, some of whom had been professional before they had left that ill-requited and chancy profession, and some of the best of these were banded in a group called the Players' Guild; one of their mainstays was Darcy Dwyer.

The Guild from time to time performed plays that demanded more bodies than the core of the membership provided and "extras" were roped in from wherever they could be found. Such a play was Josephine Preston Peabody's *The Piper*; it needed a crowd and a lot of children, and somebody whose name I have now forgotten asked me if I would like to be a German peasant of the thirteenth century for a week. I agreed, out of curiosity. I had never taken part in any of the dramatics at school, and did not consider myself a possible actor. But I was a keen patron of all the Guild's productions, and thought it would be fun to penetrate behind the curtain.

Josephine Preston Peabody's play has not endured, but in its day it won an important prize, and was widely performed. It was in four acts, written in blank verse of impeccable Bostonian solemnity (Miss Peabody was a graduate of Radcliffe), and its theme was the splendid one of the conflict between good and evil. The Piper— he was of course the Pied Piper of legend—stole the children of the stingy town of Hamelin which had refused to pay him for charming away its rats, but after immense blank-verse inner conflict, he allowed them to come back. The play was rich in characters, inevitably including a lame child, and of course this role was played by a girl, for the combination of an affliction with virgin femininity was potent at the time, and nightly at our performances tears flowed almost from the moment Elsie Polson hobbled on the stage with her pathetic little crutch.

I was not of an age to be moved by children, and I thought Elsie a little pill, for she took on airs backstage, and even eyed us poor humble "extras" with scorn. No, my eyes were fixed on Miss Wollerton, who played Barbara, the lovely daughter of the Burgomeister, and who, as the drama unfolds, becomes the wife of Michael the Sword Eater, one of the mountebank companions of the Piper. In the scene where Miss Wollerton danced, as if under enchantment, to the sound of the pipe, I thought I had never seen anything more exquisite.

The star of the piece, he who played the large-souled Piper, was Mervyn Rentoul, a big, fine-looking man capable of heaving Elsie Polson into an upstairs window without unseemly exertion. Mr. Rentoul was a man of actor-like appearance (for this was still in the days when actors were expected to have good looks, or failing that, distinction) and his voice was rich and expressive, facts of which he was perhaps a little too aware. I thought him a very fine actor indeed, but now I realize that he was of the line that descended from Irving, in which descent all the beauty and diablerie of that great player had been lost, and only the mannerisms—grunting, eye-flashing, and gnawing the nether lip—remained. I began to doubt Mr. Rentoul during the seven performances we gave of the play.

I was lurking in the wings, although that was strictly forbidden, during the great culmination of Act Three, where the Piper, grovelling before a wayside crucifix, wrestles with his soul and at last is defeated by the greater power of Christ. The theatre was full, and Mervyn Rentoul was letting them have it hot off the stove. I became aware of a figure standing just behind me, and I looked over my shoulder apprehensively, thinking it was the Assistant Stage Manager come to drive me away. But it was Darcy Dwyer, who was playing the minor role of the Burgomeister in which, his devotees in the Guild assured one another, he was quite thrown away. But there it was; he was not tall enough to boost Elsie Polson into an upstairs window (a telling piece of "business" in Act Four) and so—thrown away in a part almost anybody might have played. Well, not anybody, but one of the older men of the company, who were numerous. As the clamour of Mervyn Rentoul's soul-struggle rose to a climax, he caught my eye and held it, and as Rentoul succumbed to the divine power with a sob, Dwyer winked.

It was a sophisticated wink, not one of your grimacing

winks that contorts the whole of one side of the face. It was the slightest descent of the upper lid of the left eye, but it spoke eloquently of gentlemanly derision. It said, as plainly as speech, that Rentoul was a Ham. For me, it was a moment of enlightenment, in which I became Dwyer's slave, and remained so for some years.

[6]

WHEN IRONY FIRST makes itself known in a young man's life, it can be like his first experience of getting drunk; he has met with a powerful thing which he does not know how to handle. Of course I had been aware of irony in its superficial form, because Brocky made great use of it; but he was not a master, a subtle and gentle employer of mockery in almost every aspect of life, as was Dwyer; it was something Brocky had learned, not flesh of his flesh. Later, when I thought I had become wiser, I tried to find out what irony really is, and discovered that some ancient writer on poetry had spoken of "Ironia, which we call the drye mock," and I cannot think of a better term for it: the drye mock. Not sarcasm, which is like vinegar, or cynicism, which is so often the voice of disappointed idealism, but a delicate casting of a cool and illuminating light on life, and thus an enlargement. The ironist is not bitter, he does not seek to undercut everything that seems worthy or serious, he scorns the cheap scoring-off of the wisecracker. He stands, so to speak, somewhat at one side, observes and speaks with a moderation which is occasionally embellished with a flash of controlled exaggeration. He speaks from a certain depth, and thus he is not of the same nature as the wit, who so often speaks from the tongue and no deeper. The wit's desire is to be funny; the ironist is only funny as a secondary achievement.

One must have a disposition for irony, but it does not come without practice; like really good violin-playing, it must be practised every day. It seemed to me when I met Dwyer that I had the disposition, but I was an unpractised hand and, like a beginner on the fiddle, I suppose my squawks and screeches were painful to those around me.

Oh, I have been a fool! Have I at last outgrown my folly? My occasional hours with Esme, where she probes my memory and my sensibilities with the blunt end of her reporter's pencil, hint to me that though I have become a more complicated fool, the fool that I was as a youth still lingers somewhere inside me. I have not seen that inquisitive young woman for several weeks, but I know she will return. She smells a mouse about St. Aidan's, and she is cunning in laying out her cheese for that mouse.

[7]

"So you had a spell as an actor in your student days?"

"A modest one. I had to be moderate because after I got my B.A. I entered the medical faculty and in those days the medical faculty didn't like you to waste time on anything that wasn't medicine."

"In those days, you say. Have they changed?"

"Yes, greatly. In my day you got into medical school because you had high marks in your undergraduate work. That, and nothing else. Now they give much more consideration to what you are and what you've done. At Harvard, for instance, a candidate who hasn't some enthusiasm for politics, or the arts, or sport, or some science other than medical science doesn't stand a chance."

"They want a rounded person."

"If you put it like that, yes."

"Weren't the people you went to medical school with rounded?"

"I suppose some of them were. But it didn't matter. Getting the vast amount of information that goes with Anatomy into your head and keeping it there meant far more than a taste for pictures or foreign affairs. But by means of an elaborate range of mnemonics, some of them witty, and some obscene, and a few both, it could be managed. For instance, I can still recall that 'Some Inherit Valuable Possessions And Can Find Lucrative Foreign Investments Constantly Available,' the initial letter of which give the points of the Right Atrium of the heart—Superior caval opening, Interior caval opening, etc. The strain on memory in Anatomy, the cynicism that seemed to underlie Pharmacology, the toughness demanded by dissecting—it took a strong constitution and it changed your outlook on the world. I remember once meeting a fellow I knew in my year, and asking him what he had been doing. "Nothing special," he said; "took off a woman's head this morning, then I had lunch, and now I've really got to get down to the anatomy of the hand." That kind of thing. I met him again recently, nearly forty years later. He's made a big name as a surgeon and his divorced wife owns an almost-Picasso. But whether he's rounded or not I really couldn't say."

"But you were rounded. You were an actor."

"I was a great reader in my childhood. I knew a lot of poetry, not all of it good, but there is an astonishing amount of nutrition in second-rate poetry. So I suppose I was a little rounder than many in my year, without being positively globular. I loved the theatre. Still do."

"Let's get back to St. Aidan's. You knew this man Dwyer, who sang in the choir?"

That is a meagre way of putting it, Esme. Devoted by

day as I was to my medical studies, I seemed to live in Dwyer's pocket during my limited hours of freedom. I was apprentice to the ironist.

The theatre was a good place to study and to practise irony, and even as a medical student I hung around the university stage and became a sort of tolerated underling of the Players' Guild. A deeper irony than simple merriment underlay what went on as the plays were rehearsed and offered to their audiences. The painted and costumed figures acting out their appointed destinies in carefully calculated light seemed to be all that there was to the totality of the play. But just as much that was vital to every piece took place in the coulisses, where those who controlled the mood of the light, the thunder and lightning, the bells and trumpet-calls, and who thrust the necessary "properties" into the hands of the actors as they waited for their cues, and signalled the fall of the curtain when enough had been said, were greater figures of authority. I learned the deep satisfaction of seeing the play complete, with the illusion, the poetry, and the magic balanced against the Stage Management which set and kept it all in motion. These were the two sides of a coin, the Ying and the Yang, the opposites which Heraclitus insists are eternally flowing together and balancing one another. The result in the theatre was art, but not always fully completed art.

In time I became a frequent visitor to Dwyer's apartment, or as we called it in those days, his flat. It was small, but it had character and charm; because it was small, everything had to be chosen with care and there was no room for anything extraneous. There were a lot of books, but none on tables or on the floor; there were pictures, but they all seemed to be moving in the same direction, so to speak; nothing of the untidy heaping-up of what appealed to various aspects of a wandering taste, as at the Gilmartin house; in a tiny kitchen Dwyer prepared good things to eat, but never in excess, and there was good drink as well, but never more than the host thought it right for a guest to have. I never heard anybody ask for anything in the flat; all was provided, and it was ample and right, but there could be no choice; there was no space for choice.

Not that there was anything niggardly or domineering about it. Dwyer made everything seem so natural and right that it would have been improper to suggest any alteration. He was the most generous of hosts, but he knew precisely what he meant to do and he did it, and it seemed that it could not possibly have been otherwise.

The guests, of whom there could never have been more than three, apart from myself, were usually men; the only woman I saw there more than once was Elaine Wollerton, whom I worshipped and who did not seem to be in the least aware of it. I call her a woman but she was what we called in those days a girl—for the word had not become an offence against feminist sensibility. Was she a virgin? I pondered much on this question, because in those romantic days I set great store by virginity, and no amount of Freudian reading ever made me think ill of it. She was about twenty-two or -three, I suppose, and thus a year older than myself, but as girls normally do, she had a worldly wisdom far beyond mine. She thought of herself as an actress, even though she was an amateur one, and her conversation had the freedom popularly supposed to go with the profession. She smoked, which was not remarkable; she swore in good mouth-filling oaths, but never smutty ones, and that was uncommon. She knew the prosody of profanity, as the Montreal and Salterton girls I had met did not: she knew the tune, as well as the words. She was not a raving beauty, but she had fine eyes and a Pre-

Raphaelite air of being too good for this world while at the same time exhibiting much of what this world desires in a woman, and I suppose I gaped at her and behaved clownishly.

Or so it seems to me now. Nobody remarked on it at the time, so it cannot have been as palpable as it felt. Dwyer never told me to behave myself, and certainly he would have done so if I had been laughably callow. One remembers one's youthful behaviour as nobody else does; one blushes for gaucheries nobody else has noticed.

At first I wondered if there was some intimate relationship between Elaine and Darcy Dwyer, but even I was not so stupid as to keep that delusion for long. Dwyer was the kind of homosexual who greatly likes women's company and whom women greatly like, without any active sexual involvement. I suppose Elaine was fond of him because he was more fun to be with than any of the young men who dangled after her, of which group I was one and far from Number One. Where Dwyer was there was lots of sex in the air, but it was not likely to manifest itself in any tedious action and that is a very agreeable state of affairs, as I myself came to think later in life. The erotic tease: very agreeable.

It was in Dwyer's flat that I learned how much more there is to sex than puffing and blowing and snorting and scrambling about in the bed, or on the seashore, or in the woods. I would not say a word against the joys of physical sex, but it is not the whole story, or even half of it, as every wise man's son doth know, my dear Shakespeare.

Greatly daring, I brought this up one night when I was accompanying Miss Wollerton to her streetcar; we all used the street railway in those happy days.

"I suppose Darcy is a homosexual," said I.

"You'd better not let him hear you say that, if you

want to keep in with him," said she. "He loathes the word."

"What does he prefer to call it?"

"Not that. He calls it a barbarously hybrid word, and so it is, for the *homo* is Greek and the *sexual* is Latin. There's a kind of aptness in the word, really. An unnatural union. No; if Darcy has to speak of it—and I don't advise you to bring it up—he prefers the term 'invert.'"

"I'll watch my step."

"Not only about that. I think he has a kind of lech for you, but whether it's just a protective, educative dry lech, or the messier kind, I don't know. But perhaps you do?"

"It never entered my head."

"Make room for it now. You're not such a bad-looking fellow. Has he ever talked to you about plainsong hymns?"

"Never."

"Well, if he does, mind your eye. Do you know a fathead called Archie Featherstone?"

"No."

"I was at the flat one night when Darcy was putting the spell on Archie. He'd bring out some rare hymnbook with Latin hymns in it, and push them at the poor sap. He'd say, 'You're recently enough from school, Archie, to catch the Virgilian echo in this one. Astonishing how the tradition endured, as I'm sure you know.' Of course Archie didn't know but the flattery was going to his head, I could see. Flattery is the real expert's technique of seduction. Beats knee-squeezing forty different ways."

"Is that so? Thanks for telling me."

"Aha, the *drye mock*. You're not kidding me, young Hullah. You're learning a lot from Darcy. Just take care you don't pay too much for your lessons. Or maybe you don't mind?"

"Elaine! You don't think that?"

"Of course I don't, darling. I'm only teasing. You're a sweet boy."

"Whatever happened to Archie? Wasn't he a sweet boy?"

"I rather think Archie flunked his test. Not really Virgilian. I once mentioned him to Darcy, but he just said, 'It's no use crying over spilt milk.' Indicative?"

"Past indicative."

Of course it is pleasant to be called a sweet boy, but it does not seem to lead to anything significant with the speaker. "Darling" meant nothing. All the Guild called one another "darling."

I understood that Miss Wollerton had better fish to fry than I was, but that she liked me, and that was something of comfort. And I never ceased to marvel at the effect she produced by mingling her Pre-Raphaelite beauty with a racy sort of speech. The louche-angelic, shall I call it? It was a special charm, not imitable by the unskilled.

[8]

A FREQUENT CALLER at Dwyer's flat was Mr. Daubigny, ex-Commander in the Royal Navy and a master at Colborne. He insisted that I drop all schoolboy manners and call him Jock, although I knew very little about him except that he was rumoured to have eaten human flesh in the company of cannibals. He did not look like an Englishman, nor do I believe he was so; his appearance was distinguished and he wore a single eyeglass, which must have been the only one in Toronto at that time. His accent was slightly foreign— voice produced from some portion of his throat that was neither English nor Canadian.

He taught German at Colborne, and when *Faust* was coming up in the season offered by the Players' Guild he was often with Dwyer, taking him through the Goethe original.

The Players' Guild built its seasons with an eye to pleasing everybody, and *Faust* was to please the University. It had already done *Mary Rose* successfully, for Barrie was still a new playwright in Toronto, and Miss Wollerton was exactly right for the wistful heroine who is lost on The Island That Liked To Be Visited. Dwyer had no role in that sweetmeat. Nor had he been cast in *Pomander Walk*, a nugacity written by the industrious Louis Napoleon Parker, which had been a great success in New York in 1911. (The Guild did not blast the sensitivities of its audience with too much modernity; Barrie and Galsworthy were about as daringly contemporary as they chose to be.) *Faust* was to be the heavyweight of the season, and long beforehand Dwyer had been promised the role of Mephistopheles. He was determined to make it memorable.

The translation chosen by the Guild for its production was by a Toronto lady of an earlier generation, and she was in a dither of expectancy and requited authorship. It was not, Daubigny said, a bad piece of work, but it was not as racy and colloquial as the original; few translators capture Goethe's distinction, which he manages to achieve in an easy vocabulary, and Miss Swanwick had been too much in awe of the great man. Dwyer was determined to rid his role of Swanwickery, as he called it, and Daubigny was to help him.

"Poor Miss Swanwick was too much a lady to cope with Goethe," said Jock. "He hadn't much use for ladies, except as audiences."

"I've talked to Forsyth, and he very generously says I can alter my lines, within reason, to get an effect nearer the original."

They spent many happy hours over the work, disputing and searching for the right word, and opposing Jock's real comprehension of German to Darcy's powerful feelings about Mephistopheles. Indeed, it seemed to me that Mephistopheles was eating him up, as great works of art can do to their devotees.

This led to an odd and not really reputable adventure, in which Dwyer involved me simply because I was too curious to resist.

"The actor's art is a very great one," he said one night as we were drinking Scotch after one of the translation sessions. "It isn't really appreciated at its true worth. Mark my choice of words—its *true* worth. Of course movie stars have battalions of half-baked adorers, but who thinks acting in the movies is real acting, and who values the adoration of idiots? But the praise that is given to a great Hamlet, or a great Othello, or the infinitely rarer great Lear, is always diminished by the feeling that the chap simply goes on the stage and says what Shakespeare has written for him and draws his sword when the director tells him to. What did Mencken say? That there is something inherently disgusting in the actor's profession? I suppose he was thinking of matinee idols, who can be pretty disgusting. But the actor—why is the man who gives us Shakespeare or Ibsen or Strindberg [Dwyer pronounced this name as 'Streenberry' which was the insider's pronunciation and thought to be truly Swedish] thought to be less an artist than the man who gives us Beethoven, or Chopin, or Debussy in a way that speaks truly what the master intended? Eh? Why?"

"Oh, their lives are not so hard," said Jock. "I believe they are paid very well."

"Yes, but what honour have they? What continuing

gratitude? How many statues have been raised to great actors?"

"There's a very nice thing of Goldoni in Venice."

"Not an actor. A playwright."

"There's a statue of Irving in London." I remembered it from an early visit with my parents.

"Erected by his fellow-actors. Don't wait for the state or the public to do it. They won't."

"Maybe you should start an agitation for more statues of actors," said Jock, taking a pull at his whisky.

"Precisely what I have in mind. And I think I can count on some devout Toronto Methodists to help me," said Dwyer.

"What sort of joke is this?"

"No joke at all, my dear Jock. Will you take a little walk with me? I have something to show you."

We went with him, and as we crossed Queen's Park Dwyer held forth, waving his walking-stick like a tour-guide, on the many statues that stand in front of the Ontario Legislative Building.

"Nineteenth-century worthies," he said. "Premiers of this province, cloaked in the respectability of their frock-coats and in some cases their spectacles. Did you ever see an uglier gang of good citizens? As works of art they inspire disgust. As memorials, they are nothing. They display none of what made the man distinct from his fellow-creatures—if anything did. The heads, we may assume, are likenesses, produced by some toilsome artisan with a pair of callipers and a feeble concept of the human spirit. These are, in so far as they are any-thing at all, impeccable depictions of nineteenth-cen-tury bad tailoring. Bronze pairs of pants, bronze boots, like those dreadful babies' shoes that sentimental people have 'eternalized' at Birks. The frock-coats are lovingly moulded, and what do they say? They say, 'I'm an expensive frock-coat, worthy to be preserved for the ages.' But are these effigies evocative? Do they lift the heart and inspire the young? Would you tolerate one of them as a garden gnome? Don't trouble to answer.

"Aha, but here"—we were now on the west side of the park—"here we have something that looks like a statue. It has impact. It even has grace. It is not astonishing in terms of statuary, but it makes those bronze statesmen look like wooden Indians. Look at the pose. A man in eighteenth-century dress, wigged and ruffled, stands pointing rhetorically toward the book he holds in his hand.

"Who is he? Read the inscription. He is Robert Raikes and his dates are 1735 to 1811. Who is he? He is the man who instituted Sunday Schools in his native Gloucester, starting a movement that swept the world, spreading the Gospel and the arts of reading and writing among the very young, who were still unable to comprehend the homilies that were offered in churches. A great man? Undoubtedly. Why does he have a statue here, in Canada, in Toronto, in the place where we set up graven images of our political gods, who are the only gods Canada really acknowledges? Because the Sunday School Union decided that it should be so, and put up the money to have a replica made of the statue of Raikes that stands on the Victoria Embankment in London, where all the down-and-outs, and broken men and women may see an image of the man who was their friend.

"So there he stands. Exemplary. Deserving. A man firm in the hearts of all who hold Sunday Schools dear. But—now I am getting to our point—who does he look like?"

"He could be quite a few people," said Jock. "There is something about having your statue taken that drains the individuality out of you, unless you happen to have an Epstein on the job."

"Weren't we talking about actors? What actor does he remind you of?"

Neither Jock nor I had an answer.

"David Garrick, of course! Forget Raikes and think of Garrick. The pose, pointing at the book—mightn't it be his copy of *Hamlet*? The stout but graceful figure—isn't it Garrick as he is described? Garrick, and if his name was written at the base, you would see that it was Garrick all over!"

"Perhaps, but it isn't Garrick," said Jock.

"Await the event," said Dwyer, and would say no more on the subject.

I suppose it was a month or more later that Dwyer insisted that Jock and I spend a translating evening with him, and it was after midnight that he rose and said, "The hour has struck. Come with me."

Once again we walked across Queen's Park, but this time Dwyer had nothing to say. As we drew near the statue of Raikes, we saw a Ford truck parked a little way off. Traffic was scant.

When we were at the base of the statue a man appeared from the truck. "I'll need somebody to give me a hand," said he.

"You're the one for that, Hullah," said Dwyer. So I followed the man to the truck and helped him to unload a large rectangular slab, the edges of which were guarded by cardboard fitments; the face of it was covered with paper. We took it to where Dwyer and Jock were standing, and then the man and I heaved it into place against the plinth where Raikes's name was marked out in bronze letters. The man spread the plinth with a coating of cement, or it may have been a special glue. Quickly and expertly he produced his electric drill, connected it with a battery, and proceeded to bore holes in the face of the plinth. Then, with fine bronze spikes with flowered heads, the slab was finally fixed to the plinth. It was a job of exquisite craftsmanship. I suppose the work did not take more than twenty minutes, and when it was done Dwyer stepped forward, stripped the paper from the rectangle, and there was a piece of what I suppose was thick frosted glass, which looked wondrously like the stone of the plinth, and in which an inscription had been cut.

DAVID GARRICK
1717–1779
Actor

*I am disappointed by that
stroke of death which has
eclipsed the gaiety of
nations and impoverished
the public stock of harmless
pleasure.*

DR. SAMUEL JOHNSON
Erected by lovers of the
Player's Art

"There, a good night's work, I think, and a great wrong righted," said Dwyer.

The man, who had scarcely spoken, now approached him.

"Four hundred and fifty was the price we agreed on, including erection?" said Darcy. The man nodded. "I've added a little extra, in appreciation of your good work. And remember, not a word to a soul."

"No fear," said the man. "I could get into a lot of trouble about this."

"Now let's get to hell out of here before the police arrive," said Darcy.

But no police arrived then or for long after, so far as I know. Which raises the question: Who looks at the inscriptions on public statuary?

[9]

I SEE THAT I have scampered through several years of my university life without a mention of Charlie or Brocky; if Esme were here she would demand to know what became of them. Had I dropped them or had they dropped me? Neither; simply the familiar experience that in youth chance separates us from even the closest friends, and in the excitement of finding new ones we do not greatly notice the loss. Is this shallowness of spirit? No, in youth one must get on with one's life, lickety-split, and what might be callous indifference in an older person is simply the way in which circumstances fall out.

For a time I received long, detailed letters from Brocky about his adventures at Waverley, which did not seem especially interesting to me; I had my own adventures. The affair with Julia ravelled out and he was tedious about that. Charlie was in Quebec, at a university for English-speaking students that had a well-known theological faculty, and by various twists and turns he had been able to enter it; his engaging personality at interviews, the intervention of a friendly bishop, and the plain fact that candidates from cultivated homes were not as numerous as they had once been in the Anglican Church, stood him in good stead, and he was on his way to being a parson. He wrote from time to time; his descriptions of his fellow-theologues were funny and I especially relished his tales about their efforts to show themselves as tough, as lecherous, as foul-mouthed as any other students. It appeared that on Saturday nights some of the dominant figures among them declared their intention to go into town and explore the French part of it, expecting to "tear off a branch," which was the current slang for sexual intercourse with a prostitute. But Charlie—charitable, funny Charlie—knew very well that they sneaked into pubs and sat in a dark corner, nursing one beer, and returned to college full of vague hints, but with all their branches still in place. Charlie never wrote of his health, so I supposed he must be all right.

I wrote letters, too, but not readily. I had so much to do, and life was opening up to me in so many new ways that I did not want to sit at a desk and distil my experience into a letter. I wrote a lot, making copious notes of what I was learning and whatever seemed relevant from what I was reading, and my appetite for letter-writing was nibbled away in that sort of work.

My bedside book—not always, but often—was the *Religio Medici* Charlie had given me. It brought a sweet humanism to the gross materialism of much medical instruction.

There is no point in going into detail about my medical studies. What is relevant is fresh in my memory, and what proved not to be so has been banished to some dark cupboard in my mind—not wholly lost, but not at my fingers' ends. None of it would be of interest to Esme, or of use in her investigation of a past Toronto. I was lucky in having a good memory and the drudgery of Anatomy, for instance, was within my scope without undue strain. Very early I determined that Surgery was not to be my special work; not that I couldn't do it, in so far as I had to do it to pass my examinations. Nor was it that I was repelled by the rough stuff that goes on in the operating-room—the sawing and hammering, before much delicate work may be approached; I could saw and gouge with the best of them. But I was no surgeon by nature. It demands an extraversion of temperament which was not mine, and the irreversibility of what was done sometimes struck me as mischievous.

What I really liked was diagnosis, and early in my work I showed an aptitude for it. I knew that some of my professors had an eye on me, but for what purpose nobody said. The spirit of the medical school was firmly hierarchical; you crept upward, begging acceptance of the greater ones above you, questioning only when questioning seemed to be asked for, and if you had the makings of a True Believer, a Saved Soul, in you, you acquired a detestation of patent medicines, of osteopaths and chiropractors, of homeopaths and herbalists, of all quacks, midwives, and pretenders to medical knowledge, which was the property of your brotherhood, and you knew with whatever modesty lay in you, that you were a creature apart. The world, for you, was becoming a world divided between patients and healers.

It was odd, to me, what links were left unjoined in our training. We were assured, with sincerity, that our task in life was to relieve suffering. But never once did I hear anyone explain that the word patient really means "a sufferer." I suppose it was because so few of them groaned or wept or exhibited gross malfunctioning; the majority of them just sat *patiently* waiting for something to be done to them. But if you took a little time to talk to them—which as a student you rarely had an opportunity to do—you discovered that they were indeed suffering, and that often the suffering was simple fear.

I was impressed by what everybody else in my student group took as a joke, when we had a chance to take a peep at the bottom of a professor from the University, who had a fistula of the anus.

"We can get this right, Idris," said the professor of surgery, who was demonstrating to us what this ailment involved. "You'll soon be right as rain."

"God grant it may be so," said Professor Rowlands, obviously putting on a music-hall Welsh accent, "but don't suppose I count on it. We Welsh, you know— we're convinced that if ever we get into a hospital, the chances are strong that we'll never get out of it."

The surgeon laughed, obligingly, and so did we students, sycophantically, but I was the only one who sensed the truth beneath the joke. When educated people joke, it is a good idea to look at the underside of the joke; there may be a significant truth under there which less educated people could not cloak in a jest. Forty years later I know that what the professor said is by no means uncommon and is by no means confined to the Welsh.

What made me think that? A natural disposition to look at the underside of everything, I suppose, greatly encouraged by my exploration of *Faust*, undertaken in Dwyer's flat, under the guidance of Commander Daubigny. Goethe knew the secrets of the human heart, and would have made a fine physician if he had not been called to greater things. As it was, he was no trifler as a scientist.

One night, Mervyn Rentoul made one of our number. He was to play the great Dr. Faust, and, like every actor of that part, he faced the formidable task of topping his Mephistopheles. It is asserted by some critics that when Shakespeare wrote *Romeo and Juliet* he had to kill off Mercutio at the beginning of Act Three or Romeo would never have stood a chance of dominating the play. (Poor Romeo—between Mercutio and Juliet he has his work cut out for him!) The situation in

Faust is even worse: how many Fausts can outshine even a decent Mephistopheles? With the Devil and the pathetic Margaret sharing the stage, Faust seems rather a dull dog. So Rentoul was looking for every advantage that lay within his grasp, and because that was the kind of actor he was, he thought it could best be done through his appearance and accoutrements.

"I'll need some sort of stick, I suppose," he said.

"Are you going to totter until I renew your youth?" said Dwyer. "Better ask Angus to get you something durable, and long."

"I was thinking more of something that could later be my magician's wand," said Rentoul. "I need something to stamp me as a magician, and not simply a scholar."

"Get Angus to provide you with a proper physician's stick," said Jock. "The veritable caduceus of Hermes, with serpents twining round it."

"Don't know it," said Rentoul.

"Oh, yes you do. The staff with two snakes curling up it. You don't know it? You disappoint me. Listen—it's thousands of years old, and it comes from the days when gods trod the earth. Once when Hermes walked abroad he came on two snakes fighting furiously. To make peace and establish balance, or reconciliation or whatever, he thrust his staff between the snakes and they crawled up it, still hissing, but this time in concord, and they have remained twined about the staff of the healer to this day. And what are the snakes? You could call them Knowledge and Wisdom."

"Aha, yes—knowledge of course," said Rentoul, who liked to show himself quick in the uptake. It was also a way of keeping other people from speaking too long and distracting attention from himself.

"No, not knowledge alone," said Jock, who had been a teacher and, I suppose, a naval officer too long to be easily choked off. "Knowledge and Wisdom and they are not the same, because Knowledge is what you are taught, but Wisdom is what you bring to it. Here's Jon, he's right in the middle of it at this moment. He's being taught, and what is he being taught? Science, of course. Very fine, very splendid, very indisputable until somebody comes along with a new notion that squelches the old one. But he is also bringing to it the other snake, and we'll call it Humanism, though that doesn't rule out the gods. Don't forget that Hermes was a god, and descended from the gods of Egypt. These gods have not died, you know, because of whatever they teach in Darcy's church. They are alive, and you have only to show yourself worthy and they'll hear you."

"Go on, Jock," said I; "you'll turn my pretty head with flattery. Me, a humanist? Get away!"

"You don't know what you are, shrimp," said Jock. "I tell you you're a humanist, and if not what are you doing here listening to me explain Goethe to these stupid actors? What does the great Goethe say?

> *Grau, teurer Freund, ist alle Theorie*
> *Und grun des Lebens goldner Baum.*

Translate, Jon, translate. Did you do four years German with me and you can't translate that? Come on!"

"It means, 'My dear friend, all theory is grey—"

"Yes, yes; theory. We can't live without it and we're sunk if we live with nothing else. Go on."

"'Life's golden tree alone is green.' Correct, sir?"

"Correct, Hullah. Go to the top of the class. Easy to translate. Not easy to understand. The golden tree of life. Experience? Not just that. Experience understood, and that means quiet, calm consideration."

"That's one of my lines," said Dwyer. "I say it to that stupid student who comes for advice when I'm dressed up in Faust's doctoral robe. I have a notion for giving it a special emphasis."

"Make sure you get it across loud and clear," said Jock. "It's what every university needs to have burnt in letters of fire on every lecture-room wall."

"I'll speak to Angus about those snakes tomorrow," said Rentoul. He understood visual effects better than philosophical truths, I think. But not a bad actor for all of that.

Speak to Angus he certainly did, and Angus was not pleased, because it was fixed in his head that he knew better about costume and design than anybody else within miles of the Players' Guild. So Angus flounced and pouted, but at last said he would see what he could do.

Angus was a great enlargement of experience for me, because he illustrated how haphazardly Fate attributes names to her unoffending children. Angus McGubbin: a Scots giant, red-haired and scowling—wouldn't you think so? But though Angus was well over six feet tall, he looked not to be more than a foot and a half wide in his widest place. He weaved from side to side when you talked to him, and seemed always to be swaying in a warm breeze; his complexion was green—not a green such as one sees sometimes in patients who have been dosed with silver medicines; on close inspection I discovered that this iridescence was artificial: he powdered himself green, and then painted a blush on the cheekbones and a dusky red mouth. Strange, but looked at coolly, not a bad effect. He wore a moustache of a thinness and elegance of curve rarely seen except on the movie screen, and he assisted it with a black pencil; his manner was weary, wincing, winsome when he thought it might provoke a response in kind. Indeed, Angus was the kind of homosexual that in those days was called a "fruit." The delight of his life was his costume department at the theatre; soft fabrics, velvets and silks, furs and chamois moved him almost to ecstasy; he delighted in dressing all players, but men especially; it was a lesser sodomy to have Angus measure one's inner leg. I never saw him outside the theatre and perhaps he lived there.

No less astonishing than Angus was his wife, Vera. So tall, so dark, so slim, so pallid, she might have been his sister more credibly than his wife. But wife she was and they were devoted to one another. To achieve a perfect balance between them, she should have been a Lesbian, but she was not, and I doubt if she was sexually anything at all, though she was as green as he and not unattractive; she had a ducky little moustache of her own. She designed scenery, and helped Angus make properties. They were talented and because they loved their work they were cheap, so the Guild was lucky to have them.

One night, when perhaps I had had a little too much whisky, I raised the subject of Angus at Dwyer's, because I wanted to find out what Darcy would say about him. Angus and Darcy were both homosexuals, but could hardly have been more different. Angus, such a howling fruit, Darcy, though of conspicuous elegance, not even faintly frugiferous.

"Angus gives vice a bad name," said Jock.

"He does worse; he makes it laughable," said Darcy. "And that is a dangerous form of sin."

"Are there forms of sin that aren't dangerous?" I said, hoping it was something clever, but not having time to weigh it before it popped out of my mouth.

"Without getting into the whole question of what is sin, let's just call it folly," said Dwyer. "Angus turns his sin into folly, and so silly people think it doesn't really matter. But it does matter. Sin is very serious business."

"Ah, the sin that I have seen," said Jock, who, like me, had been getting into the drink. "All the world over. In my time I have been in three navies. Did you know that? Yes; first the Royal Navy, when I was young and had a splendid torpedo beard, in imitation of Georgie Gingerbeard, who was a fine sailor and made a pretty good king. Then, because I spoke French as readily as English—my Bosanquet family, you understand—I was lent to the French Navy as a liaison officer, and by some muddle which I never understood, they lent me to the Russians for eight months because I spoke elegant German, and anybody in the Russian Navy who could even read a barometer was a German. I was—yes, I assure you I was—an officer in the Russian Navy just before the Great War. And in those navies I travelled the globe, and I saw some things that would make your eyes start out of your skull, and was involved in certain things which I now look back on with astonishment, but without any real regret. Sins! That was why I ended up as a schoolmaster. In a boys' school the sins are all so trivial and easily comprehensible. Teaching has been a great rest from the world. And from sin."

"Jock, is it true what used to be said at Colborne, that you have eaten human flesh?"

"Oh, certainly, but that wasn't sin. That was necessity. When in Rome—you know? When among cannibals— I was shipwrecked with half a dozen other fellows—you eat whatever happens to be in the pot and you don't criticize the menu, or you might just be elected to provide an alternative."

"What was it like?"

"Not unlike horse, but not so sweet. Rather a bitter taste, as I recall it. But it would have been different if it had been a white man; we eat so much sugar I understand we make a nasty table-dish. Like a corpse, the true cannibals say. All that about missionaries being eaten is greatly exaggerated. They were prepared for the feast, but only a lick or two was consumed. Our diet— the Englishman's diet—makes for very poor feasting. Cannibals eat one another to possess whatever virtue or excellence the dead man had. They don't usually think missionaries are worth consuming because they don't want to be like them.... No, no, that was not sin. It was social custom. I have been a connoisseur of sins in my time."

"And where do you rank Angus?"

"Now you are talking like a Canadian: because Angus is unlike you, he must be wrong in some way, and his get-up suggests unacceptable behaviour. Unacceptable to whom? Anybody who is anybody is likely to be unacceptable to the nobodies. Look at our friend Darcy, here; the most obstreperous man in his religious observances you will meet anywhere. To go for a walk with him is to draw stares. If he passes a church in which he suspects that the Sacrament is reserved, he crosses himself and gabbles a *Kyrie*; if he meets a pair of nuns he sweeps off his hat to the danger of all bystanders, because nuns are the Brides of Christ and Mrs. Christ must be so honoured. His fastings are the wonder of anybody who has ever asked him to a meal; he never seems to fast from wine. But between him and Angus what is there to choose—supposing one is God, of course. They are both very much to the left of God's word as he sets it forth in Leviticus and various other gritty guides to conduct; when God writes in English— which he does with remarkable poetic force—I believe the word He uses is 'abomination.' But Darcy does not paint his face or wriggle his arse and so he is not looked upon as a sinner—simply as an eccentric. And a dear fellow. I'll just refresh my glass, if I may, Darcy."

"Go ahead, Jock. The drink talks amusingly in you. But let's be frank. You speak as though Angus and I were slightly different but essentially similar specimens of some subspecies of humanity. How would you like it if I said that you and every other retired naval officer were really the same creature—?"

"God forbid, my dear fellow! That would be abomination indeed!"

"Precisely. And I won't be lumped with Angus, who is a simple, blatant fruit and loves every minute of it. Loves the danger of being beaten up by thugs who reassure themselves about their own manliness by punching and kicking him. Except that I am sensitive to the beauty and charm of young men, and on a vastly superior aesthetic level, mind you, I have nothing in common with him. What appearance do I present?"

"Well, you are not the best judge of that, my dear fellow. But when you are not crossing and waving your hat you look like what you are—a banker."

"Exactly. Like the head of the foreign exchange department of my bank, and as level-headed, trustworthy a chap as you'd meet anywhere."

"That may be going a bit far. Since you began thinking so much about Mephistopheles you have an air of— what shall I say—of not being quite what you seem, but I assure you not an air of being in the least what we are talking about. A whiff of brimstone, shall we say?"

"Thank you Jock. That's exactly what I want—on the stage, of course, but I suppose something is bound to spill over—a whiff of brimstone. And don't worry too much about the Bible."

"I don't, I assure you."

"A fascinating book, but not the guide to conduct that extreme Protestants suppose it is. If God wrote it, what pens did he command? Some rather tough old desert characters, who ate a terrible diet, and give no evidence of having read anything except what their fellow-zealots had written. Writers, in the main, with a gigantic sense of grievance, which is very attractive, of course, because everybody has a store of grievance tucked away, waiting for something to call it forth. I'm speaking of the Old Testament. When you get to the New, another air blows through the Good Book. A Greek air. If our Blessed Saviour had not been so devoted to the cause of his own people, He would have got on admirably with the Greeks, because He had a lot of their spirit. And the Greeks had plenty of room for people like me—worshippers of beauty, who find it in the male, without in the least ignoring the part of it that inheres in the female."

"But the Bible is surely the foundation of the Church you devote so much of your best energies to," said I, because all of this was taking me out of my depth.

"I am a Church man, not a Bible man," said Dwyer. "That's where places like St. Aidan's verge away from your Low Church God-shops. And the Church has a lot of room for Greek sophistication."

"But weren't we talking about sin? Has the Church something to say about sin that the Bible didn't say first?"

"Oh, a great deal, my dear Pyke. The Church, like all great and successful rulers, has learned tolerance, which is not simply turning a blind eye to things you think are wrong. There is a lot of Law, you know, that isn't the Law of the Prophets, and it even makes fleeting appearances in our law-courts right here in Toronto. *Honeste vivere, alterum non laedere, suum cuique tribuere;* Roman law, but it came down to them from the Greeks. Do you understand what I've said?"

"I'm the only one here with a right to demand that Jon translate," said Jock. "He understands, I expect, but you tell him, Darcy, and I'll judge you on your translation."

"To live honourably, to injure no man, to render to each his own. How's that?"

"Very good. Top of the class."

"Good law and good Church, but doesn't fit easily into the Bible, you see. The Roman concept of honour wasn't a Hebrew idea at all, and they lambasted it as Pride, which to some extent it is. But Roman Law, and what the Church has taken from it, is for sophisticated, many-layered societies, and the Bible isn't. It was for a cantankerous people who had to keep their heads above water by sticking together, if I may mix a metaphor."

"So the Church has a place for people like—well, like you," said I, and was aware that for the first time Darcy and I were talking about something I hadn't thought it polite to mention.

"It had better have a place for people like me," said Dwyer, "because it needs what we artists can give it. And when I say people like me, I don't mean riff-raff like Angus; I mean Michelangelo, and Raphael, and scores of others, not forgetting the opprobriously named Sodoma. Musicians, it goes without saying. The people who have style. Because a Church with no style is a dismal affair, as is proven every Sunday in this godly city, which smugly refers to itself as The City of Churches."

"But all the artists aren't—"

"Nobody said they were. Not all, or even most. But some conspicuous examples."

"Not Bach. Not Handel. Certainly not Dr. DeCourcy Parry."

"Certainly not, Pyke. Don't be such a whole-hogger."

"No, no; but it's just that people like you so often make people like me seem clumsy and crass, and we have to struggle for our lives. Here's Jock talking about being a connoisseur of sins, and here's you talking about the Church as a guide to life that runs contrary to the Bible, and I'm just a dumb medical student from Sioux Lookout who seems not to have a leg to stand on. All I can be sure of is Gray's *Anatomy*, and that's chilly comfort, especially after a morning in the dissection lab."

"Poor old Pyke," said Dwyer, and refilled my glass. "Don't worry so. Learn to enjoy the pleasures of talk for talk's sake, without thinking you have to reshape your life every time a new idea comes along."

"What's that silly song the boys are singing in the corridors?" said Jock, and burst into stentorian bass roarings:

> *"Life is just a bowl of cherries,*
> *Don't take it serious—*
> *It's too mysterious—"*

"Precisely," said Darcy, quenching this Russian outburst (because a few months in the Russian Navy seemed to have had a deep influence on Jock's character); "precisely. All I'm getting at—apart from divorcing myself from Angus and his crew of Hallowe'en spooks and poufs—is that life needs style—style applied to everything—and religion is just the place to get it. Curious though that may seem to those whose spirits sink whenever religion is mentioned. Life is best lived according to a noble rhythm, under certain ethical restraints, and with certain metaphysical assumptions; the Church can offer that."

"Doesn't philosophy offer it, without all the flummery?" said I, for that which had made them drunk had made me bold.

"No, darling, philosophy doesn't and you have only to look at philosophers' wives, beginning with

Xantippe, to see that it doesn't. That's because philosophy excludes poetry, and the Church is wide open to poetry. And that's why I'm as happy as a sandboy."

"Why is a sandboy supposed to be happy? And what exactly is a sandboy?"

But I received no answer. Both my gurus were asleep.

[10]

I REALLY MUST put on the brakes or this Case Book, which I intend only as an *aide-mémoire*, will turn into one of those German Bildungsromanen, about the growth of a human spirit. Yet I suppose I cannot wholly escape it. My spirit was indeed growing under the guidance of Darcy and Jock, and when I look back now I see how very gentle and kind they were to me, though at the time I thought they were snubbing me and bringing me up every instant. It was not all gas and whisky. We had some good times, and now and then one of Darcy's Mephistophelian practical jokes.

As, for instance, the night we spent at the Coburg Social Parlours, where I was the victim.

The talk about sin had gone on, in a desultory fashion, for a few nights extending over two or three weeks, because I could not take every night away from my studies and Herculean feats of memorization. Darcy had maintained that there was no form of sin that could not be found somewhere in Toronto. It was not that Toronto was especially sinful; simply that after a place achieves a certain population—Toronto was now approaching the million count—every variety of human deviation will appear in it. Demand creates supply.

Jock's notions of sin were rather gloomy and Dostoevskian; he did not think there could ever be any fun in it. The argument was a self-defeating one: if something was amusing, it couldn't be sin. But Darcy spread a wider net. If something offended strongly against good taste, to say nothing of decency, it was sin.

"You don't think sin can make you laugh? Or rather, you think that if it makes you laugh it can't be sin? But what is the sin against? Morality? Taste? And where do morality and taste cease to kiss and commingle? Are you challenging me to offer you an example?"

The night the example was to be made manifest, Darcy had warned us to dress simply. Not in such a way, he said, as to identify ourselves as persons of—how could he put it?—persons who might be assumed to be of a superior caste. This was easy for me. Then, as now, a student doesn't usually have to dress down; the problem is to get him to dress up. Jock was not distinguished in dress, though his hawk-like profile and the betraying monocle could not be disguised, unless we called Angus on the job as an experienced costumier and make-up man. But Darcy was determined that nobody should spot him as the merchant banker he was, and he wore an extraordinary yellow overcoat (which I truly believe *must* have come from Angus) and a black hat with a very wide brim, pulled down to conceal his face. He looked like a conspirator in a bad amateur play, but he thought his disguise impenetrable.

"Only the owner knows me here," he whispered, as we went through the dimly lit door, gloomy with coloured glass. "Leave everything to me."

The Coburg Social Parlours, when once we had passed the poky little foyer, were brightly lit and crowded with noisy people, all of whom were sitting at tables for four, on which were glasses of beer. It looked to me like an ordinary beer-parlour, but it had a platform at one end, and there was a sense of expectation in the air.

A little man in shirtsleeves, apparently the proprietor, darted toward us as soon as we appeared.

"God, I began to think you'd forgotten," said he. "The crowd's expecting a really big night. But you've brought him? Eh? Is this him?" and he looked at Jock.

"No, that is my friend Dr. Strabismus, of Utrecht, who is travelling in Canada on a sociological expedition, and he wanted to see your place. *Here* is the judge. Young though he may look, he is the very man for the job. I present to you Dr. Jonathan Pyke, a man rapidly rising to the top of his profession as a physician, and the very person for the delicate task you are going to confront him with."

"Great!" said the little man, whose name did not seem to be worth mentioning, or was so well known that everybody ignored it. "An honour to meet you, Doc. An honour and a pleasure. Now let's get on with it. The crowd's getting anxious and the contestants are getting worried that they can't keep up to scratch. So let's not lose any time. Just come with me."

Before I could say a word I was seized by the arm and rushed to the front of the hall and up some steps onto the stage. There the little shirtsleeved man waved his arms for silence and, though the crowd may have been eager for what was to follow, it took some time to shut them up.

"Ladeez and Gen'lemen," shouted the little man. "Thank you for the patience with which you have waited during this unavoidable delay. But the wait has been worthwhile, I can assure you. Hunger is the best sauce, as they say. We have secured for tonight's contest a judge who is, I venture to say without expectation of successful contradiction, the best-qualified person in Toronto, and I would go further, and say, in Canada. The name of Dr. Jackson Peake is a household word wherever the practice of medicine is known in the civilized world, because though he is young—and I venture to say all the ladies have already noticed how young he is—and all that implies—he is at the top of the ladder in his line, which is the, uh, the medical line. So, without further ado, as they say, let's hear your welcome for Dr. Jackson Peake, who is to be judge of the Coburg's Seventh Annual Bad Breath Contest!"

I cannot avoid cliché. Clichés have become worn because they embody important truths. *My senses swam.* There's the cliché; my senses swam. Over the rows of upturned faces, like so many pink footballs in the half light, I could see Darcy and Jock in the back row, apparently hugging themselves with glee. But I had no time for thought and no chance of escape. The little man in shirtsleeves was holding me firmly by the arm while going on.

"We have this evening a large and I think uniquely gifted group of contestants. Two or three may not be in the best of health and you may think this gives them some unfair advantage in the matter of halitosis, but I am assured by reliable authorities at the Medical School in the University of Toronto, of which we are all so proud,"—he paused here for applause and as always when a skilled rhetorician does so, he got it, from an audience which couldn't have cared beans for any medical school anywhere—"that it is not so. An able-bodied halitoser may very well outstrip—or should I say outstink (*roars of laughter and some slapping of thighs*) somebody who is in really bad shape. So everybody starts even, tonight.

"Please observe that we have changed our platform arrangements from that of past years, so that you are able to observe the judge, as well as the contestants, as he sits in his seat of honour, taking his notes and making up his mind. As you observe, the contestant comes up the right-hand flight of steps, unseen by the judge whose view is cut off by these screens. The contestant kneels on this little stool here, in front of the screen in which the air-conductor is affixed. The air-conductor is, as you see, a simple megaphone, the large end of which is toward the contestant, and the sharp end directly in front of the judge, who thus gets full benefit of what each contestant has to offer. I will introduce each contestant by holding up a number, by which—and by which alone—Dr. Jason Peake will identify him or her. For in the Contest the ladies are at no disadvantage with the stronger sex. (*Homeric mirth and a serious case of choking in Seat 3, Table 7.*) There will be a brief pause between contestants, in order to permit the judge to make his notes and also to prepare himself psychologically and medically for the next contestant. And between contestants, the transmitter of the breath will be disinfected by a registered trained nurse with Listerine, so that there may be no build-up, or cumulative effect. And now, ladeez and gen'lemen, are you ready?"

The audience was clamorously ready.

"So okay, then. Blow it away!"

I suppose everybody who has lived above the cabbage level has had these moments when divine, or at least supernatural, aid seems necessary, and one calls upon it with an urgency which is as much physical as mental. I had never had any experience of appearing in public except as an unnoticeable extra in *The Piper*, and here I stood, marked as some sort of infallible authority, before an audience with the highest expectations—the expectations that are rooted in ignorance. For I was a Man of Science, a Great Authority, and what I said was golden, unless I betrayed myself irretrievably—choked on my words, wet my pants, ran from the stage weeping—

something in that order of disgrace. These calls for help from—from what?—are one of the many forms of prayer, and it was here, as judge in the Coburg Social Parlours Annual Bad Breath Contest, that I first experienced prayer as something other than what went on, ritually, in churches and meant nothing to me whatever. This was a kind of prayer that Charlie, with his Petition, Intercession, and Meditation, had said nothing about.

My prayer was answered. I gained possession of myself. Determination and daring flooded through me, as if I had had one of the miraculous injections that Dr. Romeyn spoke of as infallible in cases of shock. I would astonish my audience, and I would revenge myself on Dwyer, and rather less so on Jock, who were so pleased to have put me on the spot. I'd show 'em!

The ordeal began. I knew nothing particularly about bad breath, except as something that was part of the personalities of people like Eddu, Doc Ogg, and Père Lartigue. Something to be avoided, not studied and particularized. Mervyn Rentoul had a bad breath—or perhaps in the light of later experience, I should say a baddish breath, and nothing to the Olympic Class breaths I was to encounter in the Social Parlours—and the catty rumour at the Players' Guild was that it was his false teeth; leading ladies shrank from his caress. But here I was, at the end of the transmitter of Great Breaths.

"Number One!" shouted the man in shirtsleeves, holding up a large card on which the numeral was displayed, perhaps for the information of the deaf. From my seat behind the screens I was not supposed to be able to see the contestants, but as they approached the steps to the platform I did so, and Number One was a gangling youth who had put on his best suit for this public appearance. There was some applause from partisans and well-wishers. He scraped the stool—they all scraped the stool—that was his seat of trial, pushed his head into the megaphone's big end, and blew.

Yes, a bad breath, right enough. But how was I to rank it? Give him five out of ten on the Hullah Halitosis Scale—invented by me at that moment— and rank the others accordingly? That is what I did. The contestant left the stage amid a spattering of applause, and a woman who was, I suppose, one of the waitresses in the beer-parlour, came forward, dressed in rough parody of a hospital nurse, and gave the megaphone a thorough wipe with Listerine.

I forget most of the others. There were three or four whose personal puff was pestilential, and I awarded them eights and nines. It was a procession of, in all, seventeen men and women who had neglected teeth, disordered digestion, and, in one case, something I would have supposed to be scurvy, and as the contestant looked like a sailor from one of the lake boats, it just possibly might have been so. But the winner was unmistakable; she had the Limburger cheese hogo which my medical studies told me was associated only with seriously infected tonsils; pus, indeed. When, after I had pretended to do heavy deliberation, and casting up of figures, I told the man in shirtsleeves of my decision, he was delighted. This candidate was obviously the favourite, and a lot of money was riding, or should I say floating, on her success.

It was for me to make the announcement, and it was here, I think after all these years, that I euchred Dwyer and Jock. There had been seventeen contestants, avid for the Halitosis Crown, and by the time the puffing was completed, what with the ceremonial manner in which the man in shirtsleeves brought each one to the chair of trial, and the fuss that the phony nurse made in cleansing the megaphone, the platform reeked of

Listerine, and I doubt if the Giant Blunderbore, after a heavy meal of human flesh, could have penetrated it with his dreadful breath. It was in this heady atmosphere that I rose to speak.

"Ladies and gentlemen," said I; "my first duty is to congratulate all the contestants on their good sportsmanship and their willingness to come forward in what is, I think you will agree, an especially personal battle. (*Applause.*) For a Battle it was, I assure you. No unworthy champions appeared before you, or submitted what they had to offer to my professional judgement. I salute them all, and I know you do, as well. But before I declare the winner, I ask for your indulgence while I make a few comments on the nature of the contest. On its place of origin, so to speak." Quick, thy tablets, memory! Here it was that my unusually retentive memory bore me stiffly up, as I searched for words.

"Bad breath has always drawn the respectful attention of medical men, as an indicator of general health, and sometimes as a clue to some specific ailment. But medical men have come, with the passing of time and newer diagnostic methods, to shun an encounter with a patient's breath, because it may be offensive. Oh, shame! Shame on those who put a merely personal consideration of comfort ahead of true diagnostic practice. Shame on the physician who will not dare all for his patient's good! Modern medicine has as its banner-bearer, in this question of sampling the breath, none other than the great Sir William Osler, perhaps the most notable physician of his day, which lasted until his death in 1919. Sir William Osler who, despite the honours so deservedly showered upon him abroad, the triumphs in the United States, and later in England, where he was honoured with a knighthood by His Majesty the King (*brisk applause*), began life and was proud to define himself to the end, as a Canadian. (*Terrific applause.*) It is upon the principles laid down by Sir William that I have acted tonight, giving of Canada's best to—in the matter of bad breath—Canada's finest. And at this point may I—I know you will excuse any appearance of presumption on my part—call upon you to show your appreciation of the organizer of this contest, Mr.—"

Of course I did not know his name, but of course it was not necessary. The applause was tremendous and I had only to mumble something as the crowd cheered and some cried, "Good old Perse! Great work, boy!"

My notions of public speaking were crude, founded as they were on a handful of addresses by political spellbinders who had passed through Sioux Lookout at election times. I had flattered everybody—the contestants, the organizer, and the audience. I had raised the addled head of patriotism. Now I must impress my hearers with my own intellectual splendour. How? The historical approach seemed best.

"Bad breath is nothing new in the history of mankind. Evidence is scant, but I venture to say that when Mr. Caveman woke in the morning after a feast of raw dinosaur, Mrs. Caveman found his breath heavy, and urged him to chew a few sprigs of mint. (*Laughter and wives nudge husbands.*) Bad breath is not mentioned in many ancient documents, and we may assume that it was so common an occurrence in daily life that it was not thought worth recording. There are a few references in the Middle Ages—(*a wife nudges her husband and says audibly, 'Middle of what?' He hisses in reply, 'Olden times. Henry the Eighth and those guys.'*)—and as I do not suppose many of you trouble your heads about those, I shall mention simply that the scribe Oleaginus Silo records that the Patriarch Scrofulus of Cappadocia was sadly afflicted in this respect, but that even his best friends would not tell him. His breath was thought to arise from a rotting soul. (*This horseplay with which I had expected to rouse a laugh, is received with placid silence. The* drye mock *is not for all audiences: sometimes it falls flat.*) But now to return to Sir William Osler.

"I shall not lecture you about Sir William's definitions. Anyone who wishes to inform himself about them can easily take down his Osler from his shelves and do so. (*This was laying it on with a trowel; I don't suppose anybody in that audience owned more than six books, at an outside figure, nor was likely to have a shelf for them. But, as I say, I had heard some political speakers at Sioux Lookout, and I knew that no flattery is too gross for a general audience.*) Osler's descriptions of the *fetor oris* are truly classical, beginning with the simple bad breath of indigestion, with its associated catarrhal disturbances of the mouth, pharynx, and stomach. It is important to distinguish it from the characteristic odour of acute stomatitis, of which one of the principal causes is the excessive use of tobacco. We must keep an eye on this one, lest it be a forerunner of *pemphigoid stomatitis*, and that may quickly lead to *pemphigus vegetans* and that, as I need hardly tell an audience like this, leads straight to the graveyard."

(*Not bad policy to alarm an audience. Turn pleasure to terror for a fraction of a minute, and you have enriched the satisfaction.*)

"This brings us, as I am sure you know—for many of you will be ahead of me, I am certain—to the distinctive breath of *pyorrhoea alveolaris*, the commonest form of foul breath but not for that reason to be scorned in such a contest as this. It can be a corker, I assure you, and as I am sure many of you already know. It must not be mistaken for the odour of decayed teeth which is quite another matter.

"There follows the tonsillar infections, which can create an odour powerfully characteristic, because of the epithelial debris which accumulates in the tonsillar crypts. And finally we come to unmistakable diseases of the nose, larynx, bronchi, and lungs, and I am glad to assure you that no examples of these extreme symptoms have presented themselves tonight. No, I can assure you that all the contestants, in so far as I may judge from what I have been able to experience of them, are in good health. For bad breath is in no way incompatible with satisfactory general health, as daily experience so repeatedly makes plain.

"And now, my friends, to the winner. (*Rustle of anticipation.*) You do not, I am sure, want a clinical description of the offering, which belongs to one of the rarer categories among those I have set before you, on Osler's lines. Suffice it to say that the hogo—and I do not need to tell you that our English word comes from the French *haut gout*, for bad breath is a truly bilingual attribute as our politicians demonstrate every day (*applause and whistles*)—this hogo is one of the most remarkable I have ever experienced, and it is a scientific honour to have met with it. So, without further ado (*audiences love being assured that there has been a great deal of "ado" on such occasions*) I call upon the winner to come forward and receive the prize. Number Eleven!"

Amid clapping, whoops and whistles and cries of glee from those who had backed this easy favourite, Number Eleven trotted forward. She might have been fifty, I suppose, and she showed the characteristic dullness of expression of the mouth-breather. I pressed upon her the envelope which, I was told, contained a twenty-dollar bill and a typewritten certificate, which I signed in attestation of her success. Signed as Jason Peakc, M.D., F.R.C.P. And since there was no use leaving stones unturned, I added to these accreditations "Chevalier of the Order of Polonia Restituta."

Thus my task was done, and the audience had had all of me that it wanted. The people dissolved themselves into groups, some standing beers to unsuccessful candidates, some commiserating with them, some grouped around Mrs. Limburger Cheese, who was in high feather and who, if I may diagnose her retrospectively, had not many more years to enjoy her fame.

The man in shirtsleeves seized me by the arm; he was the kind of man who cannot establish contact with someone unless he gets his hands on them. "Come on, Doc," he said. "You done great. Great, boy. It was masterly to give it to a woman. They're always beefin' that the boys keep all the big stuff for themselves. Masterly! But I know what you need now. So come on." And he rushed me into a cluttered back office, where he poured me a big dollop of pretty good brandy. "This clears the nose," said he, and I drank it greedily. It was indeed a proper dwale.

When I joined Dwyer and Jock later, they heaped praise upon me. Didn't suppose I had it in me. Had turned up trumps. Was a prankster in their own league. My speech had been—well—Mephistophelean. And so forth. It was Dwyer who had the best news.

"We've finally completed casting for *Faust*," he said. "You, Pyke, are to understudy Wagner, and play the nice meaty little role of the Student in the scene where Mephistopheles assumes Faust's doctoral robe. We'll knock their eyes out, Pyke, my lad."

[11]

REHEARSALS FOR *Faust* took a nasty knock when Elaine Wollerton, the obvious casting for Margaret, stepped from a street-car onto an icy piece of pavement and sprained her ankle so badly that there was no chance that she could appear in the play. Consternation! Brouhaha! Run, run, and tell the King the sky is falling! On short notice—a week—the understudy, Nuala Conor, had to undertake the part. O bliss! she knew all her lines! O rapture, she had paid attention at rehearsals and knew all her moves! She would pull through, somehow, but of course she would not be La Wollerton.

No indeed. She would be much better, though nobody admits that an understudy can really be better than a star. But Nuala Conor looked like a virgin, which Elaine—good generous soul that she was—did not and had never done so. Some girls are born ready-deflowered. Nuala Conor was Irish, newly come to Canada; small, but not one of those tedious china-doll girls; pretty in an Irish style, with fine black hair and dark blue eyes set in black lashes. Best of all, she had a really beautiful voice, with a very slight Irish intonation, but nothing of the Pat-and-Mike order. An ideal Margaret, to any but unyielding Wollertonians, and they were many. She was obviously intelligent, but the director treated her like a ninny, because she had never acted before and thus must by all rules of art be a ninny. It soon became obvious that Miss Conor "came across" admirably when on the stage, and little by little most of the prejudice against her quieted down.

I fell in love with Nuala Conor, like a man falling from a precipice into an abyss which has no bottom. My feeling for Elaine Wollerton faded like the flowers cursed by Mephistopheles. I was not alone in my adoration. There were other pretenders to her charms. But by some miracle I seemed to be the first in the race, and was the one who walked her home after rehearsals.

She was the first girl I met with a genuine sense of humour. Of course I had known many girls who laughed a lot, often when there was nothing to laugh at, and behind their girlish laughter there might always be seen the mirthless faces of their mothers, grim prophecies of what those girls would in time become. Elaine Wollerton was no mean hand at the *dry mocke*, but Nuala's sense of humour was a quiet, contained but effervescent delight in the vast comedy of life. She did not laugh often, but she seemed on the brink of laughter a great part of the time, and her approach to the world—and to me, of course—was one of a charming, modest mockery. With her it was possible to talk seriously of truly serious matters, but always with a sense of laughter about to triumph. It was an enchantment I had never dreamed of, and I recall it still with tenderness. She was—and remains—the love of my life. I am sure that Freudians would have some disobliging thing to say about a man whose love becomes fixed at the age of twenty-four and never dwindles, however much time and circumstances may change it, for the rest of his life. But there are things Freudians don't know and that are known only to those of us who have fed on honey-dew and drunk the milk of Paradise.

Faust has long been the delight of scholars. However much Goethe protested that it was not a philosophical play, and that it contained no "message," and was indeed the work of a poet who was, like Shakespeare, above such leaden concerns and sought only to write what his Muse brought to him, scholars cannot leave it alone. All the scholars in Toronto who could read German seemed to haunt our rehearsals, and sometimes their hissing disputes at the back of the theatre were so distracting that the director had to threaten to turn them out. Art is always in peril at universities, where there are so many people, young and old, who love art less than argument, and dote upon a text that provides the nutritious pemmican on which scholars love to chew.

• • •

"Mervyn, old chap," calls the director from his table in the auditorium, "can you speed it up? It's dragging."

"I'm working to get the *thought* across, old boy."

"Well, let the thought take care of itself. Just pep it up."

"As you wish, old man." And sulky Mervyn gabbles.

• • •

"This is, of course, far from Goethe. So much has been cut! Have you observed?"

"Oh, indeed. I know the work intimately. But what can you expect of theatre people."

"Of course the Great Geheimrat was himself a theatre person. Managed the Weimar court theatre for twenty years. Did you know?"

"Certainly I know! What do you take me for? I took in *Faust* with my mother's milk, if you will excuse the indelicacy. But he never mounted one of his own plays. He had to put on trash to amuse the Court. He resigned at last, rather than offer *Le Chien de Montargis, ou la Forêt de Bondy.*"

"Sorry. You said—"

"*The Dog of Montargis*—by Pixérécourt. You don't know it? Well, it's a dog-drama, and stars a trick dog who unmasks the villain. Goethe wouldn't have it. Didn't like dogs."

"Ah, I see. Not my period, of course."

"My complaint is that this translation is so bad. And

as you say, cut to buggery."

"Shhh! There are ladies over there!"

• • •

"This Conor kid, you know—I don't like it. Do you suppose she's sleeping with Forsyth?"

"A girl? You're out of your skull."

"I should have preferred Dulcy Maule. She's thrown away in that miserable little part of Lieserl."

"You have a supporter in her husband, Old Decorum."

"Why do you call him that?"

"Because he's such a stick. Useful, of course, in Galsworthy. Lots of sticks there. But also because of Dulcy, don't you see? Dulcy et Decorum. Get it?"

"'Fraid not."

"Well, you remember *Dulce et decorum est pro patria mori?*"

"What's that?"

"It's Horace. I should have thought everybody knew it. 'Sweet and honourable it is to die for one's country.'"

"But what's that got to do with the Maules?"

"Christ, man! *Dulcy and Decorum*. Because her name's Dulcy, and she's so sweet, and he's so decorous. Don't you see?"

"Not much of a joke, if you ask me."

"Well I certainly won't ask you again."

• • •

"You sympathize, I am sure, vith vot I am saying: they attempt the *Walpurgisnacht* and they entirely omit the *Proktophantasmist*, the soul of the whole ting. Gone! Utterly gone! Such an omission makes the whole scene—perhaps the whole play—sheer Travestie! I shall not attend. Not on the first night, anyway."

"It would be beyond their powers to cast the *Proktophantasmist* properly—suitably—with full comprehension."

"If I had been asked, I would myself have attempted it, however greatly modesty—ah—what is it?—*dazwis chenkommen*—what is the word I want?"

"Interference? Intervened? Well, certainly a becoming modesty would have stood in your way. And you would have had to shave your beard."

"For Goethe even a beard is—how?—piffle."

"*Sehr Umgangsprachen.*"

● ● ●

Somehow, *Faust* was presented, and was widely approved because it showed that the Players' Guild was really a serious group, bent on bringing the finest in drama to the city of Toronto at a time when the travelling companies from England and the States were less frequent visitors, because of rising costs and the fierce competition of the movies. We were commended for the imagination of the settings, done with cut-outs representing Nuremberg, the Witch's Kitchen, Margaret's prison and whatever else was wanted, standing against curtains lighted with immense art and giving "impressions" rather than crude "representations." The music, which the great Dr. DeCourcy Parry had undertaken, was praised. Poor Mervyn Rentoul was brushed aside by the critics as having been "wooden"; they did not know how hard it is not to be wooden when onstage with Darcy Dwyer, who won all the notices as Mephistopheles. Nuala Conor was acclaimed as a new find by the Players' Guild, and ungallant suggestions were made that she was a pleasant change after some of the other actresses; critics have no chivalry. Quite unexpectedly, I was praised, though not in terms that thrilled me with joy, in one of the papers.

I appeared in one scene only, in an identified role, early in the play. Faust had retired, leaving his scholar's gown, which Mephistopheles puts on, and welcomes a Student who has come for advice about his studies. The student is the creepy-crawly figure, now familiar in a hundred schools of graduate studies; he defers to everything the Devil suggests. And before he departs, he asks the supposed great scholar to write something in his book. We had great irrelevant discussions as to what this book might be. Could it be an autograph album? Surely not. Probably a volume of Aristotle. Mephistopheles takes it, and the text suggests that he writes in it; it was here that Darcy had one of his best moments; he took the book and spat in it. No fake stage spit, either, but a substantial gob. And when the student takes it reverently, and reads it, it says: *Eritis sicut Deus, scientes bonum et malum.* The Satanic spew, it appears, spells out the serpent's words to Eve: *Ye shall be as gods, knowing good and evil.* The student is enraptured, and takes his leave, a man beside himself with glee.

What the Toronto *Mail* said was: "Mr. Jonathan Hullah presented a truly Gothic image as the Student, but it was not perhaps a happy inspiration on the part of the director to include his fine archaeological figure in so many of the succeeding crowd scenes."

Nuala never allowed me to forget my archeological figure from that day forward. What did it mean? Tall? Bony? Big-nosed? I accepted it as meaning Medieval rather than Classical, and have insisted on that interpretation to this day. Certainly in the *Walpurgisnacht* Scene I did my level best in the chorus of male witches, stripped to the waist and painted green. I could not persuade Angus to let me put on the green myself; he liked rubbing my chest and I had not the heart to rebuff him, though I took care he went no further.

The aftermath of *Faust* for me was a summons to the office of the Dean of Medicine. He was fatherly. Much was expected of me, it appeared. I had shown unusual promise and was now, in my fourth year, in a critical position in my studies. Too much time wasted—oh, very enjoyably and he himself liked to see a student with interests not strictly professional—but he advised me to forget about the Players' Guild until my medical work was completed and my professional status secured. Though even then, said the Dean, a medical man cannot be too careful about how he appears to the public. There was about the theatre a want of seriousness, a duplicity almost. He was sure I understood and understood also his true concern for my future.

I understood an order, even when it was enclosed in such puff pastry as this. Nose to the grindstone. Pass with honours and first in First Class, if you can manage it.

Nuala was not so gently treated. Women were still uncommon in medical studies, and she was warned in a note that if her chief interests really lay in the theatre, she had better transfer to some other work that would better fit her for such a future.

We compared notes, and cursed our elders and betters, and did as we were told.

[12]

WE HAD BECOME LOVERS in the fullest sense. The fullest sense, that is to say, that her life in a women's residence and mine in a boarding-house permitted. But love will find out a way, and our way meant that whenever we could afford it, which was not more often than every three or four weeks, we hired a room in the Ford Hotel for a Saturday afternoon, and it became a Bower of Bliss until we rose for our evening meal, eaten usually at Child's, which was good and cheap. On very great occasions we went to Miss Millichamp's on Bloor Street; she had a tender heart and I think we students received portions rather larger than the ordinary.

Nuala's father, I learned, was a lawyer in Cork, and the family seemed to be well-to-do. She wanted to study medicine, and her parents, with Catholic hearts a-quake, agreed that she might do so, and even study in North America rather than in Dublin or in England; she persuaded them that North America was advanced in medicine or at least in medical education, in a way that the homeland was not. But they had their condition: she might study in Canada, but not in the U.S.A., where a girl might more readily forget the precepts of her convent education. A scientific daughter! The Conors were half afraid and half elated. But, she confided to me, their Catholicism had been eroded by education and good fortune; they wanted her to remain firmly Catholic, as a protection of her virtue, but they themselves were not heart-and-soul children of the Church.

I took her with me to services at St. Aidan's and she declared that they were *lovely*, and far above the simplicities of Roman practice; she did not laugh, but there was an unmistakable quiver in her eyes—nothing so vulgar and Hollywood-Irish as a twinkle—when she said it. Did Father Hobbes really believe that the bread and wine at Communion became the real Blood and Body of Christ? In Ireland quite a few people took that with a grain of salt, though of course they never let on to the priest, or the uneducated people who had great solace from that belief. How *lovely* to encounter it here in

Canada, and in a church that was not quite—well, not wholly—the true Church. Oh, she quite understood why lots of people didn't want to be R.C.s, which meant swallowing the Pope, and it took a bloody strong gulp to do that, old darling that Pius XI was. Did I know that his birth-name was Achille Ratti, and that after he became Pontiff the Ratti family all suddenly blossomed into prosperity? Chicken farms, and things like that? A blessed miracle surely, that God should spread His bounty so lavishly on the kin of his Vicar on earth. The *dry mocke*.

I think our love was all the better for being stretched out by our necessity to study hard to keep up with our work. To have all the time in the world to devote to love may be idyllic for a summer, but linked sweetness long drawn out is the greater luxury. And of course Nuala returned to Ireland every summer, for she dearly loved her parents and was determined to return to her home-land for the rest of her life, when she had obtained her medical degree. This was something we did not talk about. Time would tell. During these summer absences I longed for her, and wrote to her, and loved her more than ever, abstinence sharpening the appetite.

Thus Toronto was for us a place sanctified by our love, but on my visits to Dwyer's flat I learned of another side to the City of Churches. Playing Mephistopheles had greatly affected Darcy; he had always had a turn for playing the Devil, and now he developed it to a point where it sometimes became a bore.

Sin was his great theme. What was it? How could it be identified in a world where opinions about it were so various? He took the theological line: sin was the pur-poseful disobedience to the known will of God. Aha, but how were you to know the will of God?

Jock had his own answer to that. He declared himself

to be the Last Manichaean. He believed that the world was a battleground between the forces of Good and Evil, and that Evil was a palpable reality and not just a whim-wham in the mind. The Devil was a fit opponent for God. They argued about it, sometimes interestingly and sometimes boringly. It was Jock, the self-declared connoisseur of sins, who demanded practical demonstration, and in search of evidence he and Darcy traipsed the streets of Toronto, night after night, in search of sin.

Jarvis Street was one of their accustomed beats; once a fashionable residential street, it was now the haunt of many of Toronto's whores. Why, I wondered, whenever I went with these two researchers, do people so quickly get down to sex when they talk about sin, and why does it seem to be a thing of the darkness? My Freudian enthusiasms had a great deal to say about that, but I kept my mouth shut, because I wanted to see what these lunatics might uncover, in their nocturnal mouse-hunts.

Sometimes Jock would engage a whore in conversation, questioning her about her trade. Of course the whore, thinking he was a customer, answered as well as she could, until she discovered that talk was all he wanted, and then she sometimes became abusive and we had to take to our heels. Her "friend," she shouted, would take care of us! Sons of bitches! Wasters of a girl's time! Nosy Parkers!

Jock occasionally attempted to pay for his information, but as he had a meagre schoolmaster's salary, he preferred payment in kind rather than in cash. Kind, for him, took the form of bags of humbugs, which he offered to his chosen informant, with an innocence that touched my heart.

"Have a humbug, my dear," he would say, approaching some thick-bodied woman who was too lazy to do kitchen work, and too stupid to do anything in an office.

"Talk to me a little. Let me ask you a few questions."

Of course he soon became known, and when he approached a girl she would shout, "Not for bloody humbugs!" and sweep past. Now and again the cry would go up, "Here comes the humbug man!" followed by laughter which Darcy said had a distinctly evil note. Sometimes men, ponces beyond a doubt, approached and we had to make a quick retreat.

Darcy did not himself approach the whores. His distaste for female sexuality, which never asserted itself with his women friends, became almost palpable when he encountered these street-women, who were repellent to anything but a starved appetite. As Jock sought confessions in return for humbugs, Darcy and I stood at a distance, and in our dark overcoats it was no wonder that the whores thought we must be informers, or perhaps the police themselves—cops whom they did not know and had not squared with money or with trade.

Darcy was not so simple as I thought him. Indeed I was the simple one, to suppose that he learned nothing at his work except the variabilities of foreign exchange. He knew about loans, and he knew about property values and mortgages. His bank held some mortgages relevant to the search for sin.

"What goes on in those houses? Officially we don't know. But if a bank knew nothing except what comes to it from official sources it wouldn't last long. The readiness with which the mortgage money is repaid is in itself enough to arouse suspicion. The only people who pay up so readily, so often before the due date, are either the small group of the scrupulously honest—who probably don't go in for mortgages anyway—and those who don't want investigations or questions.

"We have at least one mortgage on a house that offers children—quite small children—to interested clients.

There are people, not numerous but enough, who are willing to rent their children to that house and collect without a word being said. Of course if the child is damaged there is hell to pay, but that side of things is taken care of. Did you know, Pyke, that there is a doctor who looks after such places? Rather heavily devoted to drugs himself, and so ordinary practice is out of his scope, but he can patch and mend in a few bawdy-houses, where some of our sober citizens may become a little rough. Not a pretty way to practise medicine, but it keeps him in funds for his indulgence. A damaged child comes dear.

"There are at least two others—I can speak only of those my bank knows—where rough stuff is offered, on an as-you-like-it basis. Do you want to be strapped down on a bed and walloped by naked wenches? It comes at a price. Do you want to wallop a naked wench? Expensive but possible. Do you simply want dirty talk, because your wife is a pillar of society and won't let you say Shit when you stub your toe? There's a dirty-talker—not imaginative, but neither are most of her clients—who will give you fifteen minutes of filth for thirty dollars; she sits behind a screen because if she were seen it would dampen the lust of a gorilla. Actually, that woman could be a great hetaera, if she had what it takes, which I don't for one moment suppose she has. But if she commanded the language of sexual suggestion, she could ask a hundred dollars a half-hour from real voluptuaries of vocabulary. How many of these women know anything of the harlotry of language, the language of Théophile Gautier, for instance? What a career would lie open to her, and none of the rough-and-tumble of the harlot's couch."

"One can find that in Europe, but not I dare say on this continent," said Jock. "The Americans have rubbed the bloom off the English language. I knew a woman, once, who could bring a man off in ten minutes simply by talking to him. She lived in Winchester, just a few streets from where Jane Austen used to live. A real sorceress."

"That is the true fellatio, the real harlotry of the tongue. Jane Austen. a finer sense of language than many an acclaimed poet. Given other opportunities she might have been a great proficient at dirty talk—of the highest order. Still, we must not quarrel with what we have. Toronto is not behindhand in sin."

"But why only sexual sin?" said I. "Surely that's only a part, perhaps a small part, of what can be called sin."

"Oh quite. But it's the part most people want to hear about. Financial sin is awfully dull and to appreciate it demands a head for figures. Cruel, mind you, and disastrous for somebody, but undramatic unless there's a suicide at the end."

"Well, you certainly make my humbug research look small," said Jock. "You have established the local claim to good, run-of-the-mill sexual sin. The spirit of Ahriman is certainly felt here, at medium warmth, let us say. But has your bank a mortgage on a cucumber house, by any chance?"

"I don't know what you mean."

"Ah, well. I have told you that I spent some time in the French Navy, and indeed a few months just before I was recalled to England in 1914, in the Russian Navy. My Russian fellow-officers were very kind to me. Introduced me to their fiancées, and to their mistresses—very nice girls in both cases. I had had some experience with purchased pleasure in France, and indeed it was there that I discovered that a present of bon-bons often worked wonders with a *fille de joie* in one of the good houses. Her fee and a paper of *dragées* gave special zest to her performance. That was the reasoning that lay behind my humbug approach. The humbug is Toronto's answer to the Parisian bon-bon, don't you agree? But in St. Petersburg I met with something of which I had never dreamed. Ahriman was there, and in full power.

"One night after a mess dinner, when we were all in full dress, with fore-and-aft hats and swords and enough gold braid to keep the Stanislavsky factory working for a month, some of these young Russian aristocrats (or at least men of very good family) asked me if I would like to be introduced to a new game? An artillery game? Of course I would. So we went to a house in a quiet quarter, and very soon I found myself in a room decorated in that awful gilt and brocade style with my fellow sailors and a couple of girls, wearing only their stockings and shoes, who offered us champagne. We had already had plenty of champagne, so cognac was brought, and we had a good deal of that. Then came the artillery game. One of the girls stretched herself on a long table, while the other fetched a cucumber, and skilfully whittled it so that one half was a sharp point, and the other was in its natural green skin. Then the whittling girl thrust the point of the cucumber into the vagina of the girl who was lying on the sofa, with her legs spread and her knees raised, and everything was ready for the game.

"It appeared that this was a contest where we, each in turn, struck the reclining girl over the belly with the flat of our sword, and understandably she contracted at the blow and forced the cucumber out and across the room, where the other girl marked its place on the carpet with chalk, and the initials of the man who had struck. One by one we did this, and in the end the man whose blow had forced the cucumber farthest was declared the winner. His reward was that he had nothing to pay, and the rest of us had to stump up for the cognac and the contest. It came very high, let me tell you, and when I looked at the red belly of the girl who was the gun, so to speak, I felt that she had earned her money.

"Of course I have described it baldly, but as I have said, the spirit of Ahriman was in that room. The cigar smoke, the smell of spilled drink, the triumphant cry as each man scored his point was like nothing I have heard since, even in war. It was the laughter and chatter of hell. It was that night I became a Manichee. When we were about to leave, the leader of our party grabbed the girl who had been the gun, and kissed her heartily. I was just behind him and I saw the look in her eyes. It was not disgust, or degradation, or a sense of the brutality of what had gone on. It was simple acceptance of an evil destiny, and the look lasted only for an instant before it was replaced with the false gaiety of the purchased whore.

"That was an eye-opener to me, I can tell you. The scene recurs to me still, from time to time when people talk foolishly about sexual pleasure. For whom is it a pleasure? Who can ever say, for certain?"

"Tell me, Jock," said Darcy, and I was startled to see a hot look in his eye which I had never seen before. "Was there any blood on the girl's belly? Those swords must have been sharp."

"They were, but of course we struck with the flat of the blade. One or two of the company were not in complete command of themselves, and I think she was nicked in a couple of places. She was dabbing something on them as we left."

"How did you score, yourself?"

"Out of seven, I was third. Whatever game one plays, one plays to win, if one can."

Darcy had been drinking quite a lot of whisky. "I'll tell you a tale," he said; "something that happened in

Constantinople, before it became Istanbul, a few years ago." And he told a story about a bashaw or some such grandee, who wanted to amuse him, and offered a very nasty show involving a slave—there aren't supposed to be any slaves, but there are—and a donkey and a fine ripe fig. I would have believed it, perhaps, if I had not read the same story in Rabelais. Darcy's insistence on being wickeder than anybody else sometimes made him careless about such things. I think Jock had heard the story before, and under other circumstances, and he unkindly went to sleep as Darcy elaborated his tale of tyranny and indecency.

[13]

"YOU KNOW MY GODFATHER, Dr. Jonathan Hullah."

"We have known each other for years, Gil. Keeps an eye on my capricious lungs. You observe that I am respectful, and call him 'Doctor' as often as I can."

"And I suppose you know Hugh's stuff in the *Advocate*, Uncle Jon."

"Of course. I am a regular reader. And an admirer, may I say?"

"My God, what a mutual-admiration society we've uncovered, Gil," said Esme. "Don't you read my stuff, Uncle Jon?"

"I think I read more *about* you than *by* you, Esme. You've become a big noise in the feminist movement. And you haven't been to see me for—it must be two months."

"The series about *The Toronto That Was* is on the back burner for the time being," said Esme. "Gil's in charge. He thinks it's getting out of hand."

"I don't think anything of the sort," said Gil. "But it

is lurching toward being rather a stuffy series of reminiscences. We're a newspaper, after all, not the Dominion Archives."

"My fault, I expect," said Hugh McWearie. "Perhaps I tend to overestimate the curiosity and patience of our readers."

"That's your training on *The Scotsman*," said Gil.

"And that's why *The Scotsman* was fast going downhill," said Esme. "Had to be rescued and brightened up by a new owner. A Canadian, let me remind you."

"Who was it said that no newspaper ever went broke underestimating the intelligence of its readers?" said McWearie. "Wasn't it Mencken?"

"No longer true," said Gil. "Television has taken over the job of amusing the numbskulls. The press now has a higher purpose."

A wrangle ensued. Esme declared that Gil wanted to make the *Advocate* (or the part of it for which he was responsible, which was Arts and Books) too *New York Times*ish and nobody would stand for it. McWearie retorted by singing the praises of *The Manchester Guardian* as it was, distancing himself firmly from what it has become. Gil insisted that it was possible for a newspaper to be serious and popular and readable at once; it was simply a question of getting writers who could really *write*. I removed myself from the argument, as I knew nothing whatever about newspapers or what they might do, and thought about the people with whom I had been asked to a Saturday night supper. These people had no "Sunday nights"; they had a paper to produce for Monday.

Conor Gilmartin, my godson; child of my boyhood friend Brocky, now an honoured senior professor at Waverley and author of a handful of influential critical books about literature. Child of Brocky's wife Nuala, once the love of my life and now a regretted lost adored one, which is not so pitiful as it sounds, for every old man (and I am now, statistically and by government fiat, an old man) ought to have a regretted lost love; it goes with rims around the iris of the eyes, and hair in the ears. Child he may be of my loins, for although I have never as yet spoken of this to Nuala, it is a possibility; certainly he has my tall, rangy body, quite unlike the stocky Welsh pony build of his purported father; he even has my big nose. My son. Do I look on him with dimmed eyes, yearning to embrace him and claim him as my own? No, I don't. Things are very well as they are.

This apartment is his home with his fairly recently married wife Esme. It looks expensive, and it is expensively furnished in what I take to be chiefly Esme's taste. Everything is good but not distinguished. Such antique pieces as there are have the stamp of the fashionable antique shop on them; they come from the years between 1760 and 1820; they are small, delicate, fragile, not for use. The modern pieces have the no-nonsense air of their period, which is 1985, and are pleasant but not personal, like the staff in a good hotel. There is not a good picture in the place. Not, that is to say, a picture I would give house-room to myself. They are Canadian water-colours, in the three to four-hundred-dollar price range, and on the walls of blah colour they produce agreeable notes of blah. If there are any books they are in another room and, as Gil and Esme are both writers and he comes of a more than ordinarily literate background, there must be books somewhere. But it is not a pleasantly bookish dwelling. Why should it be? These are modern young, or youngish, people and I am an old codger with prehistoric ideas of what a son of mine should have about him.

It is the right setting for Esme. She is sufficiently

well-educated to want some pretty antiques, but not sufficiently well-educated to have any determined taste. The modern furniture reflects her spirit perfectly, for it is good, well-made, functional, and agreeably if conventionally designed, but it could belong to thousands of other young Toronto professional women without a stick or a scrap of upholstery being changed. The pictures are those of somebody who recognizes the need to have pictures that are "hand-done" but does not care a damn for pictures. The drinks and the food, however, are unexceptionable and Esme gets them on and off the table without the least fuss. There is no painful "daintiness" in evidence in the choice of foods or wine. She has good manners in the modern style: frank, no nonsense, but genuine care for what guests may want or need. A girl of a hundred good points (including good looks) and perhaps twenty bad ones and thirty more that might belong to anybody. I wish she would not call me Uncle Jon so often; she is not even an in-law and I feel the use of my name as an intrusion.

Why? Why have I a scunner against Esme that I try to fight down as unworthy and potentially mischievous? Why do I watch her, and listen to her, waiting to pounce on any unhappy phrase, any trivial solecism, any flaw? Is it because I know her parents to be humble people? If, that is, a well-run market garden in St. Catharines is humility in our egalitarian society. Have I, the boy from Sioux Lookout, become a Toronto snob? Horrible thought; why can't I treat her in my mind with the same sort of courtesy I extend to my patients? But I am sure my behaviour toward her is perfectly well-mannered. I tell myself that I am, like Dr. Samuel Johnson, well-bred to a point of needless scrupulosity.

As for Hugh McWearie, I was honest when I said I read his stuff in the *Advocate* regularly. He writes like a learned man who knows how to make his learning available to his readers without patronizing them. He writes about religion not as some journalists do, as a subject for derision, nor yet as if it deserved a kid-glove handling not accorded to science, or scholarship, or politics, or the arts; he has kept his head all through the Dead Sea Scrolls Donnybrook and he writes about fundamentalists as human beings and not as primitives deserving of pity and laughter. A first-rate journalist, in fact.

Time has done nothing to alter his appearance of chronic dyspepsia (he eats like a refugee just out of prison-camp) and his unpressed, food-spotted clothes, and his rag of a bow tie, and his scuffed shoes. But who cares? What if he does not appear to brush or wash his hair? Such thin hair does not command attention from its owner. What if his spectacles appear to have fallen into the mashed potato, and to have been imperfectly wiped? The splendid flow of his conversation, his range of ideas, his occasional new-minted phrases, his sly jokes, and his beautiful Edinburgh accent make everything else unimportant. This man is a talker to rejoice the heart of old Rhodri Gilmartin, and I am not surprised to find him a close friend of old Rhodri's grandson.

"Thank you, yes, a little more of the steak-and-kidney, Esme, if you please. Did you make it yourself? Ah, clever girl—not above domestic skills. More wine? Oh yes, I will certainly. A handsome Beaune, just the right thing to accompany the pie. We bachelors seldom dine in this degree of style, Gil. We envy you married men, don't we, Dr. Hullah?"

"Yes, yes; certainly we do."

"Don't cry a poor mouth, Hugh," said Gil. "You could dine like this every night in the week on the vast salary we pay you. So why don't you?"

"My inborn Caledonian frugality, my dear man. It

gives me positive pain to spend money on myself. It is something in the air of Scotland, I am convinced. I am an uncharacteristic Scot; my parents were very well set, because my father was a Chief Constable and had inherited some house property. A shrewd man. In childhood I had every reasonable comfort and no small degree of luxury. My education was on a very good level; I am proud to be one of the red gowns of St. Andrews. I found work without much trouble and I have always been well paid—though not, I assure you Dr. Hullah, on the scale of Sardanapalian profusion Gil pretends that the *Advocate* offers. No, mine has been a pampered life, compared with that of the legendary Scot. And yet—and yet I am as mean as the Devil and part with money as if it were not merely my blood but my marrow. I think it must be the air North of the Tweed. We pinch pennies as the Belgians eat horse-meat, because something in our genes requires it. Or am I speaking extravagantly?"

"It seems to be your one extravagance, Hugh," said Esme. "Help me carry out the plates and watch me complete the soufflé; my nose tells me the moment has come when it demands my whole attention."

"Willingly," said McWearie. He showed a gallantry toward Esme surprising in such a messy, dirty wee man.

I wish I could figure out why I do not quite like Esme. No; that's wrong. I like her well enough; I find her attractive sexually, which is unsuitable in a godfather but I might as well be honest about it, in this confidential record. But I don't fully trust her, and there again I cannot say why. Perhaps I fear that she will trick me into some confidence about that affair at St. Aidan's that I do not want to make public. And anything Esme knows will, sooner or later, be made public. She blabs to conquer.

The supper is excellent. A good clear soup before the steak-and-kidney, which was substantial without being disagreeably "hearty." Now we have a salad course while Esme is putting the finishing touches on her soufflé. And then the soufflé itself, which is perfection. Gil follows the Beaune with cognac, and the talk turns to the series, *The Toronto That Was*, which Gil was said to be delaying.

"As soon as Gil gives the word I'll be back to talk to you, Uncle Jon," says Esme.

"But why me, especially? I am no great expert on city history."

"We're not looking for history so much as atmosphere," said Gil. "This place has changed so dramatically in the past century. The almost colonial atmosphere of 1900 has virtually disappeared—"

"No, no," said McWearie. "It is still there, if you know where to look."

"Yes, but where do you look?" said Esme. "I know from what people tell me that social customs that used to be obligatory have wholly vanished. But what were they? People hum and haw and say they can't remember. Why can't they remember? It's everybody's bounden duty to remember as much as possible about everything that's come under their notice."

"I can recall two delightful elderly ladies who owned the last private horse-drawn carriage in Toronto," said I. "I think it was to be seen on the streets almost until 1930. I suppose the horses died. But I remember the Misses Mortimer-Clark saying to someone in my hearing that the Toronto they knew had utterly gone. Why, people had taken to locking their front doors when they went out! As if there might be intruders! And as if there were no servants to stop them, if by chance there should be."

"Aye, I have heard some queer tales myself," said

McWearie. "You know St. George Street? Full of decayed mansions that have become fraternity houses, and look like it? Well, somebody told me of a dinner-party he went to in one of those palaces of the plutocracy—though in fact it was the wife who had the dibs, and the husband was a clergyman and decidedly the second-in-command in that household—and my friend said it was a white-tie and spike-tailcoat affair, which had become rare in those days. It was 1925, I recollect. There were twenty guests, and they ate and drank of the best until the time came to serve the fruit and nuts, and then there was a wee tap on the door, and the hostess said, 'Come in,' and in came a wee girl in virgin white, and said, 'Mama, may I join you and your friends?' and Mama said, 'Of course, my dear; come and sit here by me.'

"And would you ever guess that this was a coming-out party? The poor little wretch had come out into society, d'you see! And there wasn't a soul in the room except herself under forty? Beat that if you can for a tribal ritual!"

"Hugh, you made that up!" said Esme.

"Not a bit of it! I'll send you a notarized transcript of that story tomorrow, if you insist."

"Golly!"

"All those old rituals have gone, and a very good thing too," said Gil.

"Not so," said McWearie. "The Hungarians still keep it up. A ball every year, where they present their daughters to the Lieutenant-Governor, which is the nearest they can get to royalty. But I believe it's falling off. Some of the girls are kicking over the traces."

"You see, Esme," said I, "Hugh is the man you should talk to about the Toronto that was. He knows far more about it than I do. I never had the entrée to these exalted circles of which he speaks so authoritatively."

"Ah, but you knew the artistic community," said Gil. "You knew the painters and especially the musicians. You used to meet them on Sunday nights at The Ladies. You told my parents about it."

"The Ladies? What Ladies are those?" said Esme. People are said, metaphorically, to "prick up their ears," and I swear I saw a stirring under Esme's hair which could have been nothing else.

"You've not heard of The Ladies?" said McWearie. "Oh, but you're a child, Esme. Hardly out of the egg. The Ladies were a very special feature of Toronto life, for God knows how long. And you were their tenant, were you not, Doctor? Your clinic was part of their property."

"I made an arrangement with them after the war," said I, and Esme laughed.

"You're showing your age, Uncle Jon. Have you any idea how many wars there have been since the one you're talking about? I suppose you mean the 1939-45 war?"

"When a man talks about The War he means the one in which he fought," said Gil. "Like my father. He had a peculiar war career; began in Intelligence, as an officer, and transferred to the Artillery because he wanted to see what the fighting was really like. And he found out. Oh yes, he found out."

"He found out enough to gain a Military Cross," said I. "But I know what you mean. It was quixotic—but your father always has been quixotic."

"You felt no inclination to follow him into the fray?" said Esme. Damned nosy girl!

"An Army doctor isn't exactly out of the fray," said Gil, who probably thought my feelings had been hurt. Did it ever occur to him that his wife had a crass streak? He was sensitive to language as she was not, and that can make a surprising difference in a marriage where both parties are writers.

"Didn't you go into the fighting right out of another kind of fighting?" said McWearie. "Darcy told me you had gone into—thrown yourself into, was his expression—some very rough medical work as soon as you qualified."

"I attached myself to the coroner's office," said I. "You remember how Darcy used to talk about the rough side of Toronto? I was curious about it."

"And that's what *I* want to uncover." Esme is a great interrupter. "The oddballs; the eccentrics. The other day an old woman in one of those Twilight Homes—I think she had been on The Game—may have been a Madam—told me there used to be a man who haunted Jarvis Street, offering the girls humbugs as payment for a lay. Can you imagine? Humbugs! The girls used to call him The Old Humbugger. Did you ever hear of him, Uncle Jon?"

"No," said I. "My Jarvis Street experience must have come later."

"Your experience? Uncle Jon, you old roué! What were you doing in Jarvis Street?"

"It was in the line of work," I said. "I had finished medical school and all the hospital work and interning and specialization, and other stuff that eats up so many years, and I thought I would like the experience of some rough work. I had done a spell in Emergency in a couple of hospitals. Saturday nights were revealing—"

"Revealing in what way?" said Esme, always the newshound.

"Crimes of passion, committed by people who usually had no words for their feelings, and took it out in action. Stabbings. Shootings. Sometimes murders. Sexual messes—"

"Like what?" Esme again.

"Like a Coke bottle stuck in somebody's rectum," said I. (She wanted it. Let her have it.) "I knew a man who invented a surgical instrument especially for their removal, and that tells you how frequent the need was. Like God knows what women had somehow got into those passages which are supposed to be of the uttermost delicacy! Like children who had been beaten up by drunken fathers—and drunken mothers too, often enough. Astonishing how people resent their young. Babies that had been treated like basketballs. Very instructive, Esme. You ought to sit in on Emergency for a few nights."

"Thanks for the tip," said Esme. "I might just do that. But why did you work for the coroner?"

"A coroner is a very busy man in a city like this. He needs a few people to go out to accidents with the police. I quickly learned how fragile the human body is, when it is subjected to the violence of some of the machines mankind has invented. When you've wandered around a roadside field in the dark for fifteen minutes, looking for a head, you get quite a different idea of the human body from what you learned in the dissecting-rooms and the anatomy classes. Or investigating a corpse that has been under the ice for the length of a hard winter. The prettiest girls quite lose their charm under those circumstances."

"So the idea of war had no terrors for you?" There was no fazing Esme. She was a modern girl, determined to be tough even if it meant being a little inhuman.

"On the contrary, my dear. Investigating an accident is not pretty work, but to expose yourself to becoming the raw material of an extremely nasty accident is frightening. And that is what war is. And I was frightened."

"But you went."

"I don't suppose anything I could say would convince

you how hard it would have been not to go. Public opinion has changed remarkably since 1939. The revulsion against war today is more powerful than I suppose it has ever been in human history. Nevertheless, I wouldn't be surprised that if a war broke out next month, all that anti-war talk would be stilled, and the old sides-taking instinct, the old killer instinct, the old find-an-enemy-and-beat-him-up instinct, would all come flooding back. In 1939 people still had a great undigested chunk of patriotism stuck in their craw. For a young man to stay out of the war would have taken even more courage than it did for me to get into it."

I had talked a good deal, and had perhaps put on the colour with a freer hand than my real feelings warranted. But I wanted to steer Esme away from talk of St. Aidan's and The Ladies, and I succeeded.

Not that I told Esme, or anybody else, the real reason why I enlisted in the Royal Canadian Army Medical Corps. It was to get away from my mother, or rather to get away from a fate she had planned for me, and in which she could see nothing but what was good for me and good for mankind. And of course good for her. Doc Ogg had died, and she wanted me to set up practice in Sioux Lookout.

Since my father's death during my third year of medical school (from pneumonia working on a growing boredom with iron pyrites) my mother had been lonely, and I had done whatever I could to help her, not stopping short of suggesting that she come to live in Toronto, though God knows I hoped she wouldn't. But Sioux Lookout had been her home for too long to make a change pleasant, and she could not see why I did not leap at the chance to establish a really modern medical practice—possibly even a modest clinic—in an area where there was now no doctor within fifty miles.

Money was not wanting. My father had left a great deal more than I thought he would and my mother, who was his sole heir, would have gladly set me up in style. But I didn't want to do it. My reasons were powerful, but not clearly defined. I admired her, and in my fashion I loved her, but I did not want to be tied to my mother's apron-strings. If my desire to marry Nuala became a reality, could I ask her to come to a backwoods practice? She was set on being a gynaecologist, and was doing well. I had my eye on more interesting work than my police and coroner's duties, though I was not yet sure in what direction it would lie. Explaining these things to my mother was not easy, and I had to be tactful when she felt no such obligation.

"If this girl you speak of has a true commitment to medicine, she would surely see the good sense of working in a deprived area where so many people, especially on the reserve, get no proper care at all."

Oh yes, she would see it, but that did not mean that she would throw herself into it. It is so easy to plan lives of humanitarian self-sacrifice for other people. And my mother could not be expected to understand that a young doctor, after something like ten years of hard work, wants to stay where there is money, as well as genuine need for medical care. Nor does such a desire mean that the young doctor is greedy or self-seeking—or at least not more so than the generality of mankind. Not everybody wants to be a saint.

There was no need for Esme or anybody else to know about that, so I simply said that I enlisted because everybody else seemed to be doing so.

I had no idea what to expect, and it was all rather easier and more pleasant for a few weeks than I had expected. As a doctor, I became a First Lieutenant right away, and was sent off to Camp Borden to be taught the rudiments of being a soldier.

For six weeks I beavered away at map-reading, marching smartly, and performing drill without a rifle, because doctors were not supposed to carry rifles or use them, although they were permitted to carry side-arms for self-defence. I learned how to look like a soldier (within reason, for I was never a "smart" officer) and how to salute and whom to salute, and how to behave when I was saluted by lesser fry. The open-air life and the unwonted exercise put me in good condition, and I was so hungry all the time that I was able to eat the dreadful food that seemed to be a part of Army life. I discovered later that the cook who prepared food for the Camp had a restaurant in the nearby town, and much of the best food that was meant for us was deflected to his restaurant kitchen. War encourages chicanery of all sorts, and in unexpected places. After I had been given this lick-and-a-promise experience of soldiering, I was promoted to the rank of Captain, and posted to a unit in Eastern Ontario, a territory beyond Salterton new to me.

It was here that I learned a few things that I had not expected to discover in the Army. The unit to which I was posted was a militia outfit, which had been fattened up by wartime enlistment. What this meant was that the privates were greenhorns, who had been workmen or farm workers, but the commissioned and non-commissioned officers were peace-time, part-time soldiers whose real occupation lay far from war or any serious Army life. The Colonel, for instance, had been the manager of a large bakery business, and what he really knew was cheap bread and confectionery. The Adjutant made a great show of military smartness, and was remorselessly jokey and cheerful; he had been the back-bone of a substantial insurance business in private life. The Major was a lawyer, of no great distinction. There was a considerable protestation of *esprit de corps*, pride in the regiment, tradition and so forth, but I would not have trusted it under any sort of stress. What became apparent quickly was that I was the most recently educated, and also the best-educated, man in the unit, and this gave me a special status.

I was the ear into which everybody's troubles were poured, and I was expected to advise and provide solutions to problems which I soon decided were insoluble.

This was not so with the privates. The Army is, and I think must be, a rigidly class-conscious organization and any attempt to make it democratic weakens its effectiveness. So I saw private soldiers, and non-commissioned officers, when they had managed to get themselves on a sick-list, which was not always easy, if the sergeant happened not to like them. Their complaints were run-of-the-mill stuff: a strain, a pulled tendon, a severe cold, fungus between the toes, constipation (a great favourite and, considering the food that was offered, inescapable), fear of having "picked up a nail" from some local prostitute when on leave, and more often than not the ills that arise from homesickness, displacement, worry about the fidelity of a wife, and simple fear. Fear arising from lost freedom; fear of what the future might hold; the fear that is looking for a cause, but exists without any apparent cause, and arises from the neurosis that is as common among enlisted men as among officers.

It was obligatory among these men to pretend to an unappeasable sexual desire. To go out for a few hours' leave without securing the prescribed issue of three condoms in a package would have been to confess to dread of sex with an unknown woman, of having no demanding sexual appetite or—and this would have been the subject of hilarity among the rougher men—fidelity to

the wife or the girlfriend at home. The idea of being a
soldier is a powerful archetype; take almost any man
and put him in the Army and the archetype of the
brutal and licentious soldiery will manifest itself and he
will behave in a way that perhaps surprises himself. I
later found out that this archetype manifests itself also
among the women who go into the armed services,
sometimes with peculiar results. The soldier-archetype
explains many things that are unaccountable in
wartime, and the idea of a brutal and licentious soldiery
is one that many men feel driven to make manifest.

It was the officers who took most of my time. Here
they were, men free from the restraints of home and
accustomed occupation, with unlimited access to a
medical adviser; they were determined to make the most
of it.

There were those with genuine problems, but I soon
discovered that most of these were inveterate and insoluble. A life which has resulted in painful feet, or a tricky
back, chronic headaches, a tendency toward severe
colds, a football knee, and indigestion in its myriad
forms, does not keep a man from becoming a militia
officer, but it is unlikely to make him a soldier that any
sensible commander would put in the field. I could do
no more for these men than their civilian doctors had
done already, but I was so readily accessible, so much a
companion in the mess, so much a part of what they
deserved for their decision to serve their country, that
they were sure I must succeed where others had failed,
and they came to me whenever I was in the little cubbyhole that was allotted to me for consultations and keeping records. I had an orderly to keep the records, but as
he was almost illiterate and naturally stupid I had to do
most of it myself.

My real work was with the neurotics, headed by the

Colonel. I had not yet faced the realization that every physician is, to some degree, a psychiatrist; his is the ear into which all woes are poured, and, although I dislike generalizations about humanity, it did seem to me during my first Army months, that the more stiff the upper lip, the more manly the bearing and the protestation when sex was discussed, the bigger the cry-baby who takes the patient's chair in the office of the Regimental Medical Officer.

The Colonel's trouble was booze, and as it was more freely available to the armed forces than to the civilian population (whom the Prime Minister, Mr. Mackenzie King, had urged to "put on the full armour of God," meanwhile reducing the alcohol content of all liquor sold in the country), the Colonel was in close touch with his bosom enemy. Why did he drink so much? It appeared to be because the big bakery of which he managed a branch was flirting with the idea of sale to a large American complex, and if that happened, what changes might not come about? Would he be kept in his position, or would he be supplanted by a younger man? And if that happened, where would he turn? He was tired of his marriage; his wife, a simple girl, had not kept pace with his rise in the social scale, and could not mix in perfect amity with the wives of other branch managers. She was a dumb-bell at bridge, and she had nothing to say at parties. Would the war settle any of his problems? He knew he would never be sent abroad; too old. Because he knew this, he convinced himself that he wanted nothing more than to plunge into the thick of battle, which he assumed would be the trench warfare of 1914-18. His life was a complexity of disappointments and worries and every Monday morning I had to do what I could to banish his hangover and still his fears.

The Adjutant's troubles were not dissimilar. His

insurance business was his own, in so far as any man's business is his own when he is obliged perpetually to show himself alert and a go-getter in the eyes of the giant companies which are his real masters. But he had built it up on his personality, which was, as he assured me I could see, that of a go-getter and a man fated for great achievement. He had left the business in the hands of his Number Two, who was a good fellow in his way, but lacked originality, was not innovative, was in fact just the sort of man a go-getter chooses for his Number Two because he presents no challenge. If the war were a long one, would the Number Two drive the business into the ground? Because in business there is no standing still; it's advance or fall back, all the time. And at home—well, he didn't know how it had come about, but it was just nag, nag, nag and gimme, gimme, gimme all the time and he had not himself had much money left over to buy the insurance he urged upon everybody else. If he had insufficient insurance, how was his retirement to be financed? Could I tell him that? Which of course I couldn't. I had no medicine for him and he had to fall back on the bottle, which was the only medicine both of us knew for what ailed him.

The Major was a relief, though not much of a relief, from these problems. His destiny lay, he was certain, in politics. He was a lawyer, and everybody knew that the law was the best preparation for a political life. He was well in with the Party, and it was only a matter of waiting for the next election for him to become a candidate for a pretty safe seat. Then along came this God-damned war, and if an election came soon, which was likely, where was he? He couldn't stand for Parliament and wear a uniform at the same time, and he saw no way of getting rid of the uniform unless I could declare that he was unfit for service. Wasn't there something he was likely to have which would manage that, without making him too unwell to face the duties of a Member of Parliament? Suppose—just suppose—he got shot in the leg during target practice, would that do it? Not easy to manage, of course; a man who gets himself between the target and the gun looks like a loser, and does anybody vote for a loser? Or was there some way he could be a militia officer at home and an efficient M.P.? Meanwhile he had headaches of an intensity that I would certainly never have encountered in my medical practice and they had him worried. Was there any way I could take a look at his brain, without a lot of X-ray and stuff that would attract undesirable attention? God, if it turned out to be a brain tumour! The only way he could get any relief from worry was by heavy drinking. I had nothing for him.

There were other officers who were perfectly sane and reasonably happy in their work, but these three at the top of the heap kept me busy at the physician's perpetual work of reassurance. Nothing is ever quite as bad as it looks, etc. I acquired a reprehensible conviction that heavy drinking was not under all circumstances a bad thing.

After that, my war experience, though extensive, was uninteresting. Whether I was bounced around from one place in Europe to another more than most medical officers I cannot say because I have not wanted to find out. But wherever I went, my work was the same, sometimes very close to danger, sometimes actually under fire, sometimes behind the guns, working in hospitals that varied from pretty well-equipped establishments that were not totally in ruins, to field hospitals where a lot of improvisation was needed. I had to do some surgery, at times when everybody who could handle a knife was needed, and there were days when I stood for ten or twelve hours with a knife in my hand, driven to make decisions about what to do in situations that called for facilities that simply did not exist where I was. I was a mediocre surgeon and had little taste for the work.

Where I shone (I suppose in the privacy of this Case Book I can tell myself that I shone) was in diagnosis and the care of men after hospital, when they had to be cajoled, or bullied, or hypnotized into a state of mind in which they could be sent back to the lines. I became the Talking Doctor, and anyone who thinks that talking under such circumstances is easy work should try it and find out the reality. Through Italy, in that dirty and difficult campaign beginning in Sicily and up The Boot all the way to the Lombard Plain I talked without cease, and inevitably developed some persuasive skill. How did I do that?

Doctors are men of substantial education, though not always men of wide culture. They develop a manner, and a vocabulary suitable to their professional status, which is sufficient in civilian life, and which is often reassuring to the uneducated patient. But sick men, and wounded men who have been patched up, who are in a strange land and often in uncomfortable and disagreeable conditions, need another kind of talk. They need a talk which is not obviously professional, and which is not couched in language that is filled with scientific terms. Friendly talk. Not patronizing talk, and not foolishly simple talk, but talk that inspires trust in men whose trust in life has been worn very thin. Talk which can reach men who have been driven to that farthest edge of the spirit we call despair. Talk that persuades a man from the prairies that as he lies in an Italian villa which is a temporary hospital, and where at every turn he comes on evidences of a Catholicism he associates with everything deceitful and morally inferior, that he has not been utterly deserted by his God, or whatever he holds as the engine of his life.

Of course the chaplains were supposed to do this, but to many of the men the chaplain was somebody with something to sell, a Holy Joe who wanted to win souls for Christ, or whatever. Some of the chaplains were first-rate. Others should have been sent home to do their mischief in civilian life. But none of them were doctors, and it was in Italy, as an Army doctor, that I first understood that the physician is the priest of our modern, secular world. The Medical Corps insignia on my sleeve promised a magic that the chaplain's Cross had lost.

It was early in 1945 that the Italian campaign ended, in so far as the Canadian Army was concerned, and we were returned to England, to await events. It was whispered—where do these whispers originate?—that we would soon get into the show in Europe. Meanwhile, reforming and reorganization and retraining under circumstances which seemed easy after the Italian battles. And first of all, some leave.

I spent my leave in London, going to the theatre and eating as well as I could in restaurants that had some—never very much—black-market food of a kind I had not eaten in over a year. I stayed at a small hotel in Russell Square, where on the night of May 2, 1945, a German bomb that had buried itself nearby without exploding, exploded at last, and my hotel suffered heavy damage. I was taking a bath at the time.

It was one of those hotels where the baths were not attached to each room, but in the old-fashioned way were at the ends of corridors. To get the use of a bathroom required some campaigning, and the hot water ran out quickly. I had been lucky and was lying in a suitably hot bath when the explosion occurred.

I cannot say precisely what happened, but it appeared

from what I later learned that the floor of my bathroom sank a few feet, and the ceiling above collapsed inward. A mass of plaster and structural wood fell on the bath, and I was lucky not to have been killed by it. As it was, I found myself imprisoned in the tub, with enough of the rubbish above me open to the sky to assure me of air, though I was unable to move except gingerly in my bath-water, which quickly began to cool.

There I remained for rather more than four days.

I could hear the workers who were trying to bring some order into the chaos of the hotel, and to remove people who had been injured, or killed. But the hotel was not the most important building to suffer damage, and the work was slow. I could hear voices, and when I did so I shouted, but was not heard.

As a medical man I knew that starvation was not imminent, but that unless I could have water, I would not last for as long as it might take for me to be discovered, or for the wreckage under me to collapse and dash me down into—what? I had water, but it was soapy water, and dirty water, and it soon became very cold water.

Late in the second day I could no longer repress a bowel movement, and my water became a cold faecal soup, of which I could not force myself to drink.

This was very bad, for if starvation was not an immediate concern, lack of water was. A physician in such a situation knows too much for his own good, and I suffered horribly from things foreseen which did not come to pass. Would I become so cold that I could not survive? If the temperature in the English spring dropped much below 50 degrees Fahrenheit I would be in serious danger. I could breathe freely, and move my legs and arms to some extent so that clotting of blood could be avoided, but it was hard to call up the will to move as much as I knew to be necessary, because as time wore on I suffered from lassitude and progressive weakness. I shivered a great deal, but this helped to maintain my bodily heat. Hunger was a torment, and I could not long keep my mind off food. After the second day my hands, my lower legs and feet began to swell. I knew perfectly well that I was *not* developing the waxy skin coating that I had so often seen in my days as a police physician on the bodies of drowned men and women, but nevertheless I feared it, and felt my body for it, and wondered if I were not indeed experiencing a novel form of drowning, while fully conscious.

But I was not fully conscious. I began to drop off to sleep at intervals, and then to recover myself with a start, recognizing the dangers of such lassitude. I thought of all I had read about courageous people who, when trapped in some situation like mine, passed the time working out problems, or composing poems, or reciting verse they had by heart. Ah—heroes every one of them, but my best efforts could not lift me to their level.

I knew the danger of despair, and fought it as hard as I could, but not with complete success. Once or twice I heard scramblings that I supposed must be rats, and all that I had ever read about prisoners plagued by filthy rodents recurred to torment me, for I knew I was weakening hourly, and had to give up shouting, for the feebleness of my own cries mocked me, and made me feel more helpless.

I thought of my totem, as Mrs. Smoke had shown it to me. But my intertwining snakes had not then assumed the strength in my psychological makeup that they were to attain later, and they did nothing for me. I thought of *Faust*, which was still fresh in my memory, but it had nothing to suggest except the inevitability of Fate, and when one's thread of life seems about to be clipped by the shears of unblinking Atropos, it demands a sturdier mind than mine to face it with courage. I remembered Mrs. Smoke and the Shaking Tent, and I longed to go into the Great Time and find help there. But how? It was in these dark hours that I knew that I needed a faith greater than the half-baked philosophy of my student days, if I were not to succumb under misfortune like this into a whimpering, ignoble creature, contemptible to myself.

Even modern warfare had not killed in me the idea that man is a noble creature, and should behave nobly under necessity. Of course in ordinary life one does not use highly charged, emotive words like "noble." Superior people laugh at such talk. But when one seems to be dying in an icy bath of one's own shit, one sees things differently, and resolves that if one escapes alive, one will never be a superior person again.

Superior? How could I be superior when my mind was invaded by rubbish from the past, and obscenities from student days? I tried to pass the time by recalling mnemonics which had helped to get me through my medical examinations, but for so many the "clean" form gave way to the form preferred by young men in excellent health whose instruction in science and medicine had done nothing to quench their natural lusts—did, indeed, encourage them.

Consider, for instance, the Twelve Cranial Nerves of the brainstem:

I	Olfactory	On	Oh!
II	Optic	Old	Oh!
III	Oculomotor	Olympus'	Oh!
IV	Trochlear	Towering	To
V	Trigeminal	Tops	Touch
VI	Aboucens	A	And

VII	Facial	Finn	Feel
VIII	Acoustic	And	A
IX	Glossopharyngeal	German	Girl's
X	Vagus	Viewed	Vagina
XI	Accessory	Some	And
XII	Hypoglossal	Hops	Hymen!

No, I could not be resolutely high-minded, and I now think that to do so would be inhuman.

Four nights and four days passed before I heard workmen near enough to hear my voice, which had become surprisingly feeble. At last I was fished out of my tank, and carried off to a hospital.

I was uninjured. Indeed, I had been all through the Italian campaign without injury, though many Medical Corps people were hurt or killed. Of course I was almost ten pounds lighter, I was dehydrated, I had some pitting oedema, the localized dropsy to be expected, and a few pressure sores. All things considered I had not come off too badly, for I was young and strong. But though physically I recovered in about ten days, I was in a bad mental state, and that recovery was slow. I had passed my time in the tank in fear, in something not like sleep but a kind of lowered consciousness, and in futile attempts to lift my spirits and shout for help. But I had what I must call a revelation in that tub and very slowly I came to some conclusions that have been important in shaping my life ever since.

As I look back at what I have written, I ask myself if I am being quite honest? Did I receive no help from anything greater than the hope that the workers outside would find me? Did I not, when the patch of sky that I could see above me turned black, think of Mrs. Smoke and her helpers? Did I not remember that in *Faust* Mephistopheles says:

Dies sind die Kleinen
Von den Meinen
Hore, wie zu Lust und taten
Altklug sie raten.

Are not these the Devil's helpers? And once Christian judgements are set aside, how does one know Mrs. Smoke's from the Devil's? Any helper, when one is in extremity, is a helper. If, as Faust says, the Devil is an egoist, who isn't an egoist when it comes to the crunch? Did I not plead, as I lay in that icy, filthy water, for Helpers, no matter whence they took their power? Were they wholly deaf? Was I not discovered in time? But my recollection is not clear.

When at last I was pronounced fit to leave hospital, where was I to go? The great ones of the Canadian Army Medical Corps were very decent in their behaviour towards me. They sent me to a hospital near Oxford, for some sensitive work that they thought I might be able to handle, or if I couldn't I could do my best.

It was sensitive work indeed. I found myself in charge of a ward of twenty-six men who had all been wounded in what has since been sardonically named "friendly fire." That is to say, they were Canadians who had been wounded by other Canadians who had misjudged their range, or their terrain, and had launched bombs, or shells or grenades, or had placed mines in circumstances where the casualties were—again the lingo is sardonic—"fratricidal." It has always been so in war, since firepower replaced the bow and arrow. Though perhaps the bow and arrow was not wholly blameless, for there were several reports of officers or sergeants who had been shot by their own men when the press of battle made it hard to know precisely what was happening, and I am sure that officers who were brutal or just intolerable fell at Crécy with "friendly" arrows between their shoulders.

Several of these men were legless, or had lost an arm, or now had a plate in the skull. The remainder were in various stages of what used to be called "shell-shock." All were in bad psychological condition and many were of the group dismissed by the unthinking as "bed-wetters." What was I to do?

I talked, of course. I saw every man for an hour or a part of an hour three times a week. When I say I talked it would be more accurate to say that they talked, for their cauldrons of resentment and fury against fate, against the Army, against anything and everything were seemingly inexhaustible, and they raged and stormed and often they wept, because they had been injured by their own people. Stupid bastards, why couldn't they watch what they were doing? (*Because they were far out of sight, far behind the area which their comrades had reached, but of which they had not been informed.*) Is this what it meant, when you sacrificed everything to come over and fight to defend a bunch of God-damned foreigners against a fate that was probably too good for them? (*Yes, this is part of what it meant, and the outbursts of self-righteousness sat ill on some of these men who had enlisted for very different reasons than those of patriotism or humanitarianism.*) Was this what it came to when you weren't twenty-five yet, and you had another fifty years to go with no legs? What kind of job was there for you? What was the girlfriend going to think when you came back in a wheelchair? She was going to think Goodbye, nice to have known you. Was this all there was in life for you now? (*Yes, in all likelihood this is all, unless you are the one in a thousand who can find a way of turning misfortune into benefit.*) With this plate in my head I get hellish headaches, and the docs don't seem to be able to do anything about it. When I get home, what am I going to do? (*If I knew, I would certainly tell you.*)

Indeed, this was sensitive work. But already I knew enough about my job to know that I was doing something just by listening and accepting whatever role the rage of these men imposed on me. I was the stupid artillery. I was the ungrateful Europe that took the best of a man's life and gave nothing in return. I was the girl-friend who did not want a crippled husband. I was the doc who couldn't solve an insoluble problem. Little by little the men, or most of them, quieted down, and though their troubles were no less, they were borne with a better courage. And slowly it became apparent that this rage, this disillusion, this disappointment was not what it seemed. It was the duct through which flowed an unhappiness and a pathos that lay at the very bottom of the spirit, and might perhaps be inborn, or, to use a more scientific and fashionable word, it was genetic. Something had to be done, and I cudgelled my brain to find out what it might be.

The large hospital camp, of which my unfortunates made a part, was near Oxford, and whenever I could get away—which was not very often—I bicycled into Oxford and refreshed myself in its excellent bookshops. It was in one of these—in Blackwell's indeed, and if the shop had not been substantially remodelled since, I could identify the very place where I stood—it was there that I had my Good Idea.

I was re-establishing my little library. I had carried a few books with me through Italy; my medical kit made it possible to disguise them because we were not supposed to have books, diaries, or anything that would possibly convey information to the enemy. But several men had books. The copy of Browne's *Religio Medici* that Charlie had given me, my three-volume Everyman edition of Robert Burton's *Anatomy of Melancholy*, and *The Oxford Book of English Verse*; these had disappeared in the bombing of the hotel. I had chosen these because they would last; they were books that could be read and reread and read again. I particularly valued crusty old Burton. Sir William Osler, my hero among medical men, had called it the greatest medical treatise written by a layman. This was because it was rooted in deep scholarship and unresting curiosity, not because it was especially scientific. Burton wrote about melancholy, he said, to dispel his own melancholy, but I don't think he can have been a serious melancholic. Such humour as his does not accord with the depression that edges toward despair. These books I had easily replaced, and I was gathering as many others as I thought I could carry in my luggage, or have shipped home across the still perilous Atlantic. But suddenly, there in Blackwell's, in the poetry section, I saw the book which for a while I called *The Golden Trashery*, until I gained too much respect for it to deny it the name of *Treasury*. It was called *The Reciter's Companion* and the title page promised that it contained pieces suitable for recitation on all occasions.

It brought into focus a notion I had been pondering for some time: what could be done to take my patients' minds off the grievance which was devouring them? The hospital had occasional visits from ENSA groups who did plays and variety shows to entertain the men, but their effect was fleeting. The men were distracted for a couple of hours, but they were not left with anything to think about, or talk about. If I were to read to them, not a novel, but something short enough to be contained within an hour, and which they could then talk about as long as they chose, would it be entertainment that lasted longer, and perhaps aroused something deeper than ENSA?

Poetry was what I wanted. But it would be patronizing lunacy to read to these men out of my *Oxford Book of English Verse*. Not to be patronizing was the secret. Not to appear to be dispensing education or "culture." Of my twenty-six patients only three had completed a High School education, and they were no advertisements for the system. I needed poetry, or better call it verse, that would catch the ear, stick in the memory, and tell a story. Bardic poetry, indeed, but not on the Gothick, Walter Scott level. A quick look through *The Reciter's Companion* showed that it was just what I needed.

So I initiated my Reading Hour. I told Corporal George that if any of the men thought they would like to hear me read, I would be in the ward at eight o'clock. Nobody who did not want to listen was under any compulsion to join the group. Corporal George was the acknowledged spokesman and leader of the ward, and he was a man with some ability as an organizer. The first night there were eighteen of the men at one end of the ward to hear me. After three nights the whole twenty-six had joined the group, and I had strong intimations of success.

My experience in the Players' Guild stood me in good stead. I could read, loud and clear, and what I read seemed to fill the bill with these men; I don't suppose any of them had heard verse read in their lives, and it was an astonishment to them.

The Reciter's Companion was aimed at just such an audience as this. I had never heard a reciter, myself, but my parents had spoken of such people with laughter; they were a terror of social life that had just been fading from view when they were young. There was the lady reciter, who imitated children and sometimes attempted a "serious" piece about Spring, or the death of a child. There was the male reciter, who was under the spell of

Henry Irving, whom he had never seen but of whom he had heard misleading stories; he recited pieces about murder and remorse, or perhaps some heroic deed like that of Grace Darling, the Light-house Keeper's Daughter. And of course there was the comic reciter, who raised gales of laughter with "How Father Papered the Parlour." But all three reciters might, if encouraged, sink themselves deep in pathos, and assault the heartstrings. I decided to go for the heartstrings, first.

When I told the men that I was going to read some verse they looked sceptical, but when I said that I would lead off with "Christmas Day In The Workhouse" they went off into fits of laughter. Everybody knew some parody of the poem, and there were roars of—

> "I wish you a Merry Christmas," said he;
> The paupers answered BALLS.

"Yes," said I; "that's what people remember now, but let me read you the original poem." And I suppose because I was an officer, and not unpopular in the ward, they quieted down and I began:

> It is Christmas Day in the Workhouse
> And the cold bare walls are bright
> With garlands of green and holly
> And the place is a pleasant sight.

And so on, as the thankful paupers receive their Christmas pudding—pudding which is provided on the rates, be it known—until there is an interruption—

> But one of the old men mutters,
> And pushes his plate aside:
> "Great God!" he cries; "but it chokes me!

For this is the day she died."

Gradually the story unfolds: the Christmas before, the wretched man's wife lay at death's door, and he had gone to the workhouse to beg for bread. He was turned away; the house offered no "out relief"; if the woman was in trouble, she must come to the house as a professed pauper, and take what the parish had to give. But the man and his wife were proud. Not the hated workhouse. No! He is tempted to steal, but his better nature intervenes and he returns to his miserable lodgings, to hear his wife cry—

> *"Give me a crust—I'm famished—*
> *For the love of God!" she groaned.*

Beside himself with grief he rushes back to the workhouse gate, crying, "Food for a dying woman!" but the answer comes, "Too late." The husband sees a dog eating a crust in the street; he wrestles with the animal, seizes the crust and returns to his wife—

> *My heart sank down on the threshold*
> *And I paused with a sudden thrill*
> *For there in the silv'ry moonlight*
> *My Nance lay, cold and still.*

His heart is torn; Nance died *alone.* Yes, there in a land of plenty lay a loving woman dead; cruelly starved and murdered for a loaf of the parish bread.

> *"At yonder gate, last Christmas*
> *I craved for a human life,*
> *You, who would feed us paupers,*
> *What of my murdered WIFE?"*

The man who has been brought down to accepting parish charity has a strain of magnanimity. He concludes:

> *"There, get you gone to your dinners;*
> *Don't mind me in the least;*
> *Think of the happy paupers*
> *Eating your Christmas feast;*
>
> *And when you recount their blessings*
> *In your smug parochial way*
> *Say what you did for me, too,*
> *Only last Christmas day."*

I gave it everything I had. My voice, which Darcy Dwyer had helped me to make firm and resonant, laid on the pathos firmly, but not with disgusting unction. It was—no getting away from it—it was a *wow*. The men clapped, some laughed, some murmured, and one or two of them seemed to be dashing aside a tear. The grim old story had hit the mark.

Had anybody anything to say? I asked. Nobody wanted to comment. But all the week that followed, in their private sessions with me, the men spoke about the poem. It was crap, of course, old stuff that nobody pays any attention to nowadays. You couldn't get away with anything like that on the radio. But God, nobody understood what a Raw Deal you got when you were hard up. Go to a bank? Don't make me laugh. Ask the boss for an advance? That'd be the first step to getting laid off. No use talking to the union; they weren't in the money-lending business and they were quick to say so. The kids demanding more and more. What gets into kids nowadays, when they have to have a quarter here, fifty cents there, all the time, and as like as not it was for something at school. If they didn't have the money like the other kids, they felt cheap and out of everything. And the wife: always complaining, never had been much of a cook, wouldn't let you have your rights in bed for fear of another young one. Christ! sometimes you just wanted to drop the whole bundle and get out. At least in the Army the wife's allowance was regular, but God, it was miserable. Ask a man to fight for what we get? Lose an arm or a couple of legs and what kind of a pension would there be? What chance has a fellow like me got, Doc? Here I am twenty-six and where am I going?

I did not harrow the men every night, but I quickly found that the verses about pathetic situations—and especially those about merit which was overlooked, or injustice nobly borne—were the favourites, and repeats were demanded. I did not scorn the patriotic string. They liked Robert W. Service. Pauline Johnson's *Canadian Born* went very well:

> *I first saw light in Canada,*
> *The land beloved of God—*

and the odd bit of Gothick thrill was much relished; of this genre Poe's "The Raven" was the favourite, but there was strong approval of Southey's "Bishop Hatto and the Rats"; it was about a wicked bishop who, when his poor neighbours pleaded with him for corn, coaxed them into a barn and burned them; they were rats, you see, who consumed the corn—or so the Bishop said; but when a thousand rats pursued him he shut himself in his tower, where the rats found him—

> *They have whetted their teeth against the stones,*
> *And now they pick the Bishop's bones,*

> *They gnawed the flesh from every limb,*
> *For they were sent to do judgement on him!*

Strong stuff. Poetic Justice, and the very thing to evoke the deep, inveterate feelings of grievance in these men, who had suffered wrong—wrong that was nobody's fault, because a surprising amount of wrong *is* nobody's fault, or certainly not the fault of anybody who can be identified.

Saturday night was "funny" night, when I read something to make the men laugh. Things went so well that one night I ventured to read Chaucer's "Miller's Tale" in a modern translation. It went, as we used to say in the Players' Guild, like a bird. The best bit of all was, understandably—

> *"Alas!" said Absolon. "I knew it well*
> *True love is always mocked and girded at*
> *So kiss me, if you can't do more than that*
> *For Jesus love and for the love of me!"*
> *"And if I do, will you be off?" said she*
> *"Promise you, darling," answered Absolon.*
> *"Get ready then; wait, I'll put something on."*

• • •

> *She flung the window open then in haste*
> *And said "Have done, come on, no time to waste,*
> *The neighbours here are always on the spy."*
> *Absolon started wiping his mouth dry.*
> *Dark was the night as pitch, as black as coal,*
> *And at the window she put out her hole,*
> *And Absolon, so fortune framed the farce,*
> *Put up his mouth and kissed her naked arse,*
> *Most savourously before he knew of this,*

And back he started, something was amiss;
For well he knew a woman hath no beard,
Yet something rough and hairy had appeared.
"What have I done?" he said. "Can that be you?"
"Teehee!" she cried, and clapped the window to.

If it is true that Chaucer read his *Canterbury Tales* aloud to his patron, King Richard the Second, I am sure that the King rolled right off his throne at that one; but he cannot have been more delighted than these Canadian Soldiers of the King five hundred years later. Chaucer was every bit as good as George R. Sims. Pretty raw, mind you. Who would expect an educated guy like the Doc to come out with a Raw One like that? You never know, eh?

The laughter roused by Chaucer was heard in high places, and on Monday morning I was summoned by the head of the hospital.

"I hear great things about what you are doing in Ward J," said he. "Could you just fill me in on what the program is?"

"I suppose in the end it boils down to this. I listen to them talk. It helps them to get things off their chest."

"I've heard about that. And you read to them. That's novel. In fact, I've never heard of such a thing before. But there are one or two disturbing rumours—nothing serious, you know, but still rumours—that you are reading some rather inflammatory stuff."

"Not a bit. Quite old stuff, as a matter of fact."

"Yes, but grievance stuff. About the government not doing enough in the way of social service. That kind of stuff."

"Grievance is what's at the root of a lot of their trouble, Doctor. Not grievance against the government, or the Army, particularly, but just a general sense of not having had a square deal from life. They get it off their chests, and their rate of recovery is improved. I can show it from my records."

"Sounds like Freud."

"Oh no, nothing as profound as that."

"Not psychoanalysis?"

"Nothing so profound."

"That wouldn't do in the Army."

"Of course not."

"Somebody hinted you were using hypnosis."

"Not now. Not after the first week. The men didn't like it. I suppose they had the usual notion that it gave me some uncanny power over them."

"Silly, of course. But perhaps unwise, with patients who aren't in a position to reject your treatment. It seems one of your men said something to somebody, who said it to somebody else, that you did use a form of hypnosis. He said he was aware of it when he had his session with you."

"I think I know the man you mean. Unusually suggestible. But I don't, you know. I just sit very still and say as little as possible. I suppose the effect may seem hypnotic to someone who has never been listened to, has never had anybody's whole attention, perhaps ever before."

"Yes. Well, don't think I'm interfering. Your results are good. Surprising, in fact. But go easy on any socialist stuff. That won't do in the Army."

Socialist stuff? I suppose to the ear of some medical colleague, like that nincompoop Norton, down the hall from Ward J, whose mind never ventured outside his medical training, "Christmas Day In The Workhouse" might have had a socialist ring. But I was an unpolitical creature, and all I knew of socialism suggested that it might very well serve as a vessel into which to pour the undifferentiated sense of grievance, the feeling of having had a Raw Deal, which was so prevalent I began to think it might be significant when a medical diagnosis was called for.

I had, indeed, found the direction in which my later medical practice was to go.

•   •   •

I had given the essence, but not the whole, of my war story to the party of Esme, Gil, and McWearie. I think I had been talking for some time and when I stopped, they were silent.

"I've never heard you talk so frankly about yourself, Uncle Jon," said Gil.

"It's your excellent Beaune, Gil. It loosens the tongue. And I am getting old, you know. We old men are garrulous."

"All that about the underlying Raw Deal," said Esme. "Of course it's true. Is it your very own?"

"Great God, no!" said McWearie. "Old as time. Anyway, as old as literature. Hinc illae lacrimae—"

"Wait!" said Esme. "Alms for the ignorant poor! What did you say?"

"'Hence the tears shed.' It's old Terence. And Wordsworth: 'The still, sad music of humanity.' Old stuff to poets, but of course brand-new to science, which is always behind literature."

"And old Burton," said I. "'If there is a hell upon earth, it is to be found in a melancholy man's heart.'"

"And that's what you've founded your medical practice on?" said Esme.

"Within the limits of reason."

"You understand now why they called him The Cunning Man," said McWearie.

"Who called him that?"

"The Ladies."

Damn! Now that cat is out of the bag. I had hoped Esme would not find out about The Ladies. But—

"I must know about The Ladies," she said.

III

Glebe House

Cockcroft Street
Toronto, Ontario
Canada

Dearest Barbara:

So long since I have written, what with one thing and another and knowing you were so tied up in the divorce business, that I don't know where to begin. As you see, we now have a permanent address (and proper paper, isn't it *smart*, done by a little man, Mr. Russell, quite close by) having taken the plunge and bought this place, which is a leap in the dark I can tell you. But everything else we tried was utterly impossible, with no place where Dear One could work with peace of mind and the space she needs. Of course I can do my scratchings anywhere (almost) but she must have space and quiet and decent light. And this place gives all of that, because the huge old conservatory is just right for a sculptor,[1] and in the winter oil stoves will keep her from freezing. But it has almost cleared us out of the ready, and neither of us is earning enough to stick in your eye.

It is called Glebe House because it stands beside

St. Aidan's Church and I suppose it was once glebe land. The builder was an Archdeacon Cockcroft who must have been one of those nineteenth-century loonies who wanted to move as much as he could of England to this extremely un-English country, so he built St. Aidan's with his own money (very Pugin in style and not at all a bad job) and built this house beside it, with a biggish garden between, which I gather he must have meant as a graveyard and there are a half-dozen tombstones in it. But the house! My dear, he must have had at least five indoor servants and the rooms are vast and draughty and we can only furnish in the sparsest way and lots of bedrooms are empty.[2] No central heating which is obligatory in this country, and we depend on stoves and fireplaces and the lugging of coal and wood you'd never believe! And behind it a huge stable block, with a tower with a clock in it and room for a cavalry regiment to stable their horses, and God be praised! this stable has been our salvation!

How? We have a tenant, a doctor who wants premises and he is prepared to do over the stables to suit his needs. And believe me, old dear, I think I have skinned the doctor good and proper, asking a *huge* rent and an agreement that if either of us is discontented with the bargain, any improvements he makes remain *our* property and he can claim *no* recompense. And he is spending a *fortune*! I don't quite know what is going into it because I don't actually like to snoop, but I know central heat, and quite a few new windows, very tactfully arranged in the Pugin style that embraces the church, house, and of course stables. Are we *Gothic*? Don't ask, as the knowing ones say around here. The glory that Archdeacon Cockcroft wanted has arrived at last. He built this whole shebang when it was still outside Toronto, hoping a parish would spring up around it, and now the city has completely enclosed it, and a very decent middle-class district surrounds us, though not really any people we want to know. Worthy, but dull, if you know what I mean (and I know you do).

The doctor is a bit of a puzzle. Long and cornery and quiet and looks like a horse with a secret sorrow.[3] Agrees with practically anything I suggest, and appears to have pots of money. Don't know what to make of him yet. Not our sort, I shouldn't think. Will have to see his pictures before we know and it will be a while before he is settled in. Meanwhile I get a lot of fun out of taking a rise out of him now and then. When first he came to ask about the stables he stood on the mat and said very politely, "Miss Raven-Hart, I presume?" rather like Stanley meeting Livingstone in the jungle. "No," sez I, "Miss Raven-Hart is working and can't be disturbed. I'm Miss Freake." You often hear about people not batting an eyelash, but he certainly batted one at that, as people always do. "Ah, yes, Miss Freake, ah—" and he seemed gravelled for lack of matter. "Don't be surprised," sez I, "Freake is a very old English name; means warrior, or hero. I'm very proud to be a Freake."[4] Having enjoyed his discomfiture, I kept it up for a while before admitting that Freake is just a Christian name, from Mummy's family—who were certainly all Freakes, whichever way you like to take it.

So there you have it. We are settled at last, until we are able to return home, which won't be until all the parents and more intractable family members are dead. I suppose our sudden departure *was* a bit of a scandal, but to use words like "bolting" and "elopement" was ridiculous and worst of all was Papa Raven-Hart's lament about having finally wangled it so that Dear One's photograph would appear in *Country Life*. Can't you see it?—"Miss Emily Raven-Hart of Colney Abbey, Bucks, will shortly be married to Captain Augustus Gryll of the Life Guards, son and heir of Sir Hamilton Gryll and the Hon. Maude Gryll of The Bossages, Hamer, Wilts." What a sweet linking of nonentities on both sides (excepting Dear One, of course) and what a prospect of a life tied to Gussie Gryll, the biggest drunk and whoremaster in the Guards. We did *right* to make a run for it, and if the Raven-Harts cut her off with the equivalent of a shilling (£150 p.a.) I at least had some money in my own right, though not a lot. Can you imagine that not one of those beasts has even *tried* to find out where we are—not that we're anxious to resume *relations* (ha,ha). So once we have established ourselves as artists in this cold country— which seems to need artists very badly—we shall be all right. But the past three years have not been easy. Still—mustn't grumble as that old cleaner at the Slade was always saying.

And that's it for the moment, just to bring you up to date, and if by chance you *do* want to set up a correspondence, Barkis is willin' *and more than that.*[5]

> Dear love from us both and dying to hear how everything works out—
>
> CHIPS

[2]

OH, ROBERT BURNS! I have never been one of your besotted admirers, but every now and then you hit the nail resoundingly on the head.

> *O wad some Pow'r the giftie gie us*
> *To see oursels as others see us!*

Me! Long, cornery, and looking like a horse with a secret sorrow! This from a woman I befriended and saved more than once from her own English beef-witted folly! But I suppose there is some justice in it. I am tall, and not fleshy; Nuala never stops reminding me of that review which spoke of my archaeological figure. But— "a horse with a secret sorrow"! If I were describing myself I might say that my face bore a certain morose splendour, but I am not describing myself; I am considering old Chips' letter about her first encounter with me, when I called to see if the stables might be rented, and renovated and made into a clinic for my work. Because at last I had decided what my work was to be.

I wanted to go on being a physician, but I came back from the war too badly used up by four years of hard and uncongenial work, topped off with a near-death imprisonment in cold water for just under four days. All right, many people have known worse things, but let them rejoice in their strength. I felt myself exhausted to the point where I never expected to be up to par again, and I wanted the rest of my life to be on my own terms. I wanted to practise medicine, but I did not want to sit all day in a dismal office with a steel desk, my diplomas on the wall in cheap frames, and a dusty bunch of paper flowers for a "homey touch," giving something like ten minutes each to a procession of patients with the same ten diseases—the colds, the coughs, the 'flus, etc. etc. until I became rich and dull-witted and disgusted with myself. God forbid that I should speak ill—or very ill— of my colleagues, but I had no wish to be like them. In

Ward J at my last military hospital, where I treated victims of "friendly fire" with a mixture of conventional medicine, advice which did not conform to psychiatry as it is defined, and the charms and releases of literature, I had discovered something which I could not define, but which I wished to pursue and examine. I knew it would take time and lead me in some unconventional directions.

Jobs were open to me. The Department of Medicine at the University invited me to lecture in pathology, or diagnosis, whichever I liked. I had cut up enough people—mostly men—to be a good pathologist and my pre-war work with the police made that possibility attractive, but I did not want the responsibility of being a crime-solver and disease-tracker. Diagnosis was also attractive and I had shown some skill in it, but I wanted to do more in that line, and do it in ways that would certainly not be useful to beginners and students who might have no real flair for the work. I wanted to go it alone, and Fate kindly opened up the way for me to do just that.

My mother died not long before I returned to Canada and all the family money came to me. It was not a vast fortune, but it was much more than I would have expected, and I popped it into an investment portfolio which brought me an annual income that would have made it unnecessary for me to do anything at all—which is what a lot of people imagine Paradise must be. There were good investment opportunities after the war.

So far then, so good. But that "secret sorrow." It was the discovery that my heart's love, Nuala, had married my old friend Brochwel Gilmartin and was, it appeared, very happy with her bargain.

"You aren't the marrying kind," she said, when we talked about it.

"That's what they say about people like Darcy Dwyer."

"Don't be obtuse, Jon. I don't mean you're a pansy. Who knows better than I that you aren't? But marriage just isn't in your stars. You are a lover, but you aren't a husband. Now Brocky is a marvellous husband—mercurial, funny, tender—all the things you aren't, and I love him dearly. But I love you dearly, too, you old fathead, and I expect I always shall. Don't you think a woman can love two men, differently but almost equally?"

"Almost equally? But which one is—?"

"Whichever happens to be on top at the moment."

"Nuala, don't be coarse."

"I didn't mean it like that. Not quite. I mean whichever one has most recently taken a new hold on my heart—mind—or both. Brocky wants children and so do I. You don't, I imagine?"

"Never thought that far."

"He'll be a wonderful father. Have you any idea what sort of father *you'd* make, Jon?"

"I thought perhaps you wanted to marry him because you liked the idea of living in Salterton."

"How can you be so stupid? And you call me *coarse*! That's offensive, Jon! I didn't calculate and weigh and choose what looked like the best bet. I followed my heart. I truly did."

"But it was a factor."

"You mean I had a chance to get into a good practice with another woman who had more than she could cope with? That was certainly tempting. And you mean that Brocky has a place in the English Department at Waverley and is virtually certain to end up as Head, if he writes all the books he has planned. So it all looked neat and tidy and irresistible. Is that what you mean? You must think I have a hatefully calculating mind."

"You're not a fool, and that means you have a certain amount of calculation in your nature."

"I worried and fussed and stewed for weeks before deciding. It was the hardest decision I've ever had to make. And Brocky knows it."

"I didn't have a fair chance to put my case. I was still abroad."

"You were very much in my mind."

"How's Brocky in bed?"

"What a question! Do you think I'm going to give you a clinical picture, as between medical colleagues?"

"That means he's not up to my standard."

"Men are always raving on and on about sex, as if it were the only thing that mattered. Let me tell you this: Brocky can talk better than any man I've ever known, and married couples talk more than they screw, even if screwing's what they think matters most. Brocky makes me laugh out loud at least once every day."

"Can Brocky talk you into multiple orgasm?"

"Laughter—real laughter—is a sort of orgasm and it gets better just when the other kind is dwindling to a few reluctant throbs. Now listen to me, Jon, I am not on the witness-stand, and I won't put up with any more of this lowbrow, jealous interrogation. There's a limit, Jon."

It did not appear that the limit precluded a splendid afternoon in bed with Nuala before she caught the late-afternoon train back to Salterton. And this was how it was. From time to time—every few weeks—Nuala's affairs called her to Toronto, and she and I lunched, and retired to bed for the afternoon.

Did Brocky know? Nuala being what she was, I supposed he did, but he never spoke of it when we met, as now and then we did. The war, and his new way of life, had made him an even more engaging companion than when first I knew him. Like me, he had had a near brush with death—a bomb that failed to go off—and it seemed to have, so to speak, integrated him. He was quite the best talker I have ever known. Not a rattle, not a buffoon, not a wit-snapper or a wisecracker, but a man whose conversation on any theme—"from grave to gay, from lively to severe"—was deft, elegant but not ornate, and witty in the sense that it was terse and apt and made brilliant but unexpected similitudes. If, as Byron said, watching Kean act was like reading Shakespeare by flashes of lightning, that was what Brocky's conversation was at its best. I'm not a great talker; a listener, really, as a good diagnostician should be. And I never seem to make anybody laugh—except behind my back, I expect.

Did I hate Brocky? Did I think of him as the man who had stolen my girl? The three of us did not live on such a primitive level. I loved Nuala. Nuala loved Brocky. Nuala loved me. I am not given to using the word "love" about my relations with men, but I suppose Brocky remained my best and closest friend. If Brocky had been called on to describe his feeling for me I am sure he would have used the word "love" but he would have known how to save it from being mawkish, or evocative of some popular magazine rubbish about "male bonding." He might even have put it in Christian terms, because he had come back from the war with profound Christian convictions, and now and then he came to Toronto to talk to Charlie, who was assistant to Father Hobbes at St. Aidan's.

Have I said that I considered Brocky my best and closest friend? No, I said I "supposed" it. Since returning to Toronto I had acquired another and in some respects more intimate friend than Brocky. He was Hugh McWearie, the editor of the religious stuff in the *Colonial Advocate*. I met him because a colleague asked me to take a look at him and give an opinion about his wheezes, which were troublesome. Of course he smoked too much and his foul old pipes made him wheeze. But was I to launch an evangelical campaign upon him, to make him ashamed of his habit, and thereby to provide him with somewhat better health but a vastly deprived life? This was the sort of problem that was now uppermost in my thoughts about my profession. Was I an apostle of health, and if so what was health? If it was bodily well-being, that was a reasonable if not a simple answer. But if it included mental well-being, or spiritual well-being, the whole thing became greatly complicated. There are people who must have their poisons, or they are not themselves. So it was with Hugh, with his whisky and his disgusting pipes.

As he was a man of broad intelligence, I explained the problem to him. I told him that if he gave up tobacco, he might expect to live longer, but would he live better? I also told him that if he did not give up tobacco he might live a long life anyhow. Lots of puffers do. I had no plan of salvation to offer him. In the end he decided on his own regime; he stopped smoking from morning till night, and confined himself to eight large pipes a day. He bought two new pipes and threw away his stinkers. He stopped getting through most of a bottle of whisky every day, and cut out entirely his habit of having a hearty snort in bed before rising. But I forbade nothing.

"I follow you, Doctor," said he. "As the old music hall song puts it—'A little o' what you fancy does you good'—but moderation must be observed. The Golden Mean, a dash of wisely applied Platonism, and a light self-discipline. I take your meaning and I thank you for not threatening me. You have reminded me of what I ought to have known myself, great gowk that I am. But one must visit a wise man from time to time to discover what one already knows. You are a doctor in a thousand."

So quite a number of people were beginning to say. Many of my patients, in their phrase, "swore by me." But many of my professional colleagues swore at me, for I appeared to them to be a heretic about health. Nevertheless, a great many of my contemporaries began to refer troublesome cases to me — cases for which they no longer felt that they could do anything helpful.

Already a legend was growing up about me. It was suggested that I used unconventional methods and there is nothing a professional group mistrusts so nervously as it does anything that appears unconventional, and that has not been thoroughly written up in the journals. It may be quackery. Worse still, it may be effective. And if it is both quackery and effective it is utterly hateful.

But I was not a quack. My dictionary says that a quack is somebody who professes a knowledge of which he is ignorant; but I profess nothing of the sort—I simply profess a knowledge of which a great many of my professional colleagues are ignorant. I suppose I might call it humanism. McWearie, when he came to know me better, called me a quodlibetarian physician, meaning that I mixed up all sorts of unlikely things to make a unity, choosing what I liked or what seemed best.

My war experience made me mistrustful of the sort of medicine that prescribes a particular remedy for a particular set of symptoms. Of course in wartime doctoring, especially when very near the fighting, that was what had to be done; there was no time for prolonged investigation, and in a few hospitals in which I worked the sole object seemed to be to get a man on his feet and back to fighting. Medicine in the peacetime world and in private practice did not drop to that level, but the weariness and boredom of the work often led to *pro forma* treatment, especially with dull or unappealing patients. For do not suppose that the attraction which so obviously happens between physician and patient does not work the other way. Very few people can be cured by a doctor they do not like and I have even heard people say that they could not be cured by a man who was obviously stupider than themselves. I myself have never responded to a doctor whom I thought illiterate, but that is sheer intellectual snobbery and of course I ought to be ashamed of it. But I'm not. However, I have never been able to do much for a patient I thoroughly disliked.

I did not reject conventional methods of treatment. I just wanted to be sure they were the right ones, which it must be clear to anybody with a grain of common sense cannot always be the case.

It was obvious to me, as I would suppose it must be to anyone, that the body is not a machine, varying only as the Ford varies from the Rolls-Royce—in quality. I have lived to see the day when worn-out organs can be replaced from another body, a form of cannibalism which sometimes works. This is a triumph of the mechanical theory of medicine. But very few people come to the point where they have to go to the body-shop for a new part.

I believe, as I discovered Paracelsus had believed before me, that there are as many stomachs, hearts, livers and lights as there are members of the human race, and that they should be treated individually to suit their special needs, whatever these might be. And those needs are not always to be found in the laboratory, but in the lay-confessional of the physician's consulting-room. Treatment must be intensely personal, and if sometimes it strays into the realm of mind, there the physician must follow it. But usually it is in that realm where mind and body mingle—where the mind affects the body and the body the mind, and where untangling the relationship is the Devil's own work, and takes time and application and sympathy—that the hard-driven general practitioner and his specialist brother cannot be expected to provide for every patient who knocks on his door.

I suppose if I were driven to describe my method of work I would call it a type of psychosomatic medicine by which I attempt to bring about change in the disease syndromes through language, and therefore through reason. And sometimes (and this was where the canker gnawed for my ultra-reasonable colleagues) in that fibrous darkness below reason. The change might never be complete, but the patient would feel much better because he—perhaps more often, she—had learned to approach the individual quality of life and the body through which life was experienced, in a different way.

No, no, *not* psychoanalysis! That marvellous but extremely limited adventure in human understanding behaves as if its patients lived principally in the mind, and as if the patients' coughs and colds and indigestions, arthritis, "bad lower back," tricky heart, asthma, skin ailments, and all the rest of their disquiets were creatures of another realm, to be dealt with by somebody else.

"Back to Paracelsus!" was McWearie's cry when I first spoke of this concept to him. But no, not to Paracelsus alone, but to other great ones, of whom Robert Burton, who wrote his *Anatomy of Melancholy* to treat his own melancholy, must be a distinguished partaker. In my work on Ward J I had discovered that a new or merely an altered way of thinking was curative. It would not restore an amputated leg, or bring back an errant girl-friend, but it would give a new look at those misfortunes and the new look was healing.

I have been known to recommend another look at religion as a way to better health, or perhaps I should say well-being. For what is health?

I say (and of late years I am astonished that the World Health Organization agrees with me) that health is when nothing hurts very much; but the popular idea is of health as a norm to which we must all seek to conform. Not to be healthy, not to be in "top form" is one of the few sins that modern society is willing to recognize and condemn. But are there not as many healths as there are bodies? If whatever we are demands certain physical frailties, why struggle to get rid of them? And what have the exemplars of health, our cherished and greatly rewarded athletes, ever done for mankind? They are entertainers, of a lesser sort. If McWearie's contribution to the public good, and his own deepest satisfaction, demands booze and stink, why try to turn him into a discontented ghost of himself, and kill him with what is popularly supposed to be kindness.

So I approach my patients intuitively, with my antennae trembling at every hint from body or speech, and when I have found out whatever I can, I do whatever seems to me to be best.

Severe disease, of course—identifiable, virulent and demanding disease—yields to rapid diagnosis, and sometimes cures or simply palliatives are available. The *vis medicatrix naturae*—Nature's healing power—is the physician's great ally with these, but every now and then he can snatch someone from the grave, and deserves every credit for doing so. But such dramatic diseases are a small part of what the doctor is expected to treat.

To practise this sort of medicine I did not want to be in one of the big buildings of medical offices; I needed space and privacy, and thus it was that I ended up in the stables at Glebe House.

It was McWearie who suggested it. "The place has just the unlikely appearance that would suit you," said he. "Over the principal entrance, which is wide enough for a Victorian carriage with a top-hatted coachman on the box, is a fine carved representation of three splendid horses, apparently in conversation. The inside finish is handsome, and upstairs is the coachman's apartment and room for a couple of grooms. It will take a lot of adapting and doing over, but it will give you premises wholly unlike anything any physician has ever had anywhere at any time. You'll have to brave The Ladies but they can't eat you and I know they need money. Go in and win."

So it happened, though I do not remember it quite as it appears in Chips' letter to her friend Barbara Hepworth, whom I presume she had known in student days in England. There are more such letters.

How did they come my way? Because in the course of time I became quite an intimate of The Ladies—or as intimate as anybody ever got with them. I was a model tenant and I must say that as time wore on they were the most kindly and generous of landladies. Chips was wrong; neither of us repented our bargain. I saw one of them into the grave and the other leave Glebe House, and in the end it was I, the horse with the secret sorrow, who acted as the executor for Pansy Freake Todhunter.

When, of necessity, I went through her desk, I found these letters neatly bundled up, with a letter from Dame Barbara's solicitor, dated 1975, saying that as Miss Hepworth had kept them it seemed proper that they should be returned to the writer. Thus it was that I came upon a strongly slanted account of much that I remembered, and a view of myself which sometimes astonished and sometimes dismayed me.

But the letters! I have never seen such letters, and I could readily understand why they had been so carefully preserved. Not for Chips' literary style, God knows, which was in the schoolgirl-slangy vein of her speech.

No: for their extraordinary beauty.

Miss Pansy Freake Todhunter was an etcher, and in that genre her work was fine, though no more thrilling—to me at least—than etchings usually are. But these letters, which were written in a minute Italic hand, in the blackest ink on Mr. Russell's beautiful buff paper, were ornamented by lovely little vignettes (so tiny in some cases that one almost needed a magnifying glass to appreciate them) that seemed to have been done with a mapping pen. And they were in a style that had nothing of the sobriety that marked Chips' serious work; they were brilliant little caricatures, reminiscent in style of some of the best *Punch* artists—Tenniel, DuMaurier, and the wonderfully funny F. H. Townshend—and they gave the letters a brilliance, a beauty, a quality of delightful hilarity that lifted Chips' awful prose to a much higher level. There was I—yes, I must face it, a horse with a secret sorrow. There were scraps and bits of Glebe House, affectionate yet mocking in their evocation of Augustus Welby Pugin's Gothic romanticism. Of course the recipient had kept them. To have destroyed one of them would have been an act of vandalism.

I cherish them yet and look at them now and then when the past recurs to me in too dark shades.

VIGNETTES
(In Chips' First Letter)

1. A sketch of the lofty old conservatory, seen from outside.
2. Glebe House, which Chips has given quite a Dickensian air, though to me it looked like a house that could only have been built in Canada by a homesick Englishman.
3. Me—the horse with the secret sorrow. Clever, perceptive, uncharitable woman!

4. But she is as hard—and as just—to herself as to me, and here she is; a Freake indeed.
5. A Freake face, lusting for letters.

[3]
Glebe House
Cockcroft Street
Toronto, Ontario
Canada

Dear Old Thing:

Overjoyed (has anybody ever been *underjoyed*, I wonder?) to have better news of you and *quite* understand long silence. There are times when one simply *can't* write, and I know how *agonizing* the whole thing must have been, when Ben is such a dear, and there were the kidlets to consider (though they must be—what?—late teens by now?) But what good news that you are still friends and that you have his encouragement and advice when you want it. Terrific about Venice! But the way of the sculptor is hard, isn't it? Dear One is still *bashing* her head against *brick walls* in this artistically God-forsaken country where their idea of a statue is something like Winston Churchill in bronze with a cigar *that really smokes* sticking out of his mouth![1] Still, odds and bits do come in, and there are one or two enlightened souls who buy some of her small stuff, and the universal and abstract vision of beauty you used to talk about is not dead in her. Though she *does* get pulled down, poor sweet!

Artistically God-forsaken—I'm not sure how fair that is, but damn it, the growth of any sort of art in a new country—once colony, now independent

but not really firm on its legs yet—is so wobbly and
slow. They have some good politicians here—sharp
as razors, and Mackenzie King (Prime Minister, just
dead if you don't know) was an old fox who could
give Disraeli lessons, but his notions about art were
primitive and he thought *If Winter Comes* the greatest novel ever written.[2] But apart from politics and
business and sport nothing is very much valued
here. The letter you quote from Kit Jones, saying
that her husband, the mighty psychoanalyst, called
Canadians "a despicable race, exceedingly bourgeois,
quite uncultured, very rude and very narrow and
pious," has to be balanced against his own experience here just before World War One (as the papers
now call it) when he offended Toronto morality by
living openly with Loe. (Remember Loe? What *can*
it have been?)[3] Of course that sort of thing is not
unknown here but Ernest hadn't the decency to conceal it, as Canadians do, and he seemed almost to be
doing it *on principle*. No proper sense of *sin*, which
Canadians like. I gather that is why they gave him
the heave-ho, which was probably the best thing for
him anyhow as he seems to have made a big Harley
Street name, and is the St. Peter to Sigmund Freud's
Christ, even if he isn't quite the Beloved Disciple.[4]
Canada isn't nearly as bad as Ernest says; just about
thirty years behind the times artistically and what he
says about being bourgeois and uncultured and
narrow and pious could just as well be said about
Nottingham or any of a dozen places we know and
keep away from.—Anyway, the going for a sculptor
is rough. I get rid of a few etchings from time to
time but they don't fetch much. But they probably
wouldn't at home, either. I'm not really a big talent,
and they think $50. is *the earth* for an etching.

Yes, it has all worked out splendidly about the doctor and the stables. We spy on him quite a lot and I'll give you the lowdown later.

But at present we are up to our necks in the nearby church, on the glebe of which this house stands. Yes, my dear, we have become quite church-mice not because we have got softening of the brain or anything but because the clergy are so *fascinating*!

St. Aidan's is terribly High, and has really wonderful music and DeCourcy Parry, who directs it, is a composer of stature. We haven't seen much of him yet, but we have hopes. His right-hand man and leader of his Chancel Choir (plainchant, and not far off Solesmes, if you can believe it) is one Darcy Dwyer[5] who has become a great chum and is gradually bringing people to this house who are the best company we have found since stepping off the boat. But the big noise at St. Aidan's is a very modest noise indeed, called Father Ninian Hobbes and he is really an old dear and pooh-poohs any suggestion that he is anything out of the ordinary. I would call him a saint if it were not for a reason I'll explain later. But Père Hobbes gives away everything he has to the poor—really fetches it up out of his pocket where he carries it in an old-fashioned leather bag. If he hasn't anything, he turns the bag inside out and blesses the beggar with a smile that is as beautiful as anything you have ever seen. Not that he is a beauty.[6] False teeth of the very falsest kind, a back-ward-looking chin and I think he cuts his own hair. He is shy of women, and we have had to coax him with food which he gives at once to his beggars. He calls them God's People—absolutely Tolstoyan! In winter he roams the back alleys around here where the down-and-outs sleep; I think he knows every refuge of the really bad kind for a mile in every direction, and he prowls the night with a flashlight, and when he finds somebody sleeping huddled up in the cold he brings him back to the Rectory and settles him down near the stove. I say "him" but he has a great following of old women, many of them manifestly mad.

His right-hand man—a curate I suppose but not a bit the limp piece of spaghetti that word suggests—is Father Iredale—Charlie to us, now. He is as feet-on-the-ground as Father Hobbes is head-in-the-air, manages everything, directs the ritual with the eye of a Reinhardt and doesn't let Father Hobbes be imposed on more than is decent for a saint. Because Charlie is determined Father Hobbes *is* a saint and I think he expects a miracle at any time. He is absolutely sweet to the old man and we admire him for it and send decent food over to the Rectory as often as we can at times when Charlie can get it on the table before Father Hobbes calls in the poor and needy, who are never full up. Oh Barbara, how I now understand Christ's words that ye have the poor always with you! And what *bores* they are, poor loves!

The other curate is Father Whimble, a decent, quiet, rather stupid dutiful man who does what Charlie tells him, and also worships Father Hobbes.

Charlie knows our new tenant who has, after rather more than two years of fastidious tinkering with our stables, got them to his liking and moved in. Charlie knows Dr. Hullah, but I thought his jaw dropped a bit when we told him Hullah had taken the old building.

But about us and the church. We go. We can't know Charlie and do what we can about Father Hobbes without going. It'd be like knowing an author and not at least buying his books, however much you hated them. But while I maintain a good deal of my original scorn for the Church and all its works—result of having been to a first-rate Anglican school—Dear One is becoming more and more involved. Not in church works, exactly (I don't think the ladies of the church would welcome us with open arms, for they mistrust English people—probably with good reason) but in actual attendance at services, and I tag along, pretty often. The music is splendid, of course, and I'd have been a musician if I had had any talent, but D.O. goes to services where there is no music, and there is a look on her dear face that I cannot very well describe—an open, fulfilled, beautiful look that moves me to tears.[7] But when we come back for breakfast she is just as much her old, witty, un-churchy self as ever.

Charlie adores her. In a priestly way, of course. He has a sharp wit, and so has she, and their conversation is marvellous. She says very sharp things, as she always has, and he pretends to be shocked or outraged and rebukes her in mock priestly terms which really egg her on to greater flights. They end up laughing their heads off, and it sets me up no end to see Dear One so happy and with somebody of her own quality. She is always urging him to get married, and he explains in hilarious terms why it would never work—unless she, the beautiful sculptress Emily Raven-Hart, would consent to be his bride. This is a great joke, of course, for although nothing is ever said I am sure he understands the situation at Glebe House perfectly.

"Ain't I volatile?" like Miss Mowcher in *David Copperfield.* And here's the end of this sheet and that must be all for now, but I shall write again after a bit.

Greatest love from us both,
CHIPS

VIGNETTES

1. A hideous realization of such a statue, the cigar the size of a baseball bat.
2. Mr. King, a wisp of hair hanging over his clever face, but, alas, his mouth, as usual, is open.
3. Loe—not a face to launch a thousand ships.
4. Ernest Jones, cocking an eye upward toward his halo, which is guttering badly.
5. Darcy to the life, with a Mephistophelean air he would have loved.
6. Poor Fr. Hobbes: why does God make so many of his most devoted servants so damnably ugly?
7. Emily Raven-Hart, seen through the eyes of her lover.

[4]

CHIPS IS RIGHT; Charlie is not best pleased that I have moved into the ambience of St. Aidan's. I suppose he wants to be free of youthful associations, as most of us do. From the frail, dreamy youth who showed such extraordinary guts when he had his fenestration operation, he has become an extremely competent, managerial sort of holy man with a talent for the ceremonial aspect of his services. He always loved that sort of thing and I remember the glee with which he described how, in some churches in the Age of Faith, a beadle with a sword stood near the altar at Communion, ready to stab any dog or cat who might wander in and gobble up a fallen crumb of the Holy Bread. Our Lord's body passing through the guts of a mongrel! The thought filled him with a delicious terror.

He seems to have outgrown such Gothic tomfoolery but the services at St. Aidan's are pretty fancy. When we meet he is civil but always too busy to stop and chat, and he sweeps away in his cassock and the becoming (he knows how becoming) flat cap he wears with it—a thing like a scholar's mortar-board with the cardboard taken out. All the clergy at St. Aidan's wear their cassocks all the time; it is against custom and I don't suppose the Bishop likes it, but he rules with a light hand.

I see more of Charlie than he sees of me, for I am now thoroughly dug in at my stable clinic, and from my private hideout and post of observation in the tower—yes, there is even a neat little tower on this archidiaconal horse-palace, to echo the larger tower of the same design on Glebe House—I see him swanning around looking at once medieval and thoroughly of the moment, a priest among his people. I also see The Ladies as they come and go, and Chips grubbing endlessly in the excellent flower and vegetable garden she has made, pausing from time to time to nag the simpleton who cuts the grass and pulls weeds (and often flowers) in the gardener's never-ending fight with the chaos of Nature. So they spied on me quite a lot, did they? I spied on them, probably just as much.

The clinic pleases me; the architect has been sympathetic in turning a grand stable into my professional premises. Lots of space and a really good waiting-room; I have always hated those wretched cubbyholes, furnished with steel-tube chairs and a table for the old magazines, frequently without any daylight, that pass as waiting-rooms in buildings given over to—what careful writer would say designed for?—the medical profession. My waiting-room is like a drawing-room, and even if that is now a little old-fashioned, it creates the atmosphere I want. I have my own consulting-room, which has one of the old stable fireplaces in it, and looks like a library and not like the ante-room of a hospital ward, as so many doctors' offices do. Off it there is a good examination-room, where I can come to grips with people who have to be stripped and gone over with every diagnostic device and trick I can command. Outside the waiting-room, and commanded by it, is the reception room, where my invaluable secretary-nurse-masseuse-hydropathologist and general healer-of-all-work, Fru Inge Christofferson, keeps an eye on everything and everybody, types letters, and issues impeccable statements of indebtedness. Off her room is the consulting-room of my junior, Dr. Harry Hutchins, who looks after anything I tell him to and is glad to get the job because he wants to do the sort of work I do, when he has had enough experience. A genial fellow and reassuring to patients who might find the place a mite forbidding.

My personal quarters are upstairs. A really good living-room with plenty of light, and from which a short spiral stair leads up to the tower, where my writing-desk is, and where, in fact, I am making these notes. A decent bedroom. A small but well-equipped kitchen for, although I am no cook, I can get my own breakfast and make a lunchtime sandwich. A bathroom of what McWearie calls Pompeian luxury, and certainly bigger than is usual in that most cramped of all domestic necessities in most of the houses where I go.

I go to a lot of houses. I make house calls, or what the grander physicians of an earlier day called "Domiciliary Attendance." I want to see where my patients live. I want to see their bedrooms, which tell much about the quality of life they experience. I always poke into their bathrooms, pretending that I want to wash my hands; are they houses of shame, privies and jakes bespeaking a disgust of bodily excretion? Is the bathtub worn down by the Toronto water so that an ugly stain extends itself from under the taps? What is in the medicine cupboard—what mess of half-consumed remedies, patent nostrums, salves and balms, mixed with razor-blades too rusty to use but too good to throw away? A whole world of habit, cast of thought, approach to health, and approach to sex can be read in a bathroom, by my sweeping eye.

What is the light in the house? Is it darkened with "drapes" and "lace curtains" so that the furniture will not be faded? Has the sofa, God forgive us all, been protected against the abrasive rumps of family and guests with a piece of plastic? Are there books, and if so what are they, and are they stowed as if they were respected and loved, or are they disposed on shelves which seem chiefly used for the display of trumpery bits of china and glass? Are there any books at the bedside, and is there any light by which they might be read?

If there is a dining-room it is usually possible to get a peep at it. Is the table left ready set for the next meal, with the condiments bunched in the middle, next to the little cluster of artificial flowers? Does it look like a room used only when "company" comes, or is it the feasting-hall of a happy family? What is the light, for the light in a dining-room is a great indicator of what the family thinks about food, and thus about a vital element in life and a principal source of pleasure.

What is the patient wearing in bed? Obviously fresh pyjamas, to greet the doctor? His undershirt? Lots of people sleep in their underwear. If the patient is a woman, does she wear pyjamas or a nightdress, and if the latter is it designed to flatter or is it of white cotton? Has she combed her hair, put on make-up—for these things tell how she regards me, and herself. Is she uncaring when I want to listen to her breathing, or does she shield her breasts? A patient's notion of modesty can be revealing, whatever meaning you choose to attach to that word.

How does the house smell? My nose is one of my principal diagnostic instruments. I can smell disease, very often. I can smell domestic disquiet. I can smell unhappiness.

Of course not all of my house calls are made in places that fit the descriptions above. Many of my patients are well-off and a few are rich. The houses of the rich are a different study. Whose notion of luxury has been responsible for what I see? Wife's or husband's? Have they risen from humbler circumstances and if so what have they learned on that very North American journey? Is the pulpy, damp hand of the interior decorator from the big shop laid too heavily over any personal taste? Is there a piano, and if so does anybody play it? I can casually strike a chord or two, while admiring the instrument, and discover if the foggy, catarrhal note of an unused instrument tells the tale of pretension, of keeping up with the Joneses. Nowadays many houses have elaborate high-fidelity reproducing machines; they cost a lot of money, but the tapes that lie around, and the compact discs tell how hi the owners fi. Is it honest sentimental stuff, dance music, rock, punk, or whatever, or is it perhaps a collection of what I think of as "real" music—the sort of thing that opens the doors of the underworld? Or is it *Gems from the Met, or Pavarotti* showing how loud he can bawl? All these details are to me elements in a diagnosis, and the only way I can uncover them is by domiciliary attendance; the doctor who refuses to make house calls cannot hope for my sort of medical awareness.

Here, in my stable, I think it all over and reach my conclusions. And when night falls, and I have come back from the hotel where I get my dinner—Toronto did not for many years have much in the way of restaurants—I settle down in my living-room to read, to listen to music, but always beneath the surface occupation to think about my patients and my work, and I am wrapped in my own sort of happiness, when nothing hurts.

[5]
Glebe House
Cockcroft Street
Toronto, Ontario
Canada

How goes it, me old Cock-Linnet?

Remember that song—"My old man said, Follow the van, and don't dilly-dally on the way. Away went the van with me few sticks in it, I followed after with me old cock-linnet..." and so on. Oh Barbara you wouldn't believe how we long for a little of that kind of easy jollity in this sober country! But mustn't grumble, as old Lucy used to say. Things haven't been too bad.

I've told you our tenant has moved in. We were simply *raving* to see what he had done but no invitation came for weeks and weeks! I suppose he was fussing. These bachelors are dreadful fussers. For weeks vans had been coming to the door—they always came to us first because it never occurred to them that anything should be delivered to the stables—with all sorts of stuff, and we knew great things must be in preparation. A fearful sort of dragon-woman turned up, bossing a lot of the work. I gather she is the doctor's nurse, or something; name of Christofferson[1] and a real tartar. Or Valkyrie.

About seven feet tall, handsome in a grenadier kind of way, and with a deep voice. I ventured a few polite remarks—hoping to see what was in some of the packages—and got a look that has left an X-ray burn. But at last we have got through the door.

My dear, you can't imagine what money must have been spent! All traces of stables quite gone, except for the dear little fireplaces in some of the rooms, where I suppose grooms rubbed up harness and told dirty stories. Quite a bit of wood panelling, not too dark, and handsome wallpapers that must have come from the States. And furniture! A room that I couldn't believe was the waiting-room—for *patients*, mind you!—with marvellous leather chairs and a really good rug on the hardwood floor and positively *books* on shelves and pictures on the walls. And what pictures! First-class prints, but the choice! Rembrandt's *Anatomy Lesson* which I would think would scare the liver and lights out of a patient, and an old Dutch one of a doctor squinting at what looks like a flask of pee, and in the consulting-room one that really knocked me back!, it was one of those *Death and the Lady* pictures; a naked female simpleton stands face to face with a skeleton, at whom she is making goo-goo eyes—and he is making rather a calculating appraisal of her pink charms.[2] What on earth does Dr. Jonathan Hullah think his patients are going to make of *that*, I'd like to know?

I put it to him. He only laughed. "Don't worry," he said; "the people who come to me will very soon accommodate to these reminiscences of an earlier and franker idea of medicine. I demand that they come to terms with several sorts of reality." He talks like that. A very queer duck indeed, but handsome in a grisly sort of way, dresses grandly—expensive cloth—and scents his hanky with Hungary water. Not Harley Street grandeur. That would never do in Toronto. But rather grand, all the same. I wished I had put on my better frock.

But the real surprise was the room off the consulting-room which was just a bit too much like a hospital; big steel table that looked as if people might be expected to lie on it and at one end a platform at the back of which was a huge sheet of frosted glass. When he tripped a switch it lighted up from behind, and on the glass were all sorts of measurements and symbols in big black lettering. "When people stand in front of that," sez he, "you'd be surprised what it is possible to discover about them. Look," sez he, picking a transparency about eighteen inches square out of a filing cabinet. It was a photograph of some poor naked wretch taken in front of that screen, probably by the dragon; the face was blacked out so I couldn't have told who it was, even if I'd had any idea. My dear, you wouldn't *believe* how pitiful that creature looked! It was a woman, hair hanging down her back, stooped, breasts sagging and belly sagging almost as badly, awful veins in her legs. He put in another film, a sideways pose. Then another, from the back, spine obviously twisted. Yet she wasn't too bad a specimen. I've seen worse on the model stand in the studio at the old Royal Coll.[3] But this was *clinical.* "Any time you feel like having your portrait done, do come in," sez he, and it would have been nasty if he hadn't smiled so nicely. They say he is a top-notch diagnostician.

Then the dragon brought us some tea. Very decent tea, too, which surprised me for some reason. Over tea we got quite chatty. We told him about how we met in the Military Transport Corps, at 39

Graham Terrace and what a scream that was. All those fashionable ladies in uniforms they had made by Hartnell, driving colonels and Cabinet Ministers all over the place, and poor Dear One being put on the job of driving wages for a Government Department to Basingstoke, where it had been settled for the duration. I drove an ambulance, you remember. More like a death-cart sometimes, because of the rule that you had to take the dead to the police before you took the injured to the hospital. And the talk! *Endless* tales of adultery in high life. And what a gang! Some Canadians, the first of the breed I ever met and very decent kids, but the high-flyers made fun of them because they always asked for leave to spend with their husbands! The idea of spending time with a *husband* was too much for our commander.[4] I kept my eye on her, because she took rather a shine to Dear One and seemed anxious to marry her off. "Of course, there are only twenty-seven *really* eligible men in the whole of England, but you never can tell what you might pick up," sez she. But even then the parents were trying to get her off with Gussie Gryll.[5] Did you ever meet Gussie? My dear, what a type! *How* it brought back those days! We don't speak of them very often. But as I was going to bed, brushing my teeth actually, I found myself humming into the toothpaste the song we used to sing in the MTC, when some of the great ladies were a little squiffed—

> *Hitler—*
>   *Has only got one ball;*
> *Goering—*
>   *Has two but very small;*
> *Himmler—*
>   *Has something sim'lar;*

> *But poor old Goebbels*
> *Has no balls at all!*

Goes to the tune of *Colonel Bogey*. Happy days!
The risk of being killed in a raid was like the
Tabasco in a sauce. Were they really happy days? For
me it was a time when to be young and alive was
enough.

> Until next time, love from us
> CHIPS

VIGNETTES

1. My nurse, Inge Christofferson, drawn by an artist
   who plainly hates her on sight.
2. An impression of *Death and the Lady*. Is it by
   chance or foreboding that the Lady looks
   woundily like Emily Raven-Hart?
3. Three lightning impressions of an unloved
   woman's body.
4. The Commander is one of those upper-class
   Englishwomen who looks like a beautiful horse.
5. If ever a caricature spoke of jealousy and hatred,
   this is it!

[6]

I REMEMBER THAT tea-party very
well. I didn't want to ask them in, but they were so
eager—at least Pansy Freake Todhunter was—that it
became inevitable. McWearie said, "The Ladies are
honing to see your place, and you'd better invite them,
if you have any hope of being asked to their Sundays." I
was not at all sure I cared about their Sundays, whatever
those might be, but there are some social obligations
that can't be avoided.

I knew they wanted to talk about the bell, and that Charlie had put them up to it. If he wanted me to silence the bell, why didn't he ask me himself? I suppose it had been many years since the stable bell had struck the hours, but when I put the place in order I had the clock mended, and when it struck each hour I was delighted; just the thing to warn patients that their appointment had run its course. It was a good bell, and I can't imagine that it would keep anybody awake when it struck during the night. But Charlie wanted my bell silenced, because it sometimes rivalled the bell on St. Aidan's, which he assumed, reasonably enough, should have first consideration. It might give out its melodious tenor note when Charlie was conducting a service—might indeed ring at the same time as his jangling sacring-bell. If he had spoken to me himself, I might have done something about my bell, but as he put The Ladies up to it, I smiled and said that the stable was now a Temple of Hygeia and as such was surely entitled to a bell, and they had no answer ready for that. I suppose they reported to Charlie that I was pig-headed, and if they did I do not care. Probably they attributed this porcinity of head to the Secret Sorrow that made me look like a horse. Quite a farmyard I must have seemed to them.

They were miffed that I did not invite them upstairs to my private quarters, but as the pictures in my professional rooms bothered them it was certainly just as well. In my sitting-room I had only two pictures, at that time, both good prints (because I would rather have a great picture in reproduction than some "hand-painted" daub of the Canadian landscape); one was Dürer's self-portrait, in which he plainly wants to look like Christ, and the other—over my mantel—was Boucher's entrancing portrait of Nelly O'Morphy, naked poppet lying face downward on what is surely the softest sofa ever painted. Nelly's pink rump has reminded me of the goodness of God after many a day dealing with such neglected carcasses as the one The Ladies had seen on the screen in my examination room.

As I sit by my fire, do I ever look around the hearth and wish that Nuala sat there, reading or knitting or day-dreaming? I refuse to give a definite answer to that question even here in the secrecy of my Case Book. Of course I long for her, but in honesty I must say that I would rather long for her than have her continually present. Travel agents assure us that "getting there is half the fun"; I might say with at least equal truth that longing is some of the best of loving. I am lonely, but do I not savour my loneliness? Nuala has become a mother; her son is a large, red infant named Conor, after her family. Do I wish that Nuala were in my little kitchen brewing up the stuff Conor eats so messily, and that Conor lay in a bassinet in my bedroom, howling his head off for some unattainable satisfaction that only a baby could want? This speculation is complicated by the knowledge that Conor may be my own son. When people are as intimate and as accustomed in their loving as Nuala and I, the precautions that mean so much to prudent people may sometimes be forgotten. Proclaim no shame, when the compulsive ardour gives the charge, and do not wait to rummage in the drawer of the bedside table to see if a prophylactic can be found.

Anyhow, as I write now, so long after these events, it is all water-over-the-dam, or condoms-down-the-loo. Conor has been a grown man for some time; sufficiently grown to have risen in his profession to be Entertainment Editor of the *Colonial Advocate.* Conor is married to Esme, who is plaguing me for revelations about the past of Toronto which cannot be divorced from revelations about my own past, and it does not matter much

who his father was. I know him. I like him and I know
he likes me, but I feel no impulse to fold him in my arms
and declare him to be my son. I do not even discuss that
possibility with Nuala. Sometimes I am ashamed of how
little family feeling I have, but I soon get over it.

Far clearer in my memory is the great Battle of the
Bell, which went on during my first three years in my
clinic behind Glebe House and adjacent to St. Aidan's.
It would seem trivial if it were not that it completed the
break between myself and Father Charles Iredale, my
old school friend and as I had thought, friend for life. It
is astonishing how such links that one supposed to be
strong, can be broken by what is comparatively a trifle.

Charlie got nowhere, putting The Ladies onto the job
of asking me to silence my bell. That merely made me
determined to let it have its voice, every hour on the
hour. Did Charlie come to me and ask me himself to
silence my bell, as friend to friend? No, he resorted to a
bit of priestcraft; he went among his parishioners and
invited them to sign a petition he had prepared (but
which he did not sign himself) asking that the police
should take action against me as the perpetrator of a
nuisance. The police took their time, but eventually
they sent me a letter saying that they had had complaints, and would I desist. Taking my own time, I
replied asking the nature of the complaints? The police,
after an interval, sent me a copy of the petition, with all
the names attached.

It was a pretty piece of work. It put forward, in tones
of gentle grievance, the claims of the old whose sleep
my bell disturbed, and the more strongly stated cases of
the chronically ill, who lay awake counting the hours.
There was some talk of the competition between my
bell and the bells at St. Aidan's, which nobody objected
to, as a bell was an appurtenance of a church which was

sanctified by time. I began to relish this neighbourhood squabble.

After an interval, I asked for an interview with somebody in the Police Force who could guide me in this matter, and had a pleasant chat with a sergeant who did not want to get too deeply into the affair, and suggested I see somebody at City Hall. After some time taken in finding out who at City Hall I should see, I met a very decent man in the City Clerk's office who said that the City would be reluctant to take action against me, and deplored the action of the police in making the names of the complainants known to me. I asked him what action the City might consider? Would they fine me? Perhaps jail me? Possess my bell? The very decent man was flustered by such suggestions, and said that nothing of that magnitude would be considered, but that something vaguely called "action" would undoubtedly result if I continued to ignore the letter which had now reached so high an authority as the City Clerk's office.

"You are committing a nuisance, you see," he said.

"Really?" I replied. "I didn't know that bells could come under that heading. I always thought it meant peeing up alleys or allowing a dead dog to deliquesce in one's backyard. So my bell is a nuisance? I'm very sorry to hear it. Really I am."

Again a masterly pause before doing anything, and then I sent a letter to Father Hobbes, which I asked him to read at such services as he thought appropriate. It read:

It reaches my ears that the bell which is part of the clock in the tower of my Clinic, at the rear of Glebe House on Cockcroft Street, is found objectionable by certain elderly neighbours, and unwell neighbours whose rest it curtails. I regret that this should

be so, and will therefore—as soon as a trustworthy
horologist can be found to whom to entrust such a
delicate operation—have the mechanism adjusted so
that in future the bell will sound only between seven
o'clock in the morning and twelve o'clock midnight,
between which hours it serves to mark the progress
of my professional appointments. I trust that this
will meet with the objections expressed to the police
and City authorities.

> Faithfully,
> JONATHAN HULLAH, M.D.,
> F.R.C.P.
> (Chevalier of the Order of Polonia
> Restituta)

I was by now a regular attendant at the eleven o'clock
High Mass at St. Aidan's every Sunday, and I waited
eagerly to hear Father Hobbes read my letter to his
flock. Dear old man, he did so with a richness of
Christian unction that made me almost sorry I was
feuding with his curate. He said he was sure everybody
would appreciate the spirit of neighbourly charity with
which I was acting, and even went so far as to say that
the tenor of my bell chimed so sweetly with the bass of
the church bell that he was always delighted to hear it.
With a coincidence that art would never dare to employ
my stable bell rang just as the old man finished the
letter. Otherwise people might have heard Charlie
grinding his teeth, but several obviously did hear the
unseemly snort from Darcy Dwyer, in his choir stall,
when he heard me defined as a Chevalier of the Order
of Polonia Restituta. I believe this distinction has long
been discontinued, but during my post-war holidays in
Europe I had purchased, in a pawn shop, the collar of

the Order and had shown it to Darcy, who recalled my triumph at the Bad Breath Contest, when I had anointed myself with that honour.

The Ladies spoke to me about the bell imbroglio that afternoon, delighted that I had euchred Charlie in this ingenious manner, they thought the whole thing a huge joke. Charlie, who had dropped in on what was now called their salon, that particular Sunday, glared at me across the room and did not speak. Indeed, the breach between us lasted for several years and was one of the aspects of the affair of Father Hobbes' sudden death that made it difficult for me to intervene as perhaps I should have done.

[7]

As I REREAD what I have written I am dismayed by the confusion of tenses and the order of time. But such an irregular record does not admit of the sort of scrupulosity I should observe if I were writing for a science journal. Here, for instance, I find a huge gap: what am I doing attending services at St. Aidan's—being in fact a regular attendant and not scanting the collection plate? How do I explain the double vision with which I observe everything that goes on in the church and around it, feeling affectionate, protective, acquiescent, ironic, amused, and satiric all at the same time? How can I think ill of Charlie for his priestly sneaking in the matter of the bell, and at the same time respect him and feel humbled by him when I receive the Bread and Wine at his hand? How can I see Father Hobbes as a saintly man and a comical, dotty old party almost at the same instant? And how can I, as a friend of Darcy Dwyer, know how carefully the services are rehearsed and performed and also be stilled and fulfilled when they take place?

That last question may not be too hard to answer. Could I not be present at the rehearsals of a great play or opera and nevertheless be brought to an admiration approaching reverence when at last I saw it in performance? But is this not something far above a performance even of a noble human creation? Is not this a service offered to the Highest, in which I am myself a humble participator? I am not a down-and-out asking God for a handout when I kneel; I am offering something, I am making a gift, a gift of myself, and the beauty and order of the ceremonial are the outward forms in which this mutuality of affection, offering, and trust are made possible.

Ceremonial. When I was young I thought, like a real Canadian of the twentieth century, that anything that was too carefully ordered was not "sincere," and I accepted sincerity—meaning life stripped of beauty though not wholly of decency—as the greatest of values. Anything goes, so long as it is "sincere," however squalid, illiterate, and confused it may seem.

The war cured me of that. I saw the sincerity, the wholehearted acquiescence, of good men fighting for a cause they could not have summed up, for a country of which they knew very little, for "values" they had never heard seriously questioned. I had seen that sincerity turned to bitterness in the men who had been brought low by "friendly fire," and who had nothing to cling to, nothing to show them that there might be something beyond the muddle of belief, or mere acquiescence, with which the best of them had gone to war. They knew no ceremonial that might light their way. Even the worldly splendour of monarchy and patriotism was denied them, because these things had been brought low by "sincere" thinkers who saw through everything that was not on the flattest level of mediocrity. Their lives brought them nothing of magnificence. And yet—did *I* believe, and if so what did I believe in?

"I take it you are not greatly impressed by 'this fable of Christ,' as the Borgias cynically called it, while they were making a very good thing out of it," said McWearie, during one of our many conversations on these matters. "Well, Jon, don't be hasty. Just about anything in history is a fable in some sense or other, and the fable of Christ has four remarkable books to support it. It's a very fine fable and you don't have to swallow it all as if it were the report of a hockey match. Remember that Christ himself was probably the finest fabulist that ever lived. The parables! What is like them? Because you can't accept Christ's economics you mustn't neglect the sublimity of his acceptance of mankind in all its variety. Is it God that sticks in your craw? Do you have a lot of heartburn about God?"

"The God of the Old Testament sticks in my craw," said I. "And he certainly does some odd things in the New."

"As he must stick in the craw of anybody with a morsel of Christian spirit. A terrible old fella a lot of the time, but an astonishingly wise father at other times. You don't know where to grasp him."

"I want none of him."

"There's no need. He's only one of a hundred gods, though we've had our noses so rubbed in his story that we have a hard time seeing beyond him. But you're not an uneducated man, Jon. You must know that when Christ walked the earth—yes, and for centuries before—there were people in India, for instance, and in Greece beyond a shadow of a doubt, to whom Christ and his Twelve fishermen would have looked like a fine bunch of hillbillies, although possessed with a good idea. You probably—if you sorted out your notions, which you are lazily inclined not to do—believe pretty much what those Greeks believed. The Perennial Philosophy, in fact."

"Leibniz," said I.

"No, not Leibniz, you gowk! He just gave it a name. What do you know about it?"

"Not much. We didn't get much Leibniz at Varsity."

"Jon, I despair of you! Have you grown up and been through a war and confronted Death and had your heart broken—lived like a man, in fact—and you still cling to the baby stuff you learned as a boy? Leibniz at Varsity!"

"Well, where should I learn philosophy if not at Varsity?"

"Learn it as the philosophers learned it—by the inward quest. Avoid philosophic systems. Idiots love them because they can all band together and piss in a quill and look down on the unenlightened majority. But nobody can teach you more than somebody else's philosophy. You have to make it your own before it's any good."

"Why can't I do that beginning with Leibniz?"

"I'd throw this bottle at you if it were empty, which God be praised it's not. Leibniz was a good chap, but he was intellectually constipated; didn't get enough olive oil in his thinking, olive oil meaning Plato. Not that Plato was the whole thing in what I'm talking about. He was the fella who linked together what the Greeks knew centuries before him—Pythagoras and Heracleitus and half a dozen more—and men who have had their heads screwed on have been with him in spirit ever since. Disraeli, now. D'you know the story about the lady who asked Dizzy what his religion was? His real religion, that's to say, because he certainly wasn't a model Jew.

And he said, 'It is the religion of all wise men.' And the woman persisted; 'What's that?' says she. 'Wise men never tell,' said Dizzy, not wanting to get into a long palaver with her."

"Hugh, that wasn't Disraeli. It was the Earl of Shaftesbury, a couple of centuries earlier."

"It sounds better as Disraeli."

"Journalism has rotted your respect for truth."

"Ah, whoever it was, he meant Platonism. You know Platonism. Did you get any of that at Varsity?"

"No. Are you going to enlighten me?"

"I'll *tell* you. Any enlightenment must come from yourself. It's rooted in the Divine Reality that we find in our minds—mind in the largest definition and not just the calculator inside your head—that recognizes and reflects the Divine Reality in all things. There is that within us which partakes of the Divine Reality, which is immanent, immemorial, and universal. There are about twenty-five centuries of experience and thinking behind it. It doesn't accommodate itself to systems or religions, but it may be approached through them—which is what you and I do at St. Aidan's, I suppose. But it isn't just St. Aidan's or what Father Hobbes gives out in his sermons, good old josser though he is. The Perennial Philosophy has much to do with beauty, and there's plenty of beauty to be going on with in St. Aidan's."

"I'd have to think a long time about that."

"Yes, but not perhaps as long as you think. This kind of medicine you practise, and which you won't define for fear somebody will contradict you, seems to me to have its roots in the Perennial Philosophy. So bite down on that, Jon, and chew until it's part of you."

That's what I did, and in time it became clearer. Platonism, or what Hugh called the Perennial Philosophy, lay at the root of my medical practice.

No—*was* the root of it.

[8]

I AM NOT GOING to include all the letters Pansy Todhunter wrote to her friend Barbara; as in all extended correspondence, much of it is dull and much also irrelevant to my own story. This letter tells what my medical practice, rooted in the Perennial Philosophy, looked like to the world around me.

Glebe House
Cockcroft Street
Toronto, Ontario
Canada

Dearest Barbara:

Queer business Dear One and I seem to be mixed up in, but surely if anything disastrous happens we as landlords cannot be involved. It's our doctor tenant, who has made himself so cosy in our stables—not that they look a bit like a stables any longer.

Of course we've been aware of the patients who visit him in substantial numbers every day, because they come right up the walk to Glebe House until they take a sharp left (indicated by a neat little sign) toward the stable area, which is a cobbled yard surrounded by neat flower-beds. (The doctor spares no expense to make his place look nice, which is for some minds almost conclusive evidence that he is a quack of some sort; proper doctors never bother about appearances, or not in Toronto.) The patients are of all kinds—invalids who have to be helped, young people looking worried, people in what used

to be called "well-worn clothes and mended gloves,"
rich people who leave classy motor cars in the street,
mostly women but a good sprinkling of men.[1]
Working in the garden I can't help but see them, and
they have to pass Dear One's conservatory studio at
the side of the house, and sometimes stare in quite
rudely. But we've never known any of them until
recently.

Now we know Miss Fothergill. I met her one
day as she was coming through the garden from the
clinic, and stopped to pet Pusey, the Anglo-Cat.—
Have I told you about Pusey? Since we have become
such church mice at St. Aidan's we thought when we
acquired a kitten—a black darling with three white
paws—that he ought to have some sanctified name.
So we thought, of course, of Father Iredale's hero,
the Rev. Edward Bouverie Pusey, one of the fathers
of the Anglo-Catholic Movement. (Newman would
also be a nice name for a cat, but as we had our
kitten removed from the temptations of sex very
early in his life we plumped for Pusey, the Anglo-Cat
and that is how he is now known—though I don't
think Father Charlie thinks it as funny as we do.)[2]
Well, anyhow, a few weeks ago Miss Fothergill
stopped to pet Pusey and that led to conversation,
and she seemed rather fagged so I asked her to step
in for a cup of tea. And what a tale she told!

She enjoys ill-health—and my dear, *how* she
enjoys it—and her own physician, exhausted and
worn out I expect, had referred her to Dr. Hullah, to
see if he could help her. A lot of doctors do that, I
gather. Hullah is a sort of Court of Last Resort and
has patients other drs. have given up, or perhaps just
found intolerable. So she made an appointment and,
she tells me, bugging her already rather bug-like eyes,

she never had such a going-over in her whole puff.

Before she even saw the great man she had quite a session with the dragon, Nurse Christofferson. All the usual details recorded on paper, and then whisked into the examination-room and ordered to strip, and not just to her undies, but ballock-naked which she made sound utterly horrible; she has an awful lot of shame for a rather small woman. Then up on that platform I told you about, and Christofferson disappeared under the black cloth of a big camera like an old-fashioned portrait camera, and turns on several cruel and searching lights and takes her picture in a wide variety of unbecoming poses. "I trust that these pictures are confidential," sez La Fothergill. "Yes," sez Christofferson with more humour than I would have suspected, "any views you want for sale or distribution must be taken elsewhere." This shook up Miss F. quite a bit. But not so much as when she was invited to lie on the big steel table (having yielded up the usual medical tribute of some pee and a few drops of blood on the way) and Dr. Hullah came in and greeted her as if she were fully clothed and in a drawing-room. He even shook hands with her! Darling, have you ever had your hand shaken when you were starkers? I suppose you have, I'm forgetting we don't live in the Fothergill world. But this was a handshake from a complete stranger.

Then he went to work. It was long and deeply embarrassing. Not that he demanded to peep up her chimney, or anything like that, for Christofferson had done all those embarrassing tests beforehand. But he stared at her until she said she blushed from head to toe. Then he poked her with an enquiring finger simply everywhere! He grabbed her tum until she thought he was trying to dislodge something inside, but it appears it was just an unusually prolonged and searching investigation of the spleen. He made her turn over and did the same sort of investigation of her back, including a prolonged parting of the buttocks while he seemed to be staring at her exit—about which she seems to be extremely secretive. He did a lot about feet. Then—and this is what really shook her—he began to sniff at her, very close up, and he sniffed her from head to foot, very slowly and even quite a lot of sniffing in that area which Miss Fothergill described as You Know Where, which was far worse than Christofferson's searching finger.[3] But after an hour or so of the most acute embarrassment she had ever suffered in her life— which seems to have been rich in embarrassment of one sort and another, for she has many areas where embarrassment is possible, social, intellectual, moral, sexual, you name it—he left and the dragon helped her to dress and even showed her a wee powder-room where she could make repairs to her make-up.

By this time Miss F. was in a perfect tizzy and when she was at last in the doctor's impressive office she wept hysterically and demanded what he thought he was doing. Securing information for a preliminary diagnosis, said he, cool as the proverbial cuke. But did he continue? Not he. It seems that he simply sat and stared at her until she could stand it no longer, and wept a lot more and at last took hold of herself and asked if he didn't want her to tell him what ailed her? But you are telling me that, sez he. Every minute you tell me more and more. Your tears are eloquent. But now perhaps you will tell me what you think ails you. And she did.

This all took a couple of hours, by which time

Miss F. was absolutely played out and was glad when the doctor said that would be all for this afternoon but he would arrange for her to have some massage and baths for a week or two, after which further diagnosis would probably be possible. And that's how it stands.

But you know how it is when you hear about something that's entirely new to you; in the course of the next few days you hear a lot more about it? So it is with Dr. Hullah and his unusual methods of diagnosis. I met one man at a party who asked me if I knew Hullah, and he said that the queerest thing Hullah did to him was to rest his head on his belly and apparently listen to what went on inside for about a quarter of an hour! All sorts of gurglings and squishings and croaks. But apparently Hullah has put him right—and not with medicines but with the ministrations of La Chris, who appears to be a whizz at massage and seems almost to rip your guts out. Whatever the doctor heard in his tum, Chris has put to rights. And I met another man who had a nasty skin ailment that the dermatologists couldn't help, and Hullah banished it in six weeks by a series of baths, again supervised by the dragon. Baths that whirl you round as imagination is said to do in Shakespeare (*Troilus and Cressida*, if you've forgotten). So if he's a quack, he is a good one. But Miss F.—who rather *haunts* us now—is sure that some day the doctor will *go too far*, whatever that dark expression may mean. But it is just the least bit alarming. I'd like to get him to take a look at Dear One, who is not a bit well—not really The Thing, as they used to say, but I know she'd shrink from the steel table and perhaps cradling the doctor's huge head on her dear tum.

Must fly—all good wishes,
CHIPS

VIGNETTES

1. Quite an extensive sketch, at least 5" x 3"—which is gigantic in Chips' terms—of a rabble of the lame, the halt, and the blind, toiling toward my clinic, on the steps of which Christofferson stands "like the blind Fury with th' abhorred shears."
2. Pusey, exquisitely done by an English animal-lover of extraordinary gifts.
3. Miss Fothergill being sniffed You Know Where. Oh, Chips, you are too funny an artist to be a real pornographer, but you might have made a fortune as a comic one. The look on my face in this vignette is that of a satyr who has had a good scientific education. Miss Fothergill is Maiden Shame grown somewhat long in the tooth.

[9]

MISS FOTHERGILL WAS more of a nuisance than most of my patients, not because of any complexity in her case but because her resistance was uncommonly strong; she fought me every inch of the way at every consultation, because she was convinced she knew how the world wagged, and any disagreement with her opinion was rooted in a defiance of all received wisdom—received, that's to say, in the Toronto district of Rosedale, of which she was a denizen. At the age of fifty-three she was alone, as her mother had died a few months before she came to see me. Saunders Graham, her family physician, had found her intolerable, and had dextrously shifted her off on me, saying he felt she needed very special attention. She didn't, but these commonplace cases are often the most inveterate.

Old Burton would have described her illness as Maids', Nuns', and Widows' Melancholy, but that would not have been quite accurate. It was not sexual experience alone she was missing, but something far broader. She exemplified, with clarity, the Revenge of the Unlived Life, the rejection of whatever possibilities had been open to her as a young woman, the abandonment of love or any strong emotion. She had never exerted her abilities (and she was not a fool) in any direction, but had devoted herself to the care and satisfaction of her selfish mother, to whom she had been companion and confidante until at last she nursed the old woman into the grave. She was convinced that her mother had been a woman of uncommon intelligence, wisdom, and social correctness, though she never offered me any evidence to justify such an opinion. And now that Mother was dead, she was high and dry without any reason to live. But the indomitable spirit of survival that exists far below the level of reason would not permit her to die (devout church-goer that she was, she was deeply afraid of death) and as her life was empty it had filled up with a variety of more or less disagreeable symptoms that convinced her she was seriously and fascinatingly unwell.

As indeed she was, measured in terms of her life and temperament. She needed waking up and a reappraisal of her situation. I didn't want to suggest that dear Mother had been an unscrupulous old blood-sucker of a quite common kind, but I wanted her to take hold of the fact that Mother was dead, and that the whole world had not thereby ground to a halt.

Treatment: Christofferson, to begin. Mineral baths that swirled her round, as Chips said, and a good enema once a week; not really necessary but it provided a sense of well-being and—this is fanciful but I allow my fancy a voice in what I do for my patients—a reminder that what was useless should be discarded. I got Harry Hutchins to make her up a tonic, reasonably helpful in providing a bit of iron but not too much (because she had an inclination toward haemorrhoids) but nasty enough to convince her that something was being done. The bottle bore a red sticker saying, "Not On Any Account To Be Taken Beyond The Prescribed Dosage." She could have swigged off a pint without much harm, but these things were supplementary to what I had to do in the consulting-room.

She must find occupation, I said. What? The Art Gallery, the Museum, the Symphony—she had no interest in those and Mother had never thought much of the kind of women who threw themselves into such causes—just seeking social advancement, Mother said. No, said I; not that sort of occupation, but mental and spiritual occupation. But she had spiritual occupation; she was a regular communicant at St. Simon's— couldn't bear St. Paul's, full of climbers and all sorts. No, said I, regular attendance at Communion was not helpful if nothing much went on between Sundays. Did she pray? Oh yes; she read out of the Book of Common Prayer every night; Mother had said she read so well. I gave her Charlie's lesson of so many years ago: her prayers seemed to be Petition, but had she ever done anything about Intercession or—this was the most significant—about Contemplation? No, she had not, and thought that sort of thing sounded unhealthy. Too much thinking about yourself. (She was happily unaware that all of her illness and her expensive visits to me were nothing but thinking about herself.) I suggested that she might make an appointment with Father Iredale at St. Aidan's, to talk about prayer, but she gave me a very old-fashioned look as if she thought that I was not merely a twat-sniffer but even more horribly a Papist. So any attempts to get her life moved on to another line by the work of religion was a failure.

What ailed her, and what I could not hope to explain to her, was that she was body and soul an heiress. Of course she had inherited all Mother's money, and she was determined to take the greatest care of it, and at last to hand it on to—to what? She didn't know. She did not approve of anything sufficiently to wish to encourage it with Mother's money. But that, and the dark old barrack in Rosedale, were not all she had inherited from Mother. The real treasure was Mother's rich body of prejudice, ill-will, and hatred. She felt it her duty to be a witness before the world of Mother's Values. It was not a light task, and she knew she must put her back into it. Which she did. And the result was that she was developing, quite rapidly, a promising case of *arthritis deformans*. Many of the ablest of my colleagues are sure this disease is caused by a virus, and it may very well be so. But there are so many viruses floating around, looking for a home, that anybody who needs one will have no trouble in picking up one that suits the need. Miss Fothergill needed something to make her firm in her beliefs (Mother's beliefs); she needed—or thought she needed—something to stiffen her, and she was in a fair way to crippling illness. Not all Christofferson's baths could do more than slightly ameliorate what was inevitable.

My consultations with her, however, might have helped if I could have persuaded her to look at her life from another point of view, which was not wholly her Mother's point of view. I urged her to read, to victual her mind for some helpful reflection. But she was not a reader. She took no pleasure in any of the arts. She was not idle. There were menus to be made out and explained to the cook; there were flowers to be "arranged"; there were letters to be written. And, of course, there was "business" to be attended to, the lawyer to be visited not less than once a month, the insurance people to be interrogated, the tax-bills to be sifted and deplored, and everything that came under the heading of "property" to be watched over. She spent her evenings poring over the annual reports of the hospitals and universities who might be worthy of her money, when—a long time hence—she could hang on to it no longer. All of this business fuelled her feeling that she was beset, beleaguered, put at bay by a world that would take advantage of her if she relaxed her vigilance for an instant. There was, it seemed to me, no way of prying her loose from the damnable inheritance she had been left by Mother. She was the keeper of Mother's opinions, and in the house in Rosedale she was the custodian of Mother's tomb.

Not all my time with Miss Fothergill was politely concealed vexation and loss. I learned something from her, and what I learned was refinement of the art of listening. Not, indeed, listening simply to her litany of complaint about the iniquities of the age, or her descriptions of her symptoms. She even at last came clean about her tiny haemorrhoid, which of course I had seen at her first examination while I was peeping between her buttocks, where it nestled like a little pink pearl. She thought it a terrible affliction, though I knew it was a trifle. Miss Fothergill knew nothing of such things, but I did, and in the army I had seen piles like bunches of grapes, which the bearers had endured for months before coming to the medical officer. ("Nobody knows de haemorrhoids I've seen/ Nobody knows but Jesus," to adapt the fine spiritual.) No, what I learned from Miss Fothergill was the tune, the cadence of her speech, which lay below the words.

Everybody's speech has a tune, and it is always revealing. For social chat it may be a light *scherzando*, but when in the consulting-room it turns to themes of lower-back pain, of haemorrhoids, of gas pains, of frequent getting-up in the night, it will turn to *andante lamentoso*; in it the attentive physician's ear discerns the cry of the infant, or the toddler who wants mother to kiss it and make it better. Or it may be the sound of deep grievance, of one who has been dealt a rotten hand in the game of life, of one who sees unworthy people prosper while he or she is sinking in illness and decline. Tunes and tunes.

Simple people speak in a simple tune, whatever they may be saying. But people of more complex mind fall into a wry tune, and sometimes when I spoke with Miss Fothergill I sensed that she thought me a very simple creature indeed.

"You have never considered marriage, I suppose," I said one day. Her tone had the chilly brilliance and edge of cut glass.

"Never. Mother was very perceptive about that. 'My dear,' I remember her saying, 'if you think of marrying a man, ask yourself this—could you bring yourself to use his toothbrush? That will tell you everything.'"

Ah, poor Miss Fothergill! Christofferson reported to me that she was *virgo intacta*. "A hymen like parchment," she said, solemnly. Nobody had passed the toothbrush test.

I am incorrigibly innocent. I frequently do not see what is under my nose. Miss Fothergill's case became clear to me when I heard, indirectly, that she had been praising me extravagantly among her acquaintances. I was the first doctor she had ever encountered who cared to understand the true nature of her ill-health. I was a man whose very presence made her feel better for hours afterward. I was a doctor who had time to *listen*. She was my trumpeter.

So, then, Miss Fothergill had found her enthusiasm, her hobby, her pursuit. It was Dr. Jonathan Hullah. The Ladies laughed their heads off, and asked me from time to time when Miss Fothergill would name the happy day, and would the wedding include a nuptial mass at St. Aidan's?

How coarse the raillery of women can be! Surely they understood that I could not discuss a patient, and certainly not joke about one. This is the sort of situation that tests a physician's character. I could milk Miss Fothergill (if such a term may be applied to a woman whose breasts looked like a couple of empty wallets hanging on her chest) for as long as she lived, flattering her, listening to her blethers, and charging her inordinate fees. Playing my cards right, I could ensure a fat legacy when she died. (I could even poison her, slowly and imperceptibly, and collect within two or three years.) Was it my own substantial fortune or my ethical scruples that deterred me? Whichever it was, I managed to reduce Miss Fothergill's appointments to one every three months, at which time I observed her gradual decline into an aching but pretty spry and cranky arthritic.

One of the unhappy things about being a doctor is that you cannot always choose your patients; it is uncommonly hard to get rid of somebody you don't like. I didn't like Miss Fothergill, though I was sorry for her. She had been foisted on me by Saunders Graham, who she thought an inconsiderate man, and not really a gentleman. But I had nobody to whom I could send her. I was a Court of Last Resort. But the astonishing thing was that I appeared to have done her a great deal of good, to have set her squarely in the sort of health she desired, and to have provided a man in her life who was in no way a sexual threat, and whose toothbrush she would never be called upon to savour.

[10]
Glebe House
Cockcroft Street
Toronto, Ontario
Canada

Dearest Barb:

In your last you say that I keep on referring to our "Sundays" but never really say what they are. Sorry. I'm a rotten correspondent. No system.

Our Sundays have become quite a Toronto institution without our ever having really done much about it. Hugh McWearie (I've told you about him) calls it our "salon" which is pitching the note too high and suggests that Dear One lies on a Récamier couch and smiles wearily at compliments, while I dominate a tremendously intellectual conversation at the other end of the room. Not a bit like that. We both work like stink from Friday through Sat., preparing the goodies, which I must say are pretty lavish—scones with jam and whipped cream are a popular item and cucumber sandwiches by the hod. Because they eat like refugees, being musicians mostly and a lot of them foreigners. Isn't it odd how much foreigners seem to eat?

But I haven't said who they are. Artists, or people somehow connected with the arts—and those managers and agents are some of the biggest eaters! We seem to specialize in musicians because they are really the most clubbable of the artistic community here. And there is one. You'd be astonished at what a lot of artists of one sort and another there are in this place, which doesn't really seem to pay much attention to them. There is even a club for them, but it doesn't prosper as our salon does. I suppose it's the food.

Why musicians? It just happens but I suppose there is some deep reason for it. The painters are a very special lot and feel themselves beleaguered because they are trying to drag Toronto taste into the twentieth century and it's an uphill pull. Sculptors hardly to be found; no call for it except effigies of dead politicians and they are getting very expensive (bronze, of course) and are generally farmed out to somebody in Montreal who specializes in that sort of thing and does it from photographs. Writers—well, we've tried with writers but no go; they are so quarrelsome, and they expect booze, which we can't run to. Certainly not the way writers guzzle it. So it's musicians, chiefly.

Not opera, though there is some. But Dear One *nauseates* opera, though I rather fancy it. Poor darling, she nauseates so many things now, it seems.

A few stage people but they are scarce on the ground and few in the pod, if you take me. Theatre here is still very much an import and the movies give most people all they want. Except for the Players' Guild, a really *good* semi-amateur group & Darcy Dwyer wants to rope us in for some design work— unpaid, of course. We get some Guild people and one or two odd bods like the woman who tries to encourage children to act, but my dear *how!* She got her early experience with Ben Greet, so you can guess what the style is—definitely not Gerald du

Maurier or Noel Coward. Dulcy and Decorum—a man and wife team, she a really good comic and he that sorry sight, a decayed *jeune-premier*, are pretty regular. And a poor old chap, Watkin Tinney, very moth-eaten, who asserts that he was Beerbohm Tree's secretary—but there must be a platoon of his ex-secs.[1] He gets himself up *á la* Henry Irving and gives the girls lessons in elocution at Moulton College. Also, I fear a toucher—$5 here and $10 there, while he is inveighing loudly against "ama-choors"—and we really can't have a toucher as one of our regulars if we must have him at all. But the poor old chap looks *so* hungry.

No, it's the musicians and I must say they are an accomplished bunch, but odd, as musicians tend to be. Is it the vibration from their instruments, do you suppose, working on the brain? All that fraught buzzing?

The very top of the heap, the star turn, is Neil Gow, who actually *is* a native born of Scots forebears as you would have guessed and could not be any-thing else.[2] He conducts the local symphony orches-tra and is pummelling them into quite decent shape. He also conducts the big choral group, so he has rather a corner on the best jobs and is very much an object of envy to the men and erotic excitement to the women who are always trying to shove him into "affairs" and sometimes putting themselves forward as likely candidates. (They have the innocent notion that "affairs" are good for art, whereas they're really only good for gossip.) But he is faithful to his Elsie, and I suspect that he relies on her to bring common sense into a complicated life. A born leader, but Dear One says not really a first-rate conductor. I wouldn't know, but certainly a leader is what's wanted. An inspirer, and that is what Neilie so triumphantly is.

You'd be surprised what an erotic undercurrent there is in the musical life here. Or probably you wouldn't. Another great focus of itchy gossip is Joyce Barma, who is a pretty good cellist but a genuine beauty in the Garbo manner—you know, as if she were rising above a quite bad pain in the gut.[3] She is married to a competent artist, Feofan Barma, so they seem exotic, though she is really an Australian, born McVittie. She is a stunner, and I must say Dear One talks about her rather a lot in a way that disturbs me. But Joyce is assotted of a young pianist, Adair Scott, who is a good ten years her junior, and of god-like beauty, so they are an astonishing pair. Poor old Feofan consoles himself with our cream scones and black-currant jam. Dwyer says, but not too loudly, that there is not a man in Toronto who doesn't long to be Joyce's cello when she takes it between her knees and makes it sing.

I've told you about Dwyer, and he certainly isn't one of those who long to be between Joyce's knees. He recruits people for our Sundays, in order, he says, that we may have the best and not just be running a soup kitchen. He and McWearie have appointed themselves our mentors and occasional chuckers-out. I *have* mentioned McWearie,[4] haven't I? Must have. He is often about the place and a great pal of Dr. Hullah.

It was Hullah who suggested that we should rate our guests on the VELAWIG Scale. You remember it? It was all the rage when we were at art school. You rate everybody with a mark out of ten on their proneness to Vanity, Envy, Lechery, Avarice, Wrath, Idleness, and Gluttony—the Seven Deadlies. But it was McWearie who said that was utterly useless unless you balanced it against a rating on the Scale of Virtues, which is Faith, Hope, Charity, Justice, Fortitude, Temperance, and Prudence—which doesn't accommodate itself to a neat acronym (McWearie throws words like acronym around very casually) like VELAWIG, which sounds positively scientific! (Named after Dr. Melchisedek Velawig of Brno.)

This provides hours of by no means harmless or edifying entertainment. I mean, look at two of our regulars, Anton Moscheles and his wife Antonia (another Australian but because of marriage to Anton has acquired a powerful Russian accent). Anton is a cellist and a member of the top local quartet. Chubby, piggy-faced but very intelligent, side-whiskers, tremulous thick *pince-nez* and always wears one of those wrap-around black stocks and a high collar, so that he looks very like Schubert. Well! Eight for Vanity, at least, the very lowest for Idleness, maybe four for Lechery (Antonia takes care of all that, I suppose), call it five for Envy, and three for Wrath—but Gluttony! A bulging, insufficient ten! ("Splendid sandwiches these, dear lady. And, my friend, I cannot resist another of those excellent scones before my slice of cake!") But on the Scale of Virtues I think old Anton must be eight on all but Temperance. And Antonia is really not far behind, if she is behind at all, except physically where she is very much behind (ha ha).[5]

Vanity is where they all score high, as I suppose all artists must do. Without vanity how could they survive? Even the austere Scot Neilie Gow rates high, though he holds it in check, and some, like Arne Gade, the Danish pianist,[6] are crafty about it. Arne plays superbly, and about sevenish on Sundays (by which time all the musicians with church duty to attend to have gone) he plays for us, pretending reluctance as we urge him. And he invariably says, "I'm not at all sure of this. Haven't looked at it for months and my memory may betray me"—and then launches into a stunning Schumann *Fantasie* or something equally demanding that several of those present have heard him practising as they passed his house on Saturday. And when he has finished, and been applauded heartily, he hangs his head and says he is sorry to have done such a poor job, and he hopes some time we will hear him play it as he hears it in his head. Tiresome, but understandable. But he is perpetually aware of his great rival Augusto DaChiesa, a Chilean who is not in the little brotherhood that runs the local Conservatory, and who plays Scarlatti like an angel. DaChiesa is said to have a pupil who will make them all sit up and take notice in a few years. But we can't get him to our Sundays; stomach is bad and he seems to live on milk and crackers—and Scarlatti, of course. Has a mistress—would you believe it?

Quite often we get the quartet, who do what they call a *hauptprobe*, a sort of dress rehearsal, for a concert they are preparing. Good chaps, really, though I'm not mad for Jean-Marie Francoeur, the leader, but Achille Moraillon, the second fiddle, keeps him from getting too pompous. George Hambrook, the viola, is a decent chap, and of course old greedy Anton is the cello. Just four varied chaps, but when they play together my dear they are *transfigured*.[7] "Because we are just the voice of Schubert," said old Anton when I raved about their performance of the Quartet in D minor—the *Death and the Maiden* one, you know. It moved me to tears, but unmusically, I'm afraid, because it made me think of Dear One (who isn't in the least ready for Death) and her struggle in this ghastly place where they haven't the least idea of her quality; it's *bloody*. And when I looked at her across the room listening so intently and looking so much her *real self*, honestly, I found myself blubbing in a most unsuitable way because of course I'm supposed to be the *strong* one.[8] Yes, the Quartet is best in Schubert, and a few weeks ago they gave us *The Trout* quintet with Arne Gade playing the piano. How do we run to a piano? The Doctor's, whose mother's it was and he didn't want it as he doesn't play. A very decent Blüthner, oldish but none the worse for that.

> So that's our Sundays.
> Dearest love from us both,
> CHIPS

VIGNETTES

1. The Child Encourager—fat but with the remains of good looks—and Watkin Tinney, a mangy caricature of Irving, in conversation.

2. Neil Gow, a Scot unmistakably, of the plump Hebridean Order. His hypnotic eye is not that of a man given to "affairs."

3. Barma—a stunner indeed and Chips' fine sketch rouses an old ache in me. A few lines suggest Adair Scott, behind her head.

4. McWearie to the life. All intelligence and wit: bad teeth, scant hair, poorly shaved—an intellectual sloven, but a dear creature.

5. Yes, Moscheles *did* look like Schubert, but I don't think he got himself up to do so. He was simply the kind of man who *must* wear a stock.

6. Arne, a seedy Grieg whose art belies his appearance, as it so often does.
7. The Quartet: an impression—but *what* an impression!—of their intent musicianship.
8. A self-caricature of Chips and most revealing—her hatred of her big, powerful, mannish figure—and her face hideous with weeping. But I remember it otherwise and its tenderness toward Emily I shall never forget.

[11]

SORRY, CHIPS, that isn't quite your Sundays. Your good heart has run away with you and your modesty has blinded you to the fact that you and Emily Raven-Hart have provided something that serves as a domestic focus for the artists who frequent it.

Neil Gow couldn't do it. Admirable man that he was, your sort of lavish, easy hospitality simply wasn't in his Scots soul. It wasn't just the scones and the cream; it was the welcome, the understanding, and after a while, the affection that made Glebe House so very special. Gow, and DeCourcy Parry, couldn't embrace these people as you did because they had to work with them, and sometimes wrangle with them, and were inevitably rivals with them.

You were patrons—not rivals but understanding friends and cheerers-on. They knew you weren't rich. They guessed—certainly Antonia and Elsie did—what slavery went into those Sunday buffets. They loved you and they mocked you behind your backs (all patrons are mocked behind their backs; it is a way artists have of maintaining self-respect) but they would not have for an instant tolerated any mockery of you by outsiders.

Besides, you mock them. Don't you? Isn't your letter

to Barbara written in terms of mockery? You fear to say what you really feel, which is that you love and pity and marvel at these people, and warm your bones at the fire of their talent, so you have to pretend that they are figures of fun. But they aren't. They make you weep when they play the *Death and the Maiden* quartet, and when Joyce Barma—yes, I saw that Emily was very much taken with her—plays the Bach D minor solo sonata on her cello, her beauty adds a grace to the music, but it certainly is not a substitute for it, so don't run Joyce down as a pretty face with a big fiddle. You don't, I know, and I understand your jealousy about Emily. Ah, Pansy my old darling, it is your upbringing makes it impossible for you to say, directly, what you feel. God, what the English do to their daughters! You had a first-rate upper-class upbringing, and it has left you crippled and tongue-tied. But how eloquently you speak in your vignettes. As for Emily—

After the Sundays at Glebe House it was usual for McWearie and Darcy Dwyer to return with me to the stables, where we rectified all that cream and jam and cake with generous bumpers of first-rate Scotch. Inevitably we talked about The Ladies.

"Extraordinary how and where the supernatural virtue of Charity manifests itself," said Dwyer, on one of these occasions. "Who would expect the Grace of God to appear as scones and whipped cream, or in a Sally Lunn, or a generous slice of cherry pound-cake? Yet it does. I assert that it does. The Ladies give, and ask nothing in return. But what they get unasked is the allegiance and respect and love of the people whom they touch by their goodness of heart. Who cares if they have sharp tongues? Not I! Judge them by what they do."

"Quite right. And I suppose in the summing-up these Sundays are their great contribution to the life around them," said McWearie. "They are artists, but that is nothing compared to what they are as human beings."

"That's for you to say," said I. "I wouldn't venture an opinion. They are sure I know nothing about art and despise my pictures. The stuff of theirs—of Emily's really—that I have seen says nothing to me, because I suppose I haven't the perception needed."

"I'll venture an opinion," said Darcy; "I know a lot about art—meaning pictures and sculptures and what-not, which seems to be what people are talking about when they talk of art—and Emily's stuff isn't really much good. It's too good to be dismissed as junk, but it really hasn't much to say for itself."

"Don't let Pansy hear you," said I. "She is sure Emily is a great unrecognized genius."

"Loyal, but wrong," said McWearie. "Dear Emily is that very sad human creature, the artist who has a lot of talent but not quite enough. The world is full of them. Some of them fake and blether their way into quite a lot of popular acceptance; they are clever talkers but poor makers. But Emily is a diminished version of—who do you guess?"

"No use asking me," said I.

"Oh, it's easy," said Dwyer. "Every little piece she does is a faint echo of Barbara Hepworth. Not imitative. Nothing cheap or me-too about it. Just the same spirit, reduced to the point where it no longer carries conviction. It is good of its sort, but it's a rather minor sort. It's school-of. So it's no use Pansy blaming Canada. It's just a sad fact."

"Do you suppose she ever knew Barbara Hepworth?" said I.

"In the world of art you never know who knows or has known who, and what is personal and what is derivative. That's part of the misery of the lesser artist. People think they copy, whereas they really just think the same way as somebody bigger, but not as effectively." Dwyer knew a good deal about art and I was ready to accept his opinion.

"This is a common tale in my consulting-room," said I. "The gift that isn't big enough to make a mark, but is too big to leave the possessor in peace. And so they can't be content to be Sunday painters, or poets who write for a few friends, or composers whose handful of delicate little settings of Emily Dickinson can't find a singer. It's a special sort of hell."

"Jon, I don't think your pictures are so dreadful," said McWearie, who had been drinking his Scotch pacing about my upstairs living-room. "Dürer letting on to be Christ—verra fine. Sweet Nelly O'Morphy looking good enough to eat with a silver spoon—yes, just the thing for over your mantel, bless her rosy little bum. I see you have a new one. What's this?"

"It's a Paul Delvaux, a Sleeping Venus now in the Tate. I had a good deal of trouble getting a suitable reproduction. It's a superb evocation of the inner world."

"Your inner world. Mine isn't so delightfully populated."

"Let's see," said Dwyer and joined Hugh in front of my picture. "Hm, yes. Another of your Death and the Lady pieces, Jon. What hold has that theme on you?"

"Oh, but Death and the Lady in very special circumstances," said McWearie. "Look—a splendid moonlit classical setting of temples and the mountains of Hellas behind them. Here in the foreground, on a gilt couch lies one verra lovely lady, nude and asleep. Ye know from the fact that she still has the hair in her armpits that she's no wee whore; she's a lady of breeding. Perhaps she's the same lady, dressed in red, who is confronting the skeleton on the left; she regards it with splendid imperturbability and the skeleton is a fine specimen of its kind—male, I should judge, though I don't know why Death always has to be male. And who are all these distracted girls raving in the middle distance—and see, here's another entering the picture from down-stage right, with her arms raised in what I would judge to be protest. A verra fine piece, Jon. You could ponder on its meaning for hours."

"If you were the kind of blockhead who looks for meaning in pictures," said Dwyer. "Meaning is *out*, Hugh."

"Then I'm out with it," said McWearie. "I cannot resist a picture that tells a story, if it's a good story. And this one seems to tell a verra fine, elusive, daft story. Something from the dream-world. A Sleeping Venus, eh? I wonder how she can sleep with all that row going on? All those shrieking girls."

"You should ask some of my patients," I said. "They hear the shrieks in their sleep."

"But you wisely keep the picture up here out of their way. Have The Ladies seen it?"

"I don't ask The Ladies up here," said I. "Their hard words about my pictures are confined to those in my waiting-room. Dearly as I love them, I can do very well without their incessant, uninvited criticism."

"I never criticize anybody's pictures," said Dwyer. "It's a liberty, and one oughtn't to take liberties, not even with good friends."

By which remark I knew that he was drunk and it was time to bring the evening to a close.

Dwyer continued to astonish me, from time to time, even though I was no longer a university lad, but a man of substantial experience. He knew so much about the way the world wagged, and it never seemed to wag simply, though it always wagged logically.

For two or three weeks I had been interested in the appearance in the tiny graveyard which was now incorporated in Pansy's garden of a man whose appearance was utterly commonplace, but who somehow drew my attention. He came only on Sundays, when one of The Ladies' evenings was about to begin—that's to say about four o'clock—and he hung about, apparently absorbed in copying the inscriptions on the tombstones. What was he up to? An amateur historian? Somebody tracing family graves? One Sunday I tackled him, because it was a rainy day and it seemed odd that he should be at his work in such unsuitable weather.

"Can I be of any help?"

"No, no, Doctor. Don't let me bother you."

(So he knew I was a doctor. Well, I suppose he read the sign that pointed the way to my door.)

"You're interested in the old gravestones."

"Yes."

"Why don't you speak to Miss Todhunter? This is her garden, you know."

"Oh, I don't want to be a nuisance."

"But it's usual to speak to the owner before you make free with a private garden, isn't it?"

"Oh, I hope I'm not intruding."

"Well, simply as a matter of curiosity, what *are* you doing?"

The conversation was beginning to take on a slight edge, and might have turned nasty if Darcy Dwyer had not turned up at that moment, and greeted the anonymous little man familiarly.

"Hullo Joe. On the job, are you?"

"Oh, nothing of that kind, Mr. Dwyer. How's everything with you?"

"As usual. Money, money, money. Jon, this is Joe

Sliter; an old business associate of mine."

"Oh, nothing as grand as that, Mr. Dwyer."

"Picking up a few names, are you? Has Mr. Wagstaff arrived yet? Or Mrs. Yarde? They'll be along soon, if they haven't come already."

"Just looking at these old stones, Mr. Dwyer—nothing in the line of business, really not."

"Come on, Joe. Everything's business with you. Working for the cops now, are you?"

"Oh heavens no, Mr. Dwyer. Nothing of that sort. I was just on my way when the Doctor spoke to me, so I'll be getting on now. Very nice to have seen you again, Mr. Dwyer." And he hurried away, seeming almost to vanish, but I suppose that was a professional accomplishment.

"Poor Joe, what an obvious ass he is," said Darcy, and would say no more at that time.

That evening was particularly fine. Neil Gow's choir was approaching its annual performance of the *St. Matthew Passion* and this evening a young tenor who was fast making a name for himself was going to sing *Ich will bei meinem Jesu wachen* with Jimmy Scrymgeour playing the *continuo* on my fine old Blüthner and Peter Erasmus playing the oboe part, which he did with an art of nuance I have never heard equalled. The noble utterance of Bach quite silenced the edge of spite in the conversation of the thirty or forty people assembled, and I was, as so often before, conscious that music made religion real to me as nothing else did. Was this triviality? If so, I must reconcile myself to being a trivial person. The music lifted me to a level which was sharply reduced when Darcy and I talked afterward in my upstairs living-room.

"Who was that fellow you introduced as Joe Something before we went into the house?"

"Joe Sliter? Just a snoop."

"What was he snooping for?"

"Information. I suppose one could dignify Joe's work by saying that he deals in information. He was checking on who went to The Ladies' evenings."

"Whatever for?"

"For people who want to know. How shallow you are, Jon. You think those things are just splendid get-togethers of artists of all kinds and friends of the arts, where we restore our souls with music and gossip. Haven't you noticed how many Jews are there?"

"So what?"

"There are a lot of people who would swear uphill and down that they are not anti-Semitic, but who have a tiny sliver of the Hitler glass sticking in their hearts. They wouldn't lift a finger to hurt a Jew, but perhaps they would not be over-zealous in defending a Jew if somebody else took a swipe at him. Jews, you see, are foreigners. Very obvious foreigners. And there is an ancient tribal suspicion of those who are not like ourselves hidden deep in most of us. Why the Jews? Why not Macedonians or Laplanders? Because the Jews tend to stick out. Their own fault, really. They simply do not assimilate and it's because they have an echo of Moses still ringing in their ears, assuring them that they are a Chosen Race. Maybe they are, though certainly God appears to have forgotten his deal with them, many and many a time. You ought to know what I'm talking about, Jon. You deal in this sort of thing in your consulting-room all the time—the hatreds and grievances that seem buried in the mythic past, but which work their way to the top at the most unexpected moments. Mistrust of the Jews is only a part of that ancient heritage, though it gets very special attention at the moment because of the ghastly mess in Germany and the uproar that we see every day in the papers from Israel."

"Darcy, these Jews we met at The Ladies' are friends. Not all of them dear friends, but friends. And in this God-forsaken northern hole they bring a breath from a warmer world and a richer heritage. They are an emollient in the structure of a raw society that needs an emollient."

"True, my dear fellow, but they are also human beings, and therefore not all white-winged angels. Talk to Jews about it, and they will be the first to tell you that some of their co-religionists are not entirely kosher in business affairs, and that the charming, sophisticated, fine-feathered men and women, and the artists of splendid achievement, are not the entire Jewish people. Many are as crass as any knuckle-headed Aryan you can find out in the boondocks. The thing about the Jews is that even on the simplest level, they tend to have style, and to have style in this, our fair land, is to be a somewhat suspicious character. They bring style to whatever they do; the Jewish lecher, the Jewish drunk (not a very common type), the Jewish con-man, is just as likely to have style as the Jewish artist or his Jewish patron. Beware of style, Jon. You show signs of developing it, and it could be your downfall."

"So that miserable little fellow is spying on the Jews?"

"No, he's spying on another bugaboo of the frightened classes—the radicals, the Reds, the threateners of Things As They Are."

"But you mentioned Cuthbert Wagstaff and Maude Yarde. What in the name of God is there to fear about them?"

"Wagstaff, editor of Canada's best political and literary weekly, and a brilliant polemicist. Maude Yarde, wife of a professor of history and a member of an old Loyalist family of unblemished repute. But both members of the recently founded Civil Liberties Association, and thus objects of suspicion to the frightened classes."

"So they get the police to track them and see where they go and who they know."

"Oh, not the police, Pyke. The banks."

"What!"

"Yes, the banks love information and need it. The police—the police have very few spies and they pay badly and grudgingly for what they call 'information,' and of course they know quite a bit, but probably not all, of the Civil Liberties Association, because they wouldn't understand what such people were concerned about. They deal in law, not opinion. But the banks—the banks need spies, and pay them quite well. Not spies in the tradition of the Italian Comedy, of course, no flamboyance, no super-subtlety, not even much brains. Just patient gumshoe work. Joe, there, will report to—never mind who—that Cuthbert Wagstaff and Maude Yarde were at Glebe House this afternoon, where there was a gathering of all sorts of people, many of them Jews and that it appeared to be a musical party although of course that could have been a cover-up. This information will eventually find itself to me, among a few others. And—understand this, my lad—I shall let Cuthbert and Maude know all about it, and they'll have a good laugh."

"This is a complication of duplicity that has my mind swimming. So you are in on this spy stuff, too?"

"I am a banker, Jon. I need to know a lot of things I can't find in the telephone directory. Wagstaff and Yarde don't interest me in that way. But there are friendships, and confidential visits, and of course unusual deposits or withdrawals from banks that do interest me very much. Me, and all the other banks, and some departments of government as well. Suicides and sudden long journeys that astonish people who are not in the financial world do not cause me to raise an eyebrow. It seems to me, my friend, that you have a very simple notion of what business really is."

"Probably. Thank God I'm not in that world."

"You are in another world, just as complex, and in some ways just as murky. There is no simplicity in any sort of significant life. I rest my spirit in the apparent complexity and actual simplicity of St. Aidan's; in that splendid ritual much of the grime and slime of daily life is washed away. That's why I give so much of my time to it. You seem to divert yourself with music and that brings you to St. Aidan's, too. We complicated people must find our repose of spirit in further complexities. We cannot retreat to blockish simplicities."

"But this spy business—it shocks me. Really, Darcy, it does!"

"Then don't call it 'this spy business.' Call it the complex exchange of confidential information in the world of business and government. It is part of the growing-up process in a society and in a city. Toronto is becoming a big place financially. It is backing Montreal into second position. And it is developing the culture appropriate to a large city, as well. I don't suppose The Ladies have any idea how vital a part they play in that. In its official histories the city will probably never mention them, but in the reality of a great city's culture their names will be enshrined forevermore."

[12]
Glebe House
Cockcroft Street
Toronto, Ontario
Canada

Dearest Barb:

You simply won't believe it! Our luck has turned, but in *such* a way—not so much turned as gone topsy-turvy![1] I have always known that life is a damned rum thing, but this is positively the *rummest*!!!

You know, I suppose, that the government in Canada is headed by a very big ceremonial wig called Governor-General. But I don't suppose you know that this time—last time—well, whenever the most recent one was appointed, it was decided that he should be a Canadian. And so he is, and all the stuffed shirts are trembling for fear he won't be completely kosher, or will lick his plate and eat peas with his knife or be in some way inferior to the grandees that have come out from home to hold the job, ever since there was a job. But not so! He is going great guns, and exerting himself more than GGs usually do, and takes to all the pomp and ceremony like a duck to water—which I suppose is not very surprising as he has been an ambassador and whatnot all his life. But the great news is that some nationalist group wants to have a head of him done in bronze for the National Gallery *and he has chosen Dear One to do it!* The very first real important recognition she has had.

But no sunshine without some rain. We had expected that she would be asked to go to Ottawa and set up a *pro tem* studio at Government House, but no—it seems His Nibs comes to Toronto often—it is where his home is or was until all this grandeur—and he will come to *her* when he can, and working with photographs and the measurements she can take it should all be done in about four actual sittings, with him posing. So far so good.

BUT—comes the great day and he is to arrive in time for tea. And so he does. Dear One and I have

fussed for three days about how to receive him. She
says we must curtsy at first meeting. I say that for an
Englishwoman to curtsy to any Canadian, however
highly placed, is against Nature and is indeed a kind
of ceremonial sodomy and *nothing* will make me do
it. She says, all right, blow my great chance, Chips,
don't let any considerations of friendship or long
association stand in your way, principle before everything—and then she weeps piteously and stabs seven
swords straight through my heart. But anyhow the
day comes and there is no question of curtsying
because His Ex walks right into the house and seizes
me by the hand and says What a pleasure Miss
Raven-Hart, and I couldn't curtsy even if I had a
mind to. Then we have to get it straightened out
who is who but the whole thing is put into utter
chaos because His Excellency proceeds to introduce
his secretary who is also his son, and then his aide-
de-camp and guess who that is? You wouldn't, not in
a thousand years. It's Gussie Gryll!!!!![2]

It seems that Gussie who should have gone back
home with the former GG, whom he had served as
aide for two years, had put in to the people in
Whitehall to stay another two years with the new
man—the Canadian man. Why? I strongly suspect
that Gussie may have blotted his copy-book at home
and wants to lie low for a bit. Can you make discreet
enquiries? Is there some ruined maiden somewhere
in the Home Counties whose father is looking for
Gussie with a horsewhip?

But anyway, there's Gussie reaching out his
hand to Dear One, smooth as a kitten's wrist and
saying, Emily Raven-Hart as I live! How are you?

None the better for seeing him, that's for certain. Dear One goes white as a sheet, but keeps her

composure, and we settle down for tea and a talk about how the great piece of work is to be done. But Gussie!—Gussie who created a situation where we had to make a run for it!

I don't suppose you ever heard. The Raven-Harts kept it very quiet. But it was like this. Dear One was never really keen to marry Gussie though both families had planned it for years—long friendship and money on his side and good family on hers. But after Dear One and I met in the MTC it was clear that the whole Gussie thing was a ghastly mistake, and that our life together was more important than anything. More important to *me*, that's to say, because my poor darling had been so brain-washed by her parents and the awful Home Counties gang they knew that she thought she *must* marry Gussie and simply couldn't see any way out of it. But she's so sensitive, and he's such a crass lout that it would have been total disaster, and after we had met, she knew it but still thought she had to go through with it. You know how strong conventional ideas are in families like that. Heart-breaking! (My heart among others.)

It came to a head when the marriage was getting close, and I was staying down at Colney Abbey because I was to be a bridesmaid. Can you imagine it? Me in one of those bloody outfits, taller and tougher than any of the dewy saps who made up the other five? And I was supposed to be Friend of the Family, helping with arrangements because I was so clever with my hands and wonderful at arranging things. Well, it was a couple of nights before the actual wedding day and Gussie had taken Dear One out into the garden for a romantic cuddle I suppose and the old folks smirked and leered and thought it was all simply divine and romantic.

They were togged up, because on impulse we'd decided to have a fancy-dress dinner and then a hop to the phonograph afterward. Dear One was wearing an Edwardian day-dress of her Gran's (because everything we wore came out of the Dressing-Up Box in the nursery) and she looked an absolute Dream, with a big hat to top it off. Gussie was a Pirate—he would—easy—just a hanky around the head and a black patch over one eye. I was *furious* because I had rigged up as a pirate myself, very much the same.[3]

Dear One has told me that Gussie was great on kissing and hugging but had never tried anything more adventurous until this night, when he had been getting a bit too heavily into Papa Raven-Hart's cognac, and they were sitting on a seat in an arbour—very romantic—and he kissed her a few times and then began to sort of snort and hugged her very close and she suddenly realized that he had his hand up her skirt and was trying to get into her panties!

Can you imagine what that must have been like for a girl like *that*, so sweet in every respect and I don't think she had any idea of what men are like or even how they're made—just the utterly uninformative stuff they dish out in Biology in school. No brothers, like mine, three Oxford Blues stamping around the house making dirty jokes all the time and going to the bath starkers and showing *everything* and laughing if I averted my maidenly eyes. But *instinct* is a great thing. Quick as a wink she whipped the long hatpin out of her Edwardian hat and gave Gussie a good jab with it—don't know where but I think it was in the arm. But that just egged him on. Some men adore resistance and he

thought she was just being flirtatious, I suppose, so
he kept on with the hand, and then Dear One seized
the dagger he had stuck in his sash and let him have
it bang in the buzzem, aiming for his heart! But
poor darling she doesn't really know where the heart
is, and so she just gashed him a bit and bent a rib.[4] I
don't know the medical details. And lucky for Gussie
the dagger was as dull as a hoe, so he was really more
bruised than wounded. But he gave a howl—outraged male lust, I suppose, and Dear One was able
to break away and get back to the house, with
Gussie in hot pursuit shouting, "Wait, Em! Hold on
a minute! You've stabbed me!"

Figure to yourself, my old one (as the French
say), the scene in the drawing-room. Bridesmaids
shrieking, groomsmen saying, "What the hell—?",
Ma Raven-Hart trying to find out what had happened, and the Colonel shouting louder than anybody, "Shut up, all of you. A chap's been wounded!
Stretcher-bearers here! Call a doctor at once! By
Gad, Gussie, you need a stiff drink—hold on a sec.
Em, you're under close arrest! Don't anyone budge
till I've had a chance to get the situation in hand, do
you hear?"[5]

Oh, the awfulness of the scene that followed! A
doctor turned up, after a while, and gave Gussie
some anti-tetanus because the old dagger was *green*,
my dear, with generations of nursery use, and if
Darkest Africa has anything more germ-ridden than
a well-used nursery, God help us all! And Dear One
was in hysterics, so I simply had to Doff the Mask
and comfort her as only I can, and I think that
astonished some of the young men—Gussie's
friends—who were hanging about with their mouths
open and probably deciding that marriage wasn't all

it's cracked up to be.

When all the shouting and hoo-ha had died down a bit one of the bridesmaids said, in a mouse's voice, "I suppose this means the marriage is off, then?[6] And you should have seen Ma Raven-Hart! She swelled to about twice her size and roared, "It most decidedly is *not* off! Everything will go forward as planned. People must come to their senses. Gussie isn't really hurt, and Emily must apologise here and now, and then off to bed, everybody, and *not a word of this beyond these walls.*"[7]

But Emily didn't apologise. She wept pitifully and I took her in charge. I must say Gussie said, "Oh, apology be blowed," which was decent.

That was it. That really put the lid on it. When everybody had gone to bed we sneaked out the garden door, found my little MG and were off, and in less than forty-eight hours we had taken ship for Canada, because it was the first booking we could get. And that's it. The Great Elopement.

And here was Gussie, large as life, behaving as though nothing at all had happened.

It's water over the dam now. No turning back. Apparently there's still no Mrs. Gussie or he wouldn't be doing this sort of duty. But I hated him worse than ever as he sat in one of our chairs, being terribly polite and deferential to His Nibs. Dear One was able to keep command of herself while she discussed how the head was to be done—a bronze job, none but the best because the Canadian Clubs of Canada are paying for it. It took just under an hour—I suppose these people work in fifty-minute hours, like psychoanalysts, and when they left, the secretary produced a uniform coat of the GG's so that the collar could be copied for the head. Gussie was all smiles and took leave of me as if he didn't hate my guts, as I'm sure he does. But Dear One had one of the *very worst* of her headaches and I had to put her to bed. And would you believe it, as I brought her a glass of hot milk she actually said, He's still very handsome, isn't he? As if it had all taken place fifty years ago, instead of five! Poor kiddie, she has such a tender heart!

And it never rains but it pours. No sooner had the GG's head been ordered than our tenant, Dr. Hullah, decided he wanted something called a caduceus in latten, of all things, made to fit on the wall in the entrance to his clinic. Wants it *four feet tall*! It'll cost the earth, sez I, ever practical. Perhaps not quite that, sez he, cool as the proverbial cuke. And he has given Dear One *carte blanche* about treatment, which means she can really do something in the modern manner. Hip, hip hurray! I am screaming out loud all the time I write, as Miss Fanny Squeers says in her famous letter.

All our love,
CHIPS

VIGNETTES

1. A smiling sun rising above the horizon, and evil-faced black clouds fleeing.
2. Gussie, even in Chips' caricature, looks quite a decent fellow. Her artist's eye disciplines her lover's prejudice.
3. Gussie and Chips—both younger—looking at each other, he with phlegmatic disapproval and she with fury. Both wear a black eye-patch, the conventional mark of a pirate.
4. Emily stabbing Gussie; she is weeping, he looks

like an astonished sheep.

5. The Colonel, purple in the face, mouth stretched for parade-ground roars. What a moustache!
6. The Bridesmaid, a mouse in very truth.
7. Ma Raven-Hart, roaring but without losing a particle of upper-class *hauteur*.

[13]
"WHAT'S LATTEN?"

"Well, Darcy, I'm delighted to inform you, because it's so rarely I know something that you don't know. Latten is an alloy of copper with zinc, lead, and tin mixed in so that when it is finished it takes on a beautiful colour which is like the softest and butteriest brass. Lighter in colour than bronze; not so aggressive as brass."

"I'd forgotten you were a bit of a metallurgist."

"Just a few things I picked up from my father."

"This caduceus—Hermes' walking-stick with two snakes curling around it—Mervyn Rentoul had one of those things made when he played Faust, do you remember? The magician's wand. Well, it'll be a nice classical touch in your reception room."

"Not entirely classical. I've asked Emily to give it a genuine Canadian treatment. The snakes will be a pair of Massassauga rattlers."

"Good God! Why?"

"They have a significance for me."

"Yes? Go on."

"Helpers and servers."

"You're being wilfully obscure."

"Totem animals."

"Pagan stuff."

"No, stuff from the Great Time, which is also where the best of your St. Aidan's stuff comes from.

When Emily is finished I shall have on my wall a constant reminder of the Warring Serpents of Hermes—Knowledge and Wisdom, balanced in an eternal tension."

"Knowledge being science and all the accumulated lore you have pumped into you at medical school; science which keeps changing and shifting all through your lifetime, like a snake shedding its old skin—"

"And Wisdom, with which you have to apply and temper the whole business, and fit it to the patient who sits before you, so that it too has a serpentine sinuosity and of course the wisdom which snakes are—quite mistakenly—supposed to possess."

"Very pretty. The snakes must be kept in balance. And is this thing you are getting Emily Raven-Hart to make supposed to explain that to your patients?"

"Not really. But it's supposed to keep me always mindful of it. It's awfully easy to become mechanical in this profession. Patients encourage it. They're so dull, most of them, poor creatures. They want something to deal with their symptoms, and they can't grasp that the symptoms and the disease are different things."

"And the disease is?"

"Burton, in his great book, calls it Melancholy—meaning a condition of the spirit, not just being down in the mouth. It shows itself in an extraordinary variety of forms. The asthmatic—is he puffed up with a sense of his own importance, or is he holding back something he dare not speak? The arthritic—is it fear of being drawn into life, or is it a grandiose rigidity of opinion? Skin ailments—are they to repel the onlooker and keep the world at bay, or are they a declaration of self-hatred and terrible humility? You have to find out. It's a matter of the finest balances, and extraverted and introverted attitudes. That's where you have to call on the Wisdom snake, and sometimes it's damned slow to tell you what you want to know. One of the worst basic ills is anger, or resentment, or simple grievance; that one can assume shapes that would astound you. And they all speak through the body, not clearly or obviously, but with a determination that can shadow a life or end a life."

"Keeps you on your toes."

"Yes. You know when the Greeks were ill they went to the temple of Hermes to pray and their prayer was, 'To which god must I sacrifice in order to be healed?' People don't do that any more. But I must do it with every patient. I must pray, 'To which god must I sacrifice in order to heal?' Then I have to wait for an answer."

"Is that what I see you praying at St. Aidan's?"

"That, yes; one temple is as good as another to those of us whose faith is the Perennial Philosophy."

"But you need a temple?"

"What's a temple for? To put you in the mood to invoke the god."

"The god?"

"The god who is present whether you call on him or not, and whom it is death to ignore. The people who ignore the god—the Undead Dead, as somebody has called them—are all about us. As thick in Toronto as anywhere else on earth."

"Are you one of those instant diagnosticians? I mean, you say it takes a long time to find out what really ails somebody, but can you spot the superficial symptoms as soon as they walk into your consulting-room?"

"Have some more Scotch. Sometimes I can, but I don't encourage myself in that trick. One mustn't become slick. But just last week a fellow came to see me who wasn't ill at all. I diagnosed him within thirty seconds as one of those Snoops you told me about."

"Really? Well, I'll be damned! And who was snooping

on you?"

"The Canadian Medical Association, I suppose. You know they have a new president. A new broom, and wants to sweep clean. Chase out quacks. Put chiropractors in the pillory. Geld osteopaths. Brand a huge H on the cheek of the homeopath. The stupider members of my profession are full of glee, because they have what they call a live wire on the job. As soon as this little fellow came into the room I thought there was something fishy about him. And the invaluable Christofferson laid a note on my desk, on which she had typed, 'N.B. the breast pocket.' And sure enough, there was the metal clip that betrays the clinical thermometer, and isn't like the clip of a pen or pencil. He was a medical man, not long graduated, I imagine, and perhaps some sort of understrapper in the Association office."

"So?"

"So I decided I had better unmask him as soon as I could. I asked him what was troubling him. A touch of heart, he said.

"I asked him to describe this 'touch of heart,' and he came up with as pretty and concise a textbook description of angina as you'd want to hear.

"'Don't you think you are rather young for what you've been describing?' I asked, soother than the creamy curd, and he, poor eager lad, fell into it at once. No, no, said he. It was beginning to be understood now that quite young people could experience angina if they were under some sort of anxiety.

"'You show some signs of anxiety at this moment,' I said. 'What is making you anxious—Doctor?'

"So there I had him. He turned quite red, and after a few more exchanges admitted that he was indeed a doctor, though a young one and inexperienced, he said. 'Why didn't you tell me at once?' I asked. Then he came out with a rigmarole about how anxious he was to study my methods of diagnosis, and he thought that perhaps if he didn't declare himself I would also provide a lesson in how to deal with a patient. And so on. He was glib, but essentially a blockhead. And I treated him with gentle courtesy."

"Did he have the gumption to see through your gentle courtesy?" said Darcy.

"Of course not. He was cheap stuff, and such people think courtesy is a sign of weakness. Did I want him to go on the table? he asked. He obviously wanted me to get him to strip, and sniff him, and listen to his foolish little gut and do all the things I sometimes do when I want to find out what's wrong with a patient. But there was nothing wrong with him, except that he needed a new heart and a new soul, which is a common enough state of affairs. So I said that no undressing would be needed.

"'I'd hoped to form some idea of your process of diagnosis,' said he, playing the role of disappointed student. He had admitted to being a doctor but so far I knew he had no idea that I was on to him as a snoop. So I decided to give him something really interesting to take back to his boss.

"'I had the good fortune to grow up in a country district,' I said. 'Perhaps country is the wrong word. Let us say a forest district and there were a great many of our native people nearby. One of them was a remarkable healer, a Mrs. Smoke, and she taught me a diagnostic method which she summed up in a story. You know the Indians love stories and parables. So listen to the story.'"

"Did Mrs. Smoke really teach you?" said Darcy. "You've mentioned her from time to time, but never as a teacher."

"Of course she didn't. She was kind to me but I think

she thought I was simple-minded. When I am pulling the wool over the eyes of a snoop, I am not speaking on oath. So I dragged in Mrs. Smoke as corroborative detail. This is what I told the snoop.

"'Long ago an Indian boy was wandering in the forest, wrapped in thought. He wanted to be a shaman, but all his friends said he was a fool, so he thought poorly of his chances. A shaman must have special wisdom. As he wandered he thought he heard a little voice, crying piteously—"Let me out! Oh, let me out!"—and when he searched he found at the root of a giant hemlock something that seemed to be a tiny bottle, like the bottles the white woodcutters carry with them, with strong waters in them. He dug the bottle out of the dirt and forest debris, and inside it he saw a small figure, which he thought must be a frog; it was gesticulating wildly and crying in its tiny voice, "Let me out!"

"'So the boy bit his teeth into the cork, and with some difficulty he pulled it out and immediately the little figure rushed through the neck of the bottle and even as it rose it seemed to grow and swell until it was a dreadful creature nine feet tall, with fiery eyes, long yellow teeth, and claws like a bear.

"'The boy was terrified, and cried out in a choked voice, "Who are you?"

"'"I am a Great Windigo," said the monster, "and I am going to eat you up."

"'"No, no—wait," cried the boy, who was not a fool. "You do not look to me like a Great Windigo. They are much bigger and have longer teeth. I think you are telling me a foolish tale to make yourself seem more frightening than you are. Can you do magic?"

"'"Of course I can do magic," said the monster. "Try me, if you have doubts."

"'"I will," said the boy. "You were small and now you

are big. If you can really do magic let me see you grow small again and slip back into this bottle. If you can do it, I will believe you are a Great Windigo."

"'With that the monster laughed, and very quickly grew small and slipped back into the bottle. Then the boy, who was not a fool, pushed the cork into the neck of the bottle as far as it would go, and the monster was imprisoned.

"'"Let me out. Let me out!" he cried, and beat piteously with his tiny claws, that were now like the quills of a humming-bird, on the glass walls.

"'"Will you eat me, if I do?"

"'"No, never; I shall reward you handsomely."

"'"Will you give me a great gift?"

"'"What do you want?"

"'"I want to be a shaman."

"'"I will make you a very great shaman."

"'"Do you swear by Ioaskeha?"

"'"By Ioaskeha!"

"'"And by Ataentsic?"

"'"Even by Ataentsic!"

"'Whereupon the boy pulled the cork again with his teeth, and immediately the Windigo stood before him. In the claws of its right hand it held what looked like a dirty piece of parchment, or bark.

"'"Take this," said the Windigo, "and it will make you a great shaman."

"'"How?" said the boy.

"'"Take it. Rub it on the blade of your axe."

"'The boy did so, and instantly the blade of the axe was beautiful, softly gleaming silver.

"'"But I want to be a shaman, not a silversmith," said the boy.

"'"Take it and be grateful," said the Windigo, "for it heals all wounds." And with that it dashed over the treetops and was lost to sight.

"'And there you have my diagnostic method,' said I. 'How do you like it?'

"The poor noodle looked very much puzzled, and swallowed hard before speaking. 'I don't think I really understand it,' he said."

"I don't understand it either," said Darcy. "But I suppose you wanted to confuse him. Well, you've confused me, too. Explain, Doctor, explain."

"What I told the noodle was this: the patient who presents himself and what ails him—what really ails him and not just his collection of symptoms—is the Windigo in the bottle. A Windigo, in case you have been too busy with plainchant to know, is a cannibal monster; like a disease, or a malady, to call it something vaguer but more accurate; it eats people up. So, by a combination of modern science, intimate and revealing conversation, and intuition, we let the Windigo out of the bottle and we know what it is. We then denigrate it a bit, just to show who's boss. Put it in perspective, so to speak. And then, when it has been reduced in size and terror, we demand that it yield up a secret that will heal. And if we're lucky it does, and if we aren't lucky at least the patient has had the pleasure of several weeks of close, kindly attention—and that can also work wonders."

"And that's what you told the snoop?"

"At somewhat greater length, for he was slow of comprehension, but substantially that is what I told him. Hear the voice; open the closed place; confront the monster; reason with him; reach a compromise. It works, Darcy. It's worked for me time and time again."

"The story is familiar."

"Should be. It's from the Grimm collection."

"Not Indian?"

"They probably have some version of it. It's one of

those universal tales that contains a great truth. I adapted it to my need."

"The Windigo seems to have been a bit stupid."

"Yes. And diseases are stupid. Powerful, frightening, but stupid."

"I wonder if the snoop understood you. Indeed, I wonder what the snoop reported to his principal."

"I don't suppose we'll ever know."

"Jon, I wish you could apply your Windigo therapy to our friend Father Iredale. I think he's getting a bit odd."

"I've been watching him—listening to his sermons. My diagnosis, not precisely in Windigo terms, is Inflation of the Ego."

"Swelled head?"

"Oh, far, far more than that."

[14]
Glebe House
Cockcroft Street
Toronto, Ontario
Canada

Dearest Barb:

You wouldn't believe the difference it has made to this house now that Dear One has a real commission—two, in fact, if you count the job for Dr. Hullah. So much so, in fact, that—this was her idea—we have given grateful thanks in St. Aidan's, and not just mouth-thanks but something solid. I have promised a chasuble—you know, one of those cloak affairs the priest wears over his alb when he is doing Mass? They have some but my dear, they are *awful* and if there is anything Em and I can do for

St. Aidan's it is to lift the level of taste and workmanship in the vestments. The nuns have made most of the outfits, and they do lovely needlework but my dear, the designs! Cor stone the crows! The worst kind of late-Victorian, feeble clapped-out trumpery. And you remember the work my Gran did years ago for the Royal School of Needlework, when she was an enthusiastic patron, not only supporting financially but actually plying the needle like billy-o. Any talent or eye I may have comes from Gran, no doubt about it. So I have designed something really stunning, to be achieved in appliqué (is that how you spell it?) work, and am hard at it. Got the material through the costume chap at the Players' Guild, so it is virtually at cost price, being wholesale; a lot of it is really upholstery material, which gives the right weight, and on it I am applying *terrific* symbols which I am copying from a book of manuscripts, big enough to make a strong impact (which the nuns simply don't understand, poor loves) and in corded silks of gorgeous colours. And some real gold thread for the visible stitchery, which costs the *earth* and is hard to work with and scuffs the fingers.[1] I am hard at it every minute I can spare. Have laid etching aside until it is done but there's lots of housework in a huge place like this, and baking for the Sundays.

This has given enormous pleasure at the church, and Father Charlie is sure we are brands snatched from the burning. Father Hobbes is not so sure and makes noises about how all this rich material might have been sold for many pence and given to the poor. But Father Charlie says the poor will be enriched when they see their priest gorgeously arrayed to serve their God, and giving to the poor needn't always mean putting ground beef patties into the gobs of the bums and layabouts Fr. Hobbes calls God's People. So poor Fr. Hobbes has to shut up and accept it, which he does with a saintly smile.

Of course I'm on Charlie's side. Beauty cannot forever be sacrificed to utility because utility—especially when it means the poor—has never had enough. There simply isn't enough to deal with all their needs. We cannot live on hamburger patties alone. The soul must be fed as well as the belly, which our pal Hugh McWearie always calls Messer Gaster, which I suppose is out of Rabelais, whom he adores. Never read him, myself, but I agree that Messer Gaster must have his due, but not everything or civilization might as well pack it in. After all, what have the poor ever done for anybody except cadge? They are a burden we better-off ones have to bear, but they can't have *everything*. Do I sound like a tough old Scrooge? You should see some of God's People hanging around the rectory and you'd know why. They would eat Fr. Hobbes right down to the cob if Fr. Charlie would allow it.

But about being a brand plucked from the burning. It's true Dear One and I have become regular attendants at St. Aidan's and even take Communion—though I simply *will not* go to Confession first. Tell Tommy Whimble what a bad girl I have been, guilty of uncharitable thoughts, etc.?[2] Not bloody likely. It's the beauty of the thing that draws us. Ever been to High Mass? I don't mean a Romanist Mass which is now pretty much in ruins, but the genuine article at a High Church Anglican place? My dear, get right around to St. Mary the Virgin, in Bourne Street next time you are in London, and you'll see what I mean.

We go to the eleven o'clock solemn High Mass, with plainsong propers sung by the Ritual Choir (that's Darcy Dwyer's lot) and a missa brevis and motet sung by the Gallery Choir, which is like angels, if angels can sing, which I suppose they do. Starts off with the introit procession, with clergy, laymen, and altar servers carrying a Cross and candles and clouds of incense from a silver censer. The three priests are the deacon (usually Whimble) in a gold silk dalmatic over an alb which is a sort of chemise with lace edging. The celebrant (Fr. Hobbes as a general thing) wearing a gold silk chasuble over an alb. Then a third, now and then a layman but usually Charlie Iredale, wearing a gold silk tunicle over an alb. And all togged out in birettas—you know, those square caps with pompons on the top, which they pop on and off every time the Holy Name crops up in the service (which I don't like— Daddy always said only counter-jumpers were always lifting their hats).[3]

For the reading, the Gospel is brought to the lectern by a little procession, wrapped in a gold silk cover with tassels, and heavily censed before the reading. They go absolutely wild with incense and sometimes it's a bit stifling but is supposed to carry prayers right up to the Throne of God. I suspect that in an earlier day before plentiful running water it was also helpful in dispelling the fearful pong of the unwashed faithful. But that's an Unworthy Thought, to which Fr. Charlie says I am prone. He doesn't know the half of it.

But my dear, this is *beauty* of a very special kind. Beauty and reverence and it is like cool water in a thirsty land. So it is for the beauty we go, and give ourselves up to it and do what we can for St. Aidan's.

Short of being utterly committed believers, that's to say. But what is belief, anyhow? Isn't our commitment to beauty of sight and sound a kind of belief?

The part of the service—it isn't part of the Mass and you can leave before it begins, but that might be thought rude in friends—that gets my goat is the Sermon. Then you come down with a bang from all the splendour of the Prayer Book and the really super prose of Cranmer to what some chap thinks it would be good for you to hear. Worst of the lot is our dear friend Fr. Charlie Iredale. Sometimes I wonder if Charlie is going right off his nut. He bangs on and on about sanctity and the necessity to live the holy life.[4] Not just doing your best in the job you have and behaving decently to everybody else, but giving up all and following Christ—as if we could kick off our shoes and tramp around Toronto in February snow exhorting and healing and mooching an occasional meal from the rich, like Jesus himself. There has to be reason in all things, even religion. And when he talks about sanctity he makes my flesh creep, because he obviously means Fr. Ninian Hobbes, who has just been celebrating Mass and is now either deep in private prayer or perhaps having a doze, within a few feet of him! What's Charlie up to, I wonder? Now and again he reads a passage out of *The Golden Legend*, and so far as I am concerned it might better be the *Arabian Nights*, and that all comes zeroing down, somehow, to Fr. Hobbes. Or Charlie tells us about the spiritual exercises of Ignatius Loyola and suggests that a few saintly push-ups would do us a world of good, and make us more worthy of the pastoral care of Guess Who. This sort of thing gets on my nerves, I can tell you.

We see Charlie quite often, and not just at our

Sundays, when he usually drops in for a cream bun and a chat with Cuthbert Wagstaff or a joke with Gerry Broom. (Did I tell you about Gerry? Came to Canada with Playfair's tour of *The Beggar's Opera*, playing Filch, liked it, saw opportunities and stayed. Sings the Narrator's role in Gow's *Matthew Passion* with superb, *tactful* reverence, and is a great joker. Usually greets Anton Moscheles with "Sorry to see your throat's still giving you trouble, Anton." Meaning Anton's handsome stock. Anton doesn't get the Joe Miller of this, but smiles forgivingly.) Now where was I? I rattle on like Miss Mowcher. Oh yes, Charlie and his whim-whams. I tackled him one day about the Loyola business. "I once heard a very learned man at Oxford say that Loyola's piety and all those Exercises may well have been a sublimation, or even a perversion, of his sexual drive. What do you say to that? I mean, nowadays, when there is so much sexual freedom and recognition of sex as something not just tied down to reproduction, and different kinds of love are being recognized as what they really are—love." But Charlie just lowered his eyelids and said, "From a Divine perspective, it could be that all this genital fulfilment and concern with sex is simply a perversion of piety!" Now what is there to say to that? I put it up to Dr. Hullah, and he said he thought Charlie might have a point, and then McWearie, who loves to take the opposition side, whatever it may be, said that Loyola was a masochist and an oddball and what did Charlie make of Loyola's campaign to reform the prostitutes of Rome, and might that not spring from repressed sexuality, as did the same odd preoccupation in the early life of Canada's great Prime Minister, W. L. Mackenzie King?[5] Charlie said that Loyola's concern with prostitutes was Christian love, and it was easy in our science-mad day to spatter everything with so-called psychology. It was getting close to being a row, and I had to quell the fever with cream scones.

But love—what is one to make of it? I look across the room at some of our Sundays and see Joyce Barma and Adair Scott, standing apart but with an adoration passing between them that is strong and beautiful and I swear, holy. And what about me and Dear One? The occasional appearances of Gussie Gryll goad me into a new awareness of how much she means to me, especially as she and Gussie have now struck up a friendship based on jokes and, God help us, mock gallantry from him and mock maidenliness from her. It's enough to drive me round the bend. But not quite yet. This is too long. Sorry.

CHIPS

VIGNETTES

1. Chips cursing over a gigantic mass of heavy material.
2. Father Whimble, eyebrows raised almost to his hairline, in the dusk of a confessional box.
3. Isometric sketch of the procession, wonderfully evocative, as it might be seen from the church's gallery.
4. Charlie in the pulpit, banging on. How wild Chips makes him look! Her artist's eye is even more perceptive than my physician's one.
5. Very odd picture of St. Ignatius and Mackenzie King exchanging knowing winks. What a pair of fixers!

[15]

CHIPS' NOTION THAT Charlie was going right off his nut was an extreme statement of an opinion that was held and debated in the congregation of St. Aidan's by all sorts of people. Some were thrilled by his vigour and exuberance and were ready to follow him in any sort of crusade. Others thought he was demanding more of them than they could reasonably give in devotion and an almost medieval approach to worship and the Christian life. But beyond a doubt St. Aidan's was very much alive under his care; no Laodiceanism, no lukewarmness could exist in his presence. A few people fell away, and went to less exigent churches, but of these almost all came traipsing back, admitting with humility that religion was more fun at St. Aidan's than anywhere else, and it bound together an unlikely group of people, ranging over Pullman-car porters and University intellectuals, with a large group of decent folk who wanted guidance and a place to put their lives, and found it in the splendid services and also in Charlie's polished, brief, and burning homilies.

He asked, as all priests do, for money, but he also demanded a change in approach to daily living, a sense of the presence of God and of Christ and the Holy Spirit in every common act.

> *A servant with this clause*
> *Makes drudgery divine;*
> *Who sweeps a room as for Thy laws*
> *Makes that and th' action fine.*

—he declared, and people who never read poetry and had never heard of George Herbert thrilled at the declaration, which ennobled—no, which almost sanctified—

their dull jobs. But he also urged a perception of beauty upon them. In such a tree-lined city as Toronto—

Towery city and branchy between towers

he declared, in the words of another great priest poet

Because the Holy Ghost over the bent
World broods with warm breast and with ah!
bright wings—

look about you, not at the drab buildings but at the sky, the trees and the gardens with which householders have striven to declare Nature's goodness which is God's goodness, and see Toronto as it truly is.

Not that beauty was a quality of Nature alone. Beauty made by man brought us into the presence of the Holy Spirit. To make this manifest Charlie found, and bought at considerable expense to himself, a fine copy of Holman Hunt's *The Light of the World*, painted by F. G. Stephens, who had been one of Hunt's pupils. The picture is familiar: Christ, crowned with thorns and haloed, stands at the door of a humble dwelling holding a lantern; His right hand is raised to knock on the door, which is partly blocked by rough growth of grass and vine; His face wears an expression of expectation, shaded perhaps by doubt. On the gold frame, as well as the name of the picture, was the text it illustrated— "Behold, I stand at the door and knock: if any man hear my voice, and open the door, I will come in unto him, and sup with him, and he with me." This was hung on one of the pillars at the main door of the church. It was a gift, Charlie said, in thanksgiving for his twenty years in the priesthood.

Of its kind it was a fine thing, and a handsome gift. If only Charlie had not made it clear to the children who came to a special youth service that it was proper to stop before the picture and bow their heads for a moment when they entered the church! This custom quickly took on, and spread to mothers who did not wish to seem behind-hand when their little girls showed reverence. Thus Charlie's picture became rather more than a picture, and that was when the Bishop thought the time had come for a mild remonstrance.

Mild remonstrance is the usual episcopal manner when things begin to go askew. Firm action is deferred as long as possible. The Bishop visited St. Aidan's once a year, for Confirmation services, and otherwise he did not appear. I think he rather liked those services for it was an occasion when he could wear a fine cope he possessed and also his mitre; he did not wear these things in churches of more evangelical leaning; a Bishop is only human, and likes to wear the full appurtenances of his office when he can do so without having to explain himself afterward to suspicious Low Churchmen, or "spleeny Lutherans" as Dwyer called them, quoting Shakespeare. The Bishop did not at this time descend upon St. Aidan's himself; that might have put too much emphasis on the rebuke he intended. He arranged in the most courteous manner that one of his trusted subordinates, the Venerable Archdeacon Edwin Allchin, should preach at morning service—or High Mass as St. Aidan's called it—late in November.

In a small body and behind an unimpressive face, Archdeacon Allchin had the spirit of a tiger. When the Bishop hinted that a rebuke was in order, Edwin Allchin girded up his loins and delivered a rebuke that the most thick-skinned transgressor could not misunderstand. He enjoyed the work, just as he enjoyed some of the rather severe financial dealings on behalf of the Church that fell to his lot; the defaulting mortgagor didn't stand a chance when he faced Allchin in his extremely businesslike office at Church House. Not that Allchin permitted many dubious mortgages or investments of Church funds. The old Anglican joke that "the Bishop is the shepherd of his flock and the Archdeacon is the crook on his staff," was often trotted out when Allchin was spoken of. This was unjust; he was not in the slightest degree dishonest, but he was tough, unforgiving and exigent as even bankers—nay, as even insurance officials or taxgatherers—rarely manage.

He disapproved of St. Aidan's, and he descended upon it on the last Sunday before Advent loaded for bear, as we used to say in Sioux Lookout.

He did not storm. Naked anger may sometimes be seen in priests of the Church of Rome, but the Church of England prefers the icy smile, the false bonhomie, the sword concealed in the palm-branch. The Archdeacon told his hearers, when he had mounted into the pulpit, that he wanted to direct their attention to one of the foundation stones of their church that was sometimes forgotten or neglected, merely because people took it for granted. He was speaking of the Thirty-Nine Articles, so discreetly placed almost at the end of the Prayer Book, and which set out the dogma of the Church of England, of which the Anglican Church of Canada was an integral part. Not that the Church cared passionately for dogma but, as we all realized, there had to be a few rules, a few guidelines, and there they were. Every good churchman and churchwoman would be wise to read them over once a year, just to be sure that the rules were not being ignored, or worn away, or simply altered.

That was one of the reasons why we have those excellent functionaries, the church wardens, whose job it is to see that rules, elastic as they are, are not forgotten. The Church has a strong democratic foundation and we clergy need somebody to keep an eye on us, ha ha. Oh, the Archdeacon was a merry man in the pulpit!

The temptation in the matter of all rules was to look for ways of getting round them; they invited that kind of ingenuity because Man (and Woman, ha ha) was a clever creature and always wanted to see what might be possible without actually going too far. Didn't we all do that as children? At school? Of course we did, but we found out that the rules were made in wisdom and love, by people who had thought a lot about it, and wanted to keep us from making silly and sometimes dangerous mistakes.

Silly and dangerous mistakes in Church affairs? Was that possible? Oh, very possible! And they came often from impulses that seemed to be of the very best—such as the love of beauty. Beauty of music—so wondrous in its effect when discreetly used, but which could so easily slide over the brink into what Allchin might call concertizing, to ravishing the spirit with sweet sounds which were loved for themselves and not as adjuncts to prayer and proper devotion. The great library of Church music of course contained much that dated from before the Reformation, and was therefore fitted to Latin texts. Oh, the temptation to sing them to those texts, so beautiful in themselves, so grateful to ears that understood the Latin tongue! But—what do we read in the thirty-fifth of the Articles? "That the Common Prayers and the Sacraments ought to be ministered in a known tongue." Was not the temptation obvious? Indeed yes. But was it excusable? The answer must be a determined No.

(It was at this point that a sound like stage thunder came from the gallery at the back of the Church where Dr. DeCourcy Parry and his Gallery Choir were awaiting the time when they would sing a motet, *Regina coeli, laetare* by Palestrina, in Latin. The noise was Dr. Parry dumping a large armful of hymnbooks on the floor, which was as near as he could come to shouting Irish obscenities at the preacher.)

Undeterred—indeed spurred on—by this show of spirit, Archdeacon Allchin went on to quote from the Homily number Six, *Against Excess of Apparel.* The dignity of God's service demanded unquestionably that his priests be dressed in seemly fashion, so that their office was made plain and their function set off from that of the people whose pastors they were. But oh, how easy it was to slide into the folly of mere dressing-up, and excessive ceremonial which he could only call play-acting. Not that he had any quarrel with play-actors. How much pleasure and indeed edification we owed to the best of them! But we knew that their function was to seem what they were not, and we certainly did not wish our priests to seem anything other than what they were—humble servants of God, and followers of a humble Saviour.

The Archdeacon had by this time stamped firmly on the corns of the church wardens, who were supposed to keep an eye on the Thirty-Nine Articles and act as brakes on headstrong parsons. DeCourcy Parry certainly did not believe that any first-rate music was out of place in what he had been heard to speak of as "his" church, and it was certainly more edifying than any amount of half-baked preaching. Charlie, the ritualist, was red in the face, not with shame but with rage. Chips, I could judge from the back of her neck, was feeling snubbed about her cope, and the splendid embroidery she was lavishing on it, and Chips did not take snubs kindly.

Only Father Hobbes seemed happy. He was nodding gently and was probably thinking about something else.

Archdeacon Allchin was coming to his conclusion.

How he smiled, how his bald head glowed, how his Adam's apple bobbed up and down as he spoke gall in words of honey! He had not meant to speak of any such thing, he said (he was a good rhetorician and knew the value of a pretended departure from his set text) but he could not help observing that as some of the members of the congregation entered the church this morning, they paused, as if in reverence, before a picture that hung near the entrance. The picture was certainly arresting in its beauty, but reverence——? He had seen some of the children, the little girls, bending a knee and the little boys bobbing their heads; did these precious little souls have any idea of the danger they were in? Let their parents consider the warning in Article Thirty-five against the peril of Idolatry.

He knew——for he was sensitive to the feeling of his hearers——that what he was saying must appear as rebuke to the good people of St. Aidan's. He would not mince words; it was indeed rebuke but certainly not in terms of a ruler. (He knew, by the bye, that the term Ruler had been revived in St. Aidan's, and he deplored such revival, for it gave a most un-Anglican impression, however it might be meant.) No, the Bishop spoke, through him, his servant Edwin Allchin, in that spirit of "quieting and appeasing" which they would find enjoined upon bishops in the Original Preface to the Prayer Book, which still had its place in the book they all possessed and loved.

And now to the Father, and to the Son, and to the Holy Ghost...Archdeacon Allchin concluded, but did not cross himself, as St. Aidan's expected a real preacher to do.

This was not simply the fat in the fire; this was a declaration of war, and the church buzzed with it like a hive of angry bees.

Business took me to the shop of a very important bee on the succeeding Monday. He was Mr. Albert Russell, who ran a very good job-printing office a few streets away. I frequented his place of business because he printed all my stationery—I seemed to need a good deal—and he was an excellent typographer. My personal writing-paper, my professional letterheads, the forms of my statements—"To domiciliary attendance—" "To private consultation—" "To auxiliary treatments and medicines—" and everything I needed, with a fine caduceus in the upper left-hand corner of each. I liked a buff paper, and a colour of ink that Mr. Russell called Ancient Red.

Mr. Russell was the Vicar's Warden at St. Aidan's.

"Did you ever hear such impudence?" said he. "Says it comes from the Bishop. I know the Bishop. Known him since he was vicar at St. Paul's. Didn't sound a bit like him. I expect the Bishop told him to step around to St. Aidan's and just suggest a little moderation. But all that detailed attack! Even griping about Father Iredale deciding to call Darcy Dwyer the Ruler; it's just an old name for whoever leads the chancel choir; it was a nice recognition of Darcy's twenty years' service to the church; I think in fact it was Dr. Parry suggested it. Means Darcy can wear a cope on big days, which of course he likes. They all like dressing up and where's the harm? Gives variety and cheers up the services. Ties in beautifully with the notion of the Christian Year—you know, all the liturgical colours on the altar and vestments. We're getting a really good selection of that stuff now at St. Aidan's, and all gifts. That job Miss Todhunter is working on now—a knockout. Let's have lots of colour. Of course, colour's part of my work, so it's no wonder I approve. But so does Milliken approve, and he's the other warden. We know our business; we don't need to be told how to be wardens by an outsider from Church House. I'll see the Bishop one of these days, and I might just drop a hint that Ed Allchin is putting words in his mouth he never intended."

Mr. Russell was annoyed, but he was a moderate man and recognized the authority of a Bishop, who was another moderate man and someone who could be talked to respectfully but forcibly.

Charlie was not a moderate man. Though I saw him now rarely, I was aware of him because of his office and his acquaintance with The Ladies. The gentle boy I had known, who possessed saintlike courage under pain, had become a determined and perhaps an arrogant man, and both his determination and his arrogance were fed by his faith. With the arrogance, which can be a good quality in a leader, there arose also a substantial measure of that snobbery which had been a quiet but firm element in his home. His professor father had an Englishman's sense of Who's Who, and his mother had been born and bred in the English-speaking society of Montreal, which in Canada is to say enough. He was angry that he had been rebuked for his determination to make the Glory of God manifest in the services he directed, and for the fact that the rebuke had come from a man whom he regarded as a vulgarian, a man of no aesthetic sense but—and more important—also a man with a stale breadandbutter notion of the Christian Faith.

In Charlie's Father's house were many mansions and he knew deep in his heart that his mansion was at a better address than that of Ned Allchin.

He began his campaign the Sunday following the Archdeacon's visit.

[16]
Glebe House
Cockcroft Street
Toronto, Ontario
Canada

Dearest Barb:

Mighty stirring here! I told you Charlie was going off his nut, and last Sunday I think quite a few other people thought the same. It was the Sunday before Advent—you know, the Christmas season in the Church—and the children call it Stir-Up Sunday because of the Collect for the Day—look at my capitals, I'm getting to be a real Church Mouse—begins Stir up we beseech thee O Lord, the wills of the faithful people—and by gum, did Charlie stir us up!

I told you, didn't I, about the visitation of a squirt called Archdeacon Allchin[1] who pranced up into our pulpit and knocked my cope, which had last week made its first appearance at High Mass, worn by the much-loved Father Hobbes and if I do say it myself looking splendid!, and he spoke nastily about just about everything that makes St. Aidan's what it is, which is to say the only church I've ever met with where a person with a crumb of artistic feeling could feel at home. But that's Toronto for you—and Canada, because this country is still pretty much pioneer in its deepest feelings and thinks art is something the women amuse themselves with in the long winter evenings—you know, knitting, tatting, and barbola—while the men drink bootleg hooch in the barn. When this kind of mind gets some education and comes to the city it discovers that art can be used to raise money for more important things, or else it can be smothered under a wonderful complexity of committees, every one with a vice-president, where endless games of organization can be played. But art never comes *first.*

Oh, but I'm as silly as Charlie. When art comes first it means that all the asses and incompetents who can paint or model or mess about in some way think they are the lords of creation, which they bloody well aren't! For the artist, the real *maker,* art is solitary. Has to be. But for those who aren't artists, but have an eye, or an ear, or the right kind of brain, it's what makes life worth having. Isn't it? Or am I wrong? You ought to know. You're the real thing and I'm just a hanger-on, I suppose. Though my cope's not half bad. I'll send you a snap.

But back to Charlie. St. Aidan's, he roared, must gird its loins for a fight with the Philistines. It must show that its devotion to art as a path to God was true religion, and not to be regulated by tea-drinkers and cookie-pushers who thought of the Church as a social centre, or pinheads who told girls preparing for Communion never to forget their date with Christ (this was a dig at a popular parson who did that sort of job for a fashionable girls' school) meaning the Eucharist, the holy centre of the Christian Faith! It must never forget for an instant that though Works were great, they were second fiddle to Faith, and Faith found its strongest voice—after Charity and Hope—in Art, in which God spoke indirectly but with His fullest plenitude.

There's always a worm under the strongest stone, of course. Charlie was deeply cheesed off because Allchin had taken a nasty crack at his *Light of the World*—the good copy Charlie gave the Church as a thanksgiving after twenty years of priesthood. It's a fine thing—all right, I give you that. But it has always given me the creeps and I'll never forget my brother Ronnie—Ronnie was lost at Dunkirk, did you know, and Ma never really got over it—saying that it looked as if Christ had got up in the night to go to the privy and found that there was already somebody inside! It's a fine piece of painting—those Pre-Raphaelites certainly could paint even if their ideas gave you the creeps—and I wouldn't say a word against it to those who really like it, and in St. Aidan's it looks just fine. So to have children warned against it as a temptation to idolatry was really insulting. But there was a personal edge to Charlie's rebuttal, and righteous wrath shouldn't be personal.

So if it were at all possible to beef up the services at St. Aidan's, they are being beefed up now. And Charlie promises a series of Advent sermons on the lives of the saints and the presence of sanctity in modern life. So up yours, Archdeacon Allchin.

The name, by the way, is something he glories in. Says it is very Old English and means Wholly Marrow, or of the Very Essence—All Chine, that's to say. Speaking as a Freake—mighty in war—I'm in no position to throw stones, but it still sounds a silly name to me.

Dear One has completed the caduceus for Dr. Hullah and very fine it looks in his entry-way, just above the Dragon's desk. Above it he has had painted something in Greek, which I told him was intolerable swank, but he laughed and talked about the decent obscurity of a learned language, which I believe is a quotation of some kind. The Dr. is a great one for the Learned Crack, which is fine if you recognize it but a bit of a snub if you don't.

So at last my cope is finished, and handsomely received and blessed, and now almost weighs down poor old Fr. Hobbes, who is getting very feeble.[2]

No more now. I'll keep you posted about the Stirring Up.

CHIPS

VIGNETTES

1. A truly libellous caricature of Edwin Allchin, malign religiosity and Christian goodwill united in a gnome-like frame.
2. Fr. Ninian Hobbes, sinking under the weight of Chips' splendid cope. Haunting the unlovely old face is some hint of Newman.

[17]

SORRY CHIPS THOUGHT I was snubbing her with my scrap of Greek. I liked the caduceus so much that I thought I would complete it with the name of the Greek concept that, with the caduceus, seemed to me to sum up my medical philosophy: the serpents of Wisdom and Knowledge, under the rule of Hermes, the medical god, and all under the domination of Fate, or Necessity. So I got a good calligrapher to paint it in red and gold on the wall above the bronze staff. And there it stood.

ΑΝΑΓΚΗ

Harry Hutchins, my assistant, was much impressed. "Looks terrific," said he, "but what does it mean, boss?"

I explained as well as I could about the domination of Fate, or grim necessity, in life, taking precedence over all the healing god could do with his wisdom and knowledge.

Harry whistled. "No freedom, eh?"

"Plenty of what looks like freedom," said I. "But in the end—of course it's not simply a physical thing; it's mysterious and dreadful and we don't often catch sight of it at work, except out of the corner of an eye. In the end, it's—well, it's the end."

"Are you going to tell your patients that?" said Harry.

"Not unless they ask, and then only if they have the philosophy to bear such knowledge."

"Quite right," said Harry. "No use frightening the timid. But the word itself—Greek to me, of course. How do you say it?"

To the surprise of both of us, Christofferson spoke up. She had been listening, sitting at her desk under the caduceus and the word.

"*Anangke*," said she.

"Well, well. Rhymes with 'a hanky,'" said Harry. "Inge, my darling, I didn't know you knew Greek."

"If that were all you didn't know, Doctor, what a wonder you would be," said she. "And have the goodness not to call me your darling. I am nobody's darling."

"Well, if you ever change your mind about that, just tip me the wink and you can be mine, like a shot," said Harry, who liked to tease her.

I suppose I am the only one who knows why Inge Christofferson is nobody's darling. Just one of the wretched tales that had their root in that awful war, of which Chips writes so cheerfully.

I liked having the word there. It kept me on the track of my medical thinking. Because I was not devising a new notion of medicine; I was seeking a very old one, a sort of perennial philosophy of the healer's art, and fatality, or necessity, was the element in life that kept me humble, for nothing I could ever do would defeat it. People must be ill, and they must die. If I could seem to postpone the dark day people thought me a good doctor, but I knew it was a postponement, never a victory, and I could secure a postponement only if Fatality, the decision of my patient's *daimon*, so directed.

Of course I could not say that sort of thing to the anxious patient sitting in the chair opposite me. (I never sit behind a desk; always in a chair opposite to the patient and no greater in importance than his.) Who wants to hear his doctor saying that he must die sometime, and the doctor cannot say when, and that anything that can be done in the meantime will not change that fact? And in virtually all cases something could be done, some physical comfort assured, some assuagement of pain or disability, until the inevitable happened.

I certainly did not scorn what drugs could do for my patients, or the ministrations of Christofferson, who was a brilliant practitioner of all the manipulative arts, and intuitive in her application of her skills. I was not a convinced believer in anything the enthusiasts for psychosomatic medicine have to say, though I was an intent listener. Of course the mind influences the body; but the body influences the mind, as well, and to take only one side in the argument is to miss much that is— in the true sense of the word—vital. Didn't Montaigne say, with that splendid wisdom that was so much his own, that the close stitching of mind to body meant that each communicated its fortunes to the other? (And didn't he immediately afterward, like the seventeenth-century sage he was, plunge into the wildest rubbish about the Evil Eye, and women marking children in the womb by their thoughts? Even my dear old Robert Burton could not escape the influence of his time, any more than my contemporaries can escape the voodoo aspect of modern science.)

Mankind, it appears to me, seeks gloves with which to clothe the iron hand of Necessity, and these gloves he calls diseases. We doctors struggle against them, but no sooner have we got the better of tuberculosis than it appears again stronger than ever: cancer is unresting and who sees an end to AIDS? Mankind must have something upon which to hang its great Dread, which is Everyman's Fatality.

I think of my patient who has now been with me for almost three years, Prudence Vizard, who seems to have a travelling malady, for it has roamed from her back to her left leg, then soared upward to the back of her neck and is now bivouacking for a while in her right arm. The pain is real and gives her a lot of disfiguring physical distress for she hobbles, then hirples, then walks with her neck twisted toward the left, and is now unable to use her right arm for anything—cannot even lift a fork to her mouth. Christofferson cannot come to grips with her, for the pain darts off to another place as soon as it has begun to show improvement in the one under treatment. She doesn't like the saline baths and says they wear out her skin—which can't be true, for Christofferson rubs pots of emollient guck into her after every bath. My attempts to get below her symptoms and track down what is really gnawing at her are ineffective, and all I can do is give her sedatives as mild as she can be persuaded to use. If I were a well-informed physician of the nineteenth century—a pupil of Charcot, for instance—I should call her an hysteric and forget about her, but that is not my way. Why is she hysterical? There must be a cause, physical or mental.

Her trouble is not Nuns', Maids', and Widows' Melancholy, for she is none of those things and seems to have a pretty satisfactory sexual life, so long as Vizard does not jog the suffering place in his infrequently permitted visitations to her privy parts. She is indifferent to sex, but has long believed that "men like it" and so it is a duty to be performed. Has orgasms, but not always. Eats well. Is fond of wine. Has no money worries (Vizard is in investment banking). Gets on as well with her children as a chronic sufferer may be expected to do. Is not unattractive, dresses well, doesn't read much but likes the movies. I suggest that she make some investigation of religion, forgetting the nonsense she was taught as a child. She goes to St. Aidan's, for which I am sorry because she is likely to tackle me after Mass about her pain, or at least to signal to me, over the heads of other worshippers, that she is bearing up bravely and, by implication, when am I going to make her well?

It is useless to talk to Prudence Vizard about *Anangke*, and it is most unlikely to kill her with the mysterious ailment she complains of. She is a Sufferer—which is what Patient means, as I have rubbed into me every day of my life—and her suffering does not yield to anything I know. Is her pain in some way a complement to her character? For character lies deeper than any question of psychosomatic medicine, and contains the key to cure—or at least to courageous endurance. Mrs. Vizard is not very courageous and her endurance lays heavy burdens on her unfortunate husband and the one son who has not yet fled the nest.

Who has character and has risen above grave misfortune? Christofferson, of course.

Her tale is briefly told. A Danish nurse, she was carried by fate from one hospital to another in the European theatre of war and was not always sure quite where she was. But in one battle area she was set upon one night after dark by four Allied soldiers—pray God they were not Canadians!—and raped. With courage she had gained from Voltaire's *Candide* (for she came of a cultivated family) she knew that rape was not invariably fatal, but the precautions she hastened to take were too late to prevent the conception of a child with an unknown father. She determined to bear it (moral scruple) but when she did so, after great trials in besieged France, the child was hydrocephalic and the prognosis was that it could not live long. But it did live long in spite of medical wisdom, and lives still, as I know very well, in a hospital for such children in Denmark, and Christofferson supports it.

I was able to offer her some help, medically and financially, and it was I who suggested that she might find a new life in Canada. She did so; I rediscovered her and was glad to have her as a colleague. I regarded her as one of my victims of "friendly fire" and treated her in the same way as the men in Ward J—but with better poetry—and she is now a woman of modest means, independent and with a variety of interests, but they do not include men. She is fiercely loyal to me, for which I am grateful. She too goes to St. Aidan's, which is not so strange to her High Lutheran upbringing as it is to many Anglicans. One of my successes, and if it were not for my continuing involvement with Nuala I might look with different eyes on Christofferson. Or would I? I don't think she would return that sort of glance.

An affair is far harder to maintain over a long period than a marriage. In a marriage the friend may gradually and without trouble alternate with or take precedence over the lover, but in an affair there must always be a pretence that heat of passion is still what keeps the thing going—or so it seems to me and Nuala has not yet contradicted me. Of course we have moved into a relationship where friendship is stronger than love, but one cannot divide the two into apples and pears in quite that easy fashion. We are like the old Emperor Franz-Joseph and his Kathi Schratt; it is the exchanged advice, the gossip over the teacups, the sympathy that really matters, though the bed also has its place. It is knowing what a woman or a man thinks, and how they think, that preserves these unions, not the "convulsive ardour" which, frankly, can become a bore if it is all there is between two people. In a real union sex becomes just another kind of happy talk, a song without words, a coming together which does not need explanations or considerations.

But Nuala is no longer young nor am I. I realized this with a start when she brought her son Conor to Toronto to enter Colborne College. He was thirteen going on fourteen and to see him with his mother was to see his mother in quite a different light. She was still as beautiful as ever—or so it seemed to me—but I could also see that in the eyes of young Conor she was not a beautiful woman at all, but a presentable mother who he hoped would not kiss him in front of other boys, or call him by a nursery name. And other boys would see her as a mother, too, and never as a woman. There is a whole large class of society—called children—to whom mothers are not women, but inescapable appendages, sometimes dear, sometimes not, and never full human beings but supporting players in their own intense drama.

Nuala a mother! Of course I had known it for all of Conor's life, but I never knew quite what it meant until I took them to lunch the day she brought him to Toronto to school.

My old school! Here was a boy who would experience at least some of what I had felt and done when I was at Colborne; he would find his Charlie and his Brochwel and think himself a fine young man of the important generation and not the generation of his parents. I was the boy's godfather—and, it was not impossible, his biological father as well—so when I drove them up to the school it was traditional, it was ritual, that I should give him a tip. And as I did so my heart sank, for I knew I had thereby entered the tipping time of life, when until then I had, without putting it in words, thought of myself as a recipient, and one of those people upon whom unexpected good luck befell.

After we had left the boy I took Nuala back to my clinic and dwelling for the usual tea, but later neither of us had any heart for bed. A touch, not quite of autumn but of a lesser summer, had come upon our lives. Young Conor, who would not have understood anything about it, had come between us without dividing us.

I have done what I suppose is "the right thing" by the boy since then. When he was in the Sixth Form he liked to have dinner with me at my club—he thought clubs rather grand and grown-up—and to go to an occasional concert or theatre. I considered taking him to one of The Ladies' Sunday receptions.

It would have been mischievously entertaining to introduce him to Charlie. Brocky's son; my godson. Charlie, the celibate, did not experience this big step as we men of the world do. He was "Father" but he was not, one hoped, a father. It would have jolted Charlie, who had the celibate's affectation of a youthful manner, to see the reality of what he feigned in this tall, handsome youth—a man in every sense except those where his fortunate birth retarded his assumption of manhood—and to understand that time was passing and that on the giant escalator he and I had made fully half our upward journey.

Why should I want to jolt Charlie? He troubled me, and as he was not my patient I was free to resent it. He preached with a tone of certainty and zeal that had just a hint of irrationality in my ear. He went on about saints and saintliness without any consideration for the obvious fact that the manner if not the matter of sainthood has changed since the days of his beloved *Golden Legend*. If it lay in his power, he would have brought back haloes, and one of the first of the saintly to be fitted for such a distinction would have been poor old Ninian Hobbes, who was certainly a good man and had been a much better man, but who was now a driveller who could barely get through the Eucharist without prompting.

The Bishop should have removed Hobbes. I suppose he thought Hobbes had not long to go and an act which might seem unkind might well await the visit of the Black Angel.

[18]
Glebe House
Cockcroft Street
Toronto, Ontario
Canada

Dearest Barb:

Extraordinary doings here. Or are they really extraordinary? Dramatic, anyhow. Poor old Father Hobbes has snuffed it, hopped the twig, kicked the bucket, and with what flair! Nobody would have thought the old man had such a sense of effect. What happened was this. On Good Friday there was an unusual ceremony at St. Aidan's, a thing called the Mass of the Pre-Sanctified, a new dodge revived from long ago by Father Charlie and DeCourcy Parry. Big crowd present. Adoration of the Cross, and Procession of the Sacrament from the Altar of Repose—because the bread and wine had been pre-pared the night before, hence pre-sanctified. Father

Hobbes was celebrant, and after the Host had been censed and elevated, the dear old chap put it in his mouth, turned toward the altar, and fell.[1] Of course everybody thought things had been too much for him—stifling incense, my heavy cope around his shoulders, all the fasting he goes in for during Lent—but when the deacons and Father Charlie rushed forward to lift him all hell broke loose. One of the deacons, a black chap who works as a technician in the hospital while qualifying as a priest, said loudly, "He's dead!" I heard Father Charlie say, "He can't be!" Dr. Hullah, our tenant, walked quickly to the altar rails, but astonishingly Fr. Charlie waved him back, and they had some sort of murmured exchange. Hullah looked black as thunder, but he stood where he was while the deacons carried the old man into the vestry.

Sensation! as they used to say in melodrama. But St. Aidan's isn't to be flummoxed by anything, and in a tick, it seemed, the Gallery Choir burst into something that certainly sounded like Bach—oh, we're not above Bach at St. A's, Lutheran though he was—which had a quieting effect and we all sat on burrs till Father Charlie made his reappearance.

He was calm, but seemed almost to glow, if you know what I mean. "Dear Father Hobbes is dead," he said, "and we who are here are greatly blessed to have been present at the death of a dearly loved father in God, and one who many of us thought a saint—not just saintly, but a saint indeed—and who we may now be assured stands in the presence of the Saviour he served humbly and greatly while he was among us. Holy Eucharist, which he began, must now be completed." And with that he turned to the altar, elevated another Host—in this sort of

Communion the priest gets a big bikky which he eats himself, and then the rest of us get a small bikky and a sip from the cup—and he ate his big bikky and then raised the cup, and the service continued. Everybody took Communion. It would have been extraordinary not to do so, after what had happened. Even Christofferson, who I would not have thought would be affected, but probably I misjudged her. More and more I think I misjudge a lot of people.

That afternoon the church was crammed for the Vigil, which takes place during the hours Christ is supposed to have hung on the Cross before he died. Everybody was thinking about Ninian Hobbes of course. I swear to you, my dear, I have never felt such holiness in any gathering, in my life. Charlie presided, but he spoke never a word about what had happened in the morning.[2]

Then Saturday, a dead day in the church. Then Easter Day itself and a Mass at seven (Whimby) and a High Mass at half past ten and such music and such ritual goings-on as you've never seen in your entire puff, and a magnificent spirit of life and love in a packed church.

You felt it even before the procession. But when the choir burst into *The strife is o'er, the battle done; / Now is the Victor's triumph won; / O let the song of praise be sung; / Alleluya!* I swear to you I felt that for the first time in my life I knew what religion really meant! It was a kind of amazing lightness in the buzzem—O hell, I can't write about it in this campy slangy way I've got into—this way that tries to turn everything into a joke! It was no joke. But it wasn't religious-serious either. It was as though I'd been renewed and wouldn't need to play the fool all the time to hide real feeling. Lots of people were blubbing. And I felt as if for the first time I could just be me, and wouldn't have to play the giddy goat so that nobody could really get near me. I don't think I'm making much sense, but I hope I'm getting it across to you that it was a revelation. Am I now a believer, a religious person? I can't tell, but I know I've never felt like that before and want to feel that way forever.

The cream on the strawberries was Charlie's sermon. Short, but the best ever. Ninian Hobbes, he declared, was a saint indeed. He had spent every waking hour since Fr. Hobbes' death thinking about the death, praying and waiting for God to speak. And he truly and humbly believed God had spoken. Not in words, but in a burning conviction that it was true. We had known a saint who had walked among us and touched our lives, and that saint was now a partaker of the splendour of God's Eternity. The man we had known and spoken with a few days ago, was now truly with God. Charlie told us this, not as a man who had himself been assured of the truth, but as one entrusted with a message for everyone his voice could reach. And we too were given the message in order that it might be told abroad. We must make it known in our city that a saint had walked among us.

Strong stuff, but you should have heard Charlie! I've told you I thought he was going off his nut, but in that sermon, which couldn't have been longer than ten minutes, he was a man transformed. We all left the church with a powerful sense that we must do what he said—tell everybody. But how?

Luckily I knew how. That Sunday afternoon we had our usual salon, as Hugh McWearie calls it—half joke, half compliment—and Hugh McWearie was there, as he always is, greedy pig! No, that's unkind, but he does eat like a refugee. Hugh is the most important lay voice in matters of religion probably in Canada. He knows what he is talking about—he's a spoiled parson—Presbyterian I believe and learned in that thorough Scots way—and he writes so even devil-worshippers pay attention, it is so interesting and unexpected. So I got Hugh cornered by a plate of my amethyst tarts—grape jelly in feathery wee tartlets and just a touch of whipped cream—and told him what had happened. Charlie's sure the old man was a saint, and everybody must be told, and that's your job Hugh, said I, so do your total utmost.

A saint, and a Protestant saint at that, said he. That's very interesting and you can be sure I'll follow it up. So I left him with the tarts with a sense of having done my bit and perhaps a little more, because I had the Ear of the Press. I had to get on with my job as hostess, and stop young Frangipani, who sounds Italian but is really Swiss and has all the Swiss determination, from making poor Arne Gade miserable by insisting that the piano is really a percussion instrument and that all Arne's exquisite phrasing and nuance is a denial of reality. (When he can get a word in Arne rebuts that Frangi can't do anything with the piano but pound and that explains his opinion.) A lot of people present had known Fr. Hobbes and really were sorry, but they didn't buy the saint bit—except as an expression meaning a really good person.

So what now? Things are looking up. Dear One's head of the Governor-General is being shown in every important city in Canada under the auspices of the Canadian Club, and thus her name is being spread Far and Wide,[3] and perhaps this break in the clouds is really a dawn at last! She gets news of it from Gussie Gryll, but I suppose there's no harm in letters.

                    Yours till Niagara Falls (ha ha)
                    CHIPS

VIGNETTES

1. A brilliant Isometric view of the Chancel at St. Aidan's, with Fr. Hobbes in the act of tumbling to the ground.
2. The chancel again, the figure of Fr. Charlie in shadow, as opposed to the rich candlelight of the morning view.
3. Emily standing beside the head, eyes modestly lowered, but looking like the cat that has swallowed the cream.

[19]

OH, MY DEAR CHIPS, I knew you were touched to the heart by Charlie's sermon and the events of the great Easter days. The afternoon of Easter Sunday, when you were stoking McWearie—yes, he does tend to gobble the sweet things, but I don't think women quite comprehend how desperate some men become for sweets—you seemed to me to be transfigured. All that awful schoolgirl, field-hockey-playing, daring-driver-in-the-Transport Corps, fake manlydom that made you look like a fool to so many people was dropped for that brief time, though it came creeping back in the days to come. (Ha ha, indeed. Oh, my poor Chips!) I was astonished that Emily Raven-Hart did not seem to share your enlargement of spirit. But I always thought that Emily was a better head and a poorer heart than you were. She was intelligent In a way you were not, under all her limp mannerisms and chronic depression. And, of course, as you say in your last paragraph, she was a success at last, even if not in quite the way she would have chosen. Nor would it be wise to discount the renewed contact with Gussie Gryll. There seemed still to be quite a bit of warmth in those ashes, and Emily did not conceal that fact from you because—did you never see it?—Emily liked to tease, and Emily rather liked to hurt. It is one of the Lesbian dreads, I suppose: some wretched man may come sneaking into Paradise, with troubling insinuation.

You were disappointed in Hugh McWearie, and I must take the blame for that. As so often, he came to my upstairs sitting-room, smoking-room, talking-room after your soirée had come to a close. It was a little earlier than usual, for so many of the musicians were tired from the demands made on them during the Easter time. Even the Jews, for during these festival times they are summoned to serenade the Christian Pantheon, and do it with artistic integrity and not a shade of an ironic smile on their faces. Hugh and I settled down, he to one of his stinking pipes (for, though under my direction he had thrown away the old ones, he had by now made disgusting a whole array of new ones) and I with an excellent cigar. And whisky, of course, for Hugh declared that whisky was one of the elements in which he lived.

He wanted to talk. He wanted to know what I thought about the death of Ninian Hobbes. He thought of me as a man who had been exposed to science, even if I had not been consumed by it, and perhaps I had not fallen so much under the Good Friday Spell as most of the others in the church.

The Good Friday Spell—yes, the atmosphere in St. Aidan's at the death, and again at the Sunday morning High Mass, might well be recalled in terms of the magic

Wagner raises in *Parsifal*, when the Grail descends. Hugh and I were both sensitive to music and that expression was a useful shorthand term for what we were talking about.

I had felt the Spell, certainly. I had observed its effect on others, and not least on Miss Pansy Todhunter. But had I felt it as the others did?

No, I could not say that. But was my failure to succumb to an extraordinary experience the result of personal pique? When Fr. Hobbes fell, I had—I thought I had broken my firehorse response to emergency, but it seemed I hadn't—I had gone at once to help. After all I knew Hobbes, respected him greatly, was a neighbour, was a doctor—why wouldn't I hasten to his side when he was plainly in great trouble? But I had been waved away by Charlie Iredale. If it had been another priest it might have been different, but Charlie and I had been through much together, and not least the dark hour when he underwent his fenestration operation without anaesthetic, and I had tried to distract him from his pain by reading from *The Golden Legend*. If we had been anywhere other than where we were, Charlie within the altar rails and I outside them, I would have told him not to be silly, and done what I could for the dying man. Was I Simon Magus, the false magician, being warned off by St. Peter, the true one? Whatever, I was warned away from the sacred precinct; my kind of magic was not wanted. I was angry.

My professional magic was wanted later, however, when Charlie sent a deacon to catch me at the church door to ask me to come and certify that the old priest was truly dead. Silly as this seems, it was required by law. I made as much of it as I could, examined the body as thoroughly as was conformable with decency, and then provided the necessary certificate that Ninian

Hobbes had indeed died of cardiac arrest. But why? Charlie knew. It was the bliss of celebrating the Eucharist once again, at the altar he knew so well, and on such a day.

I suppose bliss can be fatal, though instances of it are very few in medical literature.

Hugh had not been present on this great occasion, and he wanted to pump me for my impressions of it. Pansy, as her letter makes clear, had been hounding him about his journalistic duty to give the story a big play. He was too good a journalist for that.

"I am of the old school," said he. "My job is to give the facts, so far as I can discover them, and leave the reader to make up his own mind. I am not in the saint-making business. I shall say that many of his people regarded Fr. Hobbes as a saintly man and felt that his death at the altar was a striking culmination of a fine life. But I shall offer no opinion of my own."

I could not accept that. "Hugh," said I, "when it suits you you slant and load your stories unconscionably. The pretensions of you journalists that you deal simply in fact would be nauseating if it were not laughable."

"That is called shaping public opinion and it is actu-ated by journalistic philosophy not easily grasped by the layman," said Hugh. "You doctors deal in particulari-ties; we journalists are concerned with the broad scene. Anyhow, what do you think it would look like if I declared a saint tomorrow and some coroner finds he died of hobnailed liver on Tuesday?"

"There will be no coroner. I have declared him dead and that's all that's needed. But I wish to God I had demanded to see his false teeth."

"I saw all of them that I wanted. Did you want to see if they had 'Made in Japan' stamped on them somewhere?"

"You have no proper reverence. Journalism has covered your soul with a hard brown crust. No, I would simply have liked to analyse anything that might be clinging to them."

"Oho! What do you suspect?"

"I don't suspect anything. But I might have been able to attribute his death to something a little more interesting than cardiac arrest. That just means his heart stopped."

"I am acquainted with the term. You have a suspicion?"

"No. But I have professional curiosity. I do not like to sign legal forms simply because somebody tells me to."

"Charlie? Ah, yes; Charlie can be peremptory. Now, do you suppose he will succeed the late Father Hobbes as vicar at St. Aidan's? If he does, we must expect lively doings. Charlie is determined to take no nonsense from the Archdeacon. You heard that sermon he preached on Ceremonies? Threw the Thirty-nine Articles right back in Allchin's face. That's one of the beauties of Anglicanism; you can pretty well have things both ways. I find no fault with that. A good faith ought to leave lots of leeway. But I must get along now down to my paper to prepare the great news that a saint has died among us, for the humble folk of Toronto. My guess is that the editor will think it worth three inches on one of the duller inside pages. So don't look for a front-page spread and pictures."

I had been perfectly honest with Hugh; I did not suspect anything out of the way in the death of Ninian Hobbes, but I felt I had not been professionally careful in ascribing a cause of death. What I did suspect was that my invaluable nurse and colleague, Inge Christofferson, was developing an unexpected and wry sense of humour. She had been at Mass on that Good

Friday, and sometime when I was out she had put an envelope on my desk on which was written:

> Herewith a shard of the Host which fell from
> the lips of the Rev. Ninian Hobbes as he
> celebrated Communion on Good Friday, 1970.
> You may wish to preserve it.
> If he was truly a saint it may prove to
> be a very holy relic.

She had gone with me to the vestry to see the body when I was summoned, thinking I suppose that I might need some help, medical or secretarial. Presumably she had found this crumb in the folds of his cassock. Why had she preserved it?

I put the envelope in my desk and forgot it. I did not see any reason to get on jokey terms with Christofferson. If Charlie or The Ladies heard of it they would not like it, and as I had been snubbed by Charlie I did not want any further reason for him to think I was concerned in the matter of his saint. I settled myself to think about the Governor-General's question.

[20]
Glebe House
Cockcroft Street
Toronto, Ontario
Canada

Dearest Barb:

It never rains but it pours, doesn't it? Of course a steady flow of commissions is old stuff to you, my God you've been a Dame for ages now isn't it? but it's a blessed change for Dear One who has had such a thin time and often she has looked so sicky-pussy I wondered if she might not really be seriously ill. But the head of the G.G. has really put her on the map here, and no less than *three*, I repeat THREE banks want her to do heads of their presidents for board rooms and although this is not really very interesting work it brings in lots of lovely money.

Just at present however she can't get going on their unforgiving Scotch mugs because she has a *very special* commission from St. Aidan's church to do a bas-relief of Ninian Hobbes. A big job, the background of which is black Belgian marble on which the face is to be mounted in a palish *rosso antico* and bordered with high-relief flowers in white or yellowish, whichever way the marble turns out. May turn out to be hideous—all those colours I mean and you know how *wilful* marble can be—but it's a tremendous opportunity to show what she can really do, and maybe she can farm out some of the floral stuff to art students who would sell their souls to get at a chunk of marble. And who, you may ask, is putting up for this grandeur? Father Charlie assures us that the church will; he is going to put the screws on the faithful to commemorate their saint, and the saint must have an adequate shrine. I worry a bit about the marble. Frankly, she's rarely worked in marble. Always modelling in clay. Still, nothing venture, nothing win.

The shrine is to be in what is now a sort of cubbyhole on the right side as you look up the church, opposite the Lady Chapel. It has until now been screened off and I believe brooms and mops are kept there. But it is to be tarted up as a shrine. Father Hobbes won't be buried there, because local laws don't permit that sort of thing, but Charlie has got special permission to bury him in the old church-yard—he had to get it from us, too, because it is part of Glebe House garden—and there is just a modest but quite decent marker there. However, the affair in the church will certainly look like a shrine and Charlie says that in time that is how it will be accepted. Do you know what the old expression cock-a-hoop means? That's how Charlie is about this scheme.

Meanwhile he is hounding poor Em unmerci-fully to get the job done. It is useless to explain that it takes time to get decent marble—this has to be fetched up from the States—and when it comes you can't just start whacking the hell out of it. You have to see what it has to say for itself. But look at me telling you your business! If he wants a shrine, he will have to bide the time it takes.

But he seems almost off his head. He preaches every Sunday about sainthood, and the way in which the Anglican Church has allowed the canonization of saints to lapse ever since the Reformation. In the old Celtic church chaps became saints because everybody agreed they *were* saints. St. Deiniol and St. Asaph and all that lot down in Cornwall.[1] Why not now? Does modern life need saints? You should hear Charlie on that. Would the modern world accept saints if some were declared? He hasn't a doubt about it. So what's to be done? We must press this matter. We must stir up our Bishops and Archbishops. We must take the matter to Canterbury for serious con-sideration. It is obvious to Charlie that the whole for-ward thrust of modern Christianity depends on canonizing a few saints. What are we waiting for?

Not everybody goes along with this. Some people have left St. Aidan's but that may be because every Sunday now Charlie insists on a special collection for what he calls the Memorial Fund. Dearest Em has been getting some black looks because everybody knows she is to create the memorial and Charlie chose her out of hand without so much as putting the matter before a committee—and Canada has always been hog-wild for committees. But Charlie is implacable.

I say to Em, don't you so much as lift a chisel until you have some sort of contract for this job.[2] It's a great opportunity, but it is going to take an enormous lot of work and you must have a proper fee. When I put this to Charlie he is very soapy and tells me to trust in the Lord, and when have I ever seen the righteous forsaken or their seed begging bread? (The answer to that one is lots of times, but I don't want an outright war with Charlie.) But Em is so anxious to get her hands on all that marble that I fear she is letting herself in for a difficult time. But that's how artists are. Or a lot of the real ones, anyway. But I *do* think a price ought to be agreed on, don't you?

Surely you regard at least some part of this work as your own contribution to the memorial, says Charlie to dear Em, with one of those smiles that only parsons seem to be able to call up. And he offers to get some other work that will really bring in money.

This sounds fishy, but he actually does it. And you will never guess what it is! God, the things people think up!

You know—I don't really suppose you do, but you know what I mean—that Toronto has a huge Exhibition every autumn, a sort of fall fair on a gigantic scale. All sorts of stuff is shown, and there is great rivalry about how attractive or merely astonishing the exhibits can be. And Charlie has somehow persuaded the Daughters of the Empire (you can guess what *they* are) and the Ontario Dairy Farmers' Union to unite on a great project which is to celebrate the forthcoming birthday of the Queen Mother by having a life-size statue of her moulded in the top grade of Ontario Creamery Butter to be on show at the Exhibition!!!!! And Em is to be the sculptor!!!!!

Impossible, you'll say. Prostitution of art, and all that. Anyhow, how would you go about it?

They have the answers. First of all, a simply whacking fee, at the thought of which the senses reel—or at least mine do. As for prostitution, isn't it rather bringing Art to the People, hundreds of thousands will flock to see a popular character, realistic right down to the ferrule of her umbrella? And thirdly, you do it and show it in a sort of giant glass fridge, which has to be well below freezing, and you have to work in a kind of Arctic explorer's outfit, and the inconvenience is recognized in the fee.

So, how do you like *them* apples?

Em is attracted. There is a lot of schoolgirl still left in her, and she wants to do something outlandish and mess with unlimited butter.[3] And think of the ease with which any error or misjudgement could be corrected? And Charlie is urging her toward it, and of course expects the fee for the edible monarch to be subtracted from the costs of the marble saint.

Time will tell. Doesn't it always?

CHIPS

VIGNETTES

1. Very funny picture of four Celtic Saints, Irish, Welsh, Cornish—fat and stumpy (Irish), fat and benign (Welsh), gaunt and angry (Cornish), and one with his back turned to the rest, eating a piece of cheese, whom I take to be Breton.
2. Chips, wagging an upraised finger.
3. Emily in Eskimo dress, surveying with a speculative eye a mass of pound packages, each labelled "No. 1 Creamery."

[21]

THE GOVERNOR-GENERAL'S question did not wholly astonish me. I have been asked the same question many times by lesser folk. It was the manner in which he led up to it, and the language in which he cloaked his enquiry that surprised me and gave me unusual pleasure. It is always a pleasure—unfortunately an infrequent one—to encounter literary taste in an official personage.

The question simply put was this: could he, at his present age—which was pushing seventy—resume sexual intercourse without fearing for his heart, which was not entirely reliable? But this was cloaked in some science and much splendour. He had read the Kinsey Reports—both of them—and he knew from those sources that many people continued sexual activity into their eighties and a few into their nineties. It was true that none of these long-distance runners appeared to be people in the upper levels of education or income. They had not, it appeared, much else on their minds. But on the other hand, literature had much to say that was encouraging. Did I know the Earl of Rochester's poem "A Song of a Young Lady to Her Ancient Lover"? I didn't. He quoted with unction:

> *Ancient Person, for whom I*
> *All the flatt'ring youth defy;*
> *Long be it ere thou grow Old*
> *Aching, shaking, crazy, cold.*
> > *But still continue as thou art,*
> > *Ancient Person of my heart.*

Ah yes, charming, said I. Ah, said he, but listen to a later verse:

> *Thy Nobler Part, which but to name,*
> *In our Sex would be counted shame,*
> *By Age's frozen grasp possessed*
> *From his Ice shall be released:*
> > *And, soothed by my reviving Hand*
> > *In former Warmth and Vigour stand.*

Delightful, was it not, how a poet who was also a wit could clothe a thought of that sort in language which was explicit but never smutty?

Delightful indeed, said I, wondering when we were going to come to the Young Lady. In my experience these matters always arose in connection with some charmer, often under twenty and rarely over thirty, who had blown the sleepy ashes into flame. But it was not like that at all; he came at last to the lady herself, and it appeared that she was only a year or two younger than he, but splendidly preserved—a fine figure—and a witty, far-sighted, entrancing companion. But what about—? He had been a widower and abstinent for—good Lord—nearly twenty years. Would it now be possible to pursue with success the project which, I gathered, he had hinted at, and what might the pursuit of the right true end of love lead to, with a couple so matched in years and intellect but—one must face it—not young?

I hemmed and hawed. What else was there to do? Who could foresee whether such a mating might be a glorious winter idyll, gaining rather than losing from the accumulated years of the lovers, or whether it might be a disappointment, ending in humiliation and recrimination? Nature is cruel and the most keenly felt emotion may suddenly be made absurd by some trifle like an untimely fit of coughing, a trumpeting of flatus (rectal or vaginal) brought on by unwonted excitement, the clanking of false teeth? But I was expected to say something.

"Have you talked of this to the lady?" said I.

"I have spoken in terms that a woman of her experience and discernment could hardly misunderstand," he replied, "and she has not changed the subject nor appeared to discourage me."

I saw that all this stately minuetting would not lead us far.

"Tell me, Your Excellency," I said, "why you have chosen to come to me about this problem? You have official physicians attached to your office who could advise you—"

"But who cannot be absolutely trusted to keep their mouths shut," said he. "I do not want this to be a subject of Ottawa gossip."

"And you think I can keep my mouth shut?"

"That is the reputation you have. Also, I have heard that you are a man of unusual breadth of interest in literature. You are not a hundred-per-cent pragmatist. You are said to be able to see through a brick wall. And as you can understand that this matter is a sensitive one—which is why I have contrived this visit under cover of an appointment with our friend Miss Raven-Hart—I wanted an opinion from a doctor who is also, may I say it, a humanist."

"It sounds to me as if you really wanted to consult a fortune-teller," said I.

"That is not so far wide of the mark as you may think. A man of my temperament, as he grows older, becomes increasingly aware of influences that younger men dismiss as occult. To be frank, everything I hear of you suggests that you can give me an answer that is not tied to scientific examinations, or statistically determined probabilities. Now, Doctor, what does your intuition say to you about this matter I have broached?"

"If you put it like that, my intuition says—'Give it a go.' All for love, and if the world is lost thereby, call it the world well lost."

But don't be found dead in her bed, I wanted to add, but knew it to be impracticable advice.

"That's what I hoped you might say. And now—as I do not wish this consultation to exist on record—may we deal with the matter of your fee?"

"No fee, Your Excellency. Your confidence is sufficient reward. And now shall I let Major Gryll know that you are ready for your car?"

But when I went to speak to Gussie Gryll he was staring fixedly at an uproar in the courtyard outside my door.

"His Ex won't want to get mixed up in this," he said. "Have you got a back door, so he can sling his hook and get away without being seen?"

That was easily arranged, and the G.G. and Gussie made off with rather more than official haste to the waiting Daimler.

Christofferson put her head around the door as soon as they had left. "Miss Todhunter needs you urgently in the garden," said she.

What was going on in the courtyard? That damnable

nuisance Prudence Vizard was up to her tricks again, and had gathered fifteen or twenty people—most of them "God's people" who had depended heavily on the charity of Father Hobbes—and was defying Chips, who was using language unbecoming a lady, but entirely to be expected from an artist—even an etcher.

This was something Charlie had brought about with his sermons on the nature and the necessity of saints in our deprived North American life. Three or four weeks ago, Mrs. Vizard had left my clinic, where Christofferson had been dousing her with hot and cold, fresh and saline water, and massaging her with searching pertinacity. Did she feel refreshed, helped to endure her misery—which we had agreed to call arthritis, a grab-bag of a word for many sorts of pain—and ready to face the week ahead with courage? Not on your life. She was very much down in the mouth. But as she was walking toward the street she took a notion to look at Father Hobbes' grave—why she did not know or could not subsequently remember. She found herself looking intently at the simple stone, on which was cut—

NINIAN HOBBES
Priest
R.I.P.

followed by his dates.

She felt herself impelled to utter what she later described as "a mouthful of prayer," and then—!

And then a shooting pain of indescribable severity in her bad arm, followed by a glow of warmth—of heat, really—and relief from the misery which had pursued her through her body for years, and which had defied every doctor she had consulted, and me the last of the list.

In the Bible women who were healed of diseases issues, pains, fevers and the rest—rejoiced aloud, and so did Prudence Vizard. She howled her astonishment and delight, and flung herself face downward on the grave and wept uncontrollably. This hullabaloo roused Chips, who was weeding a bed of irises and enjoying the late spring sunshine. She hurried to the spot, which was just around the corner of her house, and hauled Mrs. Vizard to her feet, as she babbled forth the story of her miracle. She was determined that it was a miracle. The saint, of his great charity, had healed her, and though her arm was still hot—Chips felt it and it was indeed very hot— it was cured.

Chips summoned me, and fortunately I was not engaged with a patient. She appealed to Christofferson. Harry Hutchins, sensing something unusual afoot, dropped his laboratory work and came dashing to the scene in his white coat. We stood and gaped at Mrs. Vizard, and listened to her hymns of praise.

What does a physician feel when a patient over whom he has worked diligently for three years is suddenly cured by what she declares is a miracle? I felt some pique that a saint had done in a flash what I could not do in three years. I felt an unkind joy that my personal diagnosis of Mrs. Vizard, that she was an hysteric and that her roaming pain was a whim-wham of a disordered personality, had been suddenly confirmed. I was professionally interested in the flush that had come into her cheeks, and that she looked as if she had dropped ten weary years of age. I felt, well, here's a lark, and won't Charlie be pleased? And where is this likely to lead?

The immediate question was what to do with the emotionally overcharged woman? The sensible thing seemed to be to take her back into my consulting-room and give her a cup of tea, and that is what we did. Christofferson went off in search of Charlie, who was luckily in the vicarage, instructing a Confirmation class, which he was able to conclude immediately and come to the clinic. The sight of him set Mrs. Vizard going again at full steam. She repeated over and over the story of her depression, the cloud she felt over her mind and spirits—this was thickening with every repetition—and her prayer at the grave of the old priest.

"What form of prayer did you use?" asked Charlie.

"Oh, Father, the simplest. I just said, 'O God, be merciful to me, a sinner,' and then came this extraordinary feeling in my arm—like a very strong light being turned on—"

"Light? A light in your arm? How do you mean?"

"Not just in my arm. As if I were being bathed in very strong light all over—but especially in my arm, of course. Am I making myself clear? I don't suppose so. Because it was all terribly clear—wonderfully clear—but not in a way I can describe."

I had placed a thermometer in her armpit. I read it now. A surprisingly high reading. If Mrs. Vizard had not plainly been in good health I should call it a phenomenal one.

"My suggestion is that we take you home at once, and that you get as much rest as you can. We want to see if this astonishing cure persists. I'm not disparaging the power of your experience, but you understand that we must be as prudent as we can, before letting anyone else know what has happened."

"Yes, Father, I understand perfectly. But it will persist, I just know it will."

"Pray God it may be so. Dr. Hutchins, would it be an imposition to ask you to drive Mrs. Vizard home?"

When they had gone Charlie said, "What do you think?"

"I think she's an hysteric, but who can really say what that means? Lots of miraculous cures happen to hysterics, but that doesn't change the fact that they are cured, for a while at least. This may be an unusual remission. But I wouldn't for an instant dismiss the truth of what has happened. She prayed at the grave of a man she believed was a saint. She is cured for the moment. What do *you* think?"

"I hardly dare to hope. It seems such an overwhelming wonderful thing to happen here and now. Who can say what might come of it? But we must be cautious, of course."

"Very cautious indeed."

That was what had happened in the first instance. But how were we to be cautious when Prudence Vizard was so determinedly incautious? She was cock-a-hoop, in Chips' expression, at being the subject of a miraculous cure. She could not keep her mouth shut. She buttonholed people in church, and it was all Charlie could do to keep her from publicly "testifying" before the whole congregation that Father Hobbes, reaching back from the other world, had touched her. She was somewhat offensive about what my clinic had failed to do for her. She was disagreeable about Christofferson, whom she accused of being a sadist who liked to hurt people under pretence of doing them good. She was a nuisance, but not really unendurable until she began her exhortations beside Father Hobbes' grave.

[22]
Glebe House
Cockcroft Street
Toronto, Ontario
Canada

Dearest Barb:

It seems ages since last I wrote, but you will soon understand why. I write now though I am utterly fagged out, because writing to you rests me. Of course I can talk about *anything* to Dear One, but it is different talking to someone at a great distance, someone above the hullabaloo, so to speak, Because hullabaloo is precisely what we've been having for more than a fortnight past.

I told you about the strange death of old Father Hobbes, but I can't recall if I told you that he is buried in our garden. Yes, literally right under our windows because you see there is this old burying-ground, which the church used when it was still pretty much out in the country, but which has been disused for years so there is quite an *Elegy Written in a Country Churchyard* air about it. You know, mouldering headstones with almost obliterated names on them, and a good deal of clustering vine, mostly wild grape which looks stunning in autumn. When we bought Glebe House we bought the grounds, and the graveyard was part of it. Very picturesque.

Well, Father Charlie was mad to have Father Hobbes buried as near St. Aidan's as possible and so it was O please and pretty-please to Em and me, and it was proved the graveyard had never been deconsecrated. (How do you de-consecrate something? Sounds like taking the oil out of a salad dressing, if you ask me.) So we weak-mindedly agreed and now bugger-me-black the grave is a place of pilgrimage! You can guess what that means. Trampling over my garden, chattering outside the windows when Dear One is working and behaving as if the place was some kind of Mickey Mouse fun fair. And all because of a loony called Prudence Vizard.

I do not use the word *loony* loosely. For years

she has suffered from pains which I swear are all in her head, and she has lately been coming to Dr. Hullah's clinic. The Dragon has been giving her healing baths and I wish she'd drowned her. Well, one evening she was leaving the clinic just as the Angelus was ringing, which is to say sixish. She says she prayed at Father Hobbes' grave, and all of a sudden felt as if lightning had struck her and the pain in her arm vanished. She made a big fuss about it in the church and Father Charlie was delighted, to begin with, though I know he is heartily sick of her now. Because now she comes every night at Angelus to the grave, bringing with her, and assembling from all over, positively the damnedest pack of no-hopers and detrimentals you could possibly imagine, and she tells the story of her miracle—simply, she says but I swear it has grown enormously since it happened and now she says she heard a voice—and then she leads the gang in a hymn, shouting like blazes, and then she calls for prayers and offerings.

Her gang includes a few sad people whom I believe to be sincere—people who have had rotten lives. But most belong to the lot that old Father Hobbes used to encourage and who he called God's People. The Forgotten of God would be more like it.[1] Many of them are crazy, but not so crazy the police can take them down to the Provincial Asylum and commit them as being unable to take care of themselves. This is a very difficult group because most of them are quite pitiful cases but somehow they can still keep afloat in a desperate kind of way. But there are also the professionals, dyed-in-the-wool beggars and con-men (and women)—the kind of people the Jews among our Sunday guests call "schnorrers." They are a bad lot and at least one of them is a pickpocket.[2] But they shout as loud as anybody, and put the touch on whoever has gathered to see what the fuss is all about. God knows wherever there is religion there will be beggars, but this goes beyond the beyonds, as the Irish say. And this seedy pack tramp all over my garden, throw down rubbish and cigarette ends and matches and wrappers off sweets and God knows what not, and make a day's work in about half an hour.

They are destroying our Sunday salons because they lie in wait for the guests and besiege them with their cries for money. It isn't the money that keeps people away, I truly believe, but the hysterical nastiness of it all.

Of course I've complained to the police, but they say their hands are tied because a burial ground is not a place where they can intervene unless something really illegal is happening. I explain that it's part of our garden and private property and have got a lawyer on the job, but it seems that when we agreed to the burial we relinquished some right or other, and it's all a mess that will take a court case to resolve.

I have ordered them off time and again, to no effect. Once I even got into a pushing-match with Prudence Vizard but she was slippery as an eel and shrieked that I was *persecuting* her. God! She was wild and really I feared she might do me a mischief. But I was the stronger and daunted her, for the moment, at least.[3]

I think Father Charlie curses the day he ever saw Prudence Vizard, to whom he has been very decent. She now sees herself as a Holy Woman, proclaiming the sainthood of Ninian Hobbes, and it provides a focus and outlet for her nuttiness far more dramatic and exciting than simply plaguing doctors with her alleged arthritis. I think Father Charlie—and Dr. Hullah as well—hoped the "cure" would wear off and she would have to shut up, but it hasn't and my bet is that it won't so long as it brings P.V. a lot of noisy attention. The papers haven't got hold of it yet, but they certainly will if this keeps up.

Sorry to go on so! But I'm at my wit's end![4]

Love as always,

CHIPS

VIGNETTES

1. Heads of an assembly of ragamuffins and rising above them the head of Prudence Vizard, done to the life and exhorting the crowd.
2. A hand lightly groping in the rear pocket of a very tight pair of trousers.
3. Prudence Vizard and Chips in a ferocious shoving-match.
4. A distracted face of Chips.

[23]

CHIPS WAS WRONG. The papers had carried brief accounts of the goings-on at St. Aidan's and a sensational paper called *Hush* carried a picture of Prudence Vizard exhorting her assembly. This made it impossible for Hugh McWearie to ignore the matter any longer, and he wrote a very discreet article about an instance of faith-healing, but was as near silent as was possible about the part in the affair supposedly played by the late Father Hobbes. He did, however, follow it up with a report of what Prudence Vizard called her Holy Hour, which came every day at Angelus and was drawing larger and larger groups. The limit was reached when Prudence turned up one evening with a loudspeaker and a microphone; she now had a crowd of around ninety people every day, and she was riding high. Charlie asked her to desist but she replied that she was compelled to speak, and his silence was a scandal and a shame to him. That went ill with Charlie, who was resentful of any sort of criticism and was aware that his own campaign inside the church for a shrine had been overcrowed by this madwoman in the open air. The matter of Father Hobbes' sanctity had, in fact, got out of control.

I detested the whole business and gave Chips all the help I could in getting some legal restraint on the Vizard assemblies. But lawyers move like molasses in January, as my mother used to say, and there was no chance that anything would happen for weeks and probably for months. Meanwhile the flower-beds around the graveyard which were Chips' pride, were trampled to nothing, and the mess left by the crowd outside the door of my clinic was a continuing nuisance and I had to hire a man to come daily and clear it up. The church people were very loud in their disapproval; their strong sense of ritual was affronted by the Vizard evangelistic uproar. The hymns she encouraged the crowd to sing—nobody but herself seemed to know the words, but they all buzzed and hummed as she screamed—seemed like an ugly parody of the musical splendour that went on inside the church.

"Some of it inevitably rubs off," said Mr. Russell, the church warden. "She makes us look like a bunch of Holy Rollers. I don't know why the cops can't do something. Get her for unlawful assembly, or something. What are we paying taxes for?"

But nothing happened to stop Prudence Vizard.

Most decidedly nothing was to be expected from her husband. Charlie had approached him, and so had a deputation from the church. Mr. Vizard made it clear that he had no influence over his wife in such matters. He had borne with her illness for many years, and had sympathized with every manifestation of her roaming pain, and now that she was well and embarked on this new venture he preferred not to become involved. In short, he was afraid of his wife, and with good cause. She was not a brawler; she was a nagger and a weeper, which is far worse, and to top it all she was now the substance of a miracle.

Of course the trouble was the source of many discussions in my upstairs retreat in my clinic. Dwyer always came in after the salon had drawn to a close, as did McWearie. My old friend Mr. Daubigny, the humbugman, came frequently and he was a regular attendant after Prudence Vizard asserted herself. Mr. Daubigny was now an old man but his delight in the vagaries of life was unstinted.

"This business of the Holy People," he said, "is familiar to me from my Russian experience. There were thousands of them—beggars, crooks, madmen, and very possibly some deep believers. These people recall them, but they are not precisely like them. They do not smell like the Russian holy ones. Those had the unmistakable pong of people who had probably never had a bath in their lives. Of course these people of Mrs. Vizard's assemble in the open air, but we may hope for a more pungent holiness when the cold weather comes and they have to find some shelter. I saw the pickpocket at work."

"I saw the snoop at work," said Dwyer. "Didn't you see Joe Sliter, Jon? Surely you remember him. Now who do you suppose is paying Joe to mix with that rabble?"

"I wouldn't mind risking a dollar—and I'm not a

betting man, mind you—that it is the Bishop's office," said McWearie. "Ted Allchin has used private investigators before now. Always keep an eye on the man on your left at the Communion rail; he may be a snoop. Probably the Venerable Archdeacon thinks Charlie Iredale has something to do with this holy circus. That's absurd, but when has Allchin boked at absurdity?"

"Poor Charlie," I said; "he mounted a tiger when he proclaimed the sainthood of Ninian Hobbes, and now the tiger is running away with him. I've listened to Mrs. Vizard from the windows of this room; she now blasts her message through a loudspeaker. She revels in what she thinks of as the persecution from St. Aidan's. She doesn't stop at proclaiming that she is following the practice of the primitive Church."

"Well, Charlie has only himself to blame," Darcy said. "He has no discretion at all."

"That's the effect of being Charlie's sort of parson," said Hugh. "A stomachy fellow. He's the kind that knows best, and don't you contradict him. He's in the wrong Church, poor lad. He ought to have been an R.C."

"He isn't, and he talks like a fool," said I. "Did you hear him two weeks ago? You must have heard, Darcy."

"Me? Oh, I never listen to sermons," said Dwyer.

"Well, he preached right at Mrs. Vizard, who was sitting three rows from the front. He denounced the scandal of a woman pretending to special revelation. It was something not granted to her sex, he said. He denounced those who sought to 'liberalize' the faith which had been handed down to us through the ages, perfect and unchangeable. He denounced something he called Enthusiasm, which I don't think I understood, but which seems to be a dreadful threat to whatever is true and certain."

"Och, it's anathema to people of Charlie's way of

thinking," said Hugh. "It's revolution against discipline and structure in religion. It's hot and rowdy and lets the worshippers have a big part in worship instead of sitting still and letting the priest do it for them. It's fiercely personal, but of course it has to have leaders and all these popular evangelists are the sort of leaders it breeds. All the way from John Wesley (whom God preserve) to the most ignorant Bible-pounder in the American South. Its theology is simple. Say you love God—say it as loud as you can—and that's all there is to it."

"But there are often deeply interesting manifestations," said Daubigny. "The Pentecostal thing; speaking with tongues. I once heard a Russian holy creature speak incomprehensibly for ten minutes and in the end he foamed at the mouth and had a fit. The bystanders thought it was a very holy moment, because he was speaking the language the blessed ones speak in Paradise."

"We've had a snatch of that," I said. "Last week a little woman interrupted Prudence when she was in full spate and began to gabble incomprehensibly. There was a kind of power in her strange talk, too."

"I heard about her from Anton Moscheles," said Hugh. "He was on his way to Glebe House to pick up some music. He said he recognized the sound and he supposed she had gone *meshuga*—which means nutty but implies possession, as well. Anton made a run for it. It was too much like Old Russia for his delicate nerves."

"But Prudence shut her up quickly," said I. "She demanded that a couple of people take her out of the garden and into the street and make sure she could not come back. Prudence wants no rivals in sanctity. Suppose that woman had said she was bringing a message from Ninian Hobbes in his new—what's the word?—*bodhissatva*, his compassionate enlightenment? I must say she sounded a bit like Hobbes in his less coherent moments, when his false teeth weren't in perfect control."

"All this uproar about Ninian Hobbes sets my teeth on edge," said Dwyer. "He was a good old joker, but he wasn't very learned, or very wise, and he couldn't keep in tune when he was chanting. He fed the poor, did he? So do I, because I'm a taxpayer on a bigger income than Ninian Hobbes ever dreamed of."

"But he smiled on the poor," said McWearie, "and you don't smile when you pay your taxes, Darcy, and if you did our Civil Service wouldn't know how to smile back. You've got to leave some place in the world for private charity. It's a two-way thing, is charity: you give a blessing, and you receive a blessing in return. You can't do that by mail; it's a face-to-face thing. What do you receive from your taxes? Well-kept roads and snow clearance, I suppose."

"Charlie's mistake was in being so courteous to Prudence Vizard when first she declared she had been healed," said I.

"But that's Charlie all over," said Hugh. "Nothing like courtesy for keeping a woman in her place."

"Practically the first lesson we learn in the Navy," said Daubigny.

"And a very good principle," said Dwyer. "It's how we gentlemen of the special persuasion gain such a good opinion among what is sometimes called the fair sex."

"It's the way we polished villains hold our own in the sex-war," said McWearie.

"Where is it to end?" said Daubigny.

"In destruction, I fear," said Dwyer. "Places like St. Aidan's seem secure, but they are very delicately balanced. Is all that beauty, and scholarship, and real devotion to be overturned by Prudence Vizard? I have my serious misgivings."

"We shall see the outcome," said I, "and meanwhile we must await the decree of Fate. *Anangke*, which I proclaim in my entryway, is a power to rival even that of St. Aidan's."

"You are growing philosophical, and it is time for me to leave you," said McWearie. "My guess is that it will blow over. The church is an anvil that has worn out many hammers, as the church itself is verra fond of saying. St. Aidan's will pull through."

"You misunderstand me," said Dwyer. "I don't mean that anything will happen that you can see from outside. But Enthusiasm will win. At a heavy cost in some directions. I may not see it. I'm off in ten days."

"Lucky man," said Daubigny. "I wish I could afford to travel. I'm land-locked. That's fatality for you, Hullah. A sailor—and land-locked."

"I'll be gone for a couple of months. I have to look into a few things in some European branches and then the bank has very decently given me leave to spend a month in Spain."

"And you fear something decisive may happen in that time?" said Hugh.

"I know it. Archdeacon Allchin not only snoops; he is snooped upon."

"Run up the storm signals," said Daubigny.

[24]

DWYER WAS RIGHT. The Archdeacon moved swiftly and decisively. Under his urging, I suppose, the police found that Prudence Vizard was transgressing some city regulation about the assemblage of crowds numbering more than twenty-five people, without a licence, and police appeared at her

Angelus services for several days in succession and dispersed them.

When that fateful diocesan meeting occurred, as autumn began, when the Bishop announced changes in parish appointments, the Reverend Charles Iredale was transferred to a charge in the northernmost part of the diocese, a wretched post where he would be expected to serve six small country churches, the total number of parishioners numbering less than a hundred and fifty. Such charges were generally given to suckling parsons for a year or two, to give them breadth of experience; this was episcopal discipline on an unprecedented scale. The Bishop cast down his eyes as he pronounced this doom, but Archdeacon Allchin looked with perfect serenity at Charlie, who turned white but did not otherwise betray his desolation. The new incumbent at St. Aidan's was the Reverend Canon Clement Carter, a man in whom ritual enthusiasm and evangelical zeal were neatly balanced, supported by a wife admired for her adroitness in managing disparate elements in a parish. Mrs. Carter was also known to have money, which gives a parson's wife a special status.

So there were great changes at the Church House, and Mrs. Carter was exemplary in finding nice lodgings for Father Whimble with a widow who lived not too far from the church. Mrs. Carter thought it might be well to have the house fumigated before redecoration. These old houses do become rather run-down, as everybody knows, and for some months really undesirable people kept hanging around instead of going to the church's undercroft, as they ought. But after months of work, Church House was a handsome, clean, well-furnished (but no ostentation—oh dear, no) clergyman's residence. Hand-painted pictures, the work of Mrs. Carter, who was "talented" adorned the walls. Most of these were views of the Muskoka lakes, usually when the autumn colours were richest. Very choice.

Mrs. Carter's only failure was in making a happy contact with her nearest neighbours the Misses Raven-Hart and Todhunter, who were not responsive to her approaches (though perfectly civil) and never suggested that she and the Canon might drop in on one of their Sunday afternoon *belles assemblées* where there were some people (the Neil Gows, for instance—was he not said now to have a truly *international* reputation?) that the Carters would have been delighted to meet. Nor were relations really cordial with Dr. DeCourcy Parry, who seemed to think the organist in a church had an authority which was quite out of proportion to his real importance, significant though the Ministry of Music (the Canon's happy phrase) must always be. But the Canon felt that rather less ceremonial and rather more preaching of moderate doctrine was what was wanted. Was it not a pity, really, that Glebe House should be almost on top of the church, and yet not a part of it? Not under its influence, so to speak? But some very important people were seen to visit Miss Raven-Hart's studio, and that was a change from the people of the parish, who were dears, of course, and maintaining themselves in really humble positions, some of them.

Nor was Mrs. Carter any more successful in getting on close terms with that doctor who occupied what used to be the stables behind Glebe House, and who had a peculiar reputation—peculiar at least in so far as some of his diagnostic practices went. Mrs. Carter decided not to take the Canon's weak chest to Dr. Hullah, even though she had heard that the baths his nurse—formidable-looking woman—administered were effective for asthmatics. But the Canon was a shy man, and the Dragon nurse might ask him to strip, as

Scandinavians are known to do, quite casually.

All of this I heard, from one source or another, but most often from Mr. Russell, who did all the printing for St. Aidan's. Mr. Russell developed quite a turn for irony when speaking of Mrs. Carter; not a word of criticism, but all the comment seemed to tell of an east wind.

Canon Carter made short work of the plans to set up a monument to Father Hobbes. Admirable though the idea was, and a fine testimony to the devotion and kindly spirit of the people of St. Aidan's, it was quite out of the question in terms of the church's finances. Charlie had, as might be expected, made a mess of the arrangements and, in consequence, there was a big bill for marble, which had been delivered and was indeed stored in a room adjacent to the studio in Glebe House. Who was to pay? The marble had been delivered to Miss Raven-Hart and the marble company assumed that she would pay, and was prepared to take its claim to law. In the end, I weak-mindedly undertook to settle the bill, with a vague understanding that I would be repaid by The Ladies whenever they could manage it. What happened to the marble was that Emily Raven-Hart used it for portrait busts of a variety of presidents, chairmen, deans, bishops and similar dignitaries whose admirers wished to memorialize them in this handsome fashion, and Emily Raven-Hart gained quite a reputation for her work. She was said by discerning critics in banks, boardrooms, universities, and synods, to be marvellous at "catching" a likeness, though occasionally the truly critical—often the wives of the subjects—felt that "there was something not quite right about the mouth."

Dwyer had been prescient; he saw none of this. The report of his death in Gibraltar was brief and uncommunicative, but McWearie told me that he had heard that Darcy had got himself into some sort of mess with a soldier, and had been stabbed, but it was impossible to identify his murderer.

"And I suppose if you live that sort of life you must be prepared to take the rough with the smooth," said Hugh. "It is a great loss to St. Aidan's."

In a way, I suppose it was. Not quite a year after the appointment of Canon Carter, Dr. DeCourcy Parry decided that the time had come for him to retire and the Canon was loud in his regret, but of course understood all too well the workings of the artistic temperament. (His wife, you know: she *paints*.) Dr. Parry was already far beyond the usual age of retirement, and he wanted to give his last years to composition. So the two strong men of the church's music were gone, and the music was continued on a much less ambitious and artistically demanding level.

I became an infrequent attendant, as did The Ladies. I wrote to Charlie, at his new address, and so did The Ladies, but we received brief and chilly replies.

Of what follows I have no evidence but my own observation, for there are no more letters from Chips to her friend, and Emily Raven-Hart's inspiration, Dame Barbara Hepworth, for Dame Barbara died in a fire in her studio at this time, and the correspondence ended.

But the story does not end. It has rather more than ten years to go. And only during the last three of those years did Esme begin her enquiry, making me rake my memory for what had really happened and decide how much I was prepared to tell.

IV

VI

It was on a beautiful September day—my birthday indeed—that I began to suspect that I was at last an old man. A few years earlier my Government had made me an Old Age Pensioner—gave me a pension which it immediately grabbed back in taxes—but otherwise I had not heeded the passing of time.

When Christofferson made her second appearance of the morning in my consulting-room, at eleven o'clock, she brought my usual cup of coffee, and also a slice of a fine cake—not a creamy, iced cake but a butter-cake with a dusting of powdered sugar on the top.

"How kind of you to make me a cake, Chris," said I, "but however am I going to eat it all?"

"You won't," said she in her usual clipped tone. Chris had learned her English in school in Denmark and still spoke a beautiful Received Pronunciation version of the old tongue. She scorned what she called "the Toronto patois." "Half of it will go to Penley, who has children, as you know, and another third goes to The Ladies at Glebe House. So by the time I have had a slice for myself there will not be enough left to embarrass you."

Penley was my assistant. Harry Hutchins had long gone to practise for himself, and was doing very well.

Aikens had succeeded him, a dull fellow. Now Penley, a fussy little man, a born pharmaceutical chemist, had taken his place. The only human thing about Penley was that his wife had a child every year, like a repeating-gun. Chris was always diverting food from my kitchen to the Penley nursery. I didn't mind, but I rather resented being the excuse for a cake of which I would get only one slice.

"I want to talk to you," said Chris.

"What is on your mind?"

"Several things, but you are chief among them. You have no appointments after four o'clock. Shall I come then?"

That was how my sixty-fifth birthday was signalized. One slice of cake, no gifts, no telephone calls or messages of greeting. I had hoped Nuala might call, but she didn't. McWearie knows nothing of such niceties. I thought that St. Aidan's, into which I have poured money in one way and another, might have sent me a card, but under Canon Carter its chief concern was the poor and needy, a group to which I could not claim to belong. My patients would not, of course, know when my birthday was. It was all perfectly reasonable and justifiable, but nevertheless with the perversity of the human creature I felt a little neglected, somewhat overlooked, and was vaguely sorry for myself. A little self-pity, I have always found, is very agreeable, so long as one keeps it to oneself. Who would pity me, if I didn't? An old man, and apparently without a friend in the world. I was cheered after a consultation with a patient who complained of constant and medically inexplicable indigestion. I did not tell him that I was certain he was married to the cause of his indigestion, but I took some comfort in the fact that I had at least escaped the wretchedness of a bad marriage, patiently endured.

At four o'clock, when a Bell's Palsy had been shown to the door after receiving some reassurance, Christofferson presented herself. She was, as always, dressed from head to foot in white, with finely pressed white trousers; her only divergence from the dress of the ideal modern nurse was the cap she wore as evidence of her qualification in a Danish hospital. She always wore it to services at St. Aidan's, so that everyone would know that Sygeplejerske Fru Christofferson (for such was her resounding professional title) was in their midst, and a marvel of pleating and goffering it was.

"I want to talk to you about the future," said she.

"Your future?"

"Mine and yours. They are linked perhaps more than you think. You have today entered on official old age. I am several years younger, but it is time to talk."

"Well, if you want to talk about retirement, save your breath. I shall go on practising for at least another ten years. You are another matter. Do you want to give up?"

"No, no; I can take care of myself. But you will understand me when I say that I want to take care of you, as well."

"But you do. All the office work as well as your special duties fall on you. You are irreplaceable. What more could you do to take care of me?"

"I could marry you."

"But—but—."

"Don't worry. I have no intention of doing so. But it is certainly one of the solutions. Let us dismiss it and talk of other things."

"Don't misunderstand me. I don't for a moment suggest that marriage with you is a repugnant idea, but—"

"Now it is your turn to save your breath, Doctor. Do not feel obliged to be gallant. Of course you wouldn't marry me. And for that matter, I wouldn't marry you.

We are neither of us the marrying kind. It was my little joke. You have never understood my sense of humour. But about taking care of you: there I am very serious. You need to change your way of life."

"How?"

"You are getting out of condition. You take no exercise. You eat and drink and smoke too much."

"Now, Chris, I'm not going to be dieted and exercised. My constitution is strong. I shall go on as I am."

"All doctors neglect their health. I don't expect you to do anything unpleasant. But I suggest very strongly that you allow me to give you a complete massage twice a week. You know my work. I can take care of you."

"Ah, well—that's a different thing. We must talk about it."

"No, there is no need for talk. I have put your name down for appointments, beginning tomorrow. Steam bath, massage, oatmeal bath and needle shower, then half an hour's rest. To be continued until you need something more specific."

"You seem to have thought of everything."

"More than you suppose. You must take your own medicine, Doctor. What do you tell your patients? 'You must have an occupation. Something to exercise and stretch the mind, otherwise you will become mentally flabby. The inert mind is a greater danger than the inert body, for it overlays and stifles the desire to live.' Isn't that what you say? And isn't that what has helped so many of them, and made your reputation? You must have something other than your practice, and drinking with McWearie. You have come to the time of life when much happens and you must be ready for change. How are you going to meet that?"

"There I am ahead of you, Chris. I have my great work already formed as an idea. The next thing is to make a plan. Then comes the research, which will take a very long time. Oh, with the job I have before me I see myself toiling on well up into the nineties, when you will be long past your work as a masseuse."

"That will never be."

"That was my kind of joke. Do you want to hear what I have in mind?"

"I am very glad you have something planned. If you wish to tell me about it, very well."

"You promise not to breathe a word to a soul?"

"Doctor, when have I ever revealed anything you told me in confidence? You offend me."

"Sorry, Chris. I know you're no chatterbox. But this notion is so extraordinary, so far-reaching, so stupendous that I know that if it got about, somebody would steal it. It's nothing less than the next great forward step in literary criticism."

"Don't worry about your secret. I know nothing of literary criticism."

"Oh, but you must. It's in all the papers and magazines—popularizations of the newest great idea, that's to say. Surely you've heard of Deconstructionism?"

"Not a breath. What does Miss Todhunter say?—Not a peep."

"I really don't understand how people can live in such isolation. Well, anyhow—Deconstruction is a new way of looking at books. It comes from France, as so many brilliant, short-lived notions do. It's like this, you see: you take a book, and you read it, and what does it mean to you?"

"It means what it says, I suppose."

"Quite wrong. It isn't what the book says, it's what you say about what the book says that's important."

"But suppose I'm a fool and don't understand the book?"

"Doesn't matter in the least. The Deconstruction theory says that there is no meaning to be found in the actual text of a book, but only in the various 'virtual texts' constructed by readers in their search for meaning, even if they are mutually irreconcilable. Anyhow, you and ordinary readers don't come into it. This is for the élite, the critical *bon ton*. When a Deconstructionist says 'reader' he means somebody of his own stripe. The ordinary reader is irrelevant."

"You have lost me, Doctor."

"That's part of what I'm talking about. Deconstruction offers a refreshing lack of certainty about virtually everything. Let me try again to explain. This method of criticism rejects everything that traditional criticism thought important—biography, literary history, philology—they must all give place to a very close formal examination and exegetical evaluation of the texts of books themselves, exploring meanings in every mode of literary expression as they are directly apprehended by the informed modern reader. Get it?"

"No. Is this what you are intending to take up?"

"Oh, great heavens, no! Mine is an entirely different notion but no less revolutionary. It will change literature forever, and make necessary new developments and commentaries on the literature of the past. It will keep the whole critical trade hard at work for at least a couple of centuries."

"Aha.—Yes, yes. I think I see."

"How can you see when I haven't told you anything?—Oh, I understand. I read your look, my old friend. You think I've gone mad."

"Well—"

"Delusions of grandeur? Inflation of the ego? Something like that?"

"I would have expected that any big idea you had

would relate somehow to your life's work. But you seem to have deserted that for vapouring about literature."

"But my idea *is* linked to my life's work. Springs directly out of it. You'd better let me tell you in the roughest terms what it is."

"I think that would be best."

"You once told me you read a lot of history?"

"For years I have been studying Spengler. He suits my temperament exactly. Of course, sometimes—on summer vacations when I want something light—I read Toynbee; he is very good and his bias toward religion is fruitful."

"As you read the unfolding tale of man's fate, do you never wish you had more information about the medical history of those who have profoundly affected that fate?"

"No. That sounds too romantic for me."

"Oh, come on; man's fate is directly related to the ailments and disorders of those who carry it out. Don't you wish you knew more about Napoleon's haemorrhoids?"

"No. He died, as you surely know, of cancer of the pylorus."

"Of course. But it was the thrombosed haemorrhoids that cost him Waterloo. A commander who has to go on the field in a carriage, accompanied by his doctor, pausing frequently to lie down, is not at the top of his form. Don't you want to know about Washington's broncho-pneumonia—quinsy, they called it? What was it really? And Queen Anne's 'flying gout'—hopping all over her body—what do you suppose it can have been?"

"All this is well recorded. What do you intend to do with it?"

"Nothing. I'm taking an entirely different tack. You won't sympathize with it immediately, because you don't read much but Spengler, who doesn't really grab the average reader. No, I'm going to apply modern medical theory to the notable characters of literature. Why did Micawber lose his hair? Want of keratin? What were his nails like? What did Jane Eyre, as a governess in a gentleman's house, get to eat? None of the imported pineapples and grapes, I'm convinced; it was stodge, stodge, stodge for Jane every day of her life, and what had that to do with the solid little creature she became? We know that Jane Austen was fond of port; does it show up in any of her heroines? Think of the refusal to cope with normal sexuality in nineteenth-century literature.—What was the truth behind the marriage of Dorothea Brooke and Mr. Casaubon? They must have shared a bed; it was the iron custom of the time. What happened? Did anything happen? What conclusions can we draw about the menstrual cycle of Emma Bovary? How did Nana avoid having babies? Was it the old vinegar tampon, or what? What was the dental condition of the crew of the *Pequod*? I intend to go into as much of this subject as I can manage, and it will take me many happy, inquisitive years, equating literature with what we know about the medical practice that was contemporaneous with it. And—this is what I want to impress on you, Chris—the day will come when no writer will dare to offer a novel or a play to the public until he has investigated the medical history of all his characters. Very likely the great writers of the future will all be doctors. Do you follow me?"

"I think I understand you, which is not quite the same thing."

"Do you still think I'm mad?"

"Not yet."

[2]

I WAS QUITE SERIOUS in what I pro-
posed, but in describing it to Christofferson I inevitably
pitched the note somewhat too high. Her temperament
demanded it. There was that about Inge Christofferson,
so admirable in every way, that simply called for the far-
cical approach; one wanted to make her turn pale, or
squawk with dismay or amazement, or even—but this
was asking for the unattainable—to laugh. She had her
own dry wintry jokes, but was unaffected by the jokes
of others. She was a Spenglerian to the backbone. It was
his great theory of cyclic progression that had prompted
her birthday talk with me. I had, she reasoned, passed
the ages of Growth and Maturity and was now passing—with my government's sour sanction—into
Decline. Blüte, Reife, and Verfall; it was as plain as that.
In her view I had reached the Age of Regret, and spots
of food on the lapels. That anything in my temperament might change Decline into Enlightenment, and
thus inevitably into a somewhat mirthful approach to
whatever of life still remained to me, would have been
wholly inconceivable to Chris. She had a Teutonic
acceptance of authority, and Spengler was her authority.

But not mine. Admirable fellow as Spengler was
(foreseeing the disastrous consequences of National
Socialism in Germany, and standing up bravely for the
Jews) I could not tag along after his Prussian insistence
on austerity. As it appeared to me, a practising physician, life would provide all the discomfort anybody
needed, without making a principle of it. I would, so far
as possible, enjoy old age.

My great book I had decided to call *The Anatomy of
Fiction*, taking as my model Robert Burton's *Anatomy of
Melancholy*, and as his had been declared the greatest

work on medicine written by a layman, I hoped that mine might be the greatest book of literary criticism written by a physician. It would, of course, be a work of extrapolation, working from the known, as given by the author about an imaginary (but not therefore unreal) character, to well-researched and intelligently guessed-at elements which the author was probably aware of but which the conventions of his time did not permit him to describe. As a doctor, I could not conceive that he might have chosen to omit such details from reasons of literary choice; surely the health, physical state, and living conditions of his characters would be of absorbing interest to him? As they were to me.

But in the course of a life still much occupied with my medical practice, even though I was trying to diminish it, and deflect potential patients to other doctors, I had not the time for the absorbing research my book would demand. So I determined to make a note whenever an idea occurred to me, and to do so in this Case Book, even though the occasional intrusive NOTE for *ANAT.* would interrupt the flow of what was developing into a substantial narrative.

[3]

OTHER INTRUSIONS into my Case Book and Catch-All I could not by any stretch have foreseen. Such a one was the murder of my godson Conor Gilmartin.

It was Christofferson who first informed me of it. That woman seems to have assumed the character of Lachesis, the measurer of the web of life. One morning she came into my office before my first patient arrived, and laid the morning paper on my desk.

"Bad news," she said, and left.

Bad news indeed. It appeared that the night before, Gil, as we always called him, had entered his apartment, gone to his wife's bedroom where he expected to find her at work, as she usually was at that time, and was met at the door by an intruder who struck him with a heavy weapon, apparently some sort of metal cosh, and killed him instantly.

Now here I must be frank, although it may seem that my frankness does me little credit. At the moment I read the news a patient was ushered into my room by Penley—Chris would not have done it, but presumably she was not at her desk—and I gave myself, for the next fifty minutes, wholly to the concerns of that patient. By all fictional convention I should have refused to talk to old Mr. Ellworthy about his arthritis, and have rushed to the Gilmartin apartment in order to do what I could for Esme. But I didn't. I was as cool as a cucumber, and Mr. Ellworthy left much refreshed.

The shock came later. After I had telephoned, and said several things which I knew to be of no help whatever, I went to the apartment, where Esme was being "taken care of" by a distracted young woman colleague who was more bother than she was worth. Esme did not need medical attention; her own doctor had been to see her and had given her something to steady her nerves, which seemed to me to be in very good order, all things considered. I called the police and talked to the surgeon on the job, who was an old friend of mine, and was told all the medical details, which were not very revealing. I assured Esme of any help I could give, said a few bracing words to the foolish helper, and went back to my clinic. I had a full day's appointments before me, and it was not until evening and after my usual dinner at my club that I had a chance to think about Gil.

This was the man who might very well be my son,

but although I was regretful and somewhat stunned I cannot pretend that I felt any disabling grief, and I was ashamed of myself for not feeling more than I did.

Had I no decent grief in me? Or is grief something that popular opinion apportions to particular misfortunes and which may not present itself to order and in the right form? Frankness compels me to say that although I felt a certain solemnity and decent regret, I felt nothing approaching true grief and pain of bereavement until I attended Gil's funeral.

That was when I saw Nuala, and of course Brocky with her. To my eye she looked beautiful in her desolation and Brocky looked, to my dismay, quite old—older surely than I looked myself? I greeted them, but did not sit with them; that might have seemed to be claiming some equality in bereavement.

The *Advocate* had provided Gil with a funeral in high style. Esme, to my dismay, put on rather a show, going to the coffin and touching it with reverence as the priest spoke the last few words of the service. A histrionic and, of course, an un-Christian action, but not therefore insincere and I did not allow myself to judge her. Canadians, on the whole a grim-faced lot, do not show much grief in public, but that is not to say that those who do so are not giving form to true feeling.

No, the champion in grief was a man I did not know who was sitting among Gil's colleagues, and whose noisy weeping was an embarrassment. Rather a dandy he was, for as he left the chapel, leaning on the arms of two women colleagues, somebody picked up and handed him a handsome walking-stick which I assumed was his. He accepted it with a look that seemed utterly inappropriate to what was happening—a look almost as if he expected to be struck with the stick, instead of grasping it by its decorative knob.

"You'll have dinner with me tonight?" I contrived to whisper to Brocky when the funeral was over.

[4]

THUS IT WAS that we three got together at my club, the York Club, a famous refuge of the beleaguered well-to-do, and dined in the handsome dark chamber where a few others were eating and engaging in muted conversations. I had feared that talk might be difficult, but it flowed freely. Talk of the funeral, and some astonishment at the number of people present and the warmth of feeling they showed. Talk, inevitably, of the music, to which Brocky gave reserved approval. Talk of Esme's somewhat overstated performance as the widow, and it was here that I understood that Nuala and Brocky had never really liked Esme but had done their best to accept her as a daughter-in-law; it was a matter for comment that, although she had kissed them both, not warmly but with proper funeral chill, there had been no suggestion that they should meet her at any future time. They wondered what her financial situation was. (I was able to set their minds at rest; Gil had taken my advice about investment and Esme would be all right.) They did not complain, but it was clear that they felt that they might have been consulted about the funeral service, which the *Advocate* had taken unto itself and which I knew that McWearie had arranged. But at last this preliminary discussion was exhausted and we came to more important matters.

"Of course this leaves us with a problem," said Brocky. "As you can guess, my father left quite a bundle. It has been growing because we live simply, and now we have no heir. What do we do?"

"You'll want to do something about Esme, I

suppose," said I.

"Don't say we want to. Say rather that we shall," said Nuala.

"But she won't be the heir in the sense that Gil was," said Brocky; "wouldn't do at all. I haven't thought much about it, but at the moment I rather favour a large bequest to Waverley."

"But earmarked, probably for the Library," said Nuala. "Don't put it into general funds or Principal's Discretionary Fund, or those greedy scientists will blow it all on expensive toys."

"You surprise me," I said. "I thought you would favour directing the money to medical research. You—a doctor? You astonish me, Nuala."

"I know our investigative brethren just as well as you do, Jon. One of the giant industries—Cancer, or Alzheimer's, or AIDS—could gobble up everything we have and not even bother to lick its lips. And what would come of it? Damn little, so far as anyone could see. But a Library—well, a Library goes on as far as thought can reach. Who are you to talk piously about medical research? You've done some pretty good work simply using your head."

"Ah, but I don't decry research. Some fine things are done."

"Not nearly enough for the amount of money spent. Too much machinery, too much administration, and not enough brains and intuition. Research harbours a lot of second- and third-rate people."

"Aren't you being extreme?"

"Yes, and high time more people were. Those huge labs are what the monasteries were before Henry VIII took the axe to them. More humanism and less science—that's what medicine needs. But humanism is hard work and a lot of science is just Tinkertoy."

"The people at other tables are beginning to glance this way," said Brocky. "Pipe down, Nuala, this isn't your Club and you may get Jon a bad name here. Rowdy guests. But Jon, of course any ideas you have or think up during the next few weeks would be very welcome. We think of you as having a very special association with Gil."

I pricked up my ears. Was this an invitation to raise the subject that had been so much in my mind ever since the murder?

"Very special—I agree. How special, would you say?"

"You were awfully good to him during his schooldays. Formed his enthusiasm for the theatre and for literature. He spoke of you with real affection. You were very much an uncle to him."

"An uncle?"

"Don't you like the word?"

Here goes! "Brocky, I've never raised this point, but have you and Nuala never considered that I might have been Gil's father?"

Brocky stopped eating *crème brûlée* and looked me in the eye. There was a perceptible change in the atmosphere, and Nuala was part of it, though she did not move a muscle.

"Of course I know that you and Nuala were in love before you joined the Army. I suppose if things had been different, you might have married. But the gods disposed otherwise. I came back from abroad much earlier than you did; Nuala and I were both working at Waverley and were inevitably thrown together; we fell very deeply in love and married. Gil was one of the evidences of that love, if I may talk sentimentally for a moment. So I think it unlikely that you could have been Gil's father. But—that's a silly thing to say; we academics are always qualifying and diminishing things;

you simply couldn't have been."

"I suppose this is the time to get it all out, literally on the table. You'll have a cognac with your coffee?"

"Oh—should I?"

"I think you should. Speaking as a physician. You didn't know that for years after your marriage Nuala and I met very often?"

"I know her work took her often to Toronto. You mean of course that you were carrying on an affair?"

"That's one of the damnedest, silliest ways of describing what we were doing that I know."

"Just at the moment I can't think of a fancy new expression for what I mean. But listen to me; if you thought I didn't know, you underestimate me grossly. In fact, Nuala told me all about it, when things came to a head."

"You had already suspected it?"

"He knew it for a certainty," said Nuala. "He put a snoop on us."

"What!"

"A private dick named—what was that horrid little creature's name, darling?"

"The best of the lot was a worm called Joe Sliter."

"My God! Brocky—you put a tail on your own wife and your best friend? How could you do such a thing?"

"Well, when it comes to that, how could *you* do what *you* were doing? Making a cuckold of a man you think of as your best friend?"

"But—hiring a snoop!"

"What else is there to do? I don't say I'm proud of it, but you know very well we all do a lot of things we're not proud of, when it seems necessary."

"But it shows such hateful mistrust."

"Which, as is so often the case, proved to be perfectly justified."

"You're both being silly," said Nuala, "and people *are* beginning to stare. I suppose any evidence of life in here comes as a happy change. Now listen, Jon, and I'll tell you how it was. Brocky had been getting his reports from the worm, and one night he faced me with the facts."

"And raged and screamed and carried on, I suppose," said I, because now I was thoroughly angry. "Did he beat you? Slug you one? It's not unknown, you know. That's the sort of situation that brings out the caveman in professors of Eng.Lit.—usually quite a small caveman, but rough."

"Of course he didn't beat me. If he'd tried, I would have given him as good as he got. I'm wiry, Jon, as you have good cause to know. We had a very sensible discussion."

"Sensible!"

"Now who's being a caveman?"

"You know nothing about marriage, Jon," said Brocky. "People like ourselves don't go on like that. Have I worked in the world of literature for so many years, not to understand that a woman may very truly love more than one man at a time? Not the same. Not probably in equal shares, if love can be quantified. But Nuala loved you, and was sorry for you—"

"Pitied me, in fact!"

"We're all pitiable, one way or another. You must submit to being pitied, just like everybody else."

"So what came of this ultra-modern married exchange of confidences, after you had thumbed through Joe Sliter's grubby, illiterate reports?"

"Cool down. Joe wrote very plainly and suitably. No gloating. No pitying the cuckold. Just facts and times. We got out a bottle of rum, and had a long, very loving talk."

"Ending up where?"

It was Nuala's turn. "Ending up with me admitting that I had been just the teeniest scrap devious, and Brocky admitting that it wasn't very nice—"

"Though wholly justified," Brocky put in.

"To put a snoop on us, and get the goods in quite that way. It was a simple case of middle-class adultery begetting middle-class retribution, and very sensible as so much middle-class behaviour is. But then we got down to facts. I told Brocky I still loved you quite a bit, though I thought I was really still in love with the idealistic, amusing young man you had been, rather than the very successful, ironic middle-aged man you had become, and was truly in love with the wonderful Brocky with whom I had lived in such happy intimacy. Admitting, of course, that some of the dew had dried on my own personality and that being a gynaecologist does somewhat change one's attitude toward sex."

"And had being a clear-eyed gynaecologist made you certain that Gil was not my son?"

"Yes, it did."

"I never saw you taking any precautions."

"I wasn't as obvious about it as you were, when you remembered, which wasn't always. Rolling on your condom with satisfaction at filling it so well, you vain ass."

A silence followed, and at last Nuala said:

"Don't take it so hard, Jon. We've none of us been especially noble. Just human. But I don't think we've anything much to reproach ourselves with."

"Sorry. I don't have much to say. In the last few minutes I have lost the great love of my life, and also my only likelihood of a son. It takes a bit of getting used to."

"Now, now, let's have no cheap melodrama," said Brocky. "You haven't lost the great love of your life. She's still right where she has been for years—in your memory. And as for losing a son, you'd have been a rotten father, but you made a splendid weekend uncle, a Saturday-on-the-town uncle, and you had some of the best of Gil, and missed the adolescent revolt and other conventional nuisances I had to cope with. You don't suppose this Club of yours could come up with some really good rum, do you?"

"I'm certain it could. That's the kind of place it is. I am sure I could get a bottle. Then we might adjourn to my quarters."

That is what we did, and made a merry evening of it, in which our newly found situation was carefully considered, and approved, and old ties were tightened.

The odd thing was that we spoke so little of Gil. But in a very real sense, this was Gil's wake.

[5]

ARTISTICALLY, everything was wrong with the resolution of my affair with Nuala. It had been passionate love in the beginning, and those student days, and the afternoons in the Ford Hotel, were as glorious to me as anything in literature or art. The continuance of our love for several years after her marriage had for me as powerful a savour as the deception of King Arthur by his dearest friend, Lancelot of the Lake—the subjection of loyalty to passion. But the conclusion! Suspicion, and instead of a manly confrontation, resort to a private detective; a muted row in the dining-room of the York Club; a merry drunken threesome in my study, with everybody kissing everybody else and an acceptance of what, by all the rules of art, should have been utterly unacceptable. The stealing hand of old age spreading its pall over the romance of youth, so that I saw, unwillingly, my darling Nuala as a wiry gynaecologist, with a few threads of grey in her Irish black hair. I saw Brocky, with all his finely woven mantle of learning, as also a husband who had settled the hash of his wife's lover by the most conventional means, and had shown no anger. Because Nuala had said so, and Brocky had agreed as if she were stating an incontrovertible truth, I had to accept the idea that a woman could, in complete sincerity, love two men at the same time. Worst of all I saw myself not as Lancelot of the Lake, the self-hating adulterer, and decidedly not as the figure in the centre ring of the circus, but as a side-show in the lives of the two people I loved best.

Artistically I suppose I should have shot myself, leaving a message saying, "I forgive you all." But I really had no appetite for suicide and I came at last to a recognition of myself as, *in part*, a Tom Sawyer who wanted everything done according to the rules of romantic fiction, and complicated simple situations with his absurd adolescent, book-born nonsense.

In part; it is important to stress that qualification. The romantic lunatic and the shallow-witted adolescent were not the whole of Dr. Hullah, who was so successful at unravelling and re-weaving the fabric of other people's lives. How often is this so, I wonder? Turn the Wizard toward the light, and you see that he is also the Fool. The lives of the great philosophers, so far as we know them, afford ample supporting evidence.

[6]

NOTE FOR *ANAT.*: To what extent does our whole concept of the mixture of sexual attraction, elfin glamour, simple lust, and loneliness which we call love, need revision as we grow older? For there is no use pretending that love does not change with the years, in the cases when it survives the years. Fiction and poetry have little to say about this.

I have no young patients. The ills I can treat are those of middle and old age. The young have other needs. But I hear a good deal about the young, and read what they write about themselves. For them love—and I don't think they have entirely abandoned the old word—has lost virtually all of its glamour because sexual union is comparatively easy. (Though not perhaps so easy as the popular writers would suggest.) As every child knows, waiting for Christmas Dinner, hovering around the table, sniffing the wondrous scents from the kitchen and working up an appetite is immensely better than the actual consumption of the meal. Only when they have achieved some experience as gourmets does the true satisfaction of appetite arrive, and gourmets do not stuff themselves at every opportunity. So—in our time love has lost some—not all—of its glamour because it has been too much simplified. But of course lust and loneliness still play their accustomed roles. And sexual attraction, though it has found some new robes (or brought old robes out of the closet), is as potent as ever.

It was not always so.

Until quite recently the concluding experience of most popular fiction took place at the altar. With our great-grandfathers it very rarely reached the marriage bed. But oh—what we would not give to know what really happened when Mr. Rochester, in his fine linen ruffled nightshirt, lifted the cotton nightie of Mrs. R. the Second (née Jane Eyre) and set about an act which unquestionably was, for her, something new and strange.

Strange in deed. Probably not wholly strange in imagination or in daily observation. Jane cannot have lived the life she lived and remained entirely green about sex, nor could Charlotte Brontë, who was her only begetter.

Charlotte and Jane both lived in the country, and in the age of horses, and horses are not modest creatures. The dissolute Branwell Brontë must surely have dropped a few hints about his own life in the hearing of his sisters. Brothers are no friends to innocence. One of those sisters, the heroic Emily, must certainly have known how many beans made five, and what it was that—in part at least—bound Heathcliff to his youthful love Cathy; adolescent sex cannot have been unknown to a daughter of the Reverend Patrick Brontë, whose parish must have presented examples enough.

One cannot doubt that Jane Eyre went to her marriage bed a virgin, but not a fool.

What of the heroines of Jane Austen? So witty a girl as Elizabeth Bennet must have picked up a few things before her marriage to Darcy. She had the true Shakespearean heroine's combination of modesty and merry intelligence, and modesty is by no means incompatible with knowing how the world wags. Jane Austen's girls knew to a hair's breadth the fine line between merriment and simple smut.

A purity that is ignorance, when the age of childish innocence has passed, is mere stupidity, and nobody ever thought Jane valued stupidity. But later in the nineteenth century this came to pass, for there is no nonsense so gross that society will not, at some time, make a doctrine of it and defend it with every weapon of communal stupidity.

It was a convention of ordinary fiction until fairly recently that a really nice girl is not merely innocent—which is one thing—but a simpleton—which is something quite different. Amelia Sedley may have been a fool, but Becky Sharp assuredly was not. What ignorance can Becky have possessed, raised as she was? Thackeray did not write ordinary fiction.

Nor can the children in these great books have been as numbly ignorant of sex as would appear from a hurried reading. Henry James's very intelligent little Maisie knew a great deal that her biographer tells us, and undoubtedly a great many things about the sexual life of her elders which her author knew she knew, but was forbidden by convention from telling us.

Of course I, the well-read Dr. Hullah, know these things, but it is only now that my experience strikes home, and I understand that the love in literature and the love in life are one, and that the intelligent reader must bring his own experience to supplement the experience of the novel he holds in his hand. Romance, a true devotion, and simple bodily lust are all part of the same plum pudding, and there is so much more to the pudding than the delicious savour that arises from it. The proof of the pudding is in the eating, and it is only when we have eaten several mouthfuls that we begin to understand. If a book cannot stand up to this test, how good is it?

[7]

IT WAS NOT Gil's death, but the aftermath in which I had to reassess my affair with Nuala and see that the Irish enchantress of the past and the middle-aged (to be gallant, for she was not more than three or four years younger than I) and wiry gynaecological specialist of the present were two different creatures and that I was well into what the popular journals call "the youth of old age." Nor could I expect the world to sympathize with me if the world should ever hear of my trouble. The world, as represented by those who give advice on such matters in the press, would doubtless have advised me to seek a new partner, probably in the columns of those papers where "Peppy lady, 45 years young, seeks real man, fond of opera, candle-lit dinners, walks in the woods, baseball, and fly-fishing, for lasting comradeship and who knows what?" The world had, without my being strongly aware of it, changed its attitude toward sex dramatically, though not, I think, deeply. Homosexuality had become, not the love which dares not speak its name, but the love that never knows when to shut up. Words that as a boy I had seen scrawled in chalk on barns were now common-places in the daily press, and probably that is a move away from a narrow puritanism, and a foolish affecta-tion of delicacy in reportage, where there can be no deli-cacy and little decency. Nevertheless, I can never see the word "fuck" in print, or hear it on the lips of women old and young, without a start, which I have learned to con-ceal, because to me it speaks only of physical sex as it applies to a rape or commercial unions with bored hirelings. There is no other word except chilly medical circumlocutions, but to me "fuck" will always lack the elfin glamour without which the interplay of the sexes is simply hot flesh and cold potatoes—a poor meal.

Nevertheless I was kept from sinking into ancientry by my patients. Many of them belonged to the group McWearie called Hullah's Aporetics, which was his grand word for people ingenious in producing doubts and objections to virtually everything that might be expected to help them. If I prescribed a medicine they were sure to find that it was too strong, or not strong enough, or seemed to provoke new and troublesome symptoms. If I suggested that some reading, or concert-going, or hi-fi listening, or the new marvel which can bring a movie right onto your TV screen might give them a lift, they found reading "tried their eyes," or they were not "up to" getting to a concert hall, or home listening "disturbed" the rest of the household. As for the notion that films at home might raise their spirits they were more than usually ingenious in their objections. The sight of films made when they were young, or younger, were too painful because of the sense of the past they evoked; since the Holocaust all that sort of thing seemed unbearably shallow. Or else they were ridiculous because the fashions were so stupid that nobody could ever have worn them; or there was too much drinking, or cigarette-smoking, or indifference to the mounting threat of Russia, or some other thing that made the film unendurable; and of course the Marx Brothers weren't funny any more and my aporetic couldn't raise a laugh to save her life.

Did this mean that I stopped my suggestions or that they did no good? Not a bit of it. "How lucky you are, Doctor, to have such a zest for life. A poor creature like me simply has to envy you. No, the films didn't help and I've returned the machine to the shop—but I must say that what does me good is a talk with you, Doctor. You have what I heard one person call infectious mental health, and that's a great gift."

Gift! To these wretches I was a marvel of well-being. It was inconceivable to them that I might have any cares, disappointments, aches or pains, for these things were their exclusive property. My appearance of well-being was a professional manner.

Not all my patients were in this group, thank God, or I might have gone mad. But the majority were the people with infectious mental ill-health and they spread their misery to pitiable husbands, wives, unmarried daughters, and dependants and connections who could not, or would not, flee from them. I am sure I did them some good, and in doing so I earned my fee, for they were depleting company and if I had not maintained a firm professional attitude I would have laughed at them, or cursed them, for they were cumberers of the earth—poor souls.

Now and then I had a novelty, like the very pretty case of Farmer's Lung I diagnosed in a chartered accountant, whose devotion to his city garden had brought it on. It was a clear extrinsic allergic alveolitis but I thought myself rather clever to have traced it to its cause, and when he followed my advice and gave up so much intense composting, he quickly came round, and hailed me as a wonder-worker.

But there were hours when I longed for a more interesting group of patients. I had read and reread Axel Munthe's *Story of San Michele* and I wished that I too were called upon to treat crowned heads, and society beauties, and fascinating artists. True, I had a few millionaires, but they were not the interesting kind—not great pirates and rascals of finance, but just toilsome lawyers and manufacturers, every one armed with a dismal tale of how he had raised himself from humble beginnings to—it seemed to me—an intellectually and spiritually humble present. I wished for a larger life. I knew that I was just as good a physician as Munthe, looked at medicine in the same humanist light, but the interesting patients did not come my way. I was doomed to lend an ear to what Wordsworth called—

The still, sad music of humanity

which all too often degenerated into a whine. I was rich, for I had made my substantial inheritance grow by sound investment, and I had acquired a good deal by—it must be said—soaking my patients heavily for my services. The health system at that time permitted what was called "extra billing" which allowed a doctor to charge his patients something above the fee recognized by the government. I was a remorseless extra-biller, and it seemed to me that the more exacting I was, the more eager my aporetics and dismal sufferers were to reward me for my attentions.

Cynical. Inexcusable. Professionally reprehensible. My parents would not have approved. The Anglo-Catholicism which I had adopted (with substantial reservation) would not have approved. But—did I not deliver the goods? Did I not disperse my infectious mental health to those who were so eager for it? Was I not, in the term now popular, "charismatic"? As for my extra-billing, had not Sigmund Freud counselled against treatment that was too cheap, on the grounds that what came cheaply was cheaply esteemed?

But oh, I longed for a crowned head or an ailing beauty!

[8]

"Miss Todhunter has asked for an appointment."

"Extraordinary. That's never happened before."

"I know. They see Dr. Dumoulin when they see anybody."

"Any idea what it's about?"

"Yes."

"Well?"

"You'd better get it straight from her. I've given her five o'clock. Last of the day."

When Chips arrived in my consulting-room she was uneasy, and that was in itself strange. I let her go on about the weather—such a splendid autumn—for a while until she was ready to unbutton.

"It's not about myself I've come. It's about Emily. I

wish you'd have a look at her, Doctor."

"What is this 'Doctor' business, Chips? We're old friends."

"I know, but this is a professional visit, and we've never consulted you professionally. You're too expensive for us poor artists."

"I believe you are patients of Dr. Dumoulin. If you mean to go on with him, I must be reserved. No poaching. Old professional principle. But of course if you want a second opinion—"

"That's precisely what I do want. And I've come to you because you're the Cunning Man. I don't think she's getting the right sort of treatment at all."

"What is her treatment now?"

"Dumoulin keeps saying it's depression. She's become awfully hard to live with. I mean, not just the usual temperament one is used to in artists like Em. She snaps my head off about the least thing and she mopes a lot."

"I don't suppose that was what she went to Dumoulin about?"

"No. Fatigue. No chug. Run down."

"I see. Appetite?"

"Tricky. Things she used to love she won't touch. That's not like her, you know, Jon. Not a bit. It used to be that if she didn't feel like eating I could coax her, and she'd eat to please me. Now if I coax she gets very shirty and tells me not to boss her. She's losing weight, I know."

"Sleep?"

"Poorly. Reads a lot in the night."

"You share a bed?"

"Always have. So I know. And it isn't just reading. She weeps. And if I try to show any comfort she gets hysterical and tells me not to watch her all the time."

"Do you notice anything else—any unusual smells,

for instance?"

"Yes. Breaks wind a lot. But stealthily. What the Québécois call *le pet jésuite*. No noise, but of course you know. She's very ashamed of it, but can't control it."

"This is a bit personal, but what about libido?"

"Meaning—?"

"Any interest in sex?"

"Oh, that's all over. Menopause dished it. Perhaps it shouldn't have, but it did.—You *are* a nosy old thing."

"Professionally so. What does Dumoulin suggest?"

"Oh, he gives her some charcoal pills for the farts. What he really recommends is a trip of some sort. Thinks a sea voyage would help. But you know what that means nowadays—one of those bloody tours with retired simpletons. I suppose one could go on a freighter. They take passengers and I hear the Dutch ones are very good. But it's no use, anyhow. She won't hear of it. Says she must stay with her work."

"How's the work going?"

"Hardly at all. She's still messing with that banker's head she began three months ago. She puts funny faces on the clay model and then bursts into tears. Rum, Jon. What do you make of it?"

"What can I make of it when I can't see the patient? Won't Emily come and see me?"

"Not a chance. I suggested it and she blew up and said she'd be damned first. This is one of the rum things; she takes against people so unreasonably. Once she called you the Cunning Man, but now she's taken against you. You used to be on pretty good terms."

"But never on really good terms. Not like you and me. Well, Chips, you see how it is. I'd have to see her before I could say anything useful."

"But can't you say anything at all? I'm desperate, I don't mind telling you."

"With what you tell me I can't offer anything better than a medieval diagnosis. It sounds as though Emily were suffering from an excess of black bile."

"What the hell's that?"

"If the body is really governed by four humours—I say *if*—blood makes them sanguine, phlegm makes them phlegmatic, choler or yellow bile makes them choleric, and black bile makes them melancholic. The thing is to keep the humours in balance and if one begins to dominate it chooses the disease in which it will manifest itself. That's what Galen believed and Galen was no fool. Galen would say that Emily had too much black bile, which makes her melancholy and rather a lot of yellow bile, which makes her testy and sour-natured. If we take a giant leap forward from Galen into modern psychiatry, I'd say Emily was in a state of advanced denial. Her life has lost its savour. If you want a grand word for it, call it anhedonia."

"So what do I do?"

"I wish I could tell you. But unless I can put Emily on my table—"

"Yes and sniff her doings and lay your head on her dear little tum and all that nonsense—yes, yes, yes, and I tell you it won't do. Well—sorry to have wasted your time. Send me your bill."

"Chips, you wound me. What bill? We doctors treat members of the family gratis. Aren't we family, after all these years?"

"I don't know what I'm saying, I'm so worried. Yes, I suppose we are. Thanks, and I do see your point. But it's hopeless."

"Oh, nothing's hopeless to those of us at St. Aidan's."

As I showed her out she paused and looked searchingly at my fine print of Wiertz's picture of Death and the Lady in my waiting-room. She shuddered.

"Why don't you get rid of that awful thing?" she said, as she went.

It was one of those moments, and we both knew it.

[9]

NOTE FOR *ANAT.*: Only a partial estimate can be made of the quality of a life unless we know something about the defecatory habits of the patient, and that is why doctors make those tactful enquiries about the bowels, and why men patients are subjected to a dismaying examination of the prostate, with the doctor's finger jabbed as far as it will go up the rectum.

So of course, for my *Anatomy of Fiction*, what would I not give for a tickle of Mr. Pickwick's prostate? What was the condition of Miss Havisham's bowels, sitting all day in a wheelchair as she did? Intestinal stasis can have a profound influence on the personality.

Dickens, for purposes of my book, offers an almost embarrassing wealth of speculation. All those low-life characters, who lived in the streets and lay at night in Tom-all-Alone's—where did they void their bowels, when they did? In alleyways, one presumes. Those people who went on prolonged journeys by coach, did they seize the opportunity every time the horses were changed to go into the stable-yard, where they found one of those inclined troughs, emptying into a hole in the earth, for urination? Doubtless they did, considering what a lot they drank, thinking nothing of a pint of sherry—a wine substantially fortified with brandy—as a mere refresher. No wonder disease was rife. And the travelling ladies, what of them? Fiction gives no hint, but one presumes they had to ask the landlady for a room into which they could retire, with a chamber-pot.

And who dealt with that? The chambermaid, of course; it was an important part of her work.

Indeed, much of the class system of European and American life right up until the present century, rested upon the distinction between those who dealt habitually with human detritus and those who did not. Persons of gentle degree, however challenged, decidedly did not. The commodes and the chamber-pots were emptied, cleansed, and sweetened in the sun by persons who could not, for that reason, pretend to gentility. Ladies and gentlemen, even the most benevolent, drew the line at any such association. Hence the assumption that if Tom Jones impregnated a maidservant it was a trivial matter, but any attempt upon the virtue of a lady was a grave offence.

The absurdity to which such ideas might lead is satirized by Swift in his famous—for many years considered infamous—poem in which a lover steals into his adored one's bedchamber, and delights in all the pots of pomatum, scents, and ribbons he discovers there. But then, stupid ass, he investigates a pretty stool by the bed, opens it, and finds it is the commode! He rushes from the room, a man distraught, crying, "Celia! Celia! Celia shits!" Serve him right. Her personal maid could have told him other things about Celia which, though not pretty, would have given Celia a human dimension he denied her.

The line between the mistress and the maid—even Mrs. Micawber, brought low by the ill-fortunes of her beloved Wilkins, had someone to empty the chamber-pots; true the wretch was an orphan, quartered on the Micawbers for her board, which must have been scant. This orphan, who was almost certainly illegitimate, came from a workhouse and was thus virtually a non-person. Just the one to cope with the slops. And a

servant Mrs. Micawber must have, or every pretension
to gentility would disappear.

Has this line of investigation anything to do with the
shadow that has come over Glebe House? Yes, it has. If I
could have a look at Emily, and perhaps have an analy-
sis made of two or three of her stools, I might find cor-
roboration for what I already guess, and what I think
Chips fears.

[10]

Professional etiquette might
stop me from interfering in Emily Raven-Hart's treatment (though I strongly suspected that Dumoulin was
on the wrong tack) but it did not stop me from observing Emily at times when she was not aware of my presence. From my consulting-room I looked out of the
window a good deal, onto my courtyard, which was
flanked on the one side by the garden of Glebe House
and on the other by the rear portion of St. Aidan's. My
premises had lost virtually all the appearance of a stable
(except for the horses' heads so pleasingly moulded over
the main entrance) and the group of buildings was
pretty and nicely kept. As I listened to my patients I
often looked out of the window because they talked
more readily when I was not looking directly at them. I
knew that my gaze could be disconcerting.

From my window I invariably saw a few of God's
People hanging around the entrance to the crypt of the
church, which Canon Carter had developed into a
refuge for them. "Crypt" was the handsome new word
for the old, cluttered cellar; it was now fitted out with
tables and benches and a kitchen, from which good-
hearted ladies of the church, and a few retired men,
served a hot breakfast to all who came. But it was not

comfortable for those who were not eating, and so the courtyard became a hangout for them, and a few of the more venturesome went into the church itself and slept the day away on the thinly cushioned pews at the back, near the font. I disliked the use of my courtyard as a place of assembly for indigents, but there was little I could do without making a fuss and being accused of a want of charity; some of my more nervous patients did not like having to elbow their way through such a group, who did not scorn to beg from them. But my yard-man, who had little sympathy with what he called "down-and-outs," made the place as unwelcoming as he could, sweeping under their feet, and—most effective of all—asking for their help with jobs of lifting and cleaning.

This somewhat medieval arrangement undoubtedly gave an air of activity to the courtyard, but The Ladies and I could have done with less of that, and Chips became markedly hostile toward God's People when they made free with her garden, and now and then urinated in the adjoining graveyard.

My window permitted me a good view of the comings and goings of The Ladies, and at least once a day I saw Emily taking the air in the garden, or going off to do some errand. To the casual eye she showed no change from her old, pretty, and obviously well-bred self, but to my gaze she had become slower in her step, and especially when seen from the rear she seemed to droop, which was most unlike her. I made an excuse to visit the house—droppers-in were not encouraged—and although Emily was not present in the body, she was so in the spirit, to my sensitive diagnostic faculty, and I do not think I deceived myself when I caught, now and then, a smell which every physician knows but which some prefer to ignore. The spirit of Glebe House had altered significantly.

Twice a week now I lay on Christofferson's table as she searched out stiff spots, aching spots, and tense spots on my body; she was a masterful masseuse and her method was the Swedish massage of an earlier day, which at times became a sort of painful rough-house, but refreshing. Of course we talked. Attention to the body loosens the tongue.

What did she make of the situation at Glebe House, I asked.

"I have never really understood those English ladies. Of course their situation is plain enough; it's to be seen everywhere and now it's becoming quite a public cause. But in their young days it wasn't so well understood, and they always seemed as if they were united against the world. Not hostile, but ready to resist criticism. Now the hostility has gone inside the front door. For the first time since I've known them, they are at odds."

"They still sleep in the same bed."

"Yes, but the lively times are past. Now it's the hot-water-bottle-and-flannel-nightie stage of Lesbianism. Domesticity has almost choked out romance."

"Do you think they were ever very close, physically?"

"I would bet money on it. And why not? They can have some very good times together, those people, and those two are resourceful artists."

"Cunnilingus, I suppose?"

"Oh yes, and anilingus, too, I expect. Very jolly once you get the hang of it, I'm told."

"You're ahead of me, Chris. But you think that's all past?"

To my astonishment, Christofferson burst into song:

Everything passes
   In this world:
Everything makes its appearance

And dies.
But the grief in my heart, my beloved,
  Will never pass away.

"That's an old Danish song, we used to sing when I was a girl; not so good in English, but you get the idea. Am I hurting you?"

"Yes, but in an entirely beneficial way. So you think the time has come for grief at Glebe House? I agree. Miss Todhunter is very worried."

"She may well be. Of course you know what's happening."

"I think I know."

"Of course you know. And I know, too."

"But there's nothing I can do."

"Professional etiquette? Dr. Dumoulin is a man with exuberant good health; he thinks anybody who is ill needs a tonic and encouragement. A doctor's treatment is always a reflection of himself, to some degree. But Dumoulin prides himself on his twelve-minute consultations, and sometimes he misses what a slower doctor would see."

"But I can't prance into Glebe House and say, I think Emily's got cancer and I want to take a look at her, and there's no time to lose."

"No, you can't do that. Professional etiquette."

"Which can very quickly become one of the decorums of stupidity."

"You cannot fight destiny, Doctor. You have put it up in your own waiting-room. *Anangke.* If you rush in like a rescuing knight on his charger, you may make worse mischief than if you let destiny have its way undisturbed. Emily Raven-Hart is a woman of very strong character, for all her winsome, peely-whally ways, and if she has come to hate her life you must let her go her way."

"Dree her weird, as the Scotch say."

"*Anangke*. You have placed it above both wisdom and medicine, and that is where it belongs. You must take your own medicine, Doctor. Am I hurting you?"

"Yes. But helpfully."

[11]

ALL VERY WELL for Christofferson to tell me to take my own medicine but as one who had been brought up in the interfering, help-offering, Nosy Parkering tradition of modern Canada I could not entirely keep clear of my neighbours' business. I made an excuse to call at Glebe House.

Emily was there. "What have you come for?" she asked, rudely, I thought.

"Just a social call. A cup of tea, perhaps. Just to see how you are."

"I'm perfectly well, thank you. Chips is never ill, as you very well know."

"Happy to hear it. But since you have given up your Sundays I don't see as much of you as I did."

"The Sundays got to be an intolerable bore. A great deal of hard work, and for nothing, really."

"Oh, don't say that. You had a salon. It was a place of resort for the most interesting people—artistic people, that's to say—in town."

"But they've changed. Or faded so you can't recognize them. Moscheles can't even get a place in the symphony today."

"Oh, that's unjust. Moscheles doesn't want a place in the symphony. He's a quartet man if ever there was one. And he's too old now for the symphony grind."

"Just as well for the symphony. Neily Gow is out. Sir Neily, now, of course, but on the shelf. We don't know any of the new people. Don't know anything about the opera, which is struggling ahead. Nor would they want to know us, I'm sure. Those days are gone."

"But they were very good days. Something was growing, then. The arts were blossoming as never before in this city's history. There was a *Gemütlichkeit* that seems to have vanished. And your Sundays contributed greatly to that wonderful feeling."

"You're a romantic. You really believe in Bohemianism as an element in art."

"I suppose I do. But it's given place to a kind of dry artistic respectability. For example, have you heard about Jimmy Scrymgeour and Kitty? For as long as I can remember they lived together in the lurid light of bigamy, because years ago Jimmy fled from Scotland, getting on the boat just as it pulled away from the dock and leaving on the shore his alcoholic wife, raving and screaming. Everybody knew about it, and everybody approved. But a few months ago Kitty met somebody I know and declared, 'What do you think? The Woman is dead!' Mrs. Scrymgeour had apparently expired at last in a home for drunks in Dundee and Kitty and Jimmy are now respectable! And that's what has happened to music, and art generally, in Toronto: respectability has descended in a fog of Arts Councils and Foundations and, although things are better on the whole, so far as performance goes, a lot of the elfin glamour of sin-and-improvisation has been dissipated. We have become a typical American city, visited by the travelling virtuosi, used as a stepping-stone to a better orchestra by flitting conductors, and your Sunday Afternoons have given way to President's Councils, and Women's Committees, and all the paraphernalia of modern artistic strenuosity."

"You can't halt progress."

"You mean you can't halt time. I don't know that I

believe wholeheartedly in progress. Civilizations in the past have managed very well with some sort of local equivalent of your Sundays. Loving patronage I suppose is what I'm talking about. But I'm being rude. Music isn't everything. How's your work going?"

"You mean my efficient production of bronze likenesses of Nobody-in-Particular, to adorn boardrooms? Or do you hark back to my great days as a butter-sculptor?"

It was here that Chips appeared, bearing the tea-tray. "Dear Em's a bit down," said she, "but really she's doing awfully well."

"Oh, I have quite a list of presidents and chairmen to get through, if that's what you mean," said Emily.

"Darling, I keep pointing out that the great ones of the Renaissance did a lot of presidents and chairmen, but then they were called Popes and Princes," said Chips.

"Yes, but those Popes and Princes had style, and often a distinguished ugliness. Wens, and hook noses. These bankers and brokers have no style, no faces. Nobody in this God-damned country has a *face*!"

"No, but they pay on the nail, which Popes and Princes didn't often do. Forget the wens and hook noses and be glad of the lovely money."

They wrangled on, foolishly, and I thought of my own hankering for crowned heads and great beauties. At last Emily could bear no more of the reasonableness Chips could not resist pressing on her.

"Oh for Christ's sake, shut up!" she said, and ran out of the room, sobbing.

"Poor love, she's a bit down," said Chips. And then she too broke into tears, and she was not a lovely weeper, as Emily was. "Oh God, how I wish I could get her to see you!"

I felt it was time for me to go, and go I did. But not before Chips had said, at the door as I left: "Have you noticed anything funny in the courtyard?"

"Funny?"

"Queer. I'm pretty sure of what I've seen. You keep your eye peeled."

And sure enough, as I stepped from their front door, I saw what she was talking about.

[12]

NOTE FOR ANAT.: Emily had been lying—or perhaps I should say reclining—on a sofa during this passage, and I was reminded how many women in fiction spent a great part of their life on sofas. Why? What ailed them? To be in bed may signal true indisposition, but to dominate the drawing-room from a sofa suggests something else—some chronic complaint, surely. And what could it be?

I thought of the Signora Madeleine Neroni, who figures so delightfully in Trollope's *Barchester Towers*; her beauty is described as perfect and Trollope is particularly enthusiastic about her "bust," which was the modest Victorian word for her breasts. She is the centre of admiration wherever she goes and men of all sorts find her irresistible. But she spends her life on sofas, and when she goes to other people's houses her brother has to carry her immediately to the nearest, or most strategically placed, sofa. What was wrong with the Signora?

An exotic creature, surely, to be the daughter of an English clergyman, even a wealthy one, but we know that she had been married to one Paulo Neroni, an Italian who was a captain in the Papal Guard, and that he had treated her with cruelty. Thus the sofa life.

As a physician I don't believe it. Women who have been knocked about by their husbands (or who have fallen while climbing a ruin, as the Signora insisted) do not maintain quite that perfect beauty. What we do know about her, which seems to me to tell the story, is that she had a child, and it is hinted that the child was gotten out of wedlock, and was legitimized by an unwise marriage. (This child she referred to as "the last of the Neros" which was coming it strong.) My guess is that the birth of this child was botched by some cheap quack and that the Signora was left with a by no means uncommon injury of the time, a vesical fistula, a tear in the birth canal which permitted urine to seep into the vagina, which meant that the sufferer must at all times wear some sort of staunching diaper and could not enjoy normal activity. Consequence, invalidism and a sofa life. This injury was considered incurable until quite late in the nineteenth century, and as it was not something one could discuss, it accounted for a lot of mysterious female fragility.

Of course nothing of the sort ailed Emily, but her taking to the sofa brought it forcibly to my mind, and I recognized that I was falling victim to the author's obsession, which is that he relates whatever life presents to him to the book he is writing or plans to write. I have not begun on my *Anatomy of Fiction,* but it is beginning to dominate my mind, I am making notes, and I must now search the pages of novels for ladies who may have suffered from what we know was a very common mishap in childbirth before the efficiency of modern surgery made it a thing of the past.

[13]

"IF SHE IS DETERMINED to commit suicide in this particularly distressing way, my advice to you would be to let her get on with it, and not try to interfere."

This was McWearie, up to his old trick of taking the opposite side in every argument, believing that by doing so he could bring about some sort of sensible resolution.

"But Hugh, that's inhuman, surely? And for me quite impossible, because I am bound by my Hippocratic Oath to preserve life whenever I can, and not to play the philosophical jackass, which is what you are advising."

"You know, I doubt if Hippocrates ever framed that Oath."

"Perhaps not, but it embodies what he stood for, and it is a noble definition of my profession."

"Handsomely spoken. But it does trim its sails, now and then. I observe that it no longer forbids a doctor to give anything to procure an abortion, or presumably to perform one. But anybody can have an abortion nowadays. I heard of a girl not long ago who wasn't yet twenty, and she had had three."

"There must be occasional redefinitions."

"Oh, of course. We must move with the times. Well then, why don't you go to Dumoulin and tell him you think he's abetting Em Raven-Hart in a form of suicide, which may no longer be illegal but does nothing to enhance a doctor's reputation. What Em's up to isn't mercy-killing, you know; it's merciless, and not only to Em. What about Chips? Aren't you obliged to think of her?"

"I couldn't possibly go to Dumoulin. It would be—"

"Most unprofessional. And against your Oath. Aren't you sworn to be loyal to the profession, even when the profession is wrong, or just cheerfully neglectful? *The profession*! Oh Jon, don't talk that way! 'My country, right or wrong: my mother, drunk or sober.' Is that the line? I thought better of you than that."

"Very well. I'm sorry I brought the matter up."

"So you should be, you Oath-lover. Didn't you swear

that 'whatever you shall see or hear of the lives of men which is not fitting to be spoken, you will keep inviolably secret'? And here you are blathering away like some old woman at a tea-party. Shame on you, Doctor."

"Hugh, much more of that, and I'll put away the whisky bottle. You're being bloody offensive."

"Intentionally, I assure you. But can't you see I'm just trying to get at the truth? You think Em's got cancer and is neglecting it; you know that Dumoulin isn't doing anything about it, quite likely because she has never given him a hint about it and he hasn't got your famous intuition about patients; your professional loyalties keep you from interfering. So far, so good. You are aching to interfere, but your Hippocratic Oath takes precedence over your respect for Em's right to do what she likes with her life."

"Has she such a right?"

"Not by Christian reckoning. But Em's in a mess that Christianity has always found it very hard to cope with. You say she's in denial, which seems to me to mean exactly the same thing as saying that she's suffering from severe Melancholy. Now why is that, do you suppose? No, don't tell me; I want to tell *you* because I think I'll get it clearer and plainer than you will, having no Hippocratic Oath to confuse me.

"Don't you remember that years ago we went through all this with poor old Darcy? We talked about the peculiar misery of the artist who has some talent but not a talent commensurate with his aspirations? That's Em. She's pretty good. Does the heads of presidents and chairmen very well, really; a touch of real distinction. Her butter sculpture which she derides was absurd, but showed amazing skill. It's just that she's not really an originative artist; as soon as she leaves the straight and narrow path of portraiture her ideas are just slightly above the commonplace level; what is unmistakably her own in her work is not enough to lift it very high. You know her ideal was Barbara Hepworth; Em's work is imitative, not as good as B.H. but certainly never going far from her or beyond her.

"That's not too bad, really, but the misery of the thing is that Em knows she isn't quite first-rate, and it gnaws at her. The worst artistic tragedy is not to be a failure, but just to fall short of the kind of success you have marked as your own. Have you ever read the Diaries of Benjamin Robert Haydon? An interesting painter, but not good enough for the goals he had set for himself. Consequence: misery and finally suicide.

"And that's Em, I'm afraid. But where Haydon used a pistol, she's chosen a very feminine and prolonged method of ending an existence that has lost all savour for her. Ghastly, but what's one to do? It's a private affair."

"You talk as if she knows what she's doing."

"Well—doesn't she?"

"I don't suppose she does, on a conscious level. But are our most significant decisions made on the obviously conscious level? She wouldn't say, 'I'm killing myself,' but she'd say, 'I hate myself,' which might come to the same thing. I wish something could be done."

"My advice to you, Doctor, is to keep your nose out of it. If you save her, as I suppose you'd put it, what have you saved her for? More self-hatred? Don't try to play God, Doctor. Let *Anangke* take its course. As it will, you know."

"I haven't your capacity to ignore what's under my nose. And do you know what's under my nose right now, as well as Emily Raven-Hart?"

"No, but I suppose you're going to tell me."

"I am. Charlie!"

"What Charlie? Charlie Chaplin?"

"Don't play the fool, Hugh. The Reverend Charles Iredale."

"Oh, *that* Charlie. Returned from banishment, has he? Has the Bishop given him a city church?"

"He's living with the down-and-outs in the crypt at St. Aidan's."

"Oh, mercy, God! What does he say?"

"I haven't had a chance to talk with him. I've almost cornered him twice but both times he has slipped through my fingers."

"But—down-and-out! And herding with God's People! Not what one expects of a priest. How does he look?"

"Awful. Every mark of the ruined boozer. I'll corner him before long."

"I wonder if I could talk with him?"

"What for?"

"I'm religious editor of the *Advocate* in case you've forgotten. There must be a story in him. What brings a priest low? That kind of thing."

"Hugh, you are despicable."

"Not really. There'd be money in it for him. If I can help him, I will."

"Oh, will you? Not going to let Fate have its way with Charlie, but Fate can do its worst with Emily Raven-Hart?"

"Don't ask me to be consistent; it's the virtue of tiny minds. I always liked Charlie, ass though he could be. I'm human, you know, Jon. Philosophy is something to apply to outsiders, not to friends."

[14]

NOTE FOR *ANAT*.: Charlie's trouble is advanced alcohol addiction. A technical term for being a sodden boozer.

Astonishing how the notion of the Boozer as a great, free spirit has seized on the imagination of millions of people who ought to know better. He represents to them one who has soared above the shadows of daily care and whose mind is free of petty concerns. To deal with the Boozer in Lit. would mean that I should have to embark on a work of many volumes; I must be selective and concise. What could I not make of Seithenyn ap Seithyn Saidi, one of the three immortal drunkards of the Isle of Britain, as T. L. Peacock presents him? His greeting to Elphin and Teithryn when they present themselves at his castle has splendour: "You are welcome all four." And when Elphin says, "We thank you; we are but two," the great man counters, "Two or four—all is one." But Seithenyn is a creature of mythic history, and that his drunken incompetence costs Elphin his kingdom is a mythic peccadillo. The realities of drunkenness never soar so high.

Of all the great literary drunkards surely Falstaff is the chief, though we never see him overcome with drink; he is the cause that drunkenness is in other men—a very unpleasant characteristic. Generations of playgoers have adored him, and thought poorly of the prince who will not yield wholly to his spell. It is only in his brief scene with Doll Tearsheet that we see the despair beneath the jesting. Actors have loved him; stuff the pillow in the front of the breeches and speak in his richest voice and the poorest ham thinks himself splendid. And Shakespeare's genius makes Falstaff splendid. But there was one actor who seemed destined for the part, and who refused to play it; Charles Laughton had been the manager of an hotel in his youth, and he said he had been compelled to throw too many of Falstaff's kind out of the Pavilion at Scarborough to have any tolerance for the breed.

The truest portrait of Charlie's sort of drunkenness that I know in literature is Marmaladov in *Crime and Punishment*—the sodden wretch who confided to Raskolnikov that he had sold his wife's stockings in order to buy drink. The anguished repentance, the ravings of self-pity, the knowledge of the degradation to which he had sunk and the inability to rise from it, all these were Charlie's, but where Marmaladov babbled, Charlie spoke with all the practised rhetoric of the life-long preacher and exhorter.

It was plain that he had been drinking heavily for years, but like many of his kind he had not yet sunk to *mania a potu*; he had no sensations of crawling things on his body, nor did snakes or monsters menace him in the dark corners of his retreat. I had seen a few cases of The Horrors among God's People, because being the nearest doctor I was often summoned when something went amiss in the crypt. I claim no merit for answering these calls. I did not want to leave my bed and spend an hour coping with a madman, before he could be carted off to the hospital. But how does one refuse? Mine is a profession of compassion, and when compassion does not arise naturally it must be faked.

Charlie is the reality of what many writers—some of the greatest—have romanticized. I shall use the measure of Charlie against the literary drunkards I write about in my *Anatomy*.

[15]

IT WAS NOT EASY to get Charlie into my care. At first, he ran—literally ran—at my approach. Where did he go? Into the crypt, but when I followed him he was nowhere to be seen, and the other down-and-outs who happened to be there denied any knowledge of him, in the over-vehement manner that betrays the liar. But at last it came to me that he was doubtless, and very appropriately, in what Darcy Dwyer had christened the Priest's Hole.

In the penal times in Britain, when it was death for a priest of the Old Faith to be captured by the zealous Protestants, many secretly Catholic households had a hidden room, or more often a mean loft or cupboard, which was called the Priest's Hole, because it was there that the visiting priest could hide himself from searchers. Behind the antiquated furnace at St. Aidan's there was a hole in the wall, just big enough for a man to lie down in, which had at one time served as an ash-pit; there was a manhole above it, through which the ashes had once been removed. Since the conversion of the church furnace to oil-heating this miserable chamber had been cleaned out, though not very thoroughly, and was screened from the rest of the crypt by two or three sheets of corrugated iron which stood against the entrance. It was in this filthy retreat that I ran Charlie down at last.

It took some persuasion to get him to allow me to give him help. He was drenched in shame, and shame made him ugly and uncooperative. It was almost as though he were doing me a favour in allowing me to get him out of the Priest's Hole and out of the crypt, and into a succession of Christofferson's baths that finally soaked and sucked the filth out of his skin. Sucked and soaked also some of the alcohol out of his system, which left him exhausted and physically unable. The question was, what to do with him? Where to put him?

My quarters over the clinic afforded only one bedroom, which was mine and a very comfortable room indeed. There was nothing for it but to put Charlie in my room, and I had to sleep in my living-room library, on a sofa. I am sensitive to such things, and sleeping in my workroom, and having to tidy it up and stow away my bedclothes, and then settle down to a long day with my aporetics, gave me a sense of having lost caste, of having come down in the world, which was quite unreasonable but none the less real. Christofferson kept an eye on Charlie, who lay in my bed, in my pyjamas, sleeping off what must have been several years of intoxication which he had nevertheless sufficiently overcome to be able to function acceptably, if not effectively, as a priest.

I suppose I am not truly a charitable man. I do charitable things, but I can't pretend to myself that I like doing them. I could not leave Charlie to his wretchedness, but I wanted to get rid of him—or at least to get him out of my bed. I appealed to Canon Carter. He was a Professional Good Man and expressed pity and concern, but offered no solution. Had St. Aidan's no place for Charlie? I asked. Was there a spare room in Church House where he could live for a time? Unfortunately the two curates needed accommodation, as it was part of their stipend, and the paperwork that was involved in administering the parish filled all the space there was. The Canon and his wife had to occupy quite restricted quarters, to make room for the business which now seemed to be the principal concern of St. Aidan's. The Canon was very sorry, but—

Could Charlie be of any use about the church itself? Sacristan, or verger, or beadle or something? The Canon smiled a smile of deep compassion for my innocence. A former incumbent, now reduced to menial work, where many people would remember him and everybody would soon know his story? Oh, no! The Canon could not possibly subject Charlie to such ignominy. Besides, Charlie was still a priest, and in a church he must do the work of one, or do nothing. And the Canon made it very clear that Charlie would do no priesting in *his* church.

The Canon talked about people knowing Charlie's story, but he did not know it himself, and made no move to learn it. But little by little I knew it, and it was a story of a kind very familiar to me, a story, not of tragedy, but of endurance of a miserable fate, with no hint of relief to be seen. The gods destroy the heroes with a sudden blow, but they grind us mediocrities for weary, weary years.

Charlie's story cannot be told without the introduction of facts which to many people might seem trivial and snobbish, but which cause great unhappiness all the same.

The work to which the Bishop, urged by Archdeacon Allchin, banished Charlie was the care of six little churches in a part of the Province of Ontario that lacked the Boreal romance of the North, but was far removed from the amenity of the South, as we in Canada understand the word "South." This sparsely settled parish was not in the Diocese of Toronto: by a little priestly hankypanky Allchin had persuaded a neighbour-bishop, who owed him a favour, to take Charlie under his wing, but at a remote and ragged tip of that wing. The folk in the parish eked out a poor living by a little subsistence farming, a little logging, and on rare occasions, some work on the roads. They were not a prosperous or lively group. Six churches seems a great many for one man, but he was not expected to visit all of them every Sunday and two he visited only once a month. They were not far apart—not far if you have a good car that can make light of bad roads—but which are far enough apart if what you have is a second-hand motor-bicycle, sinking into the senility of its kind, and are a total innocent—what is now called a technomoron—of everything that has to do with machinery. Charlie's motor-bike was a joke to his scattered parishioners, but it was no joke to Charlie when it broke down, as it so often did, miles from anywhere that might afford expert help.

The parishioners—ah, this was where the snobbery showed itself. Charlie had been gently brought up, and expensively educated. He was no fool and he was not unreasonable. But he could not help longing sometimes for the sight of a tablecloth, and for knives and forks that were not of some metal which had gone dark with age, and between the tines of which lingered the reminders of earlier meals. He thought wistfully of bedclothes that were not masses of ragged quilts, and of sheets that were not flannelette from which all the nap had been worn; sheets that were changed more often than was the custom with Miss Annie McGruder, for it was with the McGruders that Charlie boarded.

How could it have been otherwise? The McGruders had always boarded the parson. It was one of their good works. They did not charge him what they might have charged somebody not doing the Lord's work—supposing that such a person ever applied to them for board.

They ate off oilcloth, so old that it smelled of meals long past. They ate in the kitchen. Not what city-dwellers think of as a kitchen, with pretty curtains and cupboards which have been invested by modern commercial builders with what they think of as charm, and a stove powered by gas or electricity, so pleasing in appearance that it seems hardly to be a stove at all. The McGruders knew not such Persian pomps in their kitchen; the stove was black and smelled of hot old iron when it was in full action; behind the stove a hen might be hatching out a few chicks in a cardboard box; in front of the stove two smelly old dogs, famous for their sagacity as hunters and guardians, lay comatose, farting pungently in the heat; on a special chair of its own, with its own very old cushion, slept the cat, an aged Tom. All of these creatures lent something to the compound of smells that characterized the kitchen, for all the windows were wadded firmly with newspaper to keep out the winter draughts, and it was thought to be too much trouble to free them when the warmer weather came.

Not the least element in this medley of stinks was Amos McGruder, who was not a dirty man in the sense that his face was dirty or his hands excessively dirty, but who wore the same clothes week in and week out, and who took off his shoes when he entered the house, and trod about in well-seasoned heavy socks. His smell was a powerful, masculine, farmyard smell, not unwholesome but inescapable.

Amos was a bachelor, which may have contributed a testicular element to his stench, like the cat. He lived with his sister, Miss Annie, who was by no means demonstrably insane, but who in the local parlance "lacked a round of being square." Miss Annie was quite up to keeping house, not in the highest flights of such work, but not positively squalid, though too often there was hair in the butter. She provided a cuisine of: breakfast, oatmeal porridge; dinner, stewed beef and potatoes not fully boiled; supper, bread and a variety of jams made by Miss Annie as fruits ripened in the season. All meals were washed down with stewed tea, made in a pot which was rarely emptied of leaves from which every bitter essence had been wrung.

Conversation at meals consisted of a brief weather report delivered by Amos, in which he contradicted the forecast that had been broadcast that morning on the radio; in Amos's opinion, "they never got it right." Miss Annie might mention that she had seen somebody pass on the road during the day. Otherwise she talked of religion.

Even the most devout priest can get enough of talk about religion, especially when it is untouched by theological stringency, or mystical insight. Miss Annie's talk was chiefly of her dreams; Jesus often came to her in dreams, and she described his appearance in detail. Luckily for Charlie, she did not require much of her listeners except silence and an appearance of acquiescence. Amos said nothing, but ate swiftly and passed back for more. Charlie soon learned to say nothing, and to make his plate look as much as possible as if he had eaten more than a few mouthfuls.

At the beginning of his years under the McGruder roof, Charlie had tried to institute the custom of saying grace before meat. Amos never seemed to understand why this might be done, and Miss Annie was too close to Jesus to need any such reminder. So Charlie came soon to mumbling his grace to himself, crossing himself, and then approaching the victuals that God had seen fit to grant to him. This must have been a test of faith.

Amos frowned at the crossing: to him it was something "Dogans" did.

During the day Charlie drudged at parish work, scooting around the backwood tracks on his untrustworthy steed, but when night fell he was trapped in the McGruder kitchen. He could not go to his bedroom during most of the year, for it was unheated. He could attempt to read, but Miss Annie liked to talk, and did not think that anybody could possibly want to read when she wanted to speak. Amos, from time to time, read a local paper, grunting disagreement. He had long since ceased to pay any attention to his sister.

Sunday was the day of bitterness beyond the ordinary. Charlie had to put in an appearance at two or more of his churches—small, frame buildings, obvious fire-traps, heated with stoves—and sometimes he managed to visit three. But whatever his duty might be, he had always to have midday dinner with the chief parishioner, who was probably also the Biggest Giver, and the menu and manner of these dinners was unvarying.

Now that he feeds on Christofferson's delicate and subtly flavoured broths, Charlie can permit himself to be amusing in his descriptions of those Sunday dinners. If the principal dish were not greasy fried pork chops, it was chicken pot-pie, made from superannuated hen and with dumplings of a horror he seeks to describe, searching for precisely the right word to summon up their quality; "glabrous" and "gluteal" have to be discarded because, although the sound is right, the meaning won't fit. We agree at last that "glairigenous" is as near as we can get, and indeed it is a fine word with its suggestion of stringy mucus and thick snot. The meal is completed by home-bottled stewed fruit, very sweet, and coffee, which the hostess describes, proudly, as "strong enough to trot a mouse."

Charlie had never been a big eater, nor indeed do I think he was interested in food. But etiquette demanded that he should do as his hosts did, and then, when he was away on his motor-bike to his next service, he stopped and vomited the mess by the roadside.

But this was not all that was involved in the celebration of the Lord's Day. At the McGruders' it was Parlour Night, when the parlour was opened and if it were winter, the stove—the "base burner"—was lit and after some time diffused a smelly heat and showed a cheerful glow behind the mica windows in its door. The McGruders sat in the kitchen on weekdays because it was the only heated room in the house, but on Sundays the parlour organ was needed so that Miss Annie could reveal her latest inspiration.

Miss Annie wrote hymns of praise. She did not

compose music, but she fitted her devotional rhymes to such popular tunes as she knew, and could play on the wheezing old organ; mice had been at its bellows and its voice was as vagarious as that of Miss Annie herself.

Her star piece, with which she concluded every Sunday-night concert, was set to the tune of the once-popular waltz song "Let Me Call You Sweetheart." In Miss Annie's recension it began—

Let me call you Jesus,
I'm in love with you—

and as she sang it her face wore what Charlie described as a sanctified leer, a transfiguring lust. Poor mad old maid, her innocent religiosity was heavily tinged with her ungratified desire.

Charlie's professional sense of charity and forgiveness was sorely tried by Miss Annie's warblings. His mind wandered to the music offered under the direction of Dr. DeCourcy Parry in the service of God, and he bled in spirit. But compliments were expected, and proffered.

Parlour nights went on until nine o'clock, which was late for Amos and the neighbours—Hercules McNabb and his wife Dorsy—who were the most frequent guests. The music ceased at eight-thirty, in order that there should be time for the fried cakes and strong tea before Hercules McNabb said, "Well, I guess—" and the orgy crawled to an end.

Small wonder, then, that Charlie took to drink. Small wonder that in the portmanteau strapped to the back of the motor-bike there was always a Baby Bear of the cheapest rye. Small wonder that in his bedroom, hidden in his valise which he kept locked against the inquisitive eyes of Miss Annie, there was another Baby Bear or two. Charlie was probably the most consistent and profitable patron of the government liquor store which lay just outside his pastoral district, and which he hoped, therefore, he could visit without being known or attracting attention. Vain hope. Everybody knew the parson drank.

(Does anybody now know what a Baby Bear is? The Government of Ontario used to sell spirits—usually rye or Scotch—in three sizes of bottle: the Baby Bear (12 oz.), the Momma Bear (24 oz.), and the Daddy Bear (40 oz.). The consumer was, presumably, a Goldilocks who made free with the property of all three bears. So—Charlie was a great consumer of the easily concealed Baby Bears.)

High-minded people would doubtless assure me that intellectual degeneration does not go hand in hand with physical degeneration and that neither has anything significant to do with social degeneration. I have been a physician in extensive practice too long to be deceived by such nonsense. Devout people would certainly point out to me that determined missionaries had spent years among native tribes, eating and living as did the souls they had come to save, and had acquired a high spiritual shine. But missionaries usually hunt in pairs or even larger groups; they are not utterly cut off from people of like mind; they know the tribes among whom they work to be people unlike themselves and they do not have the daily desolation of trying to live with the McGruders without in any important way offending the McGruders nor yet yielding to what might be grandly called the McGruder Ethos.

Inevitably, after nearly eight years of this sort of life, there came a crisis. One Sunday morning, when Charlie—who, of course, fasted before celebrating the Eucharist—had fortified himself with a swig from his Baby Bear before going to the first church of the day, and had then given himself another before the service, mingled with the sweet cheap wine he was preparing for Communion, was observed to be staggering as he offered the Communion cup to the seven faithful souls who had appeared to accept it, and in staggering he spilled the wine down the chin of a woman who was bending forward to receive it. Attempting to recover himself he tripped and fell and lay on the floor, moaning. The Blood of Christ slopped all down the front of his surplice. By the time two men picked him up, he had passed out. One drove him back to the McGruders' while another took charge of the senile motor-bike.

Did he sleep it off? He did not. He finished the Baby Bear and then drank all of another which he had in his valise, and lay in a stupor from Sunday until Wednesday, when he rose, set off to the nearest railway station on the motor-bike, took the day's single train to Toronto, and deserted his cure of souls forever, a priest disgraced beyond any recovery, at least in his own estimation.

In Toronto he made his way at once to St. Aidan's, as the only place in the city that was at all familiar to him. It was changed beyond belief, but he joined God's People in the crypt, and there he remained, sleeping long hours in the Priest's Hole, and drinking on the sly (so as not to have to share with others in the crypt, for there were many who would have been glad to help him with his succession of Baby Bears). How did he get money? He begged. Yes, Charlie begged with the modern beggar's cry—"Got any change?"

I suppose he had been there two weeks before I discovered him and forcibly removed him to my clinic. He was not willing to talk, but I bullied a few facts out of him: he had no resources, for his parents had left very little money and over the years it had been dissipated; the family income had depended chiefly on his mother's life interest in a family estate, and that had perished with her; the professor, a daring but unlucky investor, had lost virtually everything he had ever had, and his university pension died with him. Thus Charlie was an indigent, and in his own opinion a ruined priest.

I urged him to go to the Bishop, say his say, be properly penitent, and ask for help and work. But here Charlie's theological snobbery prevented him from doing anything of the kind; the Bishop was Low Church in the depths of his heart, and Charlie wanted no help from one so lost to reason and truth. I asked him what he thought he might do? He had no opinion on that matter. I asked him what he wanted to do, and he replied morosely that he wanted to die, but I was better able than he to judge whether or not that was likely, and I thought he was not assured but at least capable of many years of life yet. This Bishop was not the one who had banished him to the wilderness, but a new man and so far as I knew, not at all a bad sort. Meanwhile I had Charlie on my hands. Worse—I had him on my bed and I saw no hope of getting rid of him, for he had lost all power of will, and like most such people he remained a monstrous egotist: I do not think he knew what a nuisance he was.

I wrote to Brocky as being, like myself, one of Charlie's oldest friends. Had he any advice? He had none, but generous fellow that he was, he sent a handsome cheque to assist Charlie, although it was made out to me. I was so foolish as to mention this to Charlie, and he was very angry: had he reached a point where he could not be trusted to manage his own affairs? I did not quite have the cruelty to say that that was his condition. But I was firm about not letting him have more than a dollar or two in his own hand, for I knew what would happen if he could get to a liquor store. I knew

Charlie better than he knew himself, and that is always an uncomfortable situation for both parties.

[16]

NOTE FOR *ANAT*.: One of the problems surrounding Charlie's stay in my clinic was his cranky resistance to the ministrations of Christofferson, which I knew to be good for him. He could not endure to have a woman see him naked, or almost so. But I wanted him to have an oatmeal bath, following a thorough massage, every second day. Christofferson would not permit a patient to lie in a bath unless she had frequent access to the bath-chamber, for baths can be dangerous to the unable or disturbed. Charlie was one of those people in whom lingers the medieval notion that a bath is necessarily an erotic experience, and I truly believe he supposed that Christofferson looked in on him in order to feast her eyes on his naked body, and especially his privy parts. He fussed and fumed and besought me to order her to keep out of his bath-chamber, but I had no intention whatever of doing so. Modesty, in the world of medicine, is nonsense.

"Man is nothing else than fetid sperm, a sack of dung, the food of worms," I would say to him, quoting St. Bernard. "Do you suppose the admirable Fru Inge Christofferson does not know that, and values your exposed body accordingly? Do use your head, Charlie. This is a clinic, not a brothel, and Christofferson is a thorough professional at her work."

But it was useless. His attitude seemed to be that of the nineteenth century, when nakedness was not utterly decried, but was cloaked in a terrible high-mindedness. Frequently quoted was a Mrs. Bishop, a celebrated traveller, who said, "A woman may be naked, and yet behave like a lady." At the tea-table, one presumes. But it was a far, far better thing for the lady never, never to be naked. It appears that the Brownings, through all their happy married life, never saw one another naked. Did curiosity, one wonders, never assert itself? No wonder men of perfectly normal instincts resorted to brothels, where modesty was not obsessive, though beauty might be scant.

In literature the matter rarely comes up, but in the enormously popular romance *Trilby* (written, if I recall aright, in 1894 or 5) the hero is thrown into a state of nervous collapse when he discovers that the girl he adores, an artist's model in Paris, actually allows men to paint her in what was modestly called "the altogether." And his mother (Oh, those Victorian mothers!) and his sister (Oh, those Victorian mothers-in-training!) do their modest best to assuage his desolation. What, one wonders, happened on his wedding-night, when at last he had one, but not with the shop-worn Trilby? One thinks of Ruskin, who was reduced to impotence on his wedding night by the discovery that his bride—a notable beauty, be it known—had pubic hair, an adornment which had apparently never entered his consciousness in spite of his high-minded familiarity with the world's great art. He was twenty-nine at the time.

Modesty, surely, means moderation, something between the squalor of mind I recall from Eddu, and the perversity shown by Charlie, fussing lest a horrid great girl (Christofferson!) might "see" him in his bath.

But Christofferson would have none of it and insisted on drying Charlie with a large rough towel, as she knew what patchy dryers invalids can be.

"He is like a silly little boy," she said to me. Yes, and what an odd little boy I was later to learn.

[17]

AT LAST, THINGS came to a crisis with Emily Raven-Hart. She was nagged lovingly by Chips until at last she consulted Dumoulin again, to report that the pills he had been giving her were not working; they were one of the early "mood-changers" and capricious in their effect. He was finally given the proper signal by her appearance and behaviour, and insisted on an examination which showed a right breast far advanced in cancer, the nipple inverted, the flesh crêpey, and that very day she was taken to hospital and the following morning underwent a radical mastectomy and axillary node dissection. I knew very well that this might not be the complete solution of her trouble, and I arranged matters so that I happened, quite casually, to meet both Dumoulin and the surgeon later in the day, for they both lunched at my Club.

"I expect you'll get her onto radiation as soon as possible," said the surgeon, who was practising his art on a pair of lamb chops.

"Oh certainly. Not an instant's delay," said Dumoulin, who was busy with some gravy soup; "goes without saying."

"But what precisely *are* you going to say to her?" I said. I was having oysters before my chops.

"That it's the best course to pursue," said Dumoulin. "We'd be very remiss if we neglected it."

"But you won't tell her it will put her back at work, I suppose?" said I.

"That would be premature," said Dumoulin.

"Look, George," said I, "you don't have to pull your punches with me."

"Well, you are a friend of the patient, after all."

"But a physician, like yourself. It's all up, isn't it?"

"I never say that," said the surgeon, who was a large, fleshy, powerful man who looked as if he never said anything disagreeable under any circumstances. "I've seen the most extraordinary recoveries in cases where you could never have predicted them."

"But more often you've seen metastases that proliferated and made short work of things, haven't you?" said I.

"That's always a possibility, of course," said Dumoulin, "but we must wait for the X-rays. Never does to be in a hurry."

"What are you going to tell her?" said I.

"Least said, soonest mended, is what I always find. A cheerful attitude, you know. No long faces."

"A merry heart doeth good like a medicine," said I.

"Bible, isn't it? Never been put better," said the surgeon.

"But a broken spirit drieth the bones," said I, concluding the quotation.

"I think I want a cognac, to top off," said the surgeon. "It'll be my last drop for twenty-four hours. A very full schedule tomorrow. Will you fellows join me? Steward!"

They were not callous, or devious. Merely experienced in the profession which was ruled, when all the cards were down, by Fate, against which there is no armour.

[18]

IT WAS LATE in the day when Chips cornered me. "I've heard all the stuff from the doctors at the hospital," she said; "now I want you to tell me what *you* know."

"What can I add to what they've told you? They are

the men on the case. I haven't examined her, nor was I
at the operation."

"Yes, but you know *her*. They don't."

"I don't know her, Chips. She didn't want to come to
me and so, speaking as a physician, I really don't know
her."

"Jon, don't be tactful and professional with me. You'd
have spotted it, wouldn't you?"

"Well, if I'm not to be tactful or professional—yes,
I'm pretty certain I would. Quite a while ago."

"I couldn't get her to go near Dumoulin."

"It was her choice. I expect she knew."

"Of course she knew. She isn't a fool. I suppose it was
a kind of suicide bid. But Jon—she's not going to die is
she?"

"Doctors are like fortune-tellers, Chips. That's the
one question they absolutely refuse to answer."

"There's hope, isn't there? Good hope?"

"You have the hope, Chips. Has she? Has she the
wish?"

[19]

ESME REASSERTS HERSELF. Anyone
reading this Case Book might well become confused in
its time-scheme, because, while it tells a few things
about my life from its beginning, I really did not begin
to write them down until rather less than four years ago
when Miss Esme Barron of the *Colonial Advocate* came
to pump me about the history of the district of Toronto
in which I live, and in which the two principal places,
apart from domestic dwellings and a few small busi-
nesses and shops, are St. Aidan's Church (once famous
for its music) and my clinic (still famous in a quiet way
for somewhat uncommon medical practice). For me, a

lifetime: for Esme, quite a short time, made vivid by her marriage to my godson Conor Gilmartin, and his murder barely a year later, under circumstances that have never been resolved, and latest of all, by the birth of her daughter, posthumous child of Gil, to my astonishment christened in St. Aidan's with the names Marion (given by her godmother, a broadcaster friend of Esme) and Olwen (given by me as godfather, who thought Nuala's granddaughter should have a good Celtic name to sustain her through life). To my surprise and pleasure, it was Olwen that Esme chose to use when speaking of, and to, the baby—though she showed an unhappy tendency to shorten it to Ollie, in spite of my protests that this brought to mind not a stately princess, but the fat man in the Laurel and Hardy comedy team.

However, this is not a history, but a casual notebook, and as I am not writing it for other eyes—not yet, at least—enquirers will have to make of it what they can.

So, Esme reasserts herself. Recovered from widowhood, and motherhood, with surprising resilience, she is back on the job, pursuing the "story" which she believes this village-like section of Toronto contains.

She is determined to talk to Charlie, because McWearie has told her about his return, though not the circumstances surrounding it; she knows only that he is staying for a time with me, as his health is frail. Clever woman, she does not try to corner him in my clinic, but asks him to dinner, with me and McWearie as the other guests.

It was a very good affair. Olwen was in a nursery—what used to be Gil's study—and we were not called upon to admire her. Esme must be doing very well, to afford the luxury of even an eight-hour-a-day nurse, and occasional "sitters."

"What a splendid cook you are, Esme," says

McWearie, when we have come almost to the end of the meal. It was excellent, and cleverly suited to the appetite of a man like Charlie, who was still unaccustomed to civilized food.

We began with a shrimp salad, and the principal dish was a fine cheese soufflé; fruit followed. The wine was a decent Chardonnay and there was cognac with the coffee.

"Thanks, Hugh," said Esme. "Funny about cooking. Surely the most perishable of the arts. When I die, write on my tombstone, 'Here lies one whose name was written in béchamel sauce.'"

In treating alcoholics I have never denied them drink, but have imposed gentle restrictions on how much they may have. Charlie had been getting an appropriate ration at my clinic—a couple of drinks a day—so he had never suffered the agony of withdrawal. I thought that on this occasion—the first time he had met with anything more festive than a Parlour Night at the McGruders' for many years—the Chardonnay and one cognac would do no harm.

Nor did it. He talked easily and amusingly with Esme, and I remembered that it was just this charming ease with women that had always been his defence against them. How flirtatious he had been with Emily because he knew that under all the pretty speeches and easy familiarities, his priesthood and her bondage to Chips imposed a barrier which would never be seriously attacked. They had even joked about marriage, when oxen and wainropes would never have brought them to the altar. And so it was with Esme. Indeed, I envied Charlie his wonderful way with women. It was the best possible way of keeping them at a distance, and in the course of my professional life I have now and then had trouble with wistful female patients who would *not* keep matters on a professional footing.

She wanted to know about St. Aidan's in its great days and he was ready to talk. Talked of the splendid ritual so precisely and even elegantly carried out; of some of the minute details of church propriety—candles always lighted with a cigarette lighter because tradition called for flint and steel, rather than a match, for instance; of the scrupulosity about vestments; and of course about the glorious music controlled by DeCourcy Parry and to a lesser degree by Darcy Dwyer; of the crowds at Midnight Mass at Christmas, and at the Tenebrae services at Easter. There was a spirit at St. Aidan's, he said, that could not be paralleled anywhere else in the city.

All of which Esme took in quietly and surely; she was of that blessed class of journalists who do not rely on a tape-recorder, but on a first-rate memory which absorbs and edits as it listens.

"But wasn't there something about a saint?" she said.

"Where did you hear anything about a saint?" said Charlie, humorously, as if to repress a too impressionable child.

"From a Mr. Russell, who runs a little printing business near the church."

"Oh yes, Russell. A church warden at one time. Rather an opinionated fellow, as I recall. So he thought he remembered a saint, did he?"

"Remembered him very well. A Father Hobbes, who died right in the church. During a service. Russell says Father Hobbes was enormously respected—even loved—by the people."

"Quite true. A very good man."

"But the saint bit. Wasn't there a miracle or something?"

"I believe there was some foolish talk."

"A woman suddenly cured?"

"There are always hysterical people undergoing extraordinary cures. Dr. Hullah can tell you. Nothing happened in the church, or was associated with the church. And you can be sure if there had been anything miraculous, the Church would have investigated it and dealt with it rigorously—as of course it must when extraordinary things happen."

Nothing happened? Could I believe my ears? This was rewriting history indeed! Charlie certainly could not have forgotten his exhortations and assertions about the sainthood of Ninian Hobbes. He could not have wiped out all memory of that great load of marble—marble that in the end I had to pay for—which was to form the shrine of the saint. What of those gatherings at Father Hobbes' grave? What about the seven days' wonder of Prudence Vizard's miraculous cure? Of course he was covering up. Was he ashamed? Was he trying to blot out all recollection of his terrible row with Allchin, which had resulted in his banishment? What was he saying now?

"A tempest in a teapot." That was what he was saying to Esme, with a lightly dismissive laugh. As for Esme, I don't think she believed him. She had experience of people covering up inconvenient facts when talking to the press. But she was tactful. She did not turn our little dinner-party into an interview. The conversation passed on to less sensitive things.

Charlie seemed immensely refreshed by the first social occasion he had taken part in for so many years. His colour was high. He wore his new suit and Colborne Old Boys' tie with an almost dandified air. The clothes I had contrived for him were not in clerical style, and as a layman he appeared almost dashing. Christofferson's massages and baths had done him a world of good. When the time came for us to leave, he whisked into his overcoat and dashed away before me and McWearie, crying that he would find us a taxi.

But when we went into the road, he was nowhere to be seen, and after some searching I had to go home without him.

Am I of a suspicious nature? Indeed I am. It is an off-shoot of my developed intuition. As soon as I reached my quarters I looked in the drawer of my desk where there had been another cheque from Brocky—a cheque for fifteen hundred dollars which (as I had told him that Charlie resented having cheques made out to me as, so to speak, his guardian) had been made out to Charlie himself. It had been my intention to have him endorse it, and then to cash it and keep the money for use on his behalf.

So Charlie was at large with fifteen hundred dollars. I knew what would happen.

It did. After two days I called the police and asked them to keep an eye out for Charlie and bring him back to me when they found him. But ten days passed, and they brought him back, in an ambulance, dishevelled and unshaven and still in the toils of a bender of heroic proportion.

He was a relapsed alcoholic. The modest ration I had allowed him kept him stable and open to treatment but a dinner-party and agreeable female society had been too much for him and off he had gone, with plenty of money and a sharpened appetite, to gratify an over-whelming craving. The police reported that he had not been a rowdy drunk; he did not offer to treat everybody in the bars he visited; indeed he had husbanded his money carefully for his own gratification. He had not become pugnacious or tearful, and thus he had not attracted much attention. He had kept pretty well on his feet, and thus did not warn barmen that he was as drunk as he was. He had even bought a bottle of vitamin pills, eating them in the belief that they were enough to make up for the meals on which he did not want to spend his money. A crafty boozer, he had kept his celebration entirely as a personal matter, until at last he caused a commotion by seeming to die in a bar. But he was not dead, though when I had examined him with care I knew that his days would not be long.

In his ten days of freedom he had contrived to offer a massive alcoholic insult to his whole body, and he had not the resilience to overcome it. So I settled down to wait for Charlie to die.

[20]

NOTE FOR *ANAT*.: What do people die of, in fiction? As a doctor, I always long to know, but fictional illnesses are so poorly defined that I am frustrated. In Shakespeare, for instance—what really ailed Old John of Gaunt (he was only fifty-nine) who took to prophesying on his deathbed? It cannot have been a respiratory ailment, or he could never have sustained such a long dying speech. Falstaff obviously fell a victim to his boozing, and I would bet on cirrhosis of the liver; he probably had the jaundice and swollen extremities of that ailment, and he had the vastly protruding belly already. The usual decline in mental functioning would account for his ravings, his broken prayers, and his babbling, of which Mrs. Quickly tells us. But I should have liked more detail. However, Shakespeare did not write for doctors alone. He must have known something of the breed, for his darling daughter Susanna, who was said to have inherited his wit, married one, John Hall, a physician of substantial reputation, but a Puritan; was it he who put about the tale that Shakespeare died of drink? Overwork, I would suggest, at this distance.

The only character in Shakespeare I can think of before doing some research who had a specific ailment is Pandarus in *Troilus and Cressida*; he complains of "a whoreson rascally tisick," which was asthma, and that might well account for the rheum in his eyes; a man with respiratory problems. But the bone-ache about which he is so eloquent was almost certainly syphilis, which, in his line of business, he must have encountered often.

Hamlet gives us a clinical portrait of Polonius, when he talks of old men with eyes "purging thick amber and plumtree gum"; sounds like neglected conjunctivitis in a court where there were no antibiotic drops. But Shakespeare is not properly fiction.

That is where we meet the moribund ladies—David Copperfield's Dora, as an example. Fictional mothers, like Mrs. Dombey, are often disposed of in childbirth, so that their infants may be wanting in loving care. Children are frequently killed off by their authors and their deaths are pathetic, as the death of a child must surely be. But what *ailed* Little Eva St. Clair, in *Uncle Tom's Cabin*? What carried off Little Nell, who was a very young woman rather than a child, for she was sufficiently pubescent to attract the evil eye of Mr. Quilp. Nell the Nymphet. They have no clear symptoms, and seem to die of Ingrowing Virtue. Would it be possible to define in broad medical terms something that could be called Heroine's Disease, which kills with no disagreeable accompaniment other than fatigue and a dangerous increase of blood sugar? These good girls, whether wives or children, must be got rid of, but not with the accompaniments of real death, and their creators are implacable, but vague. If I had to make out a certificate of death for any one of them I suppose *myasthenia gravis* would have to do.

Of course honest Anthony Trollope killed Mrs. Proudie quickly and with comparatively brief pain by means of a heart attack, which seems to have been brought on by self-knowledge. Slowly and reluctantly Mrs. Proudie got wise to herself, and the knowledge was unendurable. Trollope as a psychologist has been shamefully neglected. Mrs. Proudie died of being herself, as in the end we all do. *Anangke*.

The wretchedness of the long death has not been much explored but Tolstoy, who is an exception to so many rules, shows us such a death in *War and Peace*. Prince Andrew Bolkonsky's thigh is shattered by an exploding shell at Borodino, and after a time he is taken to the field hospital. "One of the doctors came out of the tent in a bloodstained apron, holding a cigar between the thumb and little finger of one of his small bloodstained hands, so as not to smear it." How much that tells us! The operation is so agonizing that Prince Andrew faints, but is later brought round when water is sprinkled on his face. Astonishing detail!—"the doctor bent over, kissed him silently on the lips, and hurried away." Did the doctor's lips taste of his cigar? It is 1812, and the horrors of the field hospital are fully described by Tolstoy; the Prince had inflammation of the bowels—who is surprised?—and died at last, agonizingly, of gangrene. Chekov, a doctor and a writer, has commented on this death with wonder that in 1812 a man might die whom he himself, as the century ended, could have saved.

Tolstoy neglects no clinical details. Do I wish more authors would follow his example? On the whole, I think not. Emily Raven-Hart and Charles Iredale must die—must die of being themselves—and I, without art, must record their deaths in this my Case Book. But I shall not make a clinical report of it, in this diary-like book. Just a few facts.

[21]

CHIPS WAS DELIGHTED when Emily was permitted to leave the hospital and return to Glebe House. I took a different view of the matter; experience told me that my colleagues had done all they could for her, that the radiation treatment had not been able to overtake the metastases from the cancer, which were now spreading to her lungs and possibly to her bones. Oh, subtle, implacable cancer! She was allowed to go home in part as an act of mercy—people like Emily do not like hospitals—and partly because the overstrained hospital system needed the bed she would occupy, without any hope of recovery, for some weeks.

Chips was determined that loving care would work wonders. Emily would, of course, have to have a room to herself; bed-sharing must be postponed until she was well again. There was a room adjacent to the master-bedroom, with a connecting door; it had doubtless been a dressing-room in Victorian days. Chips took this for herself, and Emily lay alone in the big bed in the big room, but the door was open and, at the slightest call, Chips could hasten to her side. Much had been done to make the big room pretty, and when Emily was brought home, it was filled with flowers.

Emily did not now like flowers. She who had loved them and taken so much pleasure in Chips' garden found the scent of flowers nauseating. So the flowers had to be banished at once. Emily found it painful to lie in bed too long, and so she had to be helped downstairs, to walk in the long drawing-room, and on fine days in the open air. I did not visit Glebe House, because Emily did not want to see me; I suppose my gaze, which so many patients found disconcerting, troubled her. And so I kept out of the way, though at night, when Emily was in bed and trying to fall asleep, I made quiet visits to Chips, who was always anxious to know what I thought about Emily's appearance when she walked in the garden. Didn't I think she was gaining a little every day? Was she not "filling out," though she continued to eat very little. I gave what comfort I could, but to my eye Emily looked like a dying woman. She wore loose-fitting tunics, to conceal the damage of her operation, Chips said, as if Emily's little breasts were so prominent that anyone would notice that one had vanished. What could not be concealed was that her right arm was swelling with lymphadenosis, and she wore a glove to conceal the bronzing of the skin on her hand.

"Of course it's her sculptor's arm," said Chips, "and she can't use it at all—and just when I'm trying to get her to do a little work—just a little modelling in clay, to distract her. Surely they can do something?"

But "they" could do nothing. Nor could they do a great deal to ease the pain which was growing in her chest. She wheezed now, coughed, suffered shortness of breath, and even Chips could not pretend that she was not losing weight; though she had always been a small, delicately formed woman, she was now a wraith.

The disease moved rapidly, but for Emily and for Chips the time passed with leaden slowness, and every day of wretchedness made the succeeding day longer.

I really must pay tribute to Christofferson. She contrived to do all her work in my clinic, yet to visit Glebe House three or four times a day to do things for Emily that only an experienced nurse could do, or perhaps even bear to do. Emily would not hear of having a nurse on duty and she did not like Christofferson, and showed it. Emily, without I am sure meaning to do so, became a tyrant invalid, who did not notice that Chips was getting gaunt and even grey from the stress of looking after her. To her it seemed that Christofferson was merely "giving a hand" as a neighbour, and sometimes she was very rude to her. Christofferson bore it without a sign of offence; if ever a woman deserved the term "professional" it was she. When she spoke to me about Emily she was clinical in her appraisals, and not a word of pity passed her lips. But I knew her through and through and knew that her pity was of an embracing, deeply enduring quality that had no place for pettings, or endearments, or the small change of kindness. Her gaze was cold, but her hand was wonderfully light.

Emily's last days were moving toward their close when Charlie reappeared in my clinic, a mortally sick man. What was I to do? He was dying, but he might be a long time about it, and the notion that until then he was to become a fixture in my bed was repugnant to me. I suppose I could have found a bed for him in a hospital, but hospitals are busy places, distracted by the demands made on them, and finding a bed for a man who must sooner or later die, but who would postpone his last day for longer than anyone could predict, would not have been easy. Nor, though I resented his presence in my bed, did I have quite the determination to turn him out, for he was utterly miserable and his mental distress was of a character that I could not brush aside as merely a symptom of what ailed him. To put him in hospital, in quarters of clinical impersonality, would have made him miserable, and though I cursed him I could not bear to add to his wretchedness.

Oh, the tyranny of invalids! How they dominate us happy mortals who are still on our feet, able to meet in some measure the demands of life, and who feel no pain—or not very much pain. The poor wretches cannot be blamed for thinking that in an unjust world they have special privileges. They think their illnesses are visitations of a blind fate. But fate is not blind.

The problem for a Paracelsian physician like me is that I see diseases as disguises in which people present me with their wretchedness. Of course I know all that I ought to know about the clinical side of cancer, and arthritis, and osteoporosis, and muscular dystrophy and the fifty other ills that confront me, and I can order the treatment the disease calls for. But I have no faith that the treatment will heal whatever it was that gave rise to the disease. Nor am I such a fool as to think that if I could find the root of the misery, the disease would disappear. The disease is the signal, that comes late in the day, that a life has become hard to bear.

And of course there are baffling exceptions to *that* line of thinking. Paracelsus had lots of failure. He didn't know everything and, in spite of the protests to the contrary of some of my more impressionable patients, neither do I. If I am lucky, I am able to say with Ambrose Paré, "I dressed his wounds, and God cured him." Body and soul cannot be separated while life lasts.

It was Chips who solved my difficulty. "Move him across the courtyard," said she. "Put him downstairs. Might as well make a hospital of the place." Emily no longer left her room. She need not know.

That was done. Charlie was moved into the big drawing-room of Glebe House, to a single bed that seemed to lie in the embracing arm of the big piano, which nobody played any more. He did not need much nursing. Bed made freshly from time to time, such meals as he could eat produced regularly, and a little ameliorative medicine that I was able to prescribe for him—that was all the care he required. He slept for many hours, and could not endure much company.

I visited him twice a day; a morning call before I saw patients; a visit after dinner, when we chatted for a while. Even a slight measure of alcohol was out of the question; his condition was advanced alcoholic cardiomyopathy—very weak heart, in lay terms. He had spells of fluttering heartbeat, and palpitations, and these alarmed him greatly, for although he knew he was dying, he had a very human dread of doing so. But in all of this his mind was clear, and he spent his waking hours in unhappy reflection. One of our later conversations was typical.

"Made a mess of things."

"You could have done worse. Don't scold yourself."

"Been a fool."

"That's not like you, Charlie. Of all of us you seemed to be the one most sure of his way. Look at Brocky; he's done very well indeed as a scholar, but he hasn't written the great book he talked of. Look at me; the more I see of illness the less I know. But you dealt in unseen and unseeable certainties, and I suppose you do so still."

"No certainties…ghastly misunderstandings."

"Misunderstandings about what?"

"Everything important…God…His world."

"Misunderstandings about God? You wouldn't be the first."

"How do you know God from Satan?"

"I couldn't possibly tell you. Those words don't mean much to me, you know."

"You came to church."

"Yes, and I loved it. It gave a shape and a presence to so much that made life fine. But it was the beauty of the thing that reached me. A link with a noble past. Great prose; great music. An affirmation that life had a dimension compared with which all that we can seize and know is trifling. But as for God and Satan—they were part of the noble affirmation, not realities."

"Wrong....God and Satan...just shorthand for Positive and Negative...can't have one without the other...but Negative mustn't prevail...did with me."

"You were pushed too far. That was because of somebody else's Negative. Allchin's. It was a mean vengeance."

"No, no...long before that...at school."

"At school?"

"You remember those dreams?"

"No. What dreams are you talking about?"

"Erotic dreams...what the boys called wet dreams...everybody had them."

"I don't really remember much about it. I always thought you hated that sort of talk, and hated those dreams when you had them. Which you couldn't help, you know."

"I had them...but not about women....About Christ."

"What!"

"Oh, not what you're thinking...but he came to me in dreams, and was so kind....A smiling, young Christ. .No beard, even....A beautiful youth."

"Extraordinary! And were those dreams sexual?"

"Not as you might suppose....It was that poem..."

"A poem?"

"You remember Mr. Sharpe?...English master?... Read poetry in class that wasn't in the prescribed book...John Donne was his favourite....That poem... 'Batter my heart, three person'd God.'"

"Yes. Yes."

"How it ends....'Take me to you, imprison me, for I...Except you enthrall me, never shall be free...Nor ever chaste, Except thou ravish me.'"

The poem cost Charlie a great effort to speak. He

gasped for two or three minutes, and I did not urge him on. Then—

"You mean, Christ ravished you?"

"Physically...spiritually....Those dreams were terrifying—glorious...that smiling youth...the gush of my seed."

"Well, of course these things take many unaccountable forms. You were exceptional. I suppose you outgrew it?"

"No...not for years. He used to speak to me....Give commands....Ask for things."

Here there was a longish silence, for Charlie was wearing himself out. But he wanted to talk and I was eager to hear him. Christ spoke to him! Of course we know of these things, but they are the mark of the psychopath, and there was nothing in Charlie to put him in that category. Christ spoke to him! Charlie was no poet; this was not figurative language. If he said Christ spoke to him—and then something came to me, from some idle reading I had done in one of the technical journals—something about consciousness and the "bicameral mind." A sort of mind, it appeared, once common, but since superseded by a more developed consciousness. A sort of mind familiar in the ancient world, familiar in the poetry of Homer, where great heroes acted upon promptings that had for them the authority of the voices of the gods. A sort of mind not wholly vanished, but usually controlled or rebuked by the kind of intelligence it met with in other people, teachers in particular. But Charlie had never felt the need to conform to what other people thought or how they thought it.

He spoke again, faintly. "I wanted to do such great things...vain ambition....Wanted to bring about a revival of deep faith...gut faith...faith that saves a city."

"A city?"

"The great rebirths always began in a city...then spread....It seemed extraordinary....Toronto...what an unlikely place...but what pride, what impertinence to think that...as if God couldn't declare Himself in Toronto as well as anywhere else....Save my city, He said, time and again."

"Save Toronto?"

"Don't laugh....It seems absurd, doesn't it?"

"I didn't mean that. But this city has always been called Toronto the Good, the City of Churches."

"Calls itself that....Methodist humbug....But I was to make the light shine, even here."

"How? To make the light shine? How Charlie?"

"Give me a saint, He said....Give me one saint, and I shall do it."

"A tall order."

"No...there he was."

"Who was?"

"Hobbes, of course....Old Hobbes....A saint, sure enough, but people only thought him a good old man."

"Yes, of course I remember him. A very good old man. And he was to have been the saint?"

"Yes...it called for a saint's death...and that's how he died."

"On Good Friday, at Mass? I was there. I wanted to help him, but you wouldn't allow it. I always wondered about that. What did you think you were doing, Charlie?"

"Making sure....I wanted no prying...Christ had asked for a saint and I didn't want you poking your nose...into things."

"Charlie, what are you talking about? Did you arrange that, somehow?"

"Of course I did, you fool....I killed him."

What shall I say? That it was as if a light had suddenly been turned on? No, it was rather as if an annoyance, long troubling my mind, had been removed. As if a picture that had hung crooked on the wall for—how long was it?—for eight years or thereabout, had at last been put straight. But all I said was: "How?"

"The wafer....The old man always ate the whole wafer himself....If he'd given any of it to the rest of us at the altar it would have been a mass murder....But I knew he wouldn't....Never did."

"You did something to the wafer?"

"Jon...you're being stupid....I poisoned it."

"Don't be absurd! He died instantly—well within ten seconds."

"Yes....That's the kind of poison it was."

"What kind?"

"Jon...feel dreadful...can't really talk any more....Could I have a drink?"

"No, Charlie, you damn well *can't* have a drink. It could kill you. Here's a nitroglycerine tablet. Put it under your tongue. Now tell me—what was the poison?"

"It's called *ricinus communis*...comes from castor oil...a dryer...no taste, no smell, and damn near instantaneous."

Could I be unjust in thinking that Charlie was looking the least bit pleased with himself? Life is not wholly a dull fabric of commonplaces and likelihoods. He *was* pleased with himself.

"Where did you get it?"

"Russell."

"The printer? Church warden? How did he get it?"

"He makes his own inks....Point of pride....He gets it from a company in St. Louis, Missouri....The KGB used it a lot."

"And Russell gave it to you?"

"Stole it....He printed the service orders for the church....When he was out of the room I pinched a small quantity. A few drops on the wafer...no smell, no taste...and that's it."

"And Christ told you to do this?"

"I had to find the means."

"But Hobbes would have died in a year or two anyhow!"

"Not in a way that was a Sign....A saint mustn't just peg out in bed...like me."

Another pause, and during this Charlie began to look very ill indeed. At last he was weeping.

"It wasn't Christ."

"You mean it was an hallucination?"

"Oh no....It was the Negative....I've been tricked."

What followed was so confused and painful that I won't attempt to suggest Charlie's broken utterance. It was perhaps half an hour before he had fully gasped out his confession. Not Christ, though Christ may have visited him in those dreams of his boyhood, but the Negative, the Tempter, with deceptions and promises. To kill old Hobbes was surely a very minor thing in order to gain a great benefit. That was the argument. Hobbes would not live long anyway, and if he had been questioned, would he not have leapt at the chance to die at the foot of the altar, on a great day in the Christian Year, and in order that a sign might be given to a great North American city, with the salvation of not merely that city but possibly a whole continent as a consequence? Thus the voice of the Tempter.

As for Charlie himself, was not talk of murder an absurdity? Great affairs demand great actions and often there is somebody who must take a great risk. Remember Judas? The Betrayer, and the Execrated One, but could anybody seriously doubt that at this moment Judas has his place in Paradise, because he made possible the great drama upon which the world's salvation hangs? Every tragic action needs a Judas: no Hero without a Villain. Is it not the blackest ingratitude and the stupidest philosophical error to condemn that necessary figure? Charlie was not called upon to play Judas. Merely to arrange a death to the greatest advantage in the mighty work of saving mankind. We minor actors must "play as cast" and be glad of the work.

On and on Charlie raved, gasping out his words with increasing difficulty. And the final horror of the whole thing was that he was now convinced that it was not his Master, but the Adversary who had led him on this path, disappointed his great hopes, worn out his spirit in a barren place, and at last had brought him now to the threshold of what must undoubtedly be eternal damnation. Not a stupid Hell. Not an eternal burning, but a place of No Hope, in which the Mercy of God might be understood, but not enjoyed, a place of ultimate desolation.

When at last I had heard him out, I gave him a shot of morphine and went back to my own quarters, thinking what a fool I had been, so many years ago.

Of course when I was asked to sign that certificate of Father Hobbes' death, I should have asked to examine his false teeth—just in case. Would I have found the poison? Perhaps; perhaps not. If I had found it and informed the police, what then? Russell the printer would have been in trouble, I suppose, as the only person with access to that deadly stuff. And rather than see Russell implicated, Charlie would perhaps have confessed. Would anyone have been better off? What would his explanation, as I had heard it on his deathbed, have meant in a law court? He would probably have received the ultimate insult—committal to an asylum for the insane. A man whose hypnagogic visions had taken a tragic turn. No; meddling would have done little good.

[22]

IF LIFE HAPPENED along the lines of popular fiction, Charlie should have died after his confession to me, but life has a different sense of dramatic form. He lived on for another five weeks, almost to a day. He outlived Emily Raven-Hart. Each unconscious of the other they had been dying in Glebe House, each nursed by Chips and Christofferson, each surrounded by the mystery and pathos of those whom Fate allows to die in their beds. Emily was first to go; she could be seen relaxing her hold on life, and speaking, when she spoke at all, in terms of bitter stoicism. But she spoke hardly at all, and spent most of her time wearing her oxygen mask. It was obvious that she suffered a great deal of pain, as the disease spread to her bones, and her lungs; she relapsed into silence and indifference several days before at last she died. It was the coma of death but neither Dumoulin nor I stressed that because Chips, who knew precisely what was happening, nevertheless did not want to speak of it. As so often, I thought that the real heroism of death was seen in the one who stood by.

The funeral was a very quiet affair. I know a lot of old friends from the days of the salon would have come, but Chips wanted it to be as private as such things can be. There was a surprising amount of flowers, including a huge thing from the Dairy Association, which did not forget its own, and a more modest wreath from the Canadian Club. And several from banks, universities, and other bodies to whose great men Emily had given a bronze immortality. The *Advocate* published a brief obituary, headed "Butter Sculptress Dies At 57," in which the facts were in the main, correct, but the emphasis far astray. The mourners were Chips, Christofferson, McWearie, and myself, and the burial service was read by one of the curates at St. Aidan's; the Canon had meant to do it but at the last moment he had been called away to an utterly unavoidable diocesan meeting. It was as cheerless an affair as I have ever attended, and professionally I have attended many.

Hugh and I retired to my quarters for a heartening drink.

"Who's taking care of Charlie?" he asked.

"Charlie doesn't need much taking care of now. He's very low but quiet, and Christofferson will be with him soon, trying to get him to drink a little soup."

"All up, I suppose?"

"Ever since Esme's dinner-party."

"She's still on the hunt for colour stuff about St. Aidan's."

"I know. You encourage her."

"It's my profession. That series on *The Toronto That Was* needs something solid about Toronto churches, and St. Aidan's is the one I want stressed, rather than one of the evangelistic sort."

"Why don't you encourage her to do something about the salon, and The Ladies?"

"Not solid stuff. The Church is solid. She's still sure there's something in what she calls 'the saint bit' and she won't let go till she finds it."

"The less said about the saint bit now, the better."

"How do you mean?"

"Oh—nothing."

"Oh yes—something. What are you hiding, Jon?"

"Nothing that I intend to share with you, you nosy newspaperman. You blat everything you know."

"That's not true, and you know it. Charlie's told you something."

"What makes you think that?"

"Your excellent whisky. It promotes intuition. You and Charlie must have had some good talks, during the past few weeks."

"Talks, but I wouldn't call them good. But you can't sit by a man's bed and say nothing. Of course we've talked about the great days of St. Aidan's, before it fell into the Canon's ultra-modern hands and became a social centre full of live wires."

"Ah, the ritual!"

"I thought you looked on it as play-acting?"

"Nothing wrong with a bit of play-acting. The St. Aidan's ritual was in classic style; real Masterpiece Theatre. The 'sincere' stuff the Canon goes in for is Method Acting—look in your guts and fish out what you find there—and you can guess what most of it is. Ritual is a very fine guano to spread over the aridities of doctrine."

"Ritual as Charlie and DeCourcy Parry and Darcy Dwyer knew it belongs to the past, I fear."

"Balls! All eras of history are an equal distance from eternity."

"Who said that?"

"What makes you think I didn't say it just now, out of my own head?"

"Did you?"

"I've said it so often I am pretty sure it's my own. I think I was nearer to what St. Aidan's was about than you ever were, Jon. Don't forget, I was once a parson. A Presbyterian, but that's a man of faith, let me tell you. You treated Christianity at St. Aidan's the way the pagans treated mythology—as a kind of fancy wallpaper for the mind."

"It may be so. But I am not without my depths, so don't patronize me."

"Been talking to Charlie about your depths?"

"His depths."

"Jon, I can see that you are bursting to tell me something, but your Hippocratic Oath stands in the way."

"It would never do. It's a secret."

"I'll make a deal with you. I know a secret, too. A secret very near to yourself. Tell me yours and I'll tell you mine."

"It sounds like children playing in a barn: 'You show me yours and I'll show you mine.'"

"And the children emerge better informed in consequence. Come along. Out with it."

"I'm to go first? Oh, very likely! Exchanged secrets should be of equal value. How hefty is yours?"

"You want to know who murdered your godson, I suppose?"

"That was very fishy."

"Indeed it was."

"All that stuff about somebody sneaking in by way of the balcony."

"Totally improbable."

"It had to be somebody who had come into the flat through the door."

"As you say."

"So, Hugh?"

"What do you think?"

"Somebody there with Esme?"

"A possibility."

"You know, I wondered about that fellow who made such a hullabaloo at the funeral. That fellow with the fancy walking-stick."

"What did you wonder?"

"You know about the old notion that if a murderer

comes near the corpse of his victim, the body bleeds?"

"I've heard of it. But the body was very thoroughly encased, so if it bled, no one would know."

"Don't be so literal. It is simply folk-psychology for saying that murder will out."

"Well—did it?"

"I have my strong suspicions of that fellow with the walking-stick."

"Ah, Jon, you're very intuitive."

"Am I right?"

"If you knew, what would you do?"

"Do? I'd do nothing."

"Swear?"

"What would be the point? What would it mean to Esme?"

"Yes indeed. Well, there you are. A very intuitive man."

"You haven't said I'm right."

"Nor will I. I haven't leaked. But you've guessed."

"I see. Now it's your turn to guess."

"About Ninian Hobbes? Oh, I guessed long ago."

"And what, or who, did you guess?"

"My father was a policeman, you know. A very good one. Ended up as a Detective Chief Inspector. He always said that in cases of murder the first thing to do is to take a good look at the family."

"Poor old Hobbes had no family."

"Family in the sense of nearest and dearest. A son, for instance. Right-hand man. Obvious successor."

"You've got it wrong. Who would have murdered Father Hobbes to be incumbent of St. Aidan's?"

"That's what I can't figure out. Why did Charlie do it? And how did he do it? Because I'll bet any money—and I'm speaking as a Scot, mind—Charlie did it."

After that, what was there but to tell why, and how?

So there we sat, neither one having positively blabbed his secret, but with the secrets now as plainly revealed as they would ever be.

"Those hypnagogic visions," said Hugh; "they must be terribly convincing."

"Not your usual erotic dream," said I. "But those things are stupidly underestimated."

[23]

After Charlie's funeral Hugh was unable to join me for a drink to dispel the atmosphere of mourning, so I sat alone. Chips, I knew, had returned to her packing; as soon as Emily was buried she was determined to return to England.

"Nothing to keep me here, now," she said.

"Nothing to take her there, now, either," said McWearie, when he heard. "If she expects to find a pre-1939 England she is in for a dire disappointment. I've seen these people who expect to find the Land of Lost Content when they go back to England, and it never is. But she's right; there's nothing for her here, either."

I knew that better, I think, than anyone else. Ten days earlier, on the night Emily died, I had been visiting Charlie downstairs and when I was leaving an impulse made me climb the stairs and tap on the door of Emily's room. She was now so frequently unconscious that she had ceased to object to my presence, and I knew that sometimes I could lift Chips' spirits, even if only for a few minutes.

"Come," said Chips' voice.

There was only one light in the room, shining—not brightly—on the bed, where Emily lay, and the moment I saw her I knew that it was all over. The look of pain was gone, and as sometimes happens in death, it had been supplanted by a calm which looked like youth—the best of youth.

Chips sat with her drawing-board on her knees, composed as an artist is when confidently at work; she was drawing with one of her special pens—a flexible quill—and Indian ink, over a sketch that had been done so finely in pencil that it was almost imperceptible, but plain to the hand that had made it. I said nothing but sat down a little behind her so as not to disturb her concentration, and in the half-hour that followed a drawing of the dead woman's head took form on the paper, and its beauty, simplicity, and masterly command were like nothing I had ever seen from Chips' hand before.

I had known her only as an etcher, and I am not fond of etchings, and particularly not little four-by-six things showing old Toronto houses of no special interest except, presumably, to an etcher. It was not until later, when I found the letters to Barbara Hepworth, that I knew what an accomplished artist Chips was.

This was drawing in the classic mode, in which contour was indicated by line, without resort to cross-hatching or "shading." It would be romantic nonsense to say that its quality arose from love, but it may be said that love of a very special kind spoke through the artist.

"I think that will do," said Chips, coolly.

I said nothing, because in the circumstances there was nothing to be said. My praise was not needed and could only have been a clumsy intrusion on a very private estimate of a piece of work by the maker.

Chips turned to me. "I've been thinking a lot lately about all this," said she, "and I'm pretty well convinced it was all a huge mistake."

"What was?"

"The whole thing. Getting into such a fury with Gussie Gryll and having a showdown with Emily and insisting it was a choice between an elopement with me or fifty years of serving tea to the county by day and putting up with Gussie's pawing and mauling by night, and three or four kids who had to be expensively educated for just the same sort of stupid life-in-death. And forcing the choice on her because I was always the stronger one, you know—real strong prefect-guiding-the-confused-kiddie-who-has-got-herself-into-a-mess. I'm not sure our sort of life was what suited her best. Maybe she wanted a man, after all. Maybe even Gussie, ass though he was. The poor sweet wasn't really an artist, you know. Just a nice little talent. And I was so sure I could flatter and encourage and puff her up with gas until maybe the real thing would happen.

"And it was all because of love. I truly loved her, Jon. Love can be a bugger, can't it?"

[24]

IT WAS NOT LONG before I had personal assurance of the truth of Chips' harsh dictum. Spring was coming, and one morning I awoke with horror and astonishment to find that I was in love with Esme.

After the masque, the anti-masque: after the tragedy, the farce. Emily Raven-Hart and Charles Iredale had played out personal dramas that were in terms of the time, and their situation, and their limitations, tragedies. Now was the time for the harlequinade, where old, doting Pantaloon is fooled and tricked and exposed in all his senile ineptitude, to the guffaws of the mob.

I had been seeing Esme frequently because she was now completing her story about the St. Aidan's district for *The Toronto That Was* series of articles in the *Advocate*. She came to me for matters of fact and accuracy of detail, but she had ceased to pester me for information about "the saint bit" and the death of Father Hobbes.

The reason? She now had all that from a thoroughly informed source—from one who indeed had experienced the saintly charisma of Father Hobbes, one who had been present at his death before the altar, and been miraculously cured of her disabling arthritis at his grave! Yes, it was Prudence Vizard who thus reappeared. Vizard had died—died to get away from his wife, I have no doubt—and she had remarried one Serge Shepilov, a choreographer and even a dancer when a ballet dancer of fifty-five was wanted, perhaps for a television commercial. As Madame Shepilov, Prudence had developed—doubtless sympathetically—a somewhat Russian accent and was, as Esme put it, "into counselling" giving advice to married couples or couples who perhaps ought to have been married, and in some mysterious fashion Prudence Shepilov was on one of the many payrolls of the City of Toronto.

Her story was finely composed. One day, returning from a consultation with her doctor—a doctor who had shown himself utterly incompetent in his handling of her case (myself, as Prudence remembered me), she had chanced to be passing the simple grave of Father Ninian Hobbes. She was, as her custom was, praying, and her prayer was that old Orthodox one: "Father, not according to my deserts but according to Thy great mercy," and suddenly a light appeared above the grave—not a bright light, nor anything like an electric light, but a mystic light, a radiance—and the pain of her arthritis had disappeared in an instant. A blessed miracle! She had tried— God alone knows how she tried—to awaken the people in the district to the wonder that was in their midst, but in this she was thwarted by Archdeacon Edward Allchin, now Bishop of the Barren Lands, north-west of Hudson

Bay and east of the Mackenzie basin. (Allchin had thwarted or double-crossed too many senior clergy and had been kicked upstairs—kicked right into the attic, in fact—as Bishop of the Barrens.) Nevertheless, a saint had been manifested to the people of Toronto, even though that blessed people had received him with thoroughly Canadian indifference. What chance has a Saint Francis, if his Assisi is a multicultured, financial, unyieldingly secular northern city, whose lepers and other detrimentals are charges on the public purse?

Esme had accepted this story and burnished it to a high gloss. I saw no reason to trouble her with a tale of religious obsession, hypnagogic visions, deceiving Christ-figures who were in fact instruments of the Adversary, murder undertaken for the highest motives, and a deal with the Almighty that had gone tragically wrong; such a narrative would have lacked the simplicity which is vital to popular journalism. But as she talked with me in my consulting-room the warmth and charm of her personality, her youthful freshness—still glowing at the age of twenty-eight—and a softness which had not been hers when first I knew her and which I attributed to motherhood, enchanted me.

I use the word carefully. This was an enchantment. I, a physician at last admitting old age and supposing himself pretty well aware of the vagaries of the human spirit and armoured against the follies of simpler folk, had fallen in love like a boy of seventeen, and I was incapable of seeing Esme except through the deceiving-glass of that passion.

Did I blush and stammer ill-phrased compliments? Did I betray my feelings? Of course not. Outwardly, it seemed to me, I behaved to Esme as I had always done, with courteous reserve tempered by the warmth of feeling proper to a—no, not a relative, though she was the widow of my godson—but to what my mother used to call "a connection," meaning somebody who was not quite "family" but not wholly of the outer world. It seemed to me that I betrayed nothing of what I felt, but my love possessed me and interfered seriously with my work. Did Christofferson notice? Of course she knew that I was seeing Esme oftener than ever before and did not moan and protest when I saw her name on my daily list of appointments.

I felt that Christofferson disapproved of Esme. Rather sooner than one might have expected, Esme had begun to contribute a series of articles to the *Advocate* on *Coping With Widowhood* that had caused a good deal of comment and were soon to appear in a small book. Christofferson, who sifted the *Advocate* carefully every day of her life, had read these cosily phrased, grief-bravely-repressed, common-sense-triumphing-over-adversity pieces, and sometimes I observed that she was puffing from her nostrils little sounds that would have been snorts in a lesser woman. Christofferson had known adversity, and had not capitalized on it. But then, I told myself, Christofferson was not a journalist, and knew nothing of a journalist's obligation toward the greater world. But Christofferson was as icily courteous toward Esme as she was toward everybody, whenever Esme appeared for an appointment.

What did Christofferson make of the laughter which she must have heard through the door of my consulting-room? For one of Esme's principal charms was that she could make me laugh, at a time when laughter was a scarce commodity in my experience. Make me laugh not with jokes, not with journalistic wisecracks, but by oddities of phrase, drolleries of perception, wit that underlay her conversation but did not frolic on the surface of it. It seemed to me, goof that I was, that the spirit of Jane Austen lived again in Esme. It did not occur to me that Jane would never have fallen for Prudence Shepilov.

In brief, I was a fool, and an old fool. But not totally a fool. I had resort to my *Anatomy*, hoping it would have some advice for me, as I hoped that in future it would have advice for others.

[25]

NOTE FOR *ANAT.*: Fiction is rich in instances of older men falling in love with much younger women, and this is obviously because it is something literary men are prone to do. More prone than other men? Impossible to say, because other men leave no record of their experience.

Even tough old Henrik Ibsen, when he was only a little younger than I, fell like a ton of bricks for Emilie Bardach, his "summer princess," and later he was enchanted (as am I, at present) by Helene Raff, and what did he say: "You are youth, child, youth personified— and I need that for my work." And after that, Hildur Andersen—Oh, the flame did not die in Henrik, though so far as we know he was never physically unfaithful to his Susannah. (But then the thought of Ibsen rolling in the rank sweat of an enseamed bed is grotesque and pitiable, and neither description ever fitted him.)

Even Anthony Trollope, subtle Victorian psychologist, knew an autumn love, and he was psychologically astute enough to know it for what it was and to weigh it to a scruple of its worth, when he met his Kate Field.

Certainly Charles Dickens, and that duplicitous little miss Ellen Ternan, must join the club, even as it occurs to me without having done any real research on the subject. Because of his Ellen, Dickens managed to make an astonishing number of people other than himself miserable, and unlike Ibsen or Trollope he wanted a physical fulfilment of his daft passion. Whether he got it or not remains a mystery; photographs of Miss Ternan do not suggest a passionate or even a normally warm nature, but we do know that after Dickens' death she married a clergyman and occasionally gave readings from Dickens' works, but only under the most respectable circumstances and never—*never* for money. Of course he had left her a nice lump in his will, though not a fortune. No such autumnal passion appears in Dickens' novels, unless we accept the marriage of Sir Leicester and Lady Dedlock as an example.

Trollope yields more than one. His elderly lovers are given to renunciation, that Victorian enthusiasm which psychoanalysis has for the present made mockable. But it will come back. It is too good and true a feeling to be driven from the human heart by the Viennese Deconstructionists.

[26]

WHEN I READ the above to McWearie, he was not impressed. I had long ago spoken to him about the *Anatomy* because he was the only person I knew who would understand it and possibly make helpful suggestions about it.

McWearie appears in this Case Book perhaps too often as a negative figure in my life, and as a man with no existence apart from his appearances in my armchair, sponging up my whisky. Of course he was an active journalist, or as active as his task of commenting and reporting on religious topics made possible. Religion is not the liveliest of the journalistic "beats." His charm for me was as a figure against whom I could bounce ideas, knowing that they would never return to my hand precisely as they had left it. His value to the *Advocate*, I think, was that of a man with an extensive education who could, at need, compose what was professionally called "a think-piece." He was worth his salary, and it is a poor newspaper that cannot accommodate at least one eccentric on its staff.

"Your literary stuff is too selective," said he. "You brush aside the failures. Like poor Yeats, now. Arguably the greatest poet of this century, but dominated and made wretched by his longing to have carnal knowledge of the most likely of his female admirers."

"Yeats. Yes, a very interesting death by myocarditis," said I.

"Shut up, and listen to what I'm telling you. Yeats longed to be a great lover, as became a great poet, and I believe he underwent the Voronoff operation quite late in his life to forward that end—if you'll excuse the inadvertent indecency of the expression. But it was ineffective, as I believe indeed it often was, and poor Yeats was humiliated and the ladies went empty away. What a sad preoccupation for a great man! Now, what puts you on this track? You're not in love yourself, are you, Jon?"

"And if I were?" said I, attempting hauteur.

"Then I'd say, lay a cool compress of good sense on your fevered brow. No good can come of it. It's Esme Gilmartin, née Barron, I suppose?"

"What would lead you to suppose that?"

"Oh, my wee man! Love and a cough cannot be hid, as the old folks used to say. You've been seeing a lot of her about this Old Toronto business, and you've taken to wearing much smarter ties than was your habit. You now have flowers other than that horrible potted plant Christofferson maintains contrary to all aesthetic decency in your window. You know my methods,

Watson. You're in love."

"And if I am?"

"As your friend, I suppose it's my duty to get you out of it with a whole skin. You've surely seen this sort of thing in your professional work?"

Indeed I had. I remembered that visit from no less a person than the Governor-General, who asked my advice about the possibility of sexual intercourse in his state of health. Of course his love was a woman near his own age. Nevertheless, what had I said? "Give it a go"— wasn't that the message? But—what was this? I was deeply offended by the idea that I wished to have sexual intercourse with Esme. Why?

"You're being coarse, Hugh. The instances I have mentioned to you from my notes for the *Anatomy* were all, except possibly Dickens, no more than warm, intimate relationships. Men of powerful sensibility warming themselves at the sun of youth. To you love means nothing but sex. That's unworthy of you. You snub and ignore the spirit."

"What's this? I've not said a word about sex. It must be very much in your mind or you wouldn't have jumped to such a conclusion."

"Sorry. I was thinking of something else."

"You were not. But you've betrayed yourself. A Freudian slip. And don't deceive yourself about those literary characters. They were cautious, and rightly so. But don't pretend there was no sexual element in those deep flirtations, even if they didn't get beyond an occasional chaste kiss."

"I don't see the point in discussing it. It's a private matter and I don't want to talk about it. Not in the way you talk about things, which is a very rough, pragmatic, Scotch way, let me tell you."

"Insulting the Scotch won't change the subject. That's

the *argumentum ad hominem* which you ought to despise. I'm serious, and I'm a friend."

"All right. I apologize. But leave me some rags of privacy."

"Can't be done if we're to talk seriously. To get down to cases, what precisely do you want from Esme?"

"Want from her? I want to give something to her. Affection, protection, security, all that I have."

"No, that won't do. Do you remember what Stendhal says? 'When you're in love with a woman you must ask yourself what you want to do with her.' What do you want to *do* with Esme?"

What a question! And what had I wanted to do with Nuala Conor, even when our affair was at its height and she had not yet married Brocky? To be honest, I wanted to lie with her, talk and eat with her, but I could not honestly say that I had given much thought to taking her as a wife. Not, that is, until I found I couldn't have her. Of course I was young then, and now that I am old I can hardly expect a desirable woman to be my mistress simply for the pleasure of the thing, such as it might be, with one of my age and archaeological figure. To be honest and fair to myself, I had wanted the delight of Nuala's society in every possible way, including the sexual way, and that was what I suppose I wanted with Esme. But marriage? Had I ever really thought what it meant? In both cases I was enchanted by a woman of rare quality upon whom, I suppose, I had projected unreal magic. But what had seemed perfectly reasonable in youth was by no means so uncomplicated in age.

"You are not answering. That's good. That's the *argumentum e silentio*. It means you are thinking. I know I am plaguing you, Jon, and doubtless I am being impudent and coarse. But hasn't my line of questioning been very much like what you yourself have put to scores of patients, to their eventual benefit? It's never pleasant to take your own medicine, Doctor, but there it is, you see. Don't delude yourself about sex; every real love includes it, refined and chivalrous though it may be."

"What do you know about it, you finnan haddie? You've never really loved: I can tell. Gratified love is not the trivial detumescence of a petty desire, but the consummation of a longing in which the whole soul, as well as the body, has its part."

"Remember what that Frenchman said? The mucous membranes, by an ineffable mystery, enclose in their obscure folds all the riches of the infinite."

"Yes, but you're not giving fair play to the infinite. I know your intentions are all that is kind, Hugh, but you simply don't understand."

"No, and never will. Every love affair is a private madness into which nobody else can hope to penetrate. But I see a few things you don't. Your literary instances. Very carefully selected, even though I suppose the selection was unconscious. But what about old Chaucer? A fine psychologist if ever there was one, and as coarse-fibred as I am myself, and all the better for it. Don't you remember the nuptials of January and May—"

"Oh, my God, Hugh, you go too far!"

"No, no; I was about to say, before you flew off the handle, that January and May has little to do with you and Esme. But it's a general warning. No, the literary, indeed the mythical, instance that suits your case comes from an indisputably refined source, quite delicate enough in verbiage, if not in message, to please even you in your present sore state. You've read Tennyson? *The Idylls of the King*? Fine stuff, even if out of fashion. You recall Merlin and Vivien? The lovely creature who enchanted the old enchanter himself, and then locked him up in an oak tree? And for why? Because they were both themselves, and acted according to their nature and she was no less a great lady because she had tricked a very wise man, and he no less a magician because his wisdom had for a while deserted him. *Anangke* drove them both. Take heed, old magician! Take heed, Cunning Man!"

I suppose we sat for half an hour in silence. I was angry with Hugh, who had turned such a harsh light on my feelings. I was angry with myself, for seeing the good sense of what he had, with cruel Scotch directness, said about something I wanted to be secret and wholly my own. Perhaps I was most angry by his suggestion that I was driven by *Anangke*. What force had I to oppose the power against which even the gods dared not combat? I felt driven to explain, which is always a mistake.

"You're quite wrong, you know. I'm not an old lecher looking for sex—not as a principal object, certainly. I admire Esme because of her courage and her talent and something very special about her spirit, which I don't suppose you see. I want to smooth the way for her, because it could be very hard—woman alone, a child to raise, doubtless the attentions of men who wouldn't be able to appreciate her for what she is—all of that. I want to offer her protection and I want to do what I can about Olwen. Forgive me if I seem to be making pretensions to nobility; it's just that I'd like to do one really decent thing before I die, and in doing so find a warmth that my life up to now has lacked."

"Yes. Well, it's foolish to talk, and I know I talk too much. That longing for warmth and tenderness—all we old fellows miss that, unless we've grown a hard shell over our feelings. Go ahead, Jon. Do what you must. Indeed, you can't do anything else. *Anangke*, look at it how you will."

Another silence, not so long. Then Hugh said: "Do

you know when Chips is going back to England?"

"Yes. Soon."

"After nearly thirty years here…I wonder what she'll find to do."

"She doesn't have to do anything. She's quite well off, you know. Inheritances."

"Yes, but she'll need an occupation. Emily was the light of her life, as I don't need to tell you. A strange love."

"I don't agree. Strange sex, if you like. But not a strange love. A beautiful love, expressed in whirlwind activity, and a schoolgirl vocabulary, and a greatness of spirit that found its expression in jelly tartlets and exquisite little sandwiches and an unfailing charity of mind. I don't think Emily was quite up to the demands of being everything to Chips. Love lays heavy burdens on the loved one, sometimes."

"We're getting philosophical. Time I went. I'm only up to philosophy at weekends."

[27]

"I'M NOT THINKING only of myself. It will be wonderful for Olwen."

"Indeed I hope so."

"A girl needs a father—a kind of pattern, you know, against which she measures other men."

"So I understand."

"And for me, it means the end of having to struggle about a career, and be a mother at the same time; I can get on with my real writing, and look for the best in me."

"I am sure you will."

"Because I really think I'm a cut above daily journalism. I think I've got something real to say, if I can just have time to settle down to it. And that's what this makes possible."

"I sincerely hope it will."

"Suddenly, so many things are possible. Travel, for instance. Like that song in *Candide*: 'We'll live in Paris, when we're not in Rome.' Doesn't it wow you, Uncle Jon!"

"A marvellous prospect, certainly."

"And of course, I've always wanted to be close to power. And Henry is power with a capital P. Newspapers and a TV empire. Right up there with Thomson and Murdoch and Black."

"Oh, quite. I've never met him, of course. A very nice fellow, I presume?"

"Better than that. A real darling. And so *funny*!"

"A funny tycoon. Quite a novelty. What's he think about Olwen?"

"Adores her. Says he can't wait to give her her first car. Meanwhile he's settled for the biggest Teddy Bear you ever saw. Came by courier from F. A. O. Schwartz in New York. You must meet him. He's fun."

"I can't wait."

"He knows all about you."

"Indeed?"

"I couldn't get intimate with him without telling him about my dearest friend, could I?"

"Thank you, Esme. That's a great compliment."

"He wants me to do lots about you in my series about the Glebe. The Cunning Man. And what an old heart-breaker you are."

"Oh, please, Esme."

"Oh, yes. You must know. If you'd been—let's say—twenty-five years younger, I think I'd have made a play for you, Uncle Jon."

"Too bad about the twenty-five years."

"I'd have had my work cut out. I know that. You wouldn't fall for just any girl."

"You've always been a very special girl, Esme."

"Thanks. Because of Gil. Do you know—"

"Do I know what?"

"Probably it seems wacky, but sometimes I wonder what has really happened to Gil. His death was an awful accident, you know. Totally unpredictable."

"*Anangke*. Fate. Has its plan for us all."

"You think so? I never know what to think. Of course I'm not religious. Not in a church way, I mean. But every now and then I think there must be Something—"

"Well, I think you're on the right track. Perhaps after your marriage you'll be able to follow it up."

"Not right away. Henry says all that's a lot of crap. He says he believes in one thing, and that's himself. Wonderful, isn't it?"

"Enviable certainly."

"But for a woman it's different. Or I think so, anyway. For a woman. And for a really wise man like you."

"Oh Esme, I don't set up to be a wise man."

"That's a part of being wise. But other people think you are. The Cunning Man. You know they call you that?"

"Nonsense, of course."

"Not a bit. But nobody ever tells me exactly what they mean by it. There's a special meaning, isn't there?"

"It was a joke that originated with Miss Todhunter."

"Oh, The Ladies. She was the big one, wasn't she? A kind of jokey Valkyrie?"

"Yes. And Miss Raven-Hart—"

"Yes. She was the tie."

"The tie?"

"They were a collar-and-tie weren't they? That's what everybody says. But go on about the Cunning Man."

"It was a sort of person that used to be found in a lot of English villages. There was a Wise Woman or else a Cunning Man. Never both in the same place. He could set bones, after a fashion, and knew a bit of horse-doctoring, and if somebody had overlooked your cattle he could take off the spell, and maybe track down the overlooker, and then there would be a contest of wizards. A Cunning Man was a sort of village know-all."

"Not much of a name for what you are, Uncle Jon. But to get back to what we were talking about: do you think Gil *is* anywhere? Or is death simply extinction?"

"I think extinction is coming it a bit too strong. It's said energy is never lost, and there is a lot of energy in a human being, even an inferior one, and Gil certainly wasn't inferior."

"So where is that energy now?"

"If I knew that I would indeed be a Cunning Man. But of course you realize that what we're saying is wildly unscientific?"

"About the energy being somewhere, you mean?"

"About any suggestion that there is a plan, or an order, or a scheme of any kind in the Universe; no purposefulness in the evolutionary sequence whatever—not a particle. The scientific orthodoxy is that it all takes place by chance—even though it seems very odd that chance phenomena can build up systems of vast complexity. It is wholly against the law of entropy—"

"You've lost me."

"Don't worry. There is an alternative. And that's the notion of the Divine Drama. Don't worry, I'm not going to be heavy about it—not over dinner. But you know *The Mikado*? You remember Pooh-Bah who could trace his ancestry back to a protoplasmal primordial atomic globule? We can all do that, you know. And here we are, in this excellent restaurant, drinking this very good claret and eating cutlets, and not looking at all like people with such a peculiar ancestry. That's the Divine Drama. The onward march of evolution. Astonishing, so far as it's gone, but we're probably only in Act Two of a five-act tragicomedy. We are probably a mere way-station on the road to something finer than anything we can now conceive."

"Golly! And where does that put Gil?"

"I don't know. But other very wise people have guessed at something. Let me quote you some verse, but don't let anybody notice, because it isn't at all the thing to quote verse in restaurants in Toronto. Listen:

> *Then Death, so call'd, is but old Matter dress'd*
> *In some new Figure, and a vary'd Vest:*
> *Thus all Things are but alter'd, nothing dies;*
> *And here and there th' unbodied Spirit flies,*
> *By Time, or Force, or Sickness dispossest,*
> *And lodges, where it lights, in Man or Beast;*
> *Or hunts without, till ready Limbs it finds*
> *And actuates those according to their kind;*
> *From Tenement to Tenement is toss'd;*
> *The Soul is still the same, the Figure only lost;*
> *And, as the soften'd Wax new Seals receives,*
> *This Face assumes, and that impression leaves;*
> *Now call'd by one, now by another Name;*
> *The Form is only chang'd, the Wax is still the same:*
> *So Death, so call'd, can but the Form deface,*
> *Th' immortal Soul flies out in empty space;*
> *To seek her Fortune in some other Place.*

"Who wrote that?"

"It's a translation from Ovid, and Ovid was writing

about the philosophy of Pythagoras, which is very old stuff indeed, but not therefore to be dismissed. Indeed, Pythagoras has been enjoying quite a revival in this century."

"Heavy stuff. Do you think Gil is hanging around, then?"

"I don't agree or disagree. Pythagoras thought so, and Pythagoras was no fool."

"Do you think perhaps Gil hangs around his murderer?"

"That would be very disagreeable for the murderer, wouldn't it?"

"And how!"

"Well, Esme, shall I take you on to your next engagement? With your fiancé, I presume? You've told me your wonderful news and I've told you a little bit about Pythagoras, which seems a reasonable exchange."

"More than just reasonable. You're a darling, Uncle Jon."

"I do my best."

[28]

AN AUTUMN EVENING and about nine o'clock as, with Esme delivered to Henry Healy's hotel, I return to my upstairs living-room in my clinic. Autumn in my heart, too; I must not sink into easy sentimentality. But what else can I feel when I look back over the fairly recent past, during which I have lost my godson (and the only hope of a son I ever had) and what I suppose I must call my illusion about the great love of my life, Nuala, now a self-defined wiry gynaecologist, and Charlie, whom I continue to think of as the most remarkable man I have ever known (though by no means the wisest), and The Ladies, who gave so much interest to my life and whose salon was, all things considered, the most life-enhancing assembly I have ever encountered. I have lost St. Aidan's—now a thoroughly modern church, the incumbent of which does not hesitate to describe the holy edifice as "the plant."

And, this very night, this dinner on which I pinned such high hopes, but at which I had no opportunity to declare my love—so eager was Esme with her great news.

But—no gains? Has it all been loss and downhill journey? Certainly not. To have known these people was a rich experience for me. To have been the presiding genius of my own clinic and to have watched my procession of patients, some of them aporetics for a certainty, but many others who improved under my care and gave weight to my Paracelsian notion of the healing art, that was anything but trivial. To have watched my city change from a colonial outpost of a great Empire to a great city in what looks decidedly like a new empire; to have watched the British connection wither as the Brits grew weary under Imperial greatness, and the American connection grow under the caress of the iron hand beneath the buckskin glove—that was to have taken part in a great movement of history. And to have watched the paling of a Chekovian colonial social order, as new values and new heroes supplanted old manners and outworn ideals of heroism.

Was all this nothing to one who had always thought of himself as an intelligent observer of, if not a very active participator in, the life of his time? Decidedly not. Gain, every moment of it. But what remains, for autumn and winter?

The Anatomy of Fiction, of course. Ample occupation for a man now well up in years, but still in command of his wits. A commentary, a sort of footnote, to that part of the Divine Drama in which Fiction has a place. Eminently worth doing, and I'm just the man to do it.

I take down a volume of Burton, who is my exemplar in the work. It falls open at a page often read: "He that will avoid trouble must avoid the world," I read; certainly I have not done that. But I have had luck, in that I have not always gained my heart's desire. Esme, so lovely, so charming—but not meant for me. May she be happy with her Henry Healy, her tycoon. What does he want with her? Beauty, I suppose. But here is Burton: "He that marries a wife that is snout-fair alone, let him look, saith Barbarus, for no better success than Vulcan had with Venus, or Claudius with Messalina." What brutes those Jacobeans could be! Snout-fair, indeed! Was Esme "snout-fair alone"? Not alone, certainly, but—

The telephone rings. My intuition suggests a wrong number. Not that great intuition is needed; a nearby new cinema has been granted a number that is only one digit away from mine, and wrong numbers are common. This is one.

"Can you tell me the time of the last complete show?"

"You have the wrong number."

"Eh? Isn't that the Odeon?"

I decide to give a Burtonian answer.

"No, this is the Great Theatre of Life. Admission is free but the taxation is mortal. You come when you can, and leave when you must. The show is continuous. Good-night."

A must-have for Davies fans!

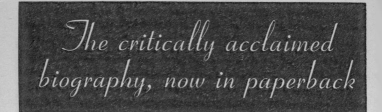

The critically acclaimed biography, now in paperback

ROBERTSON DAVIES
MAN of MYTH

A Biography by
Judith
Skelton Grant

"Meticulously researched... proves once and for all that Robertson Davies is not only unlike God, he's almost — but not quite — like the rest of us... Skelton-Grant paints a picture of a man who has spent his long life brilliantly constructing his persona... A thorough and sensible account of arguably the greatest living Canadian novelist... deserves to be on any Canadian library shelf."

— *The Toronto Star*